Y0-BCU-345

**Star Trek: The Next Generation *Genesis* Books
by John Vornholt:**

The Genesis Wave: Book One
The Genesis Wave: Book Two
The Genesis Wave: Book Three

STAR TREK
THE NEXT GENERATION®

GENESIS FORCE

John Vornholt

Based upon STAR TREK® and
STAR TREK: THE NEXT GENERATION®
created by Gene Roddenberry

POCKET BOOKS
New York   London   Toronto   Sydney

This book is a work of fiction. Names, characters, places and incidents are products of the author's imagination or are used fictitiously. Any resemblance to actual events or locales or persons, living or dead, is entirely coincidental.

POCKET BOOKS, a division of Simon & Schuster, Inc.
1230 Avenue of the Americas, New York, NY 10020

STAR TREK is a Registered Trademark of Paramount Pictures.

This book is published by Pocket Books, a division of Simon & Schuster, Inc., under exclusive license from Paramount Pictures.

ISBN: 0-7434-6502-4

First Pocket Books paperback printing April 2004

10 9 8 7 6 5 4 3 2 1

POCKET and colophon are registered trademarks of Simon & Schuster, Inc.

Cover design by Rod Hernandez
Illustration by Chris Moore

Manufactured in the United States of America

For information regarding special discounts for bulk purchases, please contact Simon & Schuster Special Sales at 1-800-456-6798 or business@simonandschuster.com

For Jean

PART ONE

ONSET

one

The screaming, the panic, the smell of blood—those he could handle. The roar of the shuttlecraft, the rioting mob, the fires burning throughout the city, the rage of his men as they fired disruptors at the populace—those he could understand. But the tingle on his brawny neck all the way to his forehead ridges—*that* terrified him. As he looked over his shoulder at the smoke blackening the skies, he could sense that something monstrous was rushing this way, searing across the heavens, destroying all in its path.

The ambassador didn't even recall what planet he was standing on with his troop of so-called peacekeepers. There had been so many doomed worlds, and every evacuation was more difficult as word spread across the quadrant of the Genesis Wave. It truly bothered him that fewer would get off this planet than should have, thanks to their unruly behavior, but he could accept their panic. What he could not accept was dying in a stupid, mindless disaster like this. It was such a waste! And trying to save the last few stragglers of a doomed race wasn't a warrior's death either. Their rescue fleet had saved over a hundred thousand on this planet alone—and a hundred million in total—but what was that, when billions stood to die?

They looked so much like humans, too. Unarmored, they died swiftly under the fiery disintegration of the disruptors.

Worried voices barked from the com medallion on his shoulder, warning him that their time was running out. Less than six minutes remained before the destruction would overtake them. From his command post on the park's sledding hill, the ambassador surveyed a city recreation area that was swollen with frightened citizens, all just realizing they were about to die. It was clear to him that the maddened and ever-growing mob would not let any more Klingon shuttlecraft land. Their transporters were working over capacity, snapping people from the crowd at random. Another two hundred or so could be saved if they let the shuttlecraft land, but at this point who could select two hundred worthy citizens from this berserk rabble? The planet's own authority and civilization had broken down, or else this mob wouldn't have swamped their position.

A rock landed at his feet, and he realized that he and his security force were under increased attack.

"Take me with you!" and "Take my child!" he heard them yell, even while they threw debris at him. It was a good thing this was a peace-loving world with few weapons. Why his superiors thought a former Starfleet officer would have better luck dealing with distraught people than a captain or an admiral, he didn't know. In the end, nothing of his experience aboard the *Enterprise* had prepared him for this grim work. Now the deadly wave had actually caught up with them, meaning that this ignominious retreat was the last chance they had to save lives. With bitterness in his heart, Ambassador Worf concluded that it was time to cut their losses and flee.

"batlh Daqawhu'taH!" he bellowed to those who were about to die. To the officers under his command, he shouted, "Squadron, regroup for transporter operations! Form ranks!"

Worf waved them to the top of the hill, and his troopers scurried to retreat, even while they fired into the crowd to keep them at bay. Worf worried that once they saw his men transporting, they would charge into the beams and disrupt the retreat. Why not? They had nothing to lose. He could see many of the doomed people screaming to the blackened sky, begging the random transporters to take them.

He tapped his com medallion and said, "Worf to Mission Command."

"Command here," answered a female officer. "Ambassador, do you know we only have five minutes before—"

"Yes," he answered testily. "Lock on to the signal of myself and the security detail. We all need to go at once, because our position will be overrun. Acknowledge."

"Acknowledged. Then we must suspend rescue operations."

"Yes," answered Worf, ducking from an errant bottle thrown his way. "Recall the shuttlecraft."

No sooner had the words escaped from his lips than one of the shuttlecraft swooped close into the crowd, attempting to land. That should have sent the mob scurrying, but instead one of them in a uniform knelt down and shot what looked like a phaser beam into the underbelly of the shuttlecraft. It exploded in a rupture of power packs and fuel that blew out the impulse engines and sent the craft plunging into the shrieking crowd. The vessel wasn't more than five meters off the ground before it dove, so no one in the path had time to get away. From the spot of the crash, a wave of shock spread among the rabble like ripples in a pool, as they tried to flee. But there was nowhere to run, because no place on the planet was safe with the Genesis Wave bearing down on them.

"Hold that transport order!" shouted Worf into his com device. "One of the shuttlecraft has crashed into the crowd—brought down by hostile fire."

Several of his officers were already shooting vengefully into the mob, trying to drive them back from the flaming wreck. It would never fly again, but the passenger cabin was built to withstand impact, fire, and planetary reentry. Despite its singed appearance, it wasn't badly damaged. There was a good chance that the two-member crew had survived the crash, but they wouldn't survive that rabid crowd for long.

"Command, lock on to the crew of the downed shuttlecraft," ordered Worf.

"Unable to, my lord," she answered. "There's a neutrino radiation leak, probably from the cryo reactants in the coil assembly. Scanner readings are unreliable, and we'd have to get them out of there fast. Of course, we have less than five minutes, anyway. Let us proceed with your transportation at once."

The locals were leaping into the flames of the wreck, and some scrambled to the top of the shuttlecraft and began to pull at latches and hatches. When his men picked them off with shots that were dangerously close to the craft, Worf yelled, "Squadron, hold your fire! Follow me to the shuttlecraft and surround it. *SuH tugh!*"

Worf waved his arm and led the charge down the hill into the crazed masses, already driven more frantic by the crash. The weight of impending doom hung over all of them, and he wondered when they would cease this denial. They had to stop rioting and prepare themselves to meet death with dignity. Then again, he thought, maybe Klingons would have behaved the same way, because it was natural to want to fight such a cruel fate. With steely reserve, he joined his men in shooting defenseless, unarmed citizens who were crowding in against them, as he fought his way toward the fallen shuttlecraft. His troops were spread out behind him, some of them too far back.

"Don't let them take your weapons!" he ordered. "Don't let them touch you—keep them back!" But the huge crowd had figured out what the Klingons were doing, and it pressed forward like an octopus wrapping its tentacles around a small fish. Despite the mayhem the Klingons unleashed upon them, this doomed populace had no reason to resist mob rule and every reason to discount death. He heard a mangled shout in Klingon and turned to see an officer at the end of the column get swamped by half a dozen rioters. His fellows tried to blast the attackers, but they couldn't fire with abandon for fear of hitting their comrade.

While Worf's attention was distracted, one man jumped him, while another grabbed his legs. He smashed the first attacker with the butt of his disruptor rifle and kicked fiercely at the second, while he sent an arcing disruptor beam through the crowd. Only turning into a berserk madman allowed him to fight his way through them, but he was determined enough to reach the smoldering wreck of the shuttlecraft. He slammed against the singed gray hull, glad that no one could reach him from behind, and pawed his com medallion.

"Worf to Mission Command!" he barked. "Evacuate as many of the away team as you can, immediately."

"Yes sir," she replied. "We cannot get a lock on you

or anyone near the shuttlecraft, because of the interference."

With relief, Worf saw the closest three of his men disappear in a sparkling mosaic of transporter molecules, and he shot a beam into the crowd to keep them at bay. Most looked confused and stunned, or contrite, and only a few were enraged to the point of insanity, but these few were enough to cause considerable trouble. He looked back at the shuttlecraft and thought he heard someone banging from inside. Then again, it could have been the mob shaking the craft from the other side.

"*MajQa'*," he told Mission Command. "Evacuate our men but keep one transporter room open for me and the survivors. Give me a countdown when we near our drop-dead departure time."

"With all due respect, Ambassador, our drop-dead countdown ended thirty seconds ago. Only the flagship remains in orbit." Her voice grew steely. "We want you back now."

"Keep taking the away team!" answered Worf, shooting a rabid citizen who rushed him with a shovel in his hands. "Give me a chance to free them—beam us up when we get away from the wreck. If you're not present then, I will understand."

"Pulling back to maximum transporter range, with best trajectory for emergency warp escape," reported Command icily, as if she were talking to a dead man. "We will remember you with honor. End contact."

Worf was glad he had fired his disruptor very little

until now, because he needed to constantly rake the crowd with the deadly beam in order to keep them away. Those in front often didn't want to come closer but were pushed by the mob from behind—everyone wanted to see the bungling Klingons who had failed to save them. More than a few wanted to tear him apart. They blamed the Federation, because this awful weapon had originated with them, even if no one knew who wielded it now. Then Starfleet had promised more help than they could deliver, even when aided by both the Klingons and Romulans. Worf didn't know who in the Federation had done all the promising to the doomed Genesis worlds, but he would look them up when this was over.

He heard a bang above his head and was alerted a second before someone slid over the top of the shuttlecraft and onto his back. The attacker tried to get his weapon, and Worf gave him the butt of it in his midsection. In fighting this close, he'd rather have a *bat'leth* than this useless rifle. Still, Worf managed to batter the attacker away, mow down a few more in the wailing crowd, and jump up on a strut. From there he scrambled to the top of the boxy craft, which was meant to carry sixteen passengers, or fourteen fully equipped warriors. Now standing atop the shuttle, Worf was bombarded by rocks and other thrown debris. He crouched down and lowered his bone-plated forehead to take most of the lumps, while his hands worked on opening the side hatch, which faced upward. It took only a few seconds to realize it was jammed shut. Brute strength wouldn't open it, and time was running out.

He banged on the hatch with his rifle and shouted, "Are you alive?"

"Yes! Yes!" He heard a faint voice, which was enough to keep him working, despite the abuse he was absorbing. There was no rear door on this vessel, and the other door was under the dirt. So he pulled a small explosive device, a *jorwI'*, from his sash, set it for five seconds, and placed it inside the recessed latch compartment. An egg suddenly hit him on the left side of his face and dribbled down his chin, but he ignored it while he drew another *jorwI'* from his sash. This charge he placed where the impact had formed a crack in the hatch's seal.

"Get back!" he bellowed to the survivors inside. "Explosive charge!"

With that, Worf armed both devices at the same instant, not seeing another crazed citizen reach the top of the craft. As Worf stood up, the local charged him and grabbed his waist, knocking the disruptor rifle out of his hands. Worf wanted to jump off before the explosion; instead he had to battle the deranged man while the seconds ticked away on the charges. Not only that, but somebody had grabbed his fallen disruptor rifle, and blasted a wild beam that went streaking over his head.

Worf whirled his attacker around just as the beam sliced into the man's back, shielding Worf from the deadly disruptor. His scream turned into a gurgle as the blast hit his body in a blazing yellow burst. Worf jumped off the opposite side of the shuttlecraft, just as another errant beam crackled through the air. The twin explosions went off, hurling Worf another few feet into the crowd. He rolled in a somersault, reached for his mek'leth, and came up slashing anyone who tried to mob him.

He fought his way back to the crushed hull of the shuttlecraft just in time to see a pilot clamber out the smoking hatch on top. A disruptor beam sheared the hull, shooting sparks, but the pilot was armed and fired back. He continued to fire at the crowd, while his comrade crawled out—she was holding her arm and had blood on her vest, clearly wounded. Still the crowd was enraged at the sight of these two would-be rescuers, who could still escape the horrible fate that awaited their whole planet. The screaming throng surged like an ocean in a storm, threatening to engulf the shuttlecraft, and Worf wasn't sure they could get far enough away from it to be rescued.

"Look at the sky!" shouted someone. Then everyone cried the same words.

Attention was diverted from the three Klingons and their wrecked vessel to the northern sky, where the gray clouds had just turned a vivid green. A flaming curtain swept over the distant mountains, throbbing and mutating as if distorted by heat. Distant majestic peaks erupted in fury, disappearing into rolling clouds of ash and steam.

"*tugh!*" shouted Worf, waving for his comrades to

follow him as he ran from the shuttle. The two pilots leaped into the crowd, many of whom had fallen to their knees in awe and supplication, and they reached Worf just as the tingle of the transporter beam gripped his spine. He felt the ground trembling and saw the buildings and monorails writhe like snakes on fire. Then mercifully their molecules disappeared from the planet just as the monstrous wall of neon fire blasted every animal, rock, and blade of grass into a churning mass of grotesque tissue.

Worf and the two shuttle pilots collapsed onto a transporter pad in a dimly lit Klingon vessel. *"Qapla'!"* exclaimed the transporter operator, as another crew member slapped him on the back. "Transporter room six to bridge," he barked. "Ambassador Worf and two crew members have been recovered. Request medical attention."

"Acknowledged," came the answer from the first officer. "Ambassador, emergency departure was successful, and we are now at warp eight, moving along the quickest route out of the path of the Genesis Wave. We have refugees to deliver at Starbase 309. After that, do you have any orders?"

Worf rose to his feet and shook the dirt and garbage off his uniform, while an underling handed him fresh ambassadorial robes. He wiped the drying egg off his face, too, and it reminded him of a Terran colloquialism. Having egg on his face was fitting, because this effort had been anything but a success. Their combined response to this terrible disaster bordered on failure, and he was supposed to be the Klingons' liaison to the Federation. They couldn't begin to move fast enough, and Starfleet had so far failed to find the source of the wave. It was too late for billions of souls—

"I want to visit one of these wrecked planets to see the aftermath," answered Worf with grim determination. "I've seen it coming straight toward me, and now I want to see what it has left behind. There will be a time of reckoning."

"As you say, my lord," agreed the first officer. "Setting course for Starbase 309."

two

From the sunrise balcony high atop the Summer Palace, Overseer Tejharet gazed down upon the central courtyard of Tejmol, the capital city of Aluwna. The flowering gardens and gleaming walkways were teeming with revelers and trinket vendors, and the trill of flutes and lyres filled the air, along with the twinkling laughter of children. In another unit of time, there would hardly be room to walk, and the smell of grilled fish would waft across the immense plaza. Blazing silver-salmon clouds silhouetted the stark spires and minarets of the city's skyline, and sun glinted off the golden pillars of the Sunrise Temple. The courtyard was lined with blue transporter booths, disgorging more pedestrians with every passing instant. No one worked more than two or three units a day, and most adults on Aluwna were artisans. His people were joyful and at peace, as they had been for millennia, and their world shined with the glow of prosperity and purpose.

In two days, all of that was going to end.

Overseer Tejharet turned back to his quaking science advisors. "Are you sure?" he asked. "Are you sure it's coming this way?"

Bereft of words, they waggled their open palms and speechless tongues. Finally one gray-haired eminence waved a device that created a holographic star chart on the sunburst design of the palace floor; a mass of stars and planets floated in the air like snowflakes caught in a whirlwind. Slicing through this delicate starscape came an ominous shaft of darkness—the shadow of death. It engulfed everything in its wake, and its black edge just barely grazed the blinking orb that represented Aluwna.

"My Overseer," said the old advisor in a quavering voice, "we have just received an update from the Federation. There can be no mistaking it: The Genesis Wave will reach Aluwna in sixty units—two dawns from today."

The monarch scowled, feeling much older than his sixty-two cycles, which still made him relatively youthful for a ruler of this courtly planet. He demanded, "What about Starfleet? They are evacuating other planets—what about *us!* They promised to send the Klingon fleet. *Where are they?*"

The advisors recoiled from the enraged monarch, and their babbling grew more intense. In the jumble of words, Tejharet could make out a few desperate excuses: "They are spread too thin!" and "They have been delayed!" or "The Klingons will arrive, but not in time to evacuate the whole planet!"

Overseer Tejharet rubbed his head ridges, which were distinguished by triple rows of silvery eyebrows. "I never trusted the damn Federation," he grumbled. "Maniacs and murderers, that's all they are. This is *their* doing—this Genesis device is *their* weapon!"

"But, sire," said the eldest advisor, "would they turn such a terrible force upon themselves? The reports from Sector 879 have been truly horrific. Twenty-three inhabited planets have been destroyed, and the death toll is over fifteen billion."

"And we are doomed to add to that total!" snapped Tejharet, dropping his hands to the sides of his brocaded satin tunic.

"Not everyone must die," a young advisor assured him. "The trade fleet and the royal yachts have been summoned, and all ships will be in orbit well before sixty units."

"What is that—ten ships? Eleven?" asked the ruler derisively. "No doubt, all of you have your seats picked out, but I'm not willing to sacrifice eighty million loyal subjects without a fight. That's eighty million innocent souls who have done nothing to deserve this cataclysm. And not just our *people*—I understand this weapon will terraform our planet and destroy our civilization! Do any of you have a single idea what to do . . . beyond saving yourselves?"

The advisors looked sheepishly at one another,

unable to admit that they had been totally dependent upon the Federation, who were nothing but a collection of bumblers and primitives. Overseer Tejharet scowled more deeply and said, "You must summon *her*."

The scientists looked more horrified by this proclamation than by the actual threat of the Genesis Wave. The elder stepped forward, his outstretched hand shaking in his billowing sleeve. "Surely, sire, you don't mean—"

"You know who I mean!" snapped the monarch of Aluwna. "Summon her immediately. By the Hand of the Divine, I pray she can save us."

With that, Overseer Tejharet turned his back on his trembling advisors, who scraped and bowed their way out of the chamber. Once again the hereditary ruler gazed out the archway at the bustling courtyard, where unsuspecting citizens laughed and talked, ate and danced, and filled the sparkling plaza in the early light. He wanted to weep for them, or at least hug each one, because they were so innocent and unaware of the mortal danger bearing down upon them.

Professor Marla Karuw ate a hearty breakfast consisting of a small game bird called a *nestarn*, plus several pinkish tubers. Unlike most of her compatriots on Aluwna, the striking brunette with six red eyebrows ate meat, and lots of it. Unlike her mealymouthed colleagues, the professor spoke her mind and did what she felt was necessary, and she maintained their respect even as she curried their antipathy. Therefore, her room in the bowels of the old hospital was more like a laboratory than a prison cell, and she had access to outside communications. Through a video terminal, she avidly followed the destructive path of the Genesis Wave, which had appeared from nowhere unexpectedly to slash a widening path through the Alpha Quadrant. From a distant video feed, she witnessed an unprepossessing rock of a planet get razed by a fiery green wall of pulsating energy, turning it into a throbbing, churning mass of monstrous new life.

Her female guard, Juwarni, sat at a small table outside the forcefield door, watching the same viewscreen that Karuw watched. The jailer put down her utensils, unable to finish her meager breakfast of porridge and greens. With shocked horror, she asked, "That isn't coming *here*, is it?"

"We'll know soon enough," answered Marla Karuw. "Of course, the instant we find out for sure, we may all be dead."

The older, stocky female scowled. "You shouldn't talk like that. Of course, you haven't got much to lose—with a life sentence and all."

"Life in a prison is preferable to *that*," answered the professor, motioning to the screen. "But that's clearly life, too. As I perceive it, the Genesis effect isn't death, really, but a reborning into something new."

"What?" asked the guard uncertainly.

The scientist shrugged. "It's hard for us to tell. Such experiments will get you imprisoned for life on our provincial planet. I should have fled to the Federation cycles ago."

"So you could make a weapon that destroys planets and kills everything in sight?" Juwarni snorted derisively.

The dark-haired woman turned and stared at her keeper with sharp golden eyes flecked with lavender. "I would like to discover all the secrets of life and death. You have only to look at this looming disaster to know that ignorance is worse than death."

Suddenly the guard bolted to attention and listened intently to orders coming through her earpiece. "Yes, sir!" she responded, then moved closer to the door. "Marla," she said, "you had better finish your breakfast, because they're coming to fetch you."

That brought a worried frown to the scientist's face. "If I were you, I'd take the rest of the day off and spend it with my family."

"Why?" asked the jailer puzzledly.

"If they are sending for me," answered Marla Karuw, "then we're in trouble." She dabbed the animal grease from the corner of her mouth and primped in front of her mirror. By the time the scientist was finished, two pale-faced elders from the Science Council arrived at the cell door, looking grim indeed.

"Marla Karuw," one of them intoned, "Overseer Tejharet requires your immediate presence, but this in no way implies that you—"

"Skip the speeches," she answered, moving toward the door. "How much time do we have?"

They looked uncertainly at one another, and she demanded again. "How much time?"

"A little over sixty units," one of them answered in a shaken whisper.

"Send Juwarni home," she ordered, motioning to her stocky guard.

"We do not take orders from you," answered the underling with a sneer.

"Oh, don't you?" Marla Karuw paused in the doorway with her arms crossed, refusing to leave her cell until they obeyed her.

With a shrug of his scrawny shoulders, the elder turned to the guard and said, "You are relieved of duty for today, but remain on call."

"Thank you," said the woman, with a worried frown. With a glance at her prisoner, she hurried away.

Wordlessly the three scientists climbed the stairs from the dungeon to the spotless yellow hospital lobby, where they stepped into three separate blue transporter booths. The staff and patrons gawked at Marla Karuw, because everyone knew the famous prisoner in the basement.

"The Summer Palace," Karuw told the computer. "Priority One."

"Bioscan complete," answered an efficient computer voice. "Marla Karuw, prepare for transport. Authorization limited to a one-way trip."

"A lot of us may go one-way," answered the scientist grimly.

As her molecules were disassembled, concentrated, and beamed across a relatively short distance to the monarch's residence, the professor decided how she would save the inhabitants of Aluwna. Or at least a good percentage of them. When she emerged from the transporter booth in the cavernous assembly room, Karuw was met by an even larger contingent of the scientific community, most of whom despised her and her forbidden work. Once again, they bombarded her with warnings and disclaimers, and she dismissed them with a wave.

"Komplum, you may come with me," she told a young scholar who had once been her student. "The rest of you stay here. I know my way to the overseer's chambers." The lad nodded, and slipped a wry smile to his stunned colleagues as he dashed after her.

The royal advisors sputtered in protest, but none of them moved to stop Professor Karuw as she climbed the grand staircase to the second story of royal suites, with young Komplum in tow. At an ornate golden door inlaid with jewels and a crest depicting the fanged beast Rahjhu, Marla was met by more sullen guards with stun sticks, and they looked as if they wanted to challenge her as well. Before they could speak, the doors opened automatically, and the professor lifted her chin and strode past them into the royal receiving room. Komplum scrambled after the deposed professor with barely a glance behind him. Marla recalled the last time she had graced this palace—the day she had been condemned for heresy—plus her many private meetings with Overseer Tejharet.

The monarch of Aluwna stood hunch-shouldered at the archway leading to his balcony, and he continued to gaze upon the unsuspecting crowd in the courtyard below. He had to tell them—he had to do *something*—because the candle wick was burning low for his beloved world. Every minute was precious, and he felt the urgent need to act now. *But what do I tell them?* he pondered. *What do I do?*

He heard an imperious clearing of a throat, and he whirled around to find Professor Marla Karuw staring at him. Tejharet almost shouted with joy. He longed to rush forward and sweep her off her feet in a passionate embrace, but his regal reserve stiffened his back and slowed his legs. He stepped toward her and took her hand in a courtly manner.

"Marla, I'm very glad you've come," rasped the ruler.

"I don't doubt it," she replied with a sniff. Hearing the happy voices and music of the crowd in the courtyard, she shook her head sadly. "They know nothing about this, do they?"

"No," said the monarch. "You know how insular most of our people are. I take it, you've been studying the outside reports?"

She nodded. "They can't stop it—they can't even find the source. How many ships do we have?"

Tejharet's shoulders slumped, and he scowled with

disbelief. "Marla, I expected more from you than 'How many ships?' I can get that from these other bookworms." He motioned to the young scholar slouching in her shadow.

"You misunderstand," said Marla, pacing thoughtfully across his brilliant mosaic floor. "The ships are only for logistical support. We can't carry millions of people in a handful of freighters, but we don't have to. We have a very mobile population and a system to move them. Why, we must have a million transporter booths dotting our countryside—"

"Two million," interjected the overseer.

She gazed at him with intense golden eyes. "Forgive me, I've been locked away for a couple of cycles. Our transporter booths are still controlled by a complex network of geosynchronous satellites, are they not?"

"Yes," answered Tejharet excitedly. He was beginning to see where she was headed with this line of reasoning.

The professor talked as she snapped her fingers, and her aide made rapid notes on his padd. "When the passengers are en route to their destinations, their patterns are stored in the transporter buffers on the satellites. True, it's seldom for more than an instant or two, but it could be much longer. There is a case in the Federation—a Starfleet engineer named Scott— whose pattern was frozen in a transporter buffer for seventy-five Terran years."

"Seventy-five years," echoed the monarch in

amazement. "Do you really think you could do that? How long can these transporter buffers last?"

Marla Karuw shrugged. "We would only need a few days, I believe . . . until the Genesis Wave passes. You are full of facts and figures, my overseer, so how many passengers can the transporter system move at full capacity?"

"Approximately ten percent of the population," he answered.

"Eight million," said the professor softly. "That is the number of lives we can save, not counting those who travel on the ships. We'll have to use our vessels to tow the satellites safely out of the way, and that will be a logistical nightmare. We'll return when it's over, but I warn you—from what I understand, this scheme will do nothing to save our planet."

She motioned around the sumptuous chamber and added somberly, "Nothing can save it. Everything you see here . . . everything on Aluwna . . . will be destroyed."

Overseer Tejharet wanted to bury his face in his hands and weep, but he couldn't allow himself that indulgence. "Yes, then our world will die. We haven't colonized other planets or joined far-flung alliances . . . it is all here on Aluwna. Please, Marla, save as many of our species as you can."

"Not just our race," she was quick to add. "We'll need lots of plant and animal samples in order to reseed the planet. We'll come back stronger than ever!"

A throat cleared in a kind of squeak, and the two elders turned to see the young scholar, Komplum, inching forward. "Professor Karuw, may I remind you that the satellite computers have living, biological components—the bioneural network. I don't think we can expect all those transporter patterns to last . . . an indefinite time."

"No, but the biological components make rapid expansion and scaling possible." Marla Karuw turned to Overseer Tejharet and crossed her arms. "So how many ships do we have?"

"Eleven full-sized vessels, a dozen shuttles and ketches."

"You must grant me a pardon and put me in command of all ships," declared Karuw. "Better yet, just give me the powers of a regent."

"My powers?" replied the monarch with a gasp. "You want me to give you *my* powers?"

"I don't have time to convince people to help me," snapped the professor. "Make me a regent, and do it now . . . unless you prefer to be the ruler of nothing."

His lips thinned, and his hands twitched; but the overseer nodded his acquiescence. After he abdicated power to the greatest thorn in his side, his subjects would all know how serious the situation was. He might never again rule this world, or these people, but he had made a decision to save the greatest number of lives possible. If Marla Karuw could not drive this desperate rescue effort to success, then no one could. He would only be in the way.

The monarch nodded, and was about to call his chancellor to make the proclamation when the side door banged open and his wife came storming into the reception room. She was in a white mourning gown, fresh from her trip to the sanctuary that sunrise. Seeress Jenoset stared in disbelief at her husband and demanded, "What is this I hear—"

When her eyes lit upon Marla Karuw, Jenoset really exploded. "What is *she* doing here? I'll call the guards!"

"No!" insisted Tejharet, actually stamping his foot at the fair-haired beauty who was his spouse. "She is here to save our world. I've just made her regent."

"Regent!" shrieked Seeress Jenoset in astonishment. "This is a joke, right? You appoint the biggest blasphemer on Aluwna as our regent? Do you want the people to overthrow you? I've got plenty of followers, and we'll call for a referendum. Or a general strike."

"They'll all be dead before you could do anything," snapped the overseer. "There's no time for dramatics, dear—the Genesis Wave is headed for Aluwna, and we're going to perform miracles just to save ten percent of the population." Before anything could stop him, he hit a communications button on his desk. "This is Overseer Tejharet, security code *rayje-teked-metsoi*. Be it known to the chancellor and all the citizens of Aluwna, I hereby pardon Professor Marla Karuw from all past crimes and convictions. Furthermore, I appoint her regent of Aluwna for an indefinite period of time, with all the rights and duties attendant to the office of overseer—"

"You fool!" screeched his wife, almost jumping across his desk to get him. "You've lost the kingdom!"

"Half true," he answered, lifting his chin. "I have both lost and saved it."

three

In the morning shadows of the immense Summer Palace, Farlo Fuzwik dashed through the crowd of merrymakers with his best friend, Candra, chasing him at full speed. Their playful game of tag had a purpose, because they often bumped into adults—romantic strollers, fat vendors, dreamy-eyed musicians, solemn artists, anyone with a beadsack. When they could easily snatch the prize and keep running, they did, but the Aluwnans weren't stupid. Most revelers had their beads of worth wrapped around their necks or waists to allow easy access to pay for trinkets and food. It was common to part with great sums in the square on a leisure day, and everyone wore the colorful beads with the intention of spending them. When Farlo and Candra couldn't steal a purse from someone laden with beads, they remembered that person for later, when they donned their tattered beggar clothes.

The stiff petticoat breeches and tunics were their "rich" clothes, the ones they wore to cavort with polite society and look as if they fit in. Or at least look as if they had parents. Farlo dashed behind a column on the shadowy side of the palisade and paused to catch a breath and inspect the two beadsacks he had swiped. For a moment, he thought he had actually escaped from his accomplice, but Candra swooped around the curve of marble and tagged his shoulder . . . hard. "You're it! Whatcha got there?"

She tried to snatch the prizes from Farlo, but he held tightly and pushed her away with a burst of strength. A cycle ago, Candra would have easily taken the beadsacks from him and left him crying, but the thirteen-cycle-old had grown in stature and muscle since those days. Candra, too, was becoming a woman, and no doubt she would have to ply the pleasure trade down on the esplanade level, or become a hostess in the resort trade. For those of low breed, there weren't a lot of opportunities. Farlo couldn't imagine growing up, because thieving and begging were all he knew. For now, he and Candra were content to be two well-dressed street urchins, trying to make a dishonest bead.

"What have you got?" she insisted, pestering him until he opened the bright purple and gold-striped bag. From long practice, he hunched down, and she moved in close and spread her arms to shield his actions from passersby.

Farlo rummaged through the meager takings. "Six

garnet beads, a sea-worm pin, and a transit pass."

"To where?" she asked with boredom.

His eyes widened as he read the runes. "Stone Spire. Hmmm, that's worth something." It was worth something only because the Bureau of Culture limited the number of visitors to the historic site.

"Another couple of garnets," she muttered, "but I'll take the pin."

Farlo intended to give her the sea-worm pin, but he hesitated, because he hadn't really inspected it yet. The pin itself was sharp and long, for holding together thick folds of fabric, and the ornament depicted a graceful sea dragon in blue enamel and golden jewels, perhaps topaz. It might be worth more than the rest of the stuff combined.

Candra held out her hand and gave him a patient smile, because she knew he always gave the girlie things to her. "Okay," he said, handing over the pin.

She promptly stuck it behind her lapel, out of sight. "We might bump into the former owner."

"No kidding," agreed Farlo with a chuckle. His voice was changing, and when he was winded he sounded like one of the yodeling warblers who entertained the crowd. "How about this other one?"

The second bag was smaller, black, frayed, and Farlo didn't hold much hope for its containing great riches. As usual, Candra moved in close to shield his actions from passing eyes. From this bag he removed a watchbug in a round crystal, three aquamarines, and a garnet, plus a curious ebony cylinder, which looked like a very expensive pillbox, or perhaps a container for makeup. Candra instantly reached for it, but he dropped the goods in his puffy laced shirt.

"You got yours," he whispered. "That pin's worth more than all the others combined. One thing's for sure, we'll have enough for a meal, a wash, and a room in the esplanade. Do you want to knock off or try for more?"

"Why don't we go see the Wishman?" asked Candra excitedly.

Farlo mulled that over. He wanted more beads, but he also wanted to hang on to these goodies for a while—to get to know them better. Candra was impatient as usual, and she wasn't much into material goods. Of course, collecting objects was pointless when you lived on the street and could hide only a few meager belongings.

"New clothes, I fancy!" said Candra, spinning about as if imitating a dancer. Her red hair flowed behind her as she spun. "Something which shows a little skin."

Farlo scowled, because they always had this argument. "Listen, you've got to keep dressing like a child. If you start to draw too much attention, we'll never be able to run our scams."

"Oh, pooh!" she answered in mock anger. "Do you really think I would attract men's attention?"

"You could land a couple of husbands right now," he said, waving his hand in dismissal. "But not with *me*—I like staying a boy. No jobs or stupid rules for me."

"You're not going to be able to stay a boy forever," she said knowingly. "Come on . . . the Wishman!"

"Oh, all right," Farlo said, giving in. He glanced around the pillar and saw the crowd indulging in their usual gaiety for a leisure day—early birds looking for bargains, diners searching for food, and would-be lovers looking for love. Nobody seemed to be looking for *them*, which struck him as odd, considering the quality of the loot they had just nabbed. Then again, it was a big crowd, and they had been moving swiftly, zigging in and out, grazing their victims without overtly mugging them.

He giggled at Candra and sprinted between two food tents into a side street, which was also choked with Aluwnans headed to the square. His friend followed him at a distance, and he had the feeling that he might be able to lose Candra if he tried hard enough. It didn't matter, because they both knew their way to the Wishman, and it was probably best if they didn't travel together. At a trash disintegrator, Farlo got rid of the beadsacks; then he jogged down an insignificant side street, keeping up his lead on Candra. For some reason, the loot in his shirt felt ponderous and bulky, and he wondered whether he should hide it rather than take it to the Wishman. Since this route was a favorite of his, he knew of a decent hiding place under a local transporter booth, where there was a loose brick. Then he could use the same machine to get to his destination.

The hiding place was on another side street in

front of a small apothecary, which was closed on leisure day. The crowd had thinned by the time he reached the narrow thoroughfare, which was good, and no one paid him any attention. Farlo crouched down behind the blue enclosure and hurriedly removed the loose brick under its back left-hand corner. The boy had dug out the ground underneath, making a perfect stash hole; but this wasn't a waterproof hiding spot, so he couldn't leave his goodies here for long. Keeping the beads for expense money, Farlo squirreled away the transit pass to Stone Spire, the watchbug, and the ebony cylinder.

But he couldn't leave the cylinder alone—he had to pick it up for one last look. When he did, he must have triggered something, because a whiff of perfume shot him in the nostrils. The boy almost sneezed, but he managed to grip his nose in time. He quickly buried the cylinder as he intended and replaced the brick.

Just as he stood up, the blue enclosure glowed with a bright green light for a moment and disgorged a constable—a strapping female with gray triple eyebrows and a four-foot-long stun stick. Farlo looked away quickly, trying not to appear interested in the peace officer, as he pretended to study a viewscreen in the window of the apothecary. From the corner of his eye, he saw the constable consult her handheld scanner and march off toward the celebration in the square.

Whew, that was close, thought Farlo with a relieved sigh. He hoped that Candra wouldn't get caught, but she probably wasn't doing anything that looked suspicious, at least not now. Before the constable came back, he slipped into the booth and said, "Watermill Station, level four."

"Transporting," said the polite computer voice, and Farlo felt the familiar tingle as his molecules were disassembled, condensed, and dispatched to another destination thirty measures away.

He felt a rush down his spine as his body was reassembled in a dingy transporter booth in the underground complex that supported the capital's main water-treatment plant. In this massive cavern, there was a square, but it wasn't warmed by glowing sunlight and filled with people. It was gray and dark with a tiled floor that was stained and damp. The sound of rushing water came from three artificial waterfalls that surrounded the plaza, and low-end shops and residences formed an outer ring around the cavern. A dozen watermill workers strolled across the expanse, headed home after their three-unit shifts.

Although there were shops and offices on this level, most were closed for the leisure day. A stretch of storefronts had been taken over by squatters, those of low breed who couldn't claim standard housing on the surface. Their little children played in the great chamber, their laughter echoing across the towering space.

Farlo stepped away from the transit booth and looked around for his friend Candra. Not seeing the vivacious redhead, he took a circuitous route behind the waterfalls to a pedestrian ramp that led upward to the surface. Here were more squatters' abodes, some he had stayed in himself. "Hello, Tagger," he said to one elder, who grinned at him toothlessly. "Keeping warm, Lonya?" he asked a thin woman who roasted urim nuts on a small stove all day long.

"Wouldn't you like to know?" she answered with a cackle. "Want a nut?"

"Just one," answered Farlo. She tossed him a steaming brown and black nut that had cracked from the heat, and he juggled it as he continued to stroll up the ramp. Even though he walked slowly and kept glancing over his shoulder looking for Candra, he never spotted his friend.

Farlo was alone when he reached a small store with a blazing sign that read WISHES. Dusty electronics, hand tools, artist's supplies, and musical instruments were hanging in the dirty display window, but he had never seen anyone purchase these used objects. A chime sounded as he entered the store, and sensors dispensed a whiff of freshener into the air, meant to hide the musty odor of the old goods. Behind a counter stood a white-haired man with six white-haired eyebrows, three of which he raised when he saw Farlo enter his establishment.

"Shhh!" cautioned the old man, putting his fingers to his lips as he slipped past the boy and gazed out the door. Content that no one had followed Farlo or was lurking on the ramp, the Wishman shut the door and locked it.

He rubbed his hands together. "Okay, boy, what have you got for me?"

The lad shrugged and looked out the window. "I don't really have much—it's Candra who has everything."

"Okay, where's Candra?" he asked impatiently. The boy shrugged again, and the old man scowled and paced across the dusty floor of his establishment. "Never trust a girl—someday you're going to have to find a new partner, a cute, small one. If she gets caught and gives my name to the Office of—"

"She won't," scoffed Farlo. "She won't ever get caught."

"I don't know," said the Wishman, nervously twisting his twelve fingers. "Something is wrong, I can feel it. Something bad is going to happen—maybe another crackdown on the low breeds. Maybe there will be a new conscription for public service. I don't know, but I can tell you that something is changing up there—I've seen too many constables today."

A rap sounded on the door, making both of them jump. They whirled around to see Candra motioning to them to unlock the door. Farlo did the honors, while the proprietor scouted the walkway.

After ducking inside, Candra hid behind a bass drum in the corner of the window. "I think I lost them," she breathed.

"Lost who?" asked the Wishman worriedly.

"Oh, some spoilers," she answered. "I don't know how they knew it was me."

"And you led them here?" shrieked the Wishman.

"I don't see anybody out there," offered Farlo. "Old man, you're acting like a third husband. Today is a normal leisure day, and everybody's happy."

The Wishman made a sign to the sky. "May the Divine Hand hear your words and move to protect us."

"I don't want to stay here long, anyway," said Candra, moving closer to the old shopkeeper. "What do you make of this." She turned back the lapel of her stiff white jacket and showed him the exquisite sea-worm pin.

"Oh!" gasped the elder, squinting at the prize. "I've never seen one like that. You must get out of here with it."

"What?" asked Candra. "But I need—"

"To leave!" he barked. "You, too, boy!" He pushed them both toward the door and yanked it open just as two broad-shouldered constables muscled their way into the store. One was female, one was male, and both looked young, strong, and determined.

"Here she is!" he said, pushing Candra toward the officers. "I told her to take her stolen goods elsewhere! We only deal in legally processed estates."

They grabbed the girl by her arms, and she struggled futilely for a moment, until the male officer jabbed her with his stun stick. Candra collapsed to the threadbare carpet as Farlo rushed to catch her. He bent over his friend to protect her from the officers.

"What is this about?" he demanded. "We're just

down here, looking for our parents. I guess they went ahead to the Summer Palace—we should meet them."

The female constable reached down and pulled the pretty pin off Candra's lapel. "This is a tracer," she said, "carried by one of our officers to catch thieves. Why don't you admit it, this time you've been fairly nabbed—and no parent would claim a low breed like you!"

His jaw set firmly, Farlo leaped to his feet and shoved the female officer out of the way. He made a break for the open door and almost got out before the other constable swung his stun stick and caught the escaping lad on the elbow. Farlo howled and tumbled through the air, already unconscious by the time he hit the ramp.

four

His vision bleary and his head throbbing dully, Farlo woke up in a hospital room. Or perhaps it was a laboratory, considering all the blinking equipment, beakers, and monitoring devices. When he tried to sit up, he found that his arms, legs, and torso were strapped firmly to the bed, and he realized it was a prison. Then he could remember all of it—the Wishman, the spoilers following Candra, the stun sticks—

The lad yanked at his bindings while he screamed, "Help! Get me out of here. I'm innocent!"

"It won't do you any good," said a weary voice.

He turned to see Candra strapped to a similar bed about two arm's lengths away. She looked tired, stunned, and several cycles older and wiser. "I've been yelling for ten minutes, and nobody's come in. Plus, they did something to us."

"What do you mean?" asked Farlo worriedly. He had heard about these kind of places, deep underground, where they experimented on orphans, criminals, and low breeds. The lad had been captured before, but he had always talked his way out of it, pretending to be a lost child. In his gut, he had known that growing older was going to be the death of him, and here was the proof.

"There's a red spot on your neck," explained Candra. "Don't you feel a little pain, a little tingle?"

Now that she mentioned it, he did, but he couldn't reach his hand to touch the spot on his neck to verify her words.

"I was waking up when they finished," said Candra. "They wouldn't explain what they were doing—they just did it. They pumped us full of something."

"No," said a voice somewhere behind Farlo, "we merely took a DNA sample. Standard procedure."

The boy craned his neck to see a handsome, white-gowned man enter the hospital room, or cell. He was groomed impeccably and smelled as if he bathed in perfume, and there was something familiar about his princely face and gracious manner, as if he were an actor from the video bands.

He strolled between the two bound prisoners and stopped to look at the girl. "Candra, I'm letting you go," he said. "Well, almost. You are to be remanded to the Bureau of Pleasure, where I believe they'll find some use for your light-fingered touch."

"No, no!" she cried, struggling desperately against

her bindings. "I want to stay with Farlo! I don't want to go to the esplanade."

"I'm sorry, the decision has been made," said the doctor, if that's what he was. He pushed a button on her bed, and a blue shroud floated down from the ceiling. As soon as she was completely covered, the shroud blazed with the eerie green of a transporter beam, and his friend Candra was spirited away.

"Will I ever see her again?" demanded Farlo, fighting back his tears.

"I sincerely doubt it," answered the man. "You are to have an altogether different destiny."

Farlo scowled, not liking the sound of that. "I was happy the way I was living."

"Society doesn't benefit from having more young thieves," said the man. "Do I look familiar to you?"

"Yes, you do," admitted Farlo. "Who are you?"

"I am the seeress consort, Padrin," he answered nonchalantly, in a tone that belied the fact that he was married to their queen. In breeding, he was the second-most-important male on the planet, the one who was supposed to guarantee the purity of the royal bloodlines if the overseer failed to produce offspring.

Farlo let a low whistle escape from his lips. "You're the seeress consort," he rasped, astounded that he should be in the presence of royalty. He had never seen a royal personage, except at great distance during a public ceremony. The boy's voice squeaked as he asked, "What do you want with me?"

Padrin smiled. "Has no one ever done a DNA test on you before?"

"No, I never got caught," he answered proudly.

The consort laughed. "It's true, we don't have any record of you. What is that name you use?"

"Farlo Fuzwik," answered the boy. "It's my real name."

"I doubt it," said Consort Padrin. "Fuzwik is a common name given to abandoned children at the Sanctuary for Public Good. Farlo is common, too. But, young man, you are not common."

"What do you mean?"

Padrin leaned close enough to inspect his prisoner. "Your breeding is a ninety-six-percent match to the chromosome particles of suzerainty. Hard to imagine this was never found before, but then homosynaptic testing wasn't widespread a dozen cycles ago. You are about twelve, are you not?"

"Thirteen," said Farlo defensively. "I don't know what any of that means, but I didn't do anything!"

"You were born," answered the seeress consort. "And your breeding is better than mine, and the equal of the overseer's."

"What?" asked Farlo, unsure if he had heard correctly. By his station in life, he had always assumed that he was of low breeding—now this popinjay was telling him that he was of equal breeding to Overseer Tejharet? "That's a bad joke," he said in a hoarse whisper.

"I wouldn't joke about such a thing," claimed Padrin

as he bent down to unfasten the straps that held Farlo to the bed. "For ten cycles, I have searched for such a match—surreptitiously, of course. Four hundred genetic engineers, an entire research facility, and an army of field agents failed to find you, because you were too busy stealing beadsacks and evading the law. My boy, you *are* the law."

His appendages freed, Farlo rubbed his wrists and slipped out of bed to stand uncertainly on the floor. "Are you saying I could become overseer?"

"It's not that simple," answered Padrin. "But your offspring stand a good chance, if you marry correctly. Will you hold still while I get a retina scan? That will put you in the system."

"Sure," said Farlo uncertainly.

The man produced a handheld device with a small white eyepiece. "Just look in here with your right eye." After the lad complied, Padrin asked him, "Do you know anything about your parents?"

Farlo shook his head. "No, I mean . . . how could someone like *me* be a high breed?"

Padrin chuckled. "Maybe you're a mutant, just a rare stroke of dumb luck from the right parents. Wild genetics often produce wild results. More than likely, you're the illegitimate offspring of two high breeds who couldn't legally marry, perhaps a brother and sister. In the circle you were born into, maybe you were too high-blooded, indicating a forbidden match, so they put you out in the street. You're lucky you found me, because in *my* circle, you're just right."

A beep sounded on one of his displays, and he tapped a button. "Padrin here."

"Sir, the seeress is here to see you," came an awed voice, and Farlo blinked with alarm.

"Send her in, of course," answered Padrin magnanimously. He winked at Farlo and said, "Just let me talk, unless Jenoset speaks to you."

"No problem," answered the boy with a gulp.

The doors to the secure examination room opened, and a stunning blond woman of uncertain age walked in. Padrin leaped forward to take her hand. "Darling, I'm glad you got my message and came so quickly." He kissed, caressed, and licked her hand, quite passionately, thought Farlo.

"There's no time for that," snapped the seeress, snatching her appendage back, "I didn't get your message, and I have no idea what you're talking about. We have an emergency."

"Can't we have good news first?" asked Padrin, grabbing Farlo by his skinny shoulders and hauling him forward. "He's a ninety-six-percent match! We've finally succeeded."

Her jaw dropped open, and her shoulders slumped, as if this was too much good news. Jenoset blinked and rubbed her head; then she awarded Farlo a glance. "Of course, it had to happen now. But perhaps the timing of this is beneficial, because we will need all the pull we've got to hold on to this kingdom, and turn it into a queendom. Do you follow Federation reports at all? Do you know about the Genesis Wave?"

Padrin seemed to pale and shrink back from her. "Yes, a little. We're not endangered, are we?"

"We're doomed," she answered gravely. "The whole planet. Tejharet has gone and appointed Marla Karuw as regent, because she has some notion of saving the people in transporter pattern buffers. Well, I wish her luck, but we can't let her continue to control the government after this crisis has passed. We must return to power in whatever form that takes."

Padrin slumped onto the bed, and Farlo felt like doing the same. But he was mesmerized by this stunning woman—the mother of future overseers—and her energy gave him hope in a crisis he didn't quite understand. "Will we even be alive?" asked the consort in a hoarse whisper.

Jenoset crossed her arms, and her auburn eyebrows fairly danced across her delicate forehead. "Yes, that is another concern—how to control the evacuation. I can't imagine that we won't protect the high-blooded first, but who can say? That . . . that blasphemer is in charge of this whole thing!"

She glanced again at Farlo, and her expression softened. "Your discovery does cast a new light on matters. If I can produce an offspring of higher blood than Tejharet's, one who is not of his loins, then we can unseat him and reclaim the throne."

"What throne?" muttered Padrin. "What will be left after this Genesis cataclysm?"

"You let me worry about that," answered Jenoset. She stepped toward the door, stopped, and pointed back at Farlo. "Prepare him for our wedding—at midday."

"Yes, my seeress," answered Padrin with a polite bow. He still looked distracted, however, as he turned to study his medical instruments. Jenoset sauntered regally into the corridor, letting the doors hush shut behind her.

His legs growing wobbly, Farlo slumped onto the bed where Candra had lain. All he could think about was his friend, now that they had become separated . . . now that both of them had become adults much sooner than they ever imagined.

From a cylindrical room on an orbital space station, Professor Marla Karuw gazed out the viewport at the dazzling blue-green planet below—the ill-fated Aluwna. Landmasses weaved in rough green bands about the vast orb, looking like fat rivers of vegetation flowing through the crystalline blue seas. Despite eighty million souls and a number of large cities, the planet was in pristine condition, owing to their determined policy of low pollution and low population. Marrying three or four men to each woman had effectively solved the population problem eons ago, and new testing procedures had allowed the bloodlines to be categorized and standardized to a degree that was unheard of before the last millennium. On that sparkling blue-green orb, everyone knew exactly where they stood in the pecking order. Their genetic code marked their rank and caste as surely as skin color, height, or wealth did on other planets.

Breedcasting was exactly the type of thing that Marla Karuw had rebelled against, and to her it wasn't even the most serious injustice on Aluwna. The grip of old dogma had stifled science, the arts, commerce, and their place among neighboring worlds. Now Aluwnans were going to pay for their isolation. *Would the Federation have made a greater effort to save us if we were under their umbrella?* wondered the regent.

Probably not, she decided. The regent had heard of their desperate attempts to save their own worlds from destruction—with spectacular failure. Given the shortage of time, no one could devise a better solution to save lives than the one she intended to use, because few other worlds had the transporter infrastructure of Aluwna. Yet moisture welled in her weary eyes, because Marla knew that even success was defeat. The best she could hope for was the death of her planet and ninety percent of the people who lived there. And what exactly was she saving? A corrupt culture and backwater pedantry were the very worst features of Aluwna, yet they would survive after all of the beauty and character were gone.

All of their venerable traditions and tortured logic had produced a world that was helpless. Had the crisis been a giant meteor, an axis shift, solar eruptions, anything on a planetary scale—the results would have been the same. They were unprepared to deal with anything that was not in their precious view of the universe.

Karuw rubbed her moist eyes, pushed back a strand of salt-and-pepper hair, and massaged her right middle eyebrow, where a dull pain had been building all morning. One thing about solitary confinement, she thought, it was low stress. This was just the opposite, and she was beginning to feel the pressure after only a few units on the job. Despite the long odds and the horror that awaited her world, win or lose, she had to think positively about her task. Nobody else wanted the responsibility, as she had already found out, and most of the populace was in denial.

With a slight shove, the regent propelled herself away from the viewport and floated across the engineering substation to another window. She caught a handle and pulled her floating body into position to gaze at the belt of satellites and orbital stations which stretched into the invisible horizon. With the naked eye, she could really see only three or four faint glimmers of machinery in the spectacular two-toned, black-blue sky, but it was comforting to know they were out there.

The com channel sounded an alert, and Marla had to look around to find the wall panel. "Karuw here," she finally responded.

"It's Komplum," said her new assistant. "The energy lab is ready to try their first test of gel-plasm power cells to replace the solar receptors on the satellites. Would you like to be there?"

"I would, but I don't have time," she answered frankly. "Tell them to be thorough and to get the results to me as soon as possible. Remind them that this is the backup power source after we get out of solar range—it must come on instantly."

"What's the primary source?" asked Komplum with interest.

"I don't know yet," she admitted. "Probably some kind of direct line we'll run from the tow ships, with frequency boosters. If you get any bright ideas, let me know. Komplum, you must make it clear to everyone that we *can't* lose power to these satellites. That's the same as murder."

"Yes, Your Regency," answered the assistant with a squeak in his voice. "I believe you have a visitor . . . he just beamed up."

"Is it Curate Molafzon?"

"Yes," whispered Komplum, "and he seems to be in the custody of two constables."

"It happens to the best of us," said Marla with a smile. "He wouldn't come any other way. Will you please have his escorts bring him in?"

"They are doing so now. Is there anything else, Your Regency?"

"No, end transmission." She tapped the com panel just as the door slid open and two beefy constables pushed a struggling, wizened old man in scarlet robes into her engineering sanctum.

"Marla Karuw!" he screeched in rage at the top of his lungs. "I should have known this was your doing— you foul beast! You blasphemer! You *charlatan*."

"That's enough," she answered with a scowl.

"You'll be quiet and listen, or I'll have them push you out an airlock."

"You can't do that!" he said with fresh horror and indignation.

"Oh, yes, I can. I'm regent of Aluwna." She motioned to the sparkling globe floating in space just outside the viewport. "I have life-and-death say over not just you—but every person, pet, or microbe on our planet."

"You're mad!" he exclaimed, aghast. "You're on a mad power rampage."

Karuw shook her head in disbelief. "I wish it was that simple and that harmless. You must know by now the Genesis Wave is headed our way."

He nodded somberly. "Yes, we are praying that it will be averted."

Marla turned away from him in disgust and motioned to the two guards. "Please leave us," she said. "I think I have another important appointment in half a unit, who will also require your assistance."

"Yes, Your Regency," said the lieutenant, bowing. The two of them pulled their weightless bodies out the opening, and the door slid shut behind them.

"Curate Molafzon," she said slowly, fixing him with a steady gaze, "whether you like it or not, this planet is going to be altered beyond recognition in fifty-seven units. I intend to save several million Aluwnans in the buffers of our satellites . . . but I don't know how to be divine and choose who lives or dies. I was hoping you would help me."

For the first time, the clergyman's expression softened a bit. "Do you really think there is *no* chance for deliverance from this dread?"

"We're in the path of the wave, and nobody knows where it began or how to stop it. Are you going to bet on a miracle, or are you going to help me?" She stared at him expectantly.

Molafzon shrugged his bony shoulders, which no amount of padding could hide. "I suppose . . . we will take the highborn first."

Karuw turned away from him and gazed out the viewport. "Is it that simple? After the danger is over, we'll have to resettle this planet. Do we really want a world in which everyone is basically brother and sister? The Divine Hand didn't create all of us with ninety percent breeding, and it might be dangerous genetically to have such a world."

He held up his hand, starting to protest her statement, and Marla quickly added, "We're not going to debate philosophy now. Just think about what we need to survive after our civilization is gone. How many high breeds are carpenters, masons, farmers, and garbage collectors? Not very many, and we'll need them far more than we need professors and administrators, such as you and me. We'll need young people with strong backs—a lot more than old people in fine clothes."

The curate fingered his satin robe, then stared at her with a mixture of fear and hope. "You will take all the clergy, won't you?"

"Every clergy?" Her brow furrowed in thought. "After I see the numbers you send me, I'll see what I can do. But should we really save an entire class of people, forsaking all others? You're in touch with the Divine Hand—I'm hoping you'll help me see the *right* thing to do. It won't be the easy thing, no matter what."

As he floated in front of her, the old clergyman rubbed his cracked lips. "I suppose you could ask for volunteers—older ones who have lived most of their lives and will make way for younger people."

"Yes," agreed Marla Karuw with a grateful smile. It wasn't much, she thought, but it was a start. "That's the kind of insight I was hoping for. Could you head this up for me—this volunteer program? I'll prepare the technology to save as many lives as possible, while you must prepare the people. It's not a job I could ask anyone else to do, but they have so much respect for you, Curate."

He nodded uncertainly, looking as if he'd been coerced into doing the devil's work. While she had the advantage, Karuw pressed on. "The overseer is due to address the populace in about a unit. Why don't you beam directly to the Summer Palace, and you can be at his side. When he's done, you make your appeal for volunteers—it will mean so much coming from you, Curate." She tapped her panel and said, "Curate Molafzon is ready to leave."

The door whooshed open, and the two constables reached inside and took the clergyman by his elbows. "Better duck, Your Holiness," one of them said as he led the elder's floating body out. He glanced back at her with an awestruck and worried expression, as if the full impact of their fate had finally hit him.

Marla's com panel chirped again, because Komplum knew this was a suitable time to interrupt her. "Regent," he began, "the Royal Biology Institute has responded to your request. They basically have a million questions about what species and genera you want to take on the transporters. At the crux is one main question—"

"Yes?" asked the regent, already certain she knew what it was.

"How many people do we leave behind in order to take plants and animals?"

Karuw took a deep breath and a long pause before replying, "This is another place I want redundancy, because we can't devote much storage space to plants and animals. We'll take the minimum needed for reproduction, favoring successful species over extremely rare ones." She pushed herself away from her instruments and drifted lazily across the small cylindrical room, while her mind worked frantically.

"For redundancy, what we need is a terraforming device that we can use to counter the effects of the Genesis Wave, whatever they may be. We know the planet will still be here, and there are reports that plants are growing on these Genesis planets. What about the chromasynthesis process? We know it can stimulate plant growth and alter genetic coding, but we've only scratched the surface. I mean, we may not be as advanced as the Federation in some respects, but nobody knows more about genetics and cultivation than we do. What an external agent can change on our beautiful planet, an external agent can put back to normal."

Komplum cleared his throat and said, "Your Regency, chromasynthesis is only in its infancy. Most of the things you're talking about have never been tested."

"What a great test!" she answered. "This isn't something we have to perfect before we go; we just have to plan for it by bringing all the pertinent data and hardware. For now, let's restrict this idea to a small number of people."

"Yes, Your Regency," answered Komplum. "There are several other urgent matters, like the commanders of the merchant fleet and the royal yachts. They've been awaiting word from you, and they're none too happy."

"Let them stew until they're all in orbit. When will that be?"

"In another six units," he answered, "all but one major vessel will be here."

Hand over hand, Marla towed her weightless body back toward her workstation. "I'll send them a memo apologizing for the delay. But they don't need *me* to report information on their tractor beams, tether lines, and power output. If they would just fill out my questionnaire, we could get somewhere."

"Yes, Regent," answered Komplum, his voice quavering at the idea of confronting these powerful commanders. "You'll handle it?"

"Yes," she assured him with a wan smile. "You're doing enough already, thank you. How many people in your family, Komplum?"

"Ten, with my sisters and fathers," he replied.

"Put them all on the list," she ordered. "Yourself too."

"The list?" he asked uncertainly. "What list is that?"

"I think you know," she answered gravely. "The ones who will be saved."

five

Long-necked yellow birds floated across the shimmering surface of the inlet, while other birds serenaded them from the willowy trees that dipped their branches into the vast mirror of water. From a colonnade that dripped with orange and lavender flowers, Farlo viewed this magnificent scene, thinking he had never seen anything so heavenly. Oh, he had visited the inlets of the Calm Ocean once before, but he hadn't been lounging in a recliner, enjoying a cool drink of nectar squeezed from the fruit that grew in profusion all around him. On that earlier occasion, he had been booth-hopping with spoilers on his tail, and he hadn't spent any time appreciating the scenery.

Now that he thought about it, the youth realized that he hardly ever devoted time to appreciating the view. Of course, he'd never had a vision like this one to appreciate. It was the Institute of Devotion, and they had arrived in a red transporter booth, which meant travel here was restricted. He turned to look at the buildings, which were every bit as grand as the natural view of the inlet. Closest to the water was a silver gazebo, which was decorated with fanciful statues of mythological beings. Behind it stood a massive building, also circular like the gazebo, but with a shining golden dome and stairs strewn with vines and flowers up the sides of it.

Every few instants, a servant would appear on the stairs, bearing trays, artwork, or armloads of flowers, which they hustled into the main entrance and the ballroom beyond. It was hard to believe that all this preparation was on account of *him*, and he tried to put that out of his mind. The idea of marriage to Seeress Jenoset was so wild that he couldn't believe they would go through with it. Surely, they would figure out they had made a mistake and put an end to this madness.

His uncle Padrin, as he had taken to calling the seeress consort, sat in a chair not far away. Armed with brush and palette, he was trying to paint an image of the inlet. He was doing a poor job, but he seemed to be enjoying himself.

The handsome man saw Farlo looking at his work, and he chuckled. "I'm woefully out of practice, I'm afraid, but I used to win awards with my painting. You wouldn't believe how hard I have worked to find somebody like you—it's been night and day. So now I'm entitled to a little relaxation, don't you think?

Although I don't know how relaxing this is going to be, with that Genesis monstrosity headed our way."

Farlo bit his lower lip, wondering if he could be blunt with his new uncle. "Sir, am I really supposed to be married to the Lady Jenoset?"

"Absolutely," answered Padrin. "She wouldn't joke about a thing like that. She only has two husbands, me and the overseer, so you should feel quite honored." He glanced at a chronometer on his chair and reported, "Only two more units until your nuptials. Oh, and it's also time for the overseer to make his announcement. Maybe he'll say this is all a bad dream, and we can wake up now."

The painter pressed a button on his chair, which turned his canvas into a viewscreen. After a few instants, the dour face of Overseer Tejharet appeared, and it took Farlo a moment to realize that he would soon be in the same family as the ruler. Thinking about that, he hardly listened to the overseer's grim account of the threat they faced. The boy's life had already been turned upside down in the space of a few units, and another complete overturn was wasted on him.

"Uncle Padrin," he said, "if it's my wedding, why can't I have at least one friend there?"

"Shhhh, boy!" hissed the consort. "Can't you see that Curate Molafzon is speaking. Does he really think that people will volunteer to die from the goodness of their hearts? He's crazy—this is going to be a mess."

"Please, Uncle," begged Farlo, "can I have one friend at my wedding? Can I invite my friend Candra?"

The man turned and scowled. "There isn't time."

"Yes, there is. You could arrange it." Farlo gave him what he thought was a winning smile. "You know they'll listen to you. Please, it would mean a great deal to me."

"Would it, now?" Padrin turned back to his screen, where the curate and the overseer were gravely shaking hands. "In these crazy times, what difference could it make if your friend comes or not?" he remarked. "People are going to stop doing their jobs, anyway."

He turned off the broadcast, and his viewscreen reverted to a virtual canvas. Then he tapped the panel on his chair. "This is Consort Padrin. Give me the Esplanade Command Center."

The canvas turned into a view of an outdoor constabulary station in the festive esplanade, only it didn't look so festive at the moment. People were gathered in solemn groups, discussing what they had just seen and heard on the overseer's address. For most of the citizens, it was the first time they had truly realized that the planet was in the path of destruction, and a majority of them would die. On the beautiful lagoon where Padrin and Farlo were lounging, it didn't seem possible that anything could spoil the idyllic calm; but in the cities, thought Farlo, fear would spread like gossip.

He listened intently as Padrin issued orders to have Candra brought to the Institute of Devotion. His new uncle also took a moment to reassure everyone he spoke to that they were important to the kingdom. Although this didn't actually promise them anything, Farlo got the feeling that the people thought their lives would be spared by their friend in the palace. From what he had heard, nobody had any control over the situation, except for the new regent, and Padrin didn't trust her.

But they couldn't be marrying him off just to kill him, figured Farlo. He and his well-born new family would be saved from this Genesis Wave, and he wanted to make sure Candra was also safe. It was all he could think of doing while he waited.

In orbit around the shimmering green-blue planet, a shuttlecraft floated beside a massive transporter satellite, which dwarfed the ship in size. Two-thirds of the satellite's wingspan consisted of its gleaming solar panels, which shifted in unison to catch the sun's disappearing rays on the curved horizon far below. Three technicians in EVA suits hovered between the satellite and the shuttle, moving on tiny thrusters. Two of them were already headed back toward the shuttlecraft, and the third one was making some final adjustments at an access panel on the satellite.

"Dyz, only eighty instants until we lose the sun," crackled the voice in the helmet of the lead technician, who was making a final adjustment to the bioneural computer banks, simulating a memory-full condition. This satellite was offline for normal transporter use and would be out of solar range in another few instants, so nothing was at risk. Like all of his comrades, Dyz wanted desperately for this to work, but it had to be a true test. The lab experiments had gone well, but the field simulation had to be as real as possible. The failures had to come now and not when they escaped planetary orbit and the sun's energy.

On the control panel, he ran through the readings of temperature, circulatory pressure, electromagnetic waves, and cell reproduction rates for the biological components. Then he rechecked the raw power levels in the gel-plasm cells, which were brand-new and fully charged. All appeared normal.

"Dyz, twenty instants," crackled the voice in his ear. "Get back here."

"Yes," said the chief, reluctantly shutting the access panel. He grabbed his handheld instruments, activated his thrusters, and slowly drifted away from the whirring solar panels, which were trying to grab the last glimmer of sunlight before shutting down. As soon as the solar power dipped below fail-safe levels, the new battery packs were supposed to activate. It would be the same if ship-based power failed during their evacuation. If all went well, the gel-plasm packs would never be used in actual conditions, but the engineer knew that things seldom went perfectly.

As the last sliver of sunlight faded over the halo of Aluwna's horizon, Chief Dyz was about halfway back to the shuttlecraft. He opened a handheld scanner and watched the satellite with both his instruments and his eyes, waiting to see its reaction. The blinking warning lights never went out, nor should they have, and the solar panels reoriented themselves to pick up the first rays of dawn in the morning, which was normal. The satellite's regular batteries performed that function, but they weren't designed to keep the memory and computer systems in active mode.

He focused his attention on the electromagnetic readings, which, for all intents and purposes, were the brain waves of the bioneural network. That level was also normal—the satellite was alive!

"All systems active!" said a joyous voice in his ears. "Dyz, did you hear me—we're a go!"

"I'm seeing it with my own eyes," he responded happily. "Are we on a countdown to see how long the batteries last?"

"Just started it," said his teammate. "If we go until sunrise, the solar panels will kick back on."

"That should be a good test," replied Dyz. "I'd be happy with that performance, as long as there's no degradation."

"We'll be watching for it," his partner said. "Congratulations, Chief."

"Don't celebrate yet," cautioned Dyz. "Let's wait a few more units. Pop the hatch for me."

"Airlock open. Prepare to terminate EVA," said the voice in his helmet.

With a glance at the silent but fully functional

satellite, the chief technician activated the tether return and let himself be reeled toward his shuttlecraft. No one could say he hadn't done all he could, trying to live up to the faith his old professor, Marla Karuw, had placed in him. He only hoped it would be enough.

On Sanoset Field, the price of shuttlecraft had just quadrupled, and then some. Not too many Aluwnans ever saw the necessity of buying a spacecraft—they thought they lived in paradise, and they knew they had a superior transporter system. So most of the vessels were owned by offworlders, governmental departments, and those few merchants who had reason to visit the other six planets in the Tejmol solar system. Rows of shuttlecraft normally stretched for measures and measures, baking in the hot desert sun, but they had been reduced to a few scattered vessels on the mostly empty field. Nervous owners had banded together to hire armed thugs to watch the vulnerable shuttlecraft, while the passengers and new owners scraped up the huge fees.

Wielding their stun sticks, the guards milled around the blue transporter booths along the fences, looking for troublemakers among the idle crowd of onlookers. The number of people showing up at the shuttlecraft field, looking desperately for salvation and hope, was starting to grow.

"But what is the point of all this?" wondered Hajhor Kanow, the pilot for a very special shuttlecraft with the crest of Rahjhu on the hull. They had their own contingent of constables guarding their ship and its crew of two, and Kanow looked at his copilot, a young woman named Ulorna. He waggled his multiple eyebrows and asked, "What's the point of wealth when the whole planet is about to be destroyed? Why are all these people scrambling like this?"

"To save their skins," answered Ulorna. "We're shuttlecraft pilots, we've got a way to escape. That reminds me, when is our drop-dead departure time?"

Hajhor glanced back over his shoulder through the open passenger hatch of his eight-person craft, and he spied the chronometer on the bulkhead. "We've got to leave in thirty-seven and a half units to beat that damn wave . . . so tomorrow night."

"And we're going to leave," said Ulorna pointedly. "Why take chances when we don't have to?"

Hajhor frowned and kicked a pebble in the dust. "You're young and unmarried," he said forlornly. "You can go to other worlds and make a new life, but I've got family here. I'm the first husband. Will we be allowed to take our families? I doubt it. What will happen to everyone . . . everything that is left behind?"

"Don't worry too much," said his partner. "A lot of people will make it anyway—in the buffers."

Hajhor looked doubtfully at the dazzling blue sky, as if he could see the satellites; then he gazed back at his sleek shuttlecraft. Their ship wasn't the royal yacht, but they got around pretty well for a little runabout. "I'll take my chances in the ketch," he said.

A voice suddenly boomed on their com channel—the restricted one—and both of them whirled around to hear, "Security alert, Sanoset Field, royal occupancy en route to shuttlecraft *Niwamol*. Arrival immediate."

The pilots jumped, and so did the constables. Within seconds, the guards had cleared away the onlookers, creating a corridor between the ship and the nearest transporter booth. Hajhor wondered who the royal personage would be, but he wasn't overly surprised to see Seeress Jenoset step from the machine and stride regally toward them, a small entourage of assistants rushing behind her. She made the most use of the shuttlecraft, often going places where the transporter network didn't even reach.

Hajhor stuck his head into the hatch and called to Ulorna in the cockpit, "Look alive! It's *her!*"

He bowed as the ravishing ruler passed by, and she nodded curtly. Jenoset looked very irritable, but he supposed even high breeds fretted when the world was about to end. "Good morning, Seeress," he said. "Are there to be more passengers?"

"No," she snapped as she stepped inside. "Just what you see. Set course for the Institute of Devotion."

"The transporters," began Ulorna, but she withered under Jenoset's glare.

"Yes, I know they go there," the ruler hissed, "but the transport system is under control of my enemy. Plus I have a feeling it's going to be closed down to regular traffic very soon. Until further notice, you and this ship are my transportation."

"Yes, Seeress," muttered Hajhor, wondering if he would ever have time to see his family again. Perhaps Ulorna was right, and they would have to make their own opportunity to escape from this cataclysm. After all, they did possess the means to save themselves.

"Get under way immediately," ordered the seeress, slipping into her special seat. "I wouldn't want to be late to my own wedding."

six

Marla Karuw stood on the holodeck room of the Summer Palace, a place she had always wanted an excuse to use for some purpose or another. This was a perfect opportunity as the holographic projectors could send the images for all the ships' captains into the blank beige room, where she could address them at once as if they were together. Most of the vessels in the small fleet of freighters and royal yachts were already in orbit, and the stragglers were coming along. Every moment was precious in her hectic schedule, and she couldn't give them the face-to-face meetings they deserved. Well, she would just tell them that, the regent decided.

She nodded to Komplum on the control panel of the holodeck, and he started the program. At once the room filled with the lifelike visages of nine starship captains. It was a rarefied job on Aluwna, befitting high breed and considerable offworld training on places like Earth and Vulcan, and the starship captains were like rulers of their own kingdoms. So they considered the regent with frowns of doubt and distrust, especially since they had been summoned at haste, then kept waiting for orders. Considering how important their cooperation was, Marla Karuw considered this her most important test yet.

"Hello, Captains," she said with a smile. "I don't begrudge you looking askance at me, because I've kept you waiting. I'm sorry, but ever since I've taken command during this time of crisis, every second has been precious. I'm sure you can relate to that. I wanted to give you my full attention, and now you have it. I'm supposed to be your superior, but I don't feel like your superior. I know that what you do, I couldn't possibly do, so I'm not asking for obedience . . . but for cooperation. By now, you've read the reports—you know how bad it is. Our world and most of the people who live here are going to perish, but we have a chance to save eight million citizens, plus animals and plants and unique species."

Marla took a moment to encapsulate what they already should have known about the Genesis Wave, then she went on, "You, Aluwna's fleet, must tow three hundred thousand satellites out of harm's way. Then we can return, resurrect our populace, and reclaim our world from this diabolical event. We have less than two days, about forty-four units, to escape. Very few of our ships have warp drive, but impulse should be enough to get away in time, since we're on the edge of the G Wave."

She paused to scan their faces, looking for dissent, but none came. "Your role in this rescue and evacuation is crucial," she continued. "It can't happen without you. You and your crews are pretty much guaranteed to survive, no matter what. The question is, do you want to survive alone? If you don't help me, you might have a few members of the royal family along with you, but you would basically be all that's left of Aluwna."

The stubbornness in their faces softened a bit, and they looked at one another as if they realized they were not in this alone. Calmly Marla Karuw went on, "There are two components to what you have to do. One is to supply energy to the satellites, to keep their computers and buffers at full, and the other is to tow as many as you can to safety. The slower ships will leave the earliest, of course, and some faster ships may be able to make two trips to our safety zone. We are constantly updating our plans as we get information from the Federation, but I feel we have enough information to proceed."

"And why can't the Federation help us?" asked one of the captains.

"They've got more ships than we do, it's true," admitted the regent. "I have asked them for help, and so has Overseer Tejharet before me. But we haven't been given much hope. Their fleets are spread all along the path of the wave, and most of their ships are already full of refugees or simply couldn't get here in time. Even if they could, it would take thousands of ships to save as many souls as your few ships can, if we store them in the pattern buffers."

"Incredible," said another captain, shaking his head. "Our entire civilization comes down to our handful of ships and this insane idea?"

"Yes," answered the regent. "Bluntly, that is it. The replicators have been ramped up to make the parts, and I know we have the technology to tether our satellites and keep them powered. The question is whether we have the will. You've received the latest guidelines from my staff, and we've already started to close down segments of the transporter network to use for testing. I hate to simply dismiss you, but I've got to keep moving—and you know what you have to do. In truth, I don't care how you do this, but *do* it. The fate of Aluwna is riding on you."

"Our families!" shouted one captain. "Will they be saved?" The others leaned forward and looked expectantly at her, as if this were the only question that mattered.

Karuw pursed her lips, trying not to show any emotion, even though this issue nagged her every waking instant. She looked at Komplum and nodded. "Yes, your families and those of your crews will be on the exempt list. They will be among the first stored in the transporter buffers. Send their names to my assistant, Komplum. Good day, my comrades, and the speed of the Divine Hand be with you."

She motioned to her assistant to end the holodeck conference, and the images of the stiff-necked captains gradually faded away. Marla Karuw let out a sigh and allowed her shoulders to slump. "That had better be all the hand-holding they need," she muttered, "because they've got to be aggressive."

Komplum cleared his throat. "You know, Your Regency, that list is becoming very long, and you've got messages from millions more, begging to be on it. We're going to need help, like a whole department devoted just to keeping the list."

"Of course," she answered with a nod. "And we'll need help from the Divine in knowing who to put on it. Every citizen who wants to apply for inclusion will have to complete a form, then we need to get the curate and the overseer to preside over the random selection. Of course, some of it won't be random, such as the families of those who help us."

"Plus the high breeds," said Komplum without a trace of sarcasm. He was simply stating a fact.

Marla Karuw didn't immediately respond, because she didn't entirely agree. "What have we heard about the battery tests?"

"So far, so good," answered Komplum, checking the notes on his handheld padd. "Still full power in the satellite systems, no biodegradation."

She strode past her assistant and toward the door, which opened at her approach. "I'm giving orders to proceed to full installation right now. Get a repair crew and tons of supplies onto every orbiter."

"But, Regent," protested Komplum, "that's not a very long test."

"We haven't got time for a very long test," she snapped. "All we have time for is hope and a prayer." She stopped and looked fondly at her young assistant. "Keep pointing things out to me—that's good. What do you think the common people will do when we turn off the transporter system?"

"Panic . . . riot," suggested the young Aluwnan. "Don't do it without warning, please."

The regent scowled. "All right, we'll give them two units to get home, but we'll suggest they don't go anywhere unless it's an emergency."

"In these times, every breath is an emergency," observed Komplum.

"You're right on that," answered Marla with a wistful sigh. "And it's only going to get worse."

"Candra!" shouted Farlo Fuzwik, rushing down the tiled walkway to the restricted red transporter booth. His old partner-in-crime looked remarkably like a woman, dressed in a diaphanous blue gown and wobbling on high heels. She staggered off the transporter platform into his arms, and they hugged in a way they had never hugged before.

Farlo pulled away, slightly embarrassed. "You look . . . grown-up! It's great that you made it—I didn't think you would."

"Look at this outfit!" exclaimed Candra, gaping at his red satin wedding uniform, with its golden epaulets, tasseled hat, striped silky trousers, and bright red slippers. They had gone from children to adults dressed in fine clothing much different from the children's threads they had worn earlier that day.

"Well, we both look terrific!" he exclaimed. "Did you . . . what was it like on the esplanade?"

"Really fun!" she answered, clapping her hands together excitedly. "I mean, I didn't do anything but try on clothes and meet some of the other girls. It was a very high-class place, from what I could tell. But then came the overseer's announcement, and a lot of people left. The customers all ran for home. I didn't know *where* I was going to go, but then the constables showed up. And here I am."

She grabbed his arms and shook him. "So that's my story, but you came out way on top, by the looks of it. What happened to you?"

Farlo started to reply but got tongue-tied about saying he was a high breed, because he had never related to Candra in that way. He had never thought she was a woman either, but she clearly was. "I'm getting married," he said sheepishly.

"Married?" Her jaw dropped. then she laughed out loud. "You *do* look like you're dressed for a wedding, but you . . . married?"

"Hey, you thought it was perfectly all right for you to service strange men, but I can't be married?" he asked indignantly. "And I'm marrying the seeress, to be her third husband, because it turns out I've got high breeding!"

Now her jaw really dropped, and she gripped his arm. "You're not making this up?"

He pointed to his elegant clothing and then at the sumptuous grounds, the glistening sea, and the mammoth building, with its outdoor staircases and madly dashing servants. "Red transporter booth," he added, pointing to the contraption she had just exited, as if he needed to explain the exclusivity.

She lowered her voice to ask, "So this means you're going to get off the planet before this energy wave hits us, but what about me?"

"Stick close to me," he advised her. "Maybe I'll have some pull with the overseer."

"Well, you should have some pull with the seeress," said Candra with a sly smile. "At least you'll get to see her alone. Very alone."

Farlo was certain he was blushing, and he was relieved when a glittering object came streaking toward them out of the sky. "Look at that," he remarked, pointing into the eastern sky. "It must be a shuttlecraft."

The servants rushed to meet the small craft when it touched down on a landing pad behind the domed building, but Farlo and Candra stayed in the garden, talking, until Uncle Padrin came to fetch them. Recognizing the handsome man from the laboratory, Candra glared at him until Farlo introduced him as the seeress consort.

"Who knew she would clean up so well," remarked Padrin, gazing at Candra with approval. "I'm sorry I sent you away, my dear, but I didn't know our whole world would be turned upside down. Rest assured, you'll be safe with us."

Frowning puzzledly, Candra asked, "Will Farlo be called the seeress consort, too?"

"I'm afraid so," he answered with a wan smile. "It works great for getting a restaurant reservation, although I don't know if that will matter in a couple of days. Come along, Farlo, your bride awaits, and she doesn't like to be kept waiting. Just nod your head and say yes. This won't be a gala wedding, given the state of emergency, but you should get a taste of your new life."

Farlo got more than a taste, and the ceremony lasted for more than a unit of time. The seeress had brought both a judge and a cleric with her, and they were surrounded by servants, minor dignitaries, and the acolytes of the Institute of Devotion. Two ceremonies were conducted—civic and religious—and both of them went by in a blur to Farlo. He couldn't take his eyes off the ravishing blond woman in the purple gown who smiled fondly at him a few times, and he couldn't imagine that she was to be his bride. Since he knew this change in his station of life was due entirely to his breeding and the children he might produce, he fretted all through the ceremonies about what his postnuptial duties would be.

Farlo scanned the crowd for Candra, to make sure she was sticking by him. Early on he saw her, watching with a concerned frown on her face, but as the ceremonies dragged on he lost sight of her. When it was over and every power on Aluwna had pronounced them husband and wife, Farlo continued to survey the crowd, looking for his friend. But Seeress Jenoset commanded his attention.

"Beloved," she told him without a trace of sarcasm, "we haven't got time to consummate our relationship at the moment, but there will be time later. You listen to your uncle Padrin and stay in this place, which is safe. If all goes well, I'll return to claim you by tonight. If there are delays, I'll know where to find you, or where to leave instructions."

Jenoset kissed him tenderly on the cheek, and he smelled her delicate perfume of fruit blossoms and autumn spices. With a swish of the stiff fabric of her gown, she turned and sauntered from the great hall, her entourage in tow. Farlo finally let his breath out, and he stared dumbly at the departing servants and guests.

"Candra!" he called. "Candra, where are you?"

When no one in the fleeing crowd answered, he found his uncle Padrin outside in the gazebo, watching the birds float idyllically across the shimmering water of the inlet cove. "Uncle," he said, "have you seen my friend Candra?"

"I saw her," answered the dapper consort, his eyes somewhat hidden and half shut. "I thought your friend came out here midway through," he answered. "Can't blame her, with all the history and religious lessons we have to hear every time one of us gets married. You know, I thought I would have no emotions when I was eventually forced to share my job. After all, we spent long enough looking for you. But now that you're here—and you're so much younger and prettier than I am—yes, I do admit to a pang of jealousy."

When Farlo sputtered something in protest, Padrin sighed and leaned against a trellis full of purple vines. "It's not your fault, lad. Why do you think we were testing street children? We knew you were out there. But will it really matter? I'm melancholy about losing our way of life. Maintaining a privileged class is not going to be a high priority on the new Aluwna, I'm afraid. Considering where you came from, you must find us stuffy and self-centered, but we have really tried to govern wisely."

After dabbing moisture from his eyes, Padrin cleared his throat and said, "Normally your fate would be blessed by this event, and no harm would ever befall you—but our world is ending. I understand they're holding a lottery for the commoners, and you must feel as if you've already won. Maybe so, but I caution you to look out for yourself, Farlo. We've lived in a bubble all these cycles, and . . . well, you know what happens to bubbles."

The boy nodded somberly, even while he scanned the beach, looking for Candra. He didn't know why, but her friendship seemed more important than anything else at the moment.

* * *

Candra hesitated before following the last of the resplendent wedding guests into the red transporter booth. Three at a time, they hurried to escape from this sylvan setting in order to do what they had to do before the disaster. *Is leaving really the best thing?* she wondered. *How can I leave my best friend when he wanted me to be here?*

The answer was clear on the face of Seeress Jenoset during the ceremony, when she gazed often at Farlo. The lady had high plans for the youth, and they didn't include his ragamuffin friends. She would only get in the way and become a hindrance to him. Then again, where could she run? Their old haunts might seem safe, but the low-bred girl knew that she would never win any kind of lottery for survival on Aluwna. She didn't even have an official existence, except for being a pleasure girl in training.

No, thought Candra, this was not the time to freelance when she finally had connections in high places. Still Candra realized it would be hard watching Farlo be married to another woman. She had never thought of him romantically, but they were a team and had been for many cycles. She would gladly share him, but that was forbidden. It was stupid—why couldn't a male marry several females? The answer, she feared, was that no man would want to marry a girl of her breeding. Desirable females were always a minority, and most men would rather be second or third husband to a high-bred wife, while they slipped off to the esplanade to pleasure themselves with females of her station.

"Excuse me, may I ask you something?" intruded a kindly male voice, interrupting her thoughts.

She turned around to see a great rarity—an off-worlder, dressed in simple but flowing brown robes, as if he were one of the acolytes. Dark gleaming hair, pointy ears, gaunt face and body, blank expression, and only one pair of eyebrows—what were they called? The girl hadn't had any formal training, but she had seen a lot of life and almost every run-down hovel in the capital city. She had seen this race before . . . Romulans, Rigelians, Klingons . . . or maybe Vulcans?

Whatever he was, Candra knew what all off-worlders wanted. "You can take this transporter booth any place that's not restricted," she told him, pointing to the red contraption.

"I know that," answered the stranger. "I have spent much time here."

The roar of thrusters sounded across the lavish gardens, and they both turned to watch a shuttlecraft climb swiftly into the azure sky. "That would be our seeress leaving," he said matter-of-factly.

With stern but not altogether unkind dark eyes, the pointy-eared man turned to regard her. "I am looking for an object I lost, and there is a reward for the one who finds it. I have my own starship, and I can offer you a coveted prize—escape from this doomed world."

"What makes you think I know where it is?" asked Candra suspiciously.

"Because you stole it," answered the man. "You and

the new seeress consort. I cannot ask him, because he is being watched too closely. Do you remember a black beadsack which you took this morning from a passerby in the courtyard of the Summer Palace?"

Candra looked down at her feet, and then she glanced at the transporter booth, wondering if she could make a break for it. But the stranger stepped in front of her and said, "My friend was careless to have it in a bag. What's done is done, and I offer no punishment, just rewards. The only thing I want from the bag is a black tubelike device about so long." He held his fingers apart a few micromeasures. "Do you remember such an ebony tube?"

"Maybe," she answered sheepishly. Since Farlo had taken all the belongings in the black bag, she didn't really know what had become of them. But Farlo ought to know.

"Here," he said, pressing a small communications device into her palm. "If you find it, you press this button to contact me. I will be waiting to hear from you. Remember, you can trust me to save your life when you can trust no one else. Pin this on your gown, like a brooch." He did the honors for her, and his hands were sure and gentle. She wondered about his age, which was hard to judge in a member of his race.

The stranger walked toward the transporter booth and said, "I hope to hear from you, Candra."

"What's your name?" she called out as he stepped into the booth.

Without giving an answer, the offworlder shook his head as the door shut after him. With a puzzled frown, Candra twisted the fabric of her gown to see the communications pin he had stuck on her. She heard a call and looked up to see Farlo running her way, and that gave her an extra boost of hope. Carefully Candra turned on her high heels and headed toward the domed building and her old friend, who was waving frantically. Things were happening so fast, but she knew that the mysterious offworlder had been right about one thing—she needed to look out for her own skin.

seven

"Turn them on! Turn on the transporters!" screamed one man just before he tossed a vase of flowers, which shattered off the side of the blue booth.

Four constables wielding stun sticks tightened ranks around the booth, but they were outnumbered about a hundred to one. Despite repeated announcements that the transporter system would shut down at midafternoon, millions of Aluwnans had been caught in places far from home—at work, at school, or at play. Most of them accepted their fate stoically, but a vocal few were becoming violent, as this video log indicated. One man taunted a smaller female constable to the point where she lashed out with her stun stick and dropped him where he stood. That sent the crowd into a frenzy; in one great surge, they overwhelmed the guards and grabbed their stun sticks, which they used against the peacekeepers.

Flush with this minor victory, the energy of the mob reached its peak, and they assaulted the transporter booth itself. Screaming and yelling, the rabble managed to uproot the box and push it over onto its side, where it exploded with a shower of sparks and smoke that drove them back. Dozens were trampled in the resulting stampede.

A synthesized voice on the fallen booth started to bemoan its fate. "The transporter booth is malfunctioning," it told the loud and deranged crowd. "Please step away. The transporter booth is malfunctioning." It exploded with a pop and belched huge clouds of smoke into the downtown air, as the crowd lustily cheered its approval.

Marla Karuw scowled and tried to look away from the disturbing sight. So the chief constable turned up the sound and made the image on the overseer's desk even larger. "Before now, we were a peaceful society," he grumbled. "So we don't have enough constables to deal with an emergency like this. According to your orders, we have to protect each and every transporter booth at all cost. Is that right, Your Regency?"

"That's right," she admitted, "every booth is crucial. But I happen to know this is a rare occurrence, and that the people are calm at most stations. In fact, more people have volunteered to stay behind than have requested to be put on the list."

"Yes, but these people just want to get home!" he exclaimed. "They don't understand or care about the logistics involved, and we'll never know which booths are going to be mobbed. Regent, we've got to have more constables. We don't have to pay them anything—we can hire all we want just by putting them on the list to be saved. My replicators are making more stun sticks, and we've got the volunteers to triple our number."

"I imagine you do," muttered Karuw sullenly. "So the only people who will be saved are the thugs we hire to protect the transporter booths?"

The chief shrugged. "My forces didn't choose this battle—we were pushed into it. With the transporters off, we face problems getting people into position, but we need the people first."

Marla Karuw sat at the desk in the overseer's receiving room and drummed her fingers on the lacquered wood. "Chief, what kind of breeding do most of the constables have? Is it high?"

He looked down at his feet and put his heels together. "Hardly. Most of them are middle breed, young and fit, about equally divided between the sexes. If you want us to find higher breeds we could, but we don't really—"

"No," she said, brushing it off. "We'll also need your constables to oversee the loading of the transporter booths, when the time comes. You're right, we aren't geared up for this, but we're learning as we go. After we get the gel packs and the power tethers installed, we should be able to reopen the transporters for official use, so keep in contact with my staff."

"Yes, Regent," he said with a bow. "So we can promise salvation to our new hires?"

"That's what I said, isn't it?" she asked testily. With a motion of her hand, Marla Karuw dismissed him, and he hurried from the receiving room, his footsteps clacking across the tiled floor.

The regent rubbed her rows of graying eyebrows, thinking that she would never get used to being a conduit for the Divine Hand—having to choose who lived and who died. Although she had always craved responsibility, this was more than any sane person would want. They *all* deserved to live, every single inhabitant of Aluwna, including every plant and animal. Nothing about this outcome was fair.

That reminded her of another task, to check in with the Biology Institute. At this point, she could do little but monitor the progress of others, and the flora and fauna of Aluwna were one area she had neglected. She tapped the com panel on the desk and said, "Regent Marla Karuw wishes to contact the chief administrator, Dr. Harlam Hazken, Institute of Biology."

"Regent, I am at your service," came a voice a moment later.

"How does it go?"

He sighed wearily. "It's difficult . . . taking some and leaving the others, but we've narrowed it down to the target number. We have all the samples, or access to them, but this is made difficult by the transporters shutting down."

"Temporary," she assured him, making new policy on the spot. "We *will* reopen a few for official use. By the way, we will also be transporting your specimens first, in about twenty units."

"Use them to test," said the biologist. "I understand."

"The time for testing is long past," answered Karuw. "We need to get the slower ships sent off as soon as possible, with easily assembled loads. Right after your menagerie are the royalty."

The biologist chuckled grimly. "I suppose *you* are having it much worse than I am."

"No comment," muttered Karuw. "We're thinking about doing some terraforming when we get back. Doctor, what do you know about the process called chromasynthesis?"

"Well, it's a way to synthesize the existence of an animal or plant down to their genetic imprinting, using standard components and cell data. A lot of raw material is required, which makes it impractical. So far it's mostly hypothetical or on a very small scale—you could maybe reproduce a grub—but chromasynthesis has the promise of a great number of uses. You also know such research is illegal?"

Marla sighed. "I didn't know for sure, but I suspected as much . . . or else we would have taken it farther. Playing with the divine, and so on. Well, we're already doing that, aren't we, Doctor?"

"Yes," he responded. "There is one man, and they say he sometimes traffics with offworlders to obtain equipment and information. He's the leading authority who's not in prison."

"Vilo Garlet?" she asked.

"Yes, Vilo, but you didn't hear that from me," cautioned the administrator. "Regent, I'd like to talk more, but I've got much to do. I've also got to plan for my passing."

"Your passing?" said Marla with alarm.

His voice cracked as he answered, "I'm eighty-seven cycles old, and my wife isn't well. Her other two husbands will apply for the list, but they're young. My wife doesn't want to be stored in a transporter buffer and resurrected on a desert, or whatever Aluwna will be. So I'll stay behind with her."

"You're a hero in many ways," said Marla hoarsely. "Thank you, old friend. I'll let you know as soon as we reopen a few transporters for official use, but it may be a secret."

"I understand. Harlam Hazken signing off."

She tapped another panel on the desk and said, "Personal records."

"Yes," answered the computer. "Please state the name or search term."

"Vilo Garlet," she answered, "formerly of the Science Council. I want an address for him."

Sunset dropped like a blazing neon curtain over the inlet of the Calm Ocean, and Farlo and Candra stopped upon a garden path to admire the brilliant orange, pink, and salmon hues, reflected in the smooth azure sea. To think that these were the final sunsets to ever be seen in the Aluwnan skies, it was almost too much for the boy and his friend to bear. They tried to talk about their good fortune, but it was clear that they had been lucky on an unlucky day.

"I can't believe it's all going to be gone," said Farlo.

"Don't think about it," answered Candra. "Whatever happens, we're going to get out of here all right."

"Yeah, I know," he muttered, thinking of all their friends, the adults who had been kind instead of cruel, and the merchants who had looked the other way when the urchins stole fruit or a roll. Most of them would be gone forever, just like this sunset and the glistening sea.

"Hey!" said Candra cheerfully. "Do you remember the loot you stole in the park this morning? What did you do with it?"

"Buried it," he said. "It was that damn loot that got us caught."

"Yes, I know," she answered, "and got you blood-tested and us on easy street. But when I was at the esplanade, I found out that those black things—that little tube—they're valuable. We should go get that thing."

He shrugged. "It was just a perfume mister. I tried it."

"Well, it's a *valuable* perfume mister," she insisted. "Where did you hide it?"

Farlo looked at her curiously. "Why should I tell

you? People are trying to save their necks—they don't care about perfume misters."

Candra grinned at him. "You hid it by the apothecary, didn't you?"

"So what if I did? You can't get there anyway—the transporters are closed, so they can get ready to grab all of our molecules and keep us in cold storage."

"Hey, let's go over to the transporter to make sure," said Candra. "Come on, I'll race you!"

She kicked off her fancy shoes and ran full speed down the path toward the red booth on the outskirts of the grounds. Farlo had no choice but to shake his head and run after his lithe companion. Even if they had left at the same time, it would have been hard to beat Candra, and he didn't stand a chance with her head start. She reached the booth several instants before Farlo did, and she hid from him on the other side of the contraption. He chased her around the enclosure a few times and tried to catch her, but she was always too swift for him; she finally ducked into the booth itself, and he followed her.

They stood panting, their short breaths echoing in the chamber, which was big enough to hold the two of them and maybe two more travelers. The lights on the control panel were blinking as if the thing worked, but they had heard from several disgruntled servants that the transporter didn't work. According to the gossip, all of them were trapped in the Institute of Devotion for the rest of their short lives, unless they made the list.

"Computer," said Candra playfully, "take us to the Blue Bird Apothecary in Tejmol."

Farlo laughed at her. "You know it won't—"

He felt the strange tingle of the transporter beam and saw his friend giggle as she began to fade away. Farlo gripped her arm and shouted, "But we can't leave—"

It was too late—they were gone, reconstituted on a side street in Aluwna's capital city. Except for the tingle and mild dizziness, the only thing that seemed to have changed was the color of the booth, because the one they exited was blue. Laughing, Candra pushed him out the door, right into the brawny arms of a constable.

"Hey, you!" he growled, grabbing Farlo roughly by the shoulders. "Don't you know that travel is restricted?"

The lad looked around at four other constables and a number of onlookers milling around the closed storefronts. He knew they had made a terrible mistake, and they would no doubt pay for it.

"It's not restricted for *us!*" claimed Candra bravely. "Don't you know who Farlo is? He's the new seeress consort. Turn him loose!"

"Sure, and I'm the new regent!" said the constable with a laugh.

"Let him go!" seconded another voice, from an officer who had stepped inside the transporter booth and was studying the control panel. "They just came from the Institute of Devotion, and the computer does identify him as Seeress Consort Farlo. Sorry, Your Highness."

The officer bowed, and so did the other constables, reluctantly. But a surly crowd was gathering around the booth to watch this bit of drama, and they didn't look impressed by the new consort, despite his exotic clothing and pretty companion.

"Hey, I thought they were shut down!" cried one woman angrily. "Hey, everyone! Look, this transporter is running!"

"Yeah, I saw them get out!" yelled a man, charging toward the brawny constable. "We can get home!"

The officer wrestled with the man for a moment and finally had to use his stun stick on him. That enraged a few loudmouths in the growing crowd, and they all pressed forward like a swelling tidal wave. The constables were quickly overwhelmed and knocked down by people rushing the transporter booth. Farlo grabbed Candra's hand and tried to make it back into the box, but they were stopped by rioters trying to squeeze in ahead of them. Then Farlo felt Candra yank her hand out of his grip, and she vanished into the frenzied crowd. He had no choice but to follow her.

Farlo caught up with his friend behind the booth, where she was digging in his secret hold. She grinned happily at him as she retrieved the small black tube, the transporter pass, and the crystal timepiece he had stashed there that morning. Some of the mob took her actions to be an effort to turn over the transporter booth, and they surrounded Candra and started pushing against the machine, even as other people battled to get inside it. The struggle turned into chaos, and all Farlo could do was grab Candra and pull her out of the melee.

"Damn, we're in for it now!" shouted the lad as he pushed his friend into the doorway of an abandoned storefront. "Look what you started!"

Triumphantly she held up the black tube and said, "I saved our lives."

"We were safe where we were," he insisted. "Now we're stuck out here . . . with everyone else. They're wrecking the transporter!"

Sure enough, the mob trying to overturn the booth was bigger and more determined than the rabble trying to enter it, and the blue enclosure tilted over and crashed into the street, accompanied by cries of horror and delight. When two explosions from the machine spewed sparks and smoke into the air, the revenge of the crowd was complete, and even Candra looked as if she was afraid.

"Come on!" she said, grabbing Farlo's arm and pulling him into the shadows. As night fell over the panicked city, two finely dressed young people dashed down a deserted street, gripping each other's hands.

Marla Karuw looked up at the flickering electric sign over the warehouse door—it read CONDEMNED BY ORDER OF PRECAUTION DEPARTMENT, and she glanced at the metal door, which was bolted and locked by an exterior device. She nodded to the cadre of constables and technicians who had accompanied her to this empty industrial park, and one of them stepped forward with a small beam emitter. Efficiently, he sliced off the lock, and it clattered to the street. Waving their stun sticks, the constables crowded around her, prepared to conduct her into the darkened building.

"No, I'll go alone," she told them as she pushed open the metal door. The odor of old solvents assaulted her nose, and she saw nothing but darkness and scattered trash on the floor.

"Regent, we urge you to reconsider," said the ranking officer. "Anybody could be living here."

"Or nobody," she suggested. "Wait here, and I'll call you if I need you. Have you got a light?"

The constable handed her a small torch which shot a bright beam into the gloomy corridor, and Marla cautiously entered. There were a few small offices on either side of the corridor, but they appeared to be deserted, except for trash. So she made her way to the double doors at the end of the hallway, and they opened at her approach. That gave her a start, but it meant that not all the power had been cut to this building, just enough to make it appear to be empty. The building had been approved for residence and light industrial work, although it didn't look inviting for either use.

Marla stepped into a large warehouse space that was empty, except for some huge packing crates in the far corner. The crates were big enough to make small apartments, and she walked slowly in that direction, letting her beam of light lead the way. In truth, she didn't have time for hide-and-seek; if her quarry was here, she wanted to see him.

"Vilo Garlet!" she called. "Listen, Vilo! This is Marla Karuw, and I'm regent now. You don't have to be afraid of me—I want to *save* your life. I need you to help me."

A wheezing chuckle sounded somewhere in the darkness, and a voice came from overhead. "I'm not afraid of you, Marla. On the contrary, I'm gladdened that they had the sense to put you in charge. On the other hand, I don't trust you any more than I trust the overseer."

She saw a slim figure moving on a catwalk against the far wall, two stories above her head. Marla walked slowly in that direction, keeping her tone of voice conversational. "We used to be colleagues, before they chased us both out. You can trust me. Don't you want to leave before the wave comes?"

"Oh, I'm leaving," he answered. "Very soon, which is why I haven't got time for *you*. Now if you and your friends outside will leave me alone, we can both get on with our lives . . . even while our homeworld dies."

"You have a way off?" asked Marla, still moving toward him. "I'm impressed."

"I have friends," he answered. "I don't want to leave right this second, but I will, if you come another step closer."

The regent stopped in her tracks and turned off her

light. "There. I won't force you to do anything, but I want to appeal to your reason. If you can help me use chromasynthesis, we may have a way to reseed this planet much more quickly than normal. Believe me, no one will go to jail, and there will be no more forbidden knowledge or heretical research."

"That's reassuring," said the figure, moving away from her. "I've only made one chromasynthetic device that's worth anything, and it was built for a very specific purpose. But it's been lost. Just when I was about to change this planet for the better, along comes this energy wave to completely wipe us out. Ironic, eh?"

"This doesn't have to be the end of Aluwna," insisted Karuw. "Help me, please."

"You and your friends do your best," said the voice from the darkness. "If I can, I'll return to Aluwna afterward and help you, but I can't risk discovery now. Good-bye, Marla."

He vanished into the shadows, and she heard a door shut. "Blast it!" muttered Karuw, feeling like a failure. How was Vilo Garlet going to leave the planet, unless he had a ship? She wouldn't put it past him, because he had often associated with offworlders.

She tapped her communications pin and said, "Regent Karuw to team leader. There's no one here, so I'm coming out. Tell the ship to prepare to beam us up."

"Yes, Regent," replied the officer with obvious relief.

"And tell the captain to scan for any offworld ships in orbit," she ordered. "If he finds any, I want them informed that they should help us."

"Yes, Regent."

"How could you *lose* him?" shrieked Seeress Jenoset, flapping her arms and stomping across the smooth tiles of the domed ballroom. Stars glistened in the night sky as seen through magnifying panels in the dome, but there were only two people in the hall, and neither one was enjoying the view.

Consort Padrin shrunk away from Jenoset's wrath, knowing he had erred badly, but he still had to offer an explanation. "The transporters were down," he said slowly, "so I didn't think it was necessary to watch Farlo every instant. How was I to know that they reopened the transporters? At least that booth at the wall they reopened—some others still appear to be closed."

The regal monarch scowled at him in disbelief and motioned to the elegant furnishings. "Are you saying they left all *this* to go back to the streets? That's hard to believe, especially with this disaster looming over us. And I don't usually lose new husbands in the space of a few units."

"I understand," said Padrin, seizing on her insecurities. "Perhaps he didn't understand *exactly* what we had to offer him. Plus it might have been a mistake to bring his little friend here, because she might have had some influence on him."

"You're right about that," snapped Jenoset, tapping her elegantly encased toe on the marble floor. "The little wench was out to destroy our marriage, I could tell with one glance. Normally I'm more careful about these things, but I was in a hurry. We've got the highest breeding stock on the planet, and he slips through our fingers. I'm so distracted by everything, I can't think!"

"Perhaps they didn't use the transporter but went on foot," said Padrin hopefully as he pointed toward the black hills, covered with night. "Perhaps they'll walk back in due time."

"Perhaps you're brain-dead," replied the seeress with a snarl. "They left—they're gone. Have you checked the log in the booth to see where the last destination was?"

He nodded vigorously. "Of course we did, and it's a small street near the Summer Palace. Yes, I would have gone after them, but the system lists that transporter booth as unavailable."

"They went to a closed station?" asked Jenoset with doubt, then she flapped her arms again. "It's all *her* fault. The regent is incompetent—she has everything in chaos!"

"Yes, My Seeress," agreed Padrin quickly.

She pointed a dark lacquered fingernail at him. "I want the exact coordinates of that place near the Summer Palace, so I can track them down. They were caught stealing near the palace, right?"

"Yes, I'll get you the coordinates," said Padrin,

backing toward the door, relieved to have a mission that took him out of the seeress's presence. She was as mad as he had ever seen her, from losing Farlo, having Marla Karuw as regent, and the rest of the crisis; and he didn't know how to console her when she got like this.

If I were a real man, he thought, *I would grab Jenoset and throw her onto her shuttlecraft, so we can escape while there's still time! To blazes with bloodlines, politics, and the rest of the royal merry-go-round—let's save our necks!*

But he was not a real man. He was just one of two consorts, and he had less guts than the new one. Padrin didn't blame the lad for running away, because it was better to die in freedom and self-respect than live in cowardice.

Most of the roofs in Tejmol were sloped or domed, like minarets, but a few had niches and cornices where two lithe young people could climb and hide, observing the whole city below them. So it was that Farlo and Candra perched on the roof of an art gallery in the old section of town, watching events transpire on the streets below them. They had borrowed some blankets from a deserted apartment and were wrapped up in them, because the night was getting cold. People should have been in bed, but they were gathered in groups, talking, complaining, and watching video logs of people volunteering to stay behind. Farther down the street, hundreds were lined up to enter their names in the lottery. A patrol of constables roamed the sidewalk, and most of the people were respectful to them. Still there was an atmosphere of panic and desperation that Farlo had never seen before.

In the starlit sky, a shuttlecraft glided slowly past their position, then wound through the sky over the Summer Palace.

"We're going to die here," muttered Farlo, "with all those other sad people. I guess I could go stand in line and tell them who I am."

"Nah," scoffed Candra, hugging the ratty old blanket tighter around her elegant gown and bare feet. "You don't have to do that. I wasn't going to tell you, but maybe I should. You look so miserable."

"Tell me what?" he demanded.

She grinned smugly. "I know an offworlder who's going to take us with him."

"What?" asked Farlo doubtfully. Normally he would have hooted at such a boast, but he knew this was no average day. After all, he'd been a homeless street child one instant, the seeress consort the next, and back to homeless.

"He wants your perfume sprayer," she whispered. "That's why we had to get it."

Farlo laughed uproariously. "You've gone crazy! We were already safe, and now we're stranded—all to get that perfume."

"I'll prove it to you," said Candra defensively. She pulled back her blanket to show him a pin she wore on her dress. "This is a communicator—all I have to do is push it, and my pointy-eared friend will answer."

"And save us?" asked Farlo. "Go ahead, I'm waiting."

Smugly the girl tapped the brooch and grinned. After a few moments, absolutely nothing happened, and she did it again. After Farlo began to laugh at her futile attempts, she tore off the jewelry and was about to hurl it twenty stories into the street below, but he caught her hand.

"No, wait," he said. "Don't turn up your nose at a gift. Let's keep that pin and see if it's at all useful in the morning. We'll keep the perfume, too. You never know—we may want to smell good when we die."

She lowered her head and muttered, "I've been stupid, haven't I?"

"Hey, we're not used to people giving us stuff," answered the boy, trying to cheer her. "They've tried to give us stuff all day, and we can't tell what's good and what's bad. The important thing is that we stick with each other—and not give up."

"I heard them talking," said Candra, "and we have until tomorrow night. That's when the ships have to leave to beat the energy wave."

"We'll find a way," vowed Farlo.

eight

From the cockpit of his runabout, *Klamath*, the pointy-eared alien looked back at the sleeping Aluwnan in the passenger seat. He wanted to make sure that Vilo Garlet was asleep before he broke security and made contact with his superior. It was a shame he'd had to flee from Aluwna at warp speed before getting the sample he had gone to find, but that girl wasn't likely to come through for him. Besides, the information he had gathered was almost as valuable as the sample. So was the passenger sleeping in a backseat and snoring contentedly.

Using a special, encrypted subspace band, the pilot opened a direct channel and carefully enunciated, "Specialist Regimol on starship vessel *Klamath* to Admiral Nechayev, access code 'Bakus aurora thirteen' urgent protocol."

Regimol sat back in his seat, inspecting his fingernails. He never got through immediately, especially not in these troubled times, so he used these leisure moments to remove a bit of the pale makeup he wore to look more Vulcan than Romulan. Later he would wash the dye out of his hair and let the gray that revealed his age show through. Finally his instrument panel beeped, and he leaned forward to make contact with his superior.

Only it wasn't the admiral on the screen—it was her taciturn Andorian aide, Commander Dakjalu. "Sorry, *Klamath*, but the admiral is in the field and is indisposed."

"In the field during the Genesis Wave?" asked Regimol. "I don't like the sound of that. Where is she exactly?"

Even the stone-faced Andorian seemed to flinch as he answered, "She's on Myrmidon with members of the *Enterprise* crew, seeing if the interphase generators work during exposure to Genesis."

"That's seeing them at awfully close range, isn't it?" muttered Regimol. "An interphase generator is fine for walking through walls, but for saving a planet? I don't know. We really don't know if she's alive or dead?"

"That is correct," answered the commander. "But she did leave orders for you, if you checked in. You are to report to Deep Space 9 and await further orders."

The renegade Romulan scowled. "Hurry up and wait? What about my passenger . . . and the mission I'm already on?"

"Since Aluwna has been determined to be in the path of the Genesis Wave, we no longer suspect that rebels on Aluwna are involved."

"But this research of theirs is very exciting," countered Regimol. "And it might vanish along with the planet, if we don't grab it first."

"You have your orders, Specialist Regimol," said the taciturn Andorian. "I will update you when we receive word of Admiral Nechayev's status. I will inform her that you made contact. Starfleet out."

The screen went blank, and the Romulan cursed under his breath. "Stupid bureaucrats . . . worse than the Romulan Senate. Besides, I work for Nechayev, not Starfleet." He plied his controls and brought the runabout out of warp drive.

"Vilo!" he shouted. "Wake up! We're headed back to Aluwna."

"Huh? What?" muttered the sleepy Aluwnan. "Are you crazy? We'll barely get back before the wave hits. And they're already looking for us!"

"Then it's only fair to let them find us," answered Regimol, setting a new course for the doomed planet.

"But I tell you, I'm Farlo Fuzwik, the new seeress consort," insisted the young man to the official in the temporary kiosk set up to register citizens for the lottery. Despite their snide comments of the night before, by midday both Farlo and Candra realized they had better get registered. The more ways to escape the disaster, the better. "Look up my name," urged the lad. "I married Seeress Jenoset just yesterday!"

"It doesn't matter—we aren't using names," snapped the official. "You were standing in line for over two units—you could read the brochure on how this all works."

"They were out of brochures," said Candra, trying to act seductive and almost making Farlo laugh. "Can't you just put us on the list?"

"I can register you for the random lottery," answered the man, working his board and smiling slightly. "You just married Seeress Jenoset! That's a good one, thanks for the laugh. We're taking retina scans and matching them to a microscopic homing device, which I'll implant under your skin. If the homing device beeps and lights up, you've been selected—you can prove who you are later with another retina scan. If it doesn't light up, well, maybe they're wrong about how bad it will be. So, my seeress consort, look into this eyepiece with your right eye."

As Farlo obeyed and gazed into the white circle, the official readied a hypospray that was connected by a tube to his medical computer. "Almost done, hold still." He jabbed Farlo in the left forearm, implanting a small tracking device just under his skin. The lad rubbed the bump, which was kind of tingly and itchy.

"Next, young lady, come on," said the man wearily. Candra stepped forward and began the same procedure.

"How long until the random selection?" she asked

nervously, while putting her eye to the machine.

"As soon as we get everyone done. Should be three or four units." He punctured her arm and shooed her out of the way. "Move on."

"Are *you* going?" asked Candra, staring the man in the eyes.

He didn't say anything, but his smirk told them the answer. "Next!" he called, getting the attention of the constables who were standing nearby.

The two youths shuffled away from the line at the kiosk, not knowing what to say to each other. It was hard to be enthusiastic about being frozen in a pattern buffer for an indefinite time, no matter what the alternative was. Plus they had been treated like royalty yesterday, and today they were like the rest of the dregs, begging for a chance to live.

"Did you hear what the odds are?" asked Candra. "I mean, for getting a safe spot. One in twenty, I heard them say."

"I thought it was one in ten," said Farlo with surprise.

She snorted. "Not after you figure the high breeds and all the people who are working this scam, like that spoiler back there. You've got all the clerics and constables going, and how many of *them* must there be? No, all of this is just to keep us quiet while we wait for the end."

She lowered her head and added, "You should be going with the seeress—I'm sorry I screwed up."

"Don't worry about it," said Farlo, mustering more

bravado than he felt. His mind was whirring, trying to figure out how to beat those odds and return to find protection, with the seeress or Uncle Padrin if need be. "If we could only find a working transporter—to get back to the Institute of Devotion—we'd be all right."

"But how do we know which ones work?" she asked. "We came through a red one, so maybe the red ones—"

"Yes, we'll find another restricted booth!" whispered Farlo excitedly. "Good idea, Princess!"

She bowed regally. "And how will we do that, Seeress Consort?"

He held up his transporter ticket for the Stone Spire and said, "There's one here—it's restricted. All we have to do is walk there. Maybe we'll find another one before we reach the Stone Spire."

"Can we steal some food along the way?" asked Candra.

"Sure," answered the lad, but in truth they didn't have to steal food. The merchants and vendors were giving it away, along with everything else. Everyone who was condemned could have a free last meal.

It was a surreal walk through city streets that were often crowded but seemed empty, with people wandering, some weeping, some making grim jokes. Farlo could spot those like him and Candra who were walking determinedly toward a destination. He figured most of them were just trying to get home in time. Their anger had been dulled by the promise that they could still be saved under a system that was fair to all, and not too dangerous. Everyone looked with hope at the transporter booths, all guarded by tight-lipped constables, some of whom didn't fit their uniforms very well.

We've trusted transporters our whole lives, thought Farlo, *so it's logical to trust them now.* Even with this promise, a large number of people wandering the byways of Tejmol looked like the walking dead, far beyond the stages of denial or hope.

"I don't like the looks of this," said Chief Dyz to himself, as he grabbed one of the solar panel struts on the satellite and stopped floating in his EVA suit. The technician was tethered to his orbital craft, along with four others from his augmented crew; they were busy attaching power cables to their first test subject. Then it would be filled with precious data and whisked away.

Like a floating mountain, behind the workers and the transporter satellite hung a massive gray freighter. Dented and dirty, it took up half of the blue-black, two-toned sky. The other half was taken up with the cometlike tail of satellites strung behind the immense freighter. Their pattern buffers were already filled with precious living samples of the planet's great beasts and small butterflies, plus grains, thorny weeds, and the most prized herbs Aluwna had to offer.

Despite the marvels around him, Chief Dyz was concentrating on a stranger kind of animal, the bioneural network that formed the bulk of the satellite's computer system and data storage. On this first test unit, they hadn't beefed up the memory or installed new biological components; they wanted it to be a typical satellite of common functionality and condition. Now he was beginning to doubt the wisdom of that, because the satellite's operating temperature had dropped two degrees, according to the built-in scale. It wasn't much, but it was enough to make the chief frown behind the transparent mask of his helmet.

"Dyz to orbiter. Lazmon, are you at the console?" he asked aloud.

"Yeah," answered his pilot, the only one who was not on EVA at the moment.

"Double-check my readings on the bioneural network. Has it gone down two degrees?"

After a moment, the voice came back, "Yes, two degrees from optimum, although contents reading stable."

"I know that," muttered the chief. "I don't want to cause waves, but make an urgent report of this. Tell them we can't keep monitoring the test satellite, because they're going to fill it for real and take it out of orbit. Remind them it was running all night on plasma gel packs."

"Yeah," said the pilot, "so it's probably normal."

"Nothing's normal when you've never done it before," muttered the chief. "Better yet, bring me back. I'll make the report."

"Aye, Chief."

* * *

Marla Karuw tapped her chin thoughtfully when she read the dispatch from the test satellite. She had been watching for degradation in the system while it ran under the plasma gel packs, and she thought they would be home free. But they weren't. This was a small glitch, however, and it came after a full night and part of a day running on the emergency power. More important, the data contents were still stable, and that was the stat that really mattered. The regent frowned at the report as she read it again, because she had no backup plan to the backup plan. So she reluctantly filed the log on the computer of the royal yacht, *Darzor*, and moved on to other matters.

One of them was waiting on the other side of the bulkhead, kicking up a fuss, and she knew she couldn't keep him at bay much longer. She tapped the com panel on her desk in the royal library, which was now her private office. "Komplum, is he still out there?" she asked.

"Oh, yes," answered her assistant. "He claims he won't go away until he sees you, and he kicked one of the constables in the shin."

"I did not!" shouted a voice in the background. "He's a liar!" That was followed by more invective, most of it directed at the regent personally.

"Send Curate Molafzon in," she ordered with a sigh. "Send the constables with him."

"Yes, Your Regency."

A moment later, the door to the library slid open,

and the wizened clergyman strode into the room, fire burning in his eyes and his six gray eyebrows twitching. "You promised me!" he yelled, wagging a finger at her. "You said you would take *all* of my clergy and acolytes!"

"I never said that," replied Marla firmly. "In fact, I questioned the wisdom of saving an entire class of people, when so many other were dying. I automatically took all of the clergy who are under thirty and put all the others in the lottery, so many more will be saved."

"I'll fight you!" vowed the curate, shaking his fist at the regent. She moved back as two brawny constables surrounded the holy man, whose stream of invective was anything but holy. She couldn't tell the curate that she *had* saved an entire class of people, but they were constables who kept the peace. It was a matter of practicality, she told herself, not of worth or morality. The new Aluwna wouldn't need swollen ranks of clergymen when the entire planet had to be rebuilt, but she said none of these things, because Curate Molafzon wasn't listening to her.

"I'll rally the masses against you!" he shouted. "I'll go on all the bands and tell everyone how you *tricked* me into helping you. I'll reveal you for the megalomaniac you are!"

He rushed her and actually had his hands around her neck when the two constables moved in to restrain him. For an elder man, the curate was strong and enraged, and he fought the two constables to a standstill while Marla tried to escape behind her desk. It was shocking, but every moment of life was shocking—and decisions had to be made.

"Stun him!" she shouted at her guards.

One of them finally found his stun stick and dropped the maddened clergyman into unconsciousness. They all stood panting for a moment, even Molafzon, who was curled up asleep on the deck.

"Throw him out an airlock," said Marla Karuw, her jaw tightening.

The constables stared at the regent as if they hadn't heard her correctly. "You want him in the brig?" asked one officer uncertainly.

"That's not what I said," she replied through clenched teeth. "We'll never be able to reason with him—he'll do nothing but cause trouble, and he could upset the whole plan. Listen, I can't appease *him* and let all of you constables live, too. To be blunt, I haven't got time to fight problems when I can eliminate them, so do what I say."

They gaped at her, and the younger officer finally rasped, "But that would be . . . murder!"

Marla Karuw scowled as she circled her desk to face them. "I've already committed murder seventy million times today—my hands are drenched in blood! Yours will be, too, before this is all over." She pointed at the well-dressed, gray-haired figure lying on the deck. "I don't want him on the new Aluwna, and I have the say over who is there. If the two of you won't throw him out an airlock, I'll take your names off the list and find two people who will."

They blinked at each other but said nothing, and the regent moved to a computer console on her desk. "I'll inform the captain that we need to open airlock three, which is just down the corridor. Take him away, do it quickly, and don't tell anybody, not even my staff or your superiors. We'll let history decide if we're villains or heroes. You're dismissed."

After a glance at each other to fortify their courage, the constables holstered their stun sticks and picked up the unconscious curate. They had no difficulty hauling the slender elder out of the library and into the corridor, while Marla sent word to the bridge that they would need to open an airlock. She had essentially taken over the royal yacht since arriving on board, and nobody could question her orders. People were coming and going in a mad rush, occupying the ship's transporters almost every instant, and they could easily lose track of one old man. By the time queries rolled in, so would the Genesis Wave, making Molafzon's disappearance an obscure footnote. When so many died, who would notice one more?

Despite the logic and pragmatism of her decision, the regent sat at her desk, buried her face in her hands, and began to weep.

nine

In downtown Tejmol, Overseer Tejharet's immense, stricken face appeared on the wall of a twenty-story building, on a screen that a mural of farm life usually occupied. Slightly behind him stood Curate Molafzon, and the entire body of the Science Council stood behind them. In this prerecorded message, the overseer urged the populace to remain calm and to volunteer to stay behind. Farlo had seen it a dozen times that afternoon, and so had everyone else. But they kept watching the building screens, because they knew that the overseer would eventually show up to announce the end of the lottery and a final list.

After walking all afternoon until the early dusk, he and Candra finally reached the Stone Spire. Eons ago, this crude minaret of bricks and mortar had noted the first incursion of the Divine Hand into this region, which had been held by pagans. The sanctuary stood on a funny little hill on the outskirts of the city, where it had withstood attacks in its early cycles. The crude fortress had been rebuilt many times and was a famous but fragile monument to the Dark Ages. Farlo didn't know why it had seemed important to come here, because they had probably passed other restricted booths behind the walls of government buildings. They had needed a destination, and this seemed a logical one.

Now arriving at the ruin and seeing the crowds, he realized they had made a mistake. People choked the narrow streets leading to the place, and a large contingent of constables stood behind the black metal gate. If there was any transporter booth inside, it was behind the old gray walls, which looked as difficult to assault now as they had been in the Dark Ages.

"They're not going to let us in there," muttered Farlo. "This trip has been a waste of time."

"Would you prefer to sit around and wait for the end?" asked Candra. "Come on, let's see if they know anything."

By moving patiently and trying not to anger people, the two youths worked their way to the tall metal gates, where the watchful constables kept an eye on the crowd. More constables stood on the parapets above, and it was obvious that this was some kind of staging area. Near the gate were two kiosks for lottery registration; they were empty, although the retina scanners had been removed and set up just inside the metal bars. Farlo rubbed the bump on his arm where the tracking device had been implanted, as if assuring himself he was still included.

"Move along!" growled a constable even before Candra and Farlo had stopped. "No loitering."

"But I've got a ticket to go in here," said Farlo, producing the transporter stub. "If I could just use the transporter for one second, I could go back to the Institute of Devotion and—"

"Get out of here!" Laughing, the guard took a swipe at him through the bars with his stun stick, and Farlo had to duck out of the way. Beside him, Candra moved like a flash and caught the constable's wrist in both her hands. Since he was on the other side of the barred gate, she could pull his arm backward until he screamed in pain, which she did. They always knew what the other one was thinking, so Farlo instantly lunged to grab the stun stick away from the constable. While the other guards shouted and tried to grab him through the bars, the two wrested the weapon away from the constable. It dropped to the ground, and Candra picked it up and ran.

As they scampered off with their prize, the crowd lustily cheered its approval. Two days earlier, thought Farlo, this kind of violence would have been met with absolute shock and indignation, no one ever having seen such a thing. Now the constables were objects of hate and fear, and the street thieves were the heroes.

"Give me that!" shouted the wronged constable.

Three layers of shaggy eyebrows sloped angrily down his brow. "We'll come after you!"

"Yeah, right!" scoffed Candra. "As if any of you have the guts to come out *here!*"

The gathering mob laughed and hooted, getting squarely on the side of the young punks in their tattered, satin clothes. Some in the crowd argued that authority had to be maintained, and various shouting matches broke out, with the wronged constable still bellowing the loudest.

Farlo gripped Candra's spare hand, being careful to avoid the stun stick. "Come on, I know another way in." He pulled her away from the milling crowd, which was pressing forward to see what all the commotion was about, and they dashed down a narrow, winding stairway made of rocks.

"The orphanage brought us here once," he said. "They took us in a back way." When he nearly bumped into her stun stick, he asked, "Does that thing turn off?"

"I suppose it must," she answered. They ducked into the shadow of an alcove and carefully studied the weapon, avoiding the charged end. On the curved rod, there was a small panel for power readouts, a dial, and a button. Upon pushing the button, they got a message saying that the stick was turned off.

"Look, here's a name," said Candra, pointing to a shiny label with the words WARLIN BETZEL.

"I bet Warlin is ticked off," added Farlo with a grin. "Come on, it's just down here. If there's only one guard, I've got a plan." He told her as they ran.

The stone passageway, built during the Dark Ages, was so low, stooped, and dank that nobody wanted to be in there, and even the two young people had to duck. Whatever sheen was left on their fine clothes was now dulled forever, and Candra's bare feet were covered in mud. Just as Farlo hoped, the metal bars at the far end were guarded by only one constable, there being no room for more than that in the cramped tunnel.

"Remember what I told you," whispered Farlo, taking the stun stick, turning it on, and hiding it behind his back, being careful not to poke himself.

As they stepped from the shadows, the constable snarled at them through the bars. "Hey! Nobody's allowed down here! Go back where you came from."

Candra held out the transporter ticket and said tearfully, "Our father's in there. Can you just get him a message, when you're able?"

"Right, and *who* is your father?" he asked, sounding doubtful.

"Warlin Betzel," she answered with a sniff. "We're his children, but we got separated . . ." She began to weep. "Oh, it's so sad—"

"Warlin's children?" he whispered, aghast. "Why aren't you at the arena with the other constables' families?"

"It's a long story," answered Candra, her voice choked with emotion. "If you could just give our father this."

She held out the slip of paper in trembling hands, stopping short enough of the gate that the lawman had to reach through the bars to take the offering. Farlo had been edging forward, and that was when he brought the stun stick sweeping upward between his legs to jab the constable on the wrist. With a groan and a thud, the big man slumped against the bars and slid to the cobblestone walkway. Both Farlo and Candra reached through the bars into the man's uniform. Skilled at rifling through clothes, in a matter of seconds they found his identification, com device, a few beads, and a ring with two keys. These were old-fashioned keys, befitting an old-fashioned lock, and Farlo reached through the bars and tried one of them on the ancient gate. It took all of his strength from the awkward angle, but he was finally able to pop the lock. Groaning on its hinges, the aged portal creaked open.

The youths dragged the unconscious constable outside the gate, closed it, and locked it. Now they were inside the walls of the Stone Spire, but a transporter booth was nowhere in sight, not even a blue one. Sunset was coming, and long shadows stretched across the narrow byways and rustic stone walls of the restored ruin, making the place seem like a labyrinth. Hearing footsteps, they ducked into a niche and waited until a party of constables marched past, and they picked up a few snippets of conversation:

"A quarter unit before the announcement," said one. "Then the fireworks will really start."

"The ones going will be on our side," offered another. "The rest will keep calm, I bet."

"You haven't heard what happened on—"

"Shut up back there!" snapped a female voice. "No more talking."

After they were gone, Candra whispered, "Once they start beaming people up, we'll never get inside a transporter."

Farlo stepped in front of her, hefting the stun stick as he had seen the constables do it. "Let's just march around until we find it. Keep close to me."

Motioning his arm forward, he led the way out of the labyrinth onto a wider pathway which sloped upward toward the old sanctuary. Constables were stationed above them along the walls, but they were watching the people outside and not the ones inside. Within the narrow walkways of the old fortress, they avoided being seen as long as they avoided bumping into anyone, and their luck lasted until they reached the courtyard and saw the outline of an open hand chiseled into the aged rock floor. The thumb was pointing directly toward a red transporter booth, which no one was watching or guarding.

The two young people dashed straight into the enclosure and heaved sighs of relief. Farlo set the stun stick in the corner, while Candra said very clearly, "Institute of Devotion, please."

Nothing whatsoever happened. The computer didn't even say they weren't cleared for that destination—the booth acted as if it were turned off.

"Okay, now what?" asked Candra.

"Unless you have a better idea, we wait," answered Farlo. "Nobody can see us while we're in here. Don't open the door."

The next few instants dragged by like an eternity, then they heard voices and running footsteps. Farlo lifted the stun stick to defend himself, but nobody charged into the booth to confront them. Instead they heard a familiar voice booming from the speakers inside the enclosure and seemingly everywhere at once:

"Citizens of Aluwna, I thank you for your patience and understanding," said Overseer Tejharet. "Our greatest thanks goes to those millions of you who have opted to stay behind—no words can convey our respect and admiration for your courage. Now many more of you will have to be courageous. You can join hands with your friends and neighbors and family . . . and face this great change with the knowledge that your sacrifice is saving millions of our people, our plants and animals, and our very civilization."

The overseer paused as if gathering his own courage. "The results of the lottery are complete, and those of you who are leaving with us have been chosen. In a few instants, your implants will activate if you have been so chosen, and you should report immediately to the nearest transporter booth. Bring no belongings, just the clothes on your back. To all who have not been chosen, your names will be honored forever in the Halls of the Divine." At the last words, his voice choked with emotion.

Farlo held his breath and looked at his arm. A moment later, there was a dull red glow under his skin and a barely perceptible beeping. With a grin, he looked excitedly at Candra and asked, "And you?"

She shook her head glumly, because there was no change in the bump on her arm. Shouts of relief and screams of anguish rose over the walls of the Stone Spire, telling them that others were facing this moment of truth.

"Yours was supposed to light up," said Farlo with a nervous gulp. "You'll go—we'll find a way!"

"No," answered Candra, brushing a tear from her eye. "You were meant to go . . . you *have* to go. Don't let anyone stop you, not even me." Weeping, she lowered her head and moved toward the door.

"No, Candra!" he said, gripping her arm. "I'll tell the seeress . . . I'll explain to her."

"Let go of me!" she yelled, wrenching her arm away. "I *want* to stay behind." With that, she dashed from the enclosure, leaving Farlo stunned.

Slowly he moved after her, but the transporter booth suddenly activated with a rash of lights, a low hum, and a calm voice which said, "Prepare to transport."

Before Farlo could even gasp, he began to dematerialize, and his body was whisked away into the unknown.

"Wonderful! You made it!" shouted Uncle Padrin as he pulled Farlo Fuzwik out of the red transporter booth and gave him a crushing hug. "I thought we had lost you forever!"

Dazed, Farlo looked around and found himself back in the beautifully kept gardens of the Institute of Devotion, with the domed building, the gazebo, and the shimmering sea dominating the horizon. Darkness was almost upon this part of the world, and it was eerie to think this would be the last night on Aluwna.

"I told you it would work," said a snide voice, and he turned to see Seeress Jenoset, smiling smugly. "It was dumb of you to run away, but at least you had the brains to register for the lottery. That's how we found you."

"My friend . . . Candra," he said weakly. "Can't we take her, too? She won't be any trouble, and she's just back at the Stone Spire."

"A place we're not going," said Jenoset, checking an exquisite timepiece hanging from her golden sash. "As of now, every transporter is off-limits to regular travel, because they're filling up the satellites. I personally don't have much faith in the regent's crazy scheme, but I'm not going to worry about it—because we're leaving by shuttlecraft, not in a transporter buffer."

The seeress sniffed with disdain and touched the sleeve of Farlo's soiled garments. "What have you been doing, rolling in the mud? Padrin, get him cleaned up a bit, in new clothes, then meet me at the shuttlecraft. Don't delay, because our optimum departure time is in half a unit."

"Yes, Seeress," said the handsome man with a regal bow. He gripped the boy's arm and dragged him toward the institute, whispering under his breath, "You're the luckiest boy on the whole damn planet, and you almost threw it away!"

Farlo sniffed back tears, thinking that he didn't feel like the luckiest boy when he had just lost his best friend.

"Evacuation proceeding as planned," reported the chief constable over Marla Karuw's com link. The regent was still ensconced in the library of the royal yacht, *Darzor*, studying a bank of status monitors connected to the satellites, the transporters, and the vessels under her command. One of the slower freighters had already gotten under way to the safety zone, and that test case was the one she was most concerned about. Nevertheless, she switched her attention from those readouts to the readouts from the transporter system.

"Thank you, Chief," she said, trying to sound calm. "Have there been any problems?"

"A few outbreaks," he answered with a shrug, "but we're handling them. It was smart not to use the retina scanners to double-check the passengers, because that would have slowed us down immensely."

"I just wanted everyone to *think* they were in use," answered Karuw, "so people wouldn't try to steal the implants from each other. When do we estimate we'll be done with the evacuation?"

"Three units for the upload, and the satellites are already tethered. We'll be on schedule."

"Thank you, Chief," she said, mustering a wan smile. "If there's nothing else, I've got four starship captains waiting to talk to me."

"One more thing," said the lawman. "Is Curate Molafzon on your ship? We've had reports that the curate has gone missing."

"No," she answered, tight-lipped. "He was here, but he left some time ago."

"Do you know where he went? He's dropped out of the system . . . completely out of sight."

"I've got eight million people to keep track of," she answered testily. "If he shows up here or contacts me, I'll tell him to check in."

"Thank you, Regent. Central Constabulary out."

With relief, she punched the Off switch on that viewscreen and turned back to the others. *One old man,* she told herself, *among tens of millions—it was a necessary sacrifice.*

The process had to go smoothly, especially this complex evacuation, because the last starship and the last satellite had to depart before midnight. Nothing could stand in the way of that goal.

As darkness dropped decisively over the Calm Ocean and the picturesque islet where the Institute of Devotion stood like a perfect mountain, the shuttle-craft lifted from the landing pad. Still sniffing back tears, Farlo gazed out the viewport at a dark strip of land that quickly disappeared beneath them, to be replaced by a velvet sky sprinkled with stars like spun sugar. The boy had never flown anywhere, but this unique experience was muted by his sorrow. His world, his friends, his haunts—this was the last time he would ever see any of them.

The lad heard another sniffle, and he turned to see Seeress Jenoset staring out the viewport on the other side of the aisle. He wanted to hold her hand and comfort her, because he knew how she felt. The seeress glanced at him for a moment, her lovely face puffy from crying, and she shook her head.

"What a waste," she said hoarsely. "Now life will be a battle."

"At least you're alive, my dear," said a voice from the front. It was Uncle Padrin, trying to sound composed and failing. There were also three strangers on the shuttlecraft, family of the pilot, Farlo had been told. They huddled in silence, cowed by the presence of royalty. It was ironic, thought Farlo, that so much had changed that the pilot of a shuttlecraft made demands to the seeress of Aluwna and was appeased.

If they could be saved, why couldn't Candra? he wondered glumly.

There was no answer, no answer at all—just the soft hum of the shuttlecraft's impulse engines fleeing from the ill-fated planet.

ten

"It is done," said Overseer Tejharet, looking fifteen cycles older than he had before freeing Marla Karuw from arrest and inviting her to his chambers. There he had asked her to save the world, when all she could save was a small chunk of it. Now the regent had summoned the overseer to *her* chambers on the *Darzor*, where she wanted him to state for the ship's log that he had appointed her regent with full custodial powers of the overseer. For better or worse, her ragtag fleet would soon be all that was left of Aluwna and a noble civilization, at least temporarily. The ship's log, not the soon-to-vanish computers and scrolls on the planet, would be the instrument of record.

On her viewscreen, they had both watched the final gathering of the satellites by the fastest of the yachts, the *Darzor* herself. Now they were finally under way. The last vessel to leave orbit, and they were only a few instants over deadline. Crammed with two hundred passengers and crew, dragging a tail of tethered satellites in the cocoon of a tractor beam, the sleek yacht sped away from Aluwna at half-impulse. That was as slow as they could go and still escape in time.

"How did you do it?" he asked, shaking his head. "How did you choose who would go?"

Marla was taken aback by the question, because Tejharet was the first person who was blunt enough to ask it. "We never announced it officially," she answered, "but half the lottery selection were children. We'll have a great many orphaned children to raise as our own. Other choices were made for me by circumstances, such as bringing so many constables, but they fit a general profile of what I wanted. I mean, what I thought would be best for the new Aluwna."

"And they will be loyal to you," said the overseer pointedly. "I could quibble with you, Marla, but I could not have done what you did. Nobody else could have devised this plan and seen it through in the time you had. We all owe you a debt of gratitude."

She smiled wanly. "Many people pitched in to help—another large contingent of those we took. To tell you the truth, I feel more like a mass murderer than a savior."

"So do I," he answered, folding his hands before him and looking stooped and tired. "But what else could we do?"

"We're not saved yet," said the regent grimly.

"Thus far, everything has gone remarkably well, considering. I would like to think it would stay that way, but I'm too much of a realist for that. So I need you to redo your proclamation making me regent one more time—for the ship's log."

He blinked in surprise. "That is why you succeed—you think ahead. Should I do it orally?"

"No, I've written it out this time," said Marla Karuw, bringing up the document on one of her screens. "It's verbatim what you said in the Summer Palace. Don't worry, I'm sure there will come a time when you can reclaim your throne."

"I doubt it," said Tejharet stoically. "You have no intentions of ever returning power to me and the monarchy. You've always hated the hereditary system—found it unfair and regressive. Yes, it is. Of course, it's also a tradition that has seen us through eons of peace and prosperity, but that never made much difference to you. Here you've struggled for decades to revolutionize our society, and an outside force has done it for you."

Marla was speechless for a moment, unsure whether he was complaining or stating the simple truth. This was a man she had once loved, despite their differences, so she found it hard to hate him—even if she hated what he represented.

"I'm playing it by ear," she said honestly. "In truth, I would like things to be so simple that I could just walk away from this responsibility, but I doubt that will happen for a long time."

"Let me sign your document," said the overseer quietly. "I don't wish to stand in your way, and I am indebted to you—we all are. Just don't give me reason to oppose you."

Marla Karuw clenched her teeth together and said nothing as he entered an electronic signature and once again turned over all his power to her. When he was done, she asked, "Where is your wife?"

The overseer shrugged. "Jenoset left in a royal shuttlecraft with her new husband and her old husband."

"She's taken a third mate?" asked the regent with mild amusement. "Now?"

"The new one is very high-bred, I understand," answered the overseer. "Perhaps now she'll deign to have a child. You know, this document I signed doesn't mean anything to *her.*"

"I'll deal with that when the time comes," answered the regent. "Thank you again for speaking to the people in this time of need. They respect you a great deal."

"That doesn't mean much when ninety percent of them will be dead by morning," he answered hoarsely. "I think I need some sleep, and you, too. Perhaps we'll share a meal in the morning, like the old days. We'll both need some company then."

"I would like that," said Marla Karuw. "Good night."

"Good night." The overseer shuffled toward the door, stopped, and looked back. "You will keep the ones in the satellites alive, won't you?"

"I'm trying my best," she answered.

Left alone, under way on their journey, and with no immediate concerns, Marla decided to take the overseer's advice and get some sleep. She curled up on the couch in the library and was out in less than a heartbeat.

What seemed like a moment later, someone shook Marla Karuw's shoulder, dragging her out of a heavy sleep. "Regent Karuw, please wake up!" urged a youthful voice.

She blinked wearily and focused on the face of her young assistant, Komplum. From his grim expression, she knew that he hadn't woken her for a trivial reason.

"What is it?" she asked, sitting up and swinging her legs over the edge of the couch.

"They need you on the bridge," replied Komplum. "The captain says it's urgent."

Without even wiping the sleepiness from her eyes, Karuw charged out of the library and down the corridor. Komplum hurried to keep up with her.

"What time is it?" she asked.

"Six units after midnight."

"What!" she snapped. "How could you let me sleep so long?"

He stammered, "Well, I, uh . . . you never gave me any orders to wake you. I didn't even know you were asleep, and the captain tried to hail you."

"I'm sorry," she answered. "When you spend a few

cycles in a cell, you're used to getting lots of sleep."

They charged onto the sumptuous bridge of the yacht, which looked more like a parlor on the esplanade than a ship's command center to Marla's eye. From the grim look on Captain Uzel's face, she knew they were in some kind of serious trouble. Every station was manned by a crew member, which was also unusual.

"What is it?" she asked.

"The main impulse engine is failing," he answered grimly. "We didn't anticipate the drain it would be on the reactor to maintain the tractor beam—and power the satellites—for this long. The tractor beam is for short haul at these speeds."

"Now you tell me," she muttered. "How fast are we going?"

"We're at a dead stop," he answered gravely. "That was the only way to recharge the deuterium tanks. I thought our momentum would carry us, but we had to make some course adjustments for a meteor shower. Our shields don't extend all the way out to the satellites, so we have to be careful. I could have awakened the overseer, but I assumed you would want to know first. At any rate, we're in serious trouble."

"What's our position?" she asked, leaning over the shoulder of the conn officer. "How close are we to the safety zone?"

"Still two units of travel time, and that is approximately when the Genesis Wave is due to hit." The captain gulped and looked ashen as he uttered those words. "That's not the worst of it—the other two yachts report similar problems. Only the freighters are going to make it unscathed."

"Do we have any options?" asked Karuw. "Any at all?"

The captain winced as he answered, "Yes, one option. We can shed the satellites."

"And kill seven hundred thousand people," she rasped. "Are you insane?"

Captain Uzel bristled at that suggestion. "If our ship goes down, they'll die anyway."

"What about cutting power to the satellites and letting them run off the plasma packs?"

"We've already done that," answered the captain grimly.

The regent exploded in anger, shouting, "Without my authorization, you cut the power?"

"I'm the captain of the *Darzor,*" he answered imperiously. "My first allegiance is to this vessel. We had to rest and recharge the impulse engine before we could continue."

Marla took a deep breath and tried to calm herself. "I'm sorry," she said. "I know you've done all you can, Captain. Listen, can we tow the satellites without the tractor beam?"

The gray-haired master shook his head. "Not at the speed we'd have to travel. We'll have to go at full impulse just to make it out of here in time. I'm sorry, Regent, but unless we cut loose the satellites, we're all going to die. And that goes for the other two yachts as well."

"Two million people." The regent scrunched her eyes shut and almost screamed in anguish. "I suppose you put out a distress signal?"

"Oh, yes, some time ago," he answered. "But who is going to be cruising around out here in the path of the Genesis Wave? Nobody." The captain turned to his engineering station and asked, "What's the reactor status now? Can we go?"

"Not with the added drain on the engine," answered the crewman.

Captain Uzel nodded gravely. "Make ready to sever tethers and power lines. I'm sorry, Your Regency, but as captain of this ship, I have the authority to do anything it takes to save it."

Marla Karuw hung her head, feeling utterly defeated.

"Captain," said the tactical officer puzzledly, "I'm receiving a hail."

"Which one of our ships?"

"Not one of ours," answered the officer in amazement. "It's the *Doghjey*, a Klingon vessel."

"Klingon?" asked Marla, hope rising in her breast. "Put them onscreen."

Everyone stopped what they were doing—almost stopped breathing—as they turned their attention to the small screen above the bow viewport. When the image blinked on, they saw the fearsome visage of a Klingon warrior, with prominent head ridges, dusky skin, and shoulders broader than a landing pad.

"I am Ambassador Worf, aboard a Klingon vessel but representing the United Federation of Planets," he said in a thunderous voice. "Do you need assistance?"

"Do we ever," breathed Marla Karuw. "I am Regent Marla Karuw of Aluwna, and we've evacuated eight million people from our planet, but they're stored in the pattern buffers of our transporter satellites. Our main impulse engine is failing, and two other ships are in distress."

"We have them on our sensors," said the big Klingon. "I have a fleet of seven warships, and we are at your disposal. We can accommodate your vessels and the satellites you are towing."

Marla felt a chill rush up and down her spine at this news, and crew members behind her cheered. Her voice was a croak as she added, "But the Genesis Wave—"

"We're tracking it as well," said the Klingon ambassador. "We can tow you at warp speed if you can maintain your tractor beams. You will not need to use your engines for propulsion."

Marla Karuw lowered her head and sniffed back tears, unable to speak. Captain Uzel stepped to her side and said, "We'll send you coordinates . . . where our other ships will be waiting for us. What should we do to help?"

"Leave everything to us," answered the big Klingon. "Are you going to return to Aluwna after the wave has passed?"

"Yes," the captain answered.

"We will go with you," promised the ambassador. "I regret we were unable to come sooner and do more. Worf out."

As soon as the transmission ended, Marla turned to the captain and said, "Get power back to the satellites."

"Yes, Regent," answered the captain cheerfully. "I always heard that Klingons were rude and unpleasant, but I think they're wonderful."

"Me, too," she said with a wide grin. "Klingons are beautiful."

PART TWO

AFTERMATH

eleven

In the central square of the Summer Palace, thousands of Aluwnans joined hands, lifted their arms toward the darkening sky, and sang spiritual songs. Hundreds more recited poetry, played musical instruments, and danced tearfully. Artists sketched pictures of the gathering, trying to capture this moment of togetherness for a posterity they would never see. Naysayers, who deemed the evacuation a great hoax, halted their speeches in midsentence. Even the rioters and those driven insane with fear stopped their pointless destruction of the palace to watch and wait. Parents hugged their children and tried to comfort them, ignoring the questions they couldn't answer. The wind seemed to stop blowing, and the boughs of the trees stood perfectly still as well. The end was at hand.

When the ground trembled, the screaming and

praying began in earnest. Believers raised their voices to the heavens, begging forgiveness and mercy. But neither one was forthcoming. In an instant, the sky turned from blue-black storm clouds into a hellish blaze of vivid purple and green, like a festered wound. The horizon quivered and undulated, and distant mountains exploded with barbarous fury, shooting monstrous waves of ash into the sky. Like a wildfire set loose in a parched forest, a neon green curtain of fire roared across the plains, bearing down on the city. As geysers erupted, the stone and earth liquefied into a churning quagmire that consumed the flailing people and crumbling buildings alike. As fiery green embers scorched the air, the planet of Aluwna turned into a morass of sludge, which throbbed and quaked like a living thing.

Abruptly, the subspace video feed from Aluwna ended, leaving Worf gasping for air as if he had been there for the conflagration. He turned to see his hosts on the *Darzor*, Regent Karuw and Overseer Tejharet, who gripped each other to keep from collapsing. All over the bridge of the royal vessel there was silence, punctuated by an occasional whimper from a crew member. The Klingon felt like roaring with outrage at this mindless destruction, but all he could do was maintain his stiff-backed composure. There was certainly nothing he could say to alleviate the horror and helplessness they all felt.

"Every power in the Alpha Quadrant is looking for the ones who unleashed this force," said Worf. "We will find them and destroy them."

"Precious good that will do Aluwna now," rasped Marla Karuw, slumping into the seat at an empty console.

"I hope you're right, Ambassador," said Overseer Tejharet, who was more given to good manners and graciousness than his regent. "What could possibly be the point of this devastation?"

Choosing his words carefully, Worf answered, "The original Genesis project was a rapid way to terraform a planet. One Starfleet theory is that this wave is designed to prepare a planet for invasion."

"Invasion?" Marla Karuw gaped at him, her six eyebrows arching upward. "Are you saying that we're going to have to fight invaders to win back our world? Aluwnans are not fighters."

"Klingons are," he assured her. "But perhaps you would prefer to relocate."

Overseer Tejharet shook his head and said, "We're not empire builders or colonizers. The only world we've ever known is Aluwna. We want to return and rebuild." He looked at his regent for confirmation, and the tight-lipped woman nodded forcefully.

"We'll do more than that," vowed Regent Karuw. "We'll restore Aluwna to the way it was. We've got specimens of almost all plant and animal life stored in the transporter buffers, plus we have living specimens on one of our ships. We happen to be experts at genetics, and we can do our own terraforming."

Worf granted her a slight smile. "I was hoping you would say that. I would like to visit one of these

Genesis planets, and win it back for its rightful inhabitants."

"When can we return?" asked Karuw bluntly. "The sooner the better, because we can't maintain the pattern buffers in our satellites indefinitely. We need to get back there soon."

The Klingon nodded solemnly. "We shall send probes into your solar system to see what we can learn. As I understand it, the most devastating effects of the wave—wholesale molecular changes—occur once and are over."

"What do you mean by 'wholesale molecular changes'?" asked Tejharet worriedly.

"What you saw on your video feed," answered Worf. "This wave causes more than destruction—it takes the existing matter and converts it into something new. Even the sun in your solar system has been changed. I have not yet seen these effects firsthand, but we will see them together."

"There's no time to waste," insisted Marla Karuw.

"Very well." The Klingon touched the com medallion on his sash and said, "Worf to Captain Kralenk of the Doghjey."

"Kralenk here," came the reply. "Ambassador, I was just about to contact you. We've received a message from Starfleet saying the source of the Genesis Force has been discovered and neutralized. We don't have any other information, but Starfleet says we should proceed with extreme caution into any areas affected."

"Send probes into the Aluwnan solar system," replied Worf. "If it is safe, we will proceed as soon as possible. Worf out." He turned to his hosts and said, "That is good news."

"Good news that's too late for us," muttered Marla Karuw. "Can you ask your ships to help us maintain the integrity of the transporter buffers? I know that a Starfleet officer was supposed to have lasted seventy-five Terran years in a transporter buffer, but I'm not convinced."

"I can assure you it happened," answered Worf. "I was serving aboard the ship that rescued a retired Starfleet engineer named Montgomery Scott, who survived a fatal crash by suspending himself in a transporter. I am very impressed that you came up with such a novel solution."

"We were desperate," answered Karuw. "And we still are."

"We will do what we can," promised Worf. "In a way, I feel like Noah."

"Who's Noah?" asked the regent.

"The hero in an epic story from Earth," answered the Klingon. "I will send it to you—you may draw inspiration from the tale. Now I had best return to my ship. Should I direct-beam?"

"Please," answered the regent. "We haven't got any power to spare for transporter operations."

"Very well." The big Klingon again tapped his com device. "Worf to *Doghjey*. Beam me back to the ship."

"Yes, Ambassador."

* * *

Marla Karuw watched the fearsome-looking Klingon disappear from their bridge, having promised the Aluwnans to help them return to their home-world. But she wasn't mollified, nor was she reassured by the sight of seven huge Klingon warships just off the port bow of the royal yacht. This normally empty stretch of space was crammed with ships at the moment—eight freighters, three royal yachts, the Klingon task force, and a ragtag collection of shuttle-craft and other small vessels that had helped them escape the disaster. None of them meant as much as the thousands of transporter satellites tethered to the Aluwnan ships; that was where the future of their world awaited, suspended in the bioneural networks of their computers.

"Marla, you look so grim," observed Overseer Tejharet. "I know nothing can replace the great loss we have suffered, but your plan worked. We made it to safety, and now we have help."

"We were lucky," she grumbled. "I guess I wasn't ready to hear that we would have to fight to reclaim Aluwna. I thought we could simply return, rebuild, and reseed—but it's not going to be that easy. I'm afraid to go back there . . . and see what has become of our beloved home."

The overseer moved to the bridge station where the regent was seated and gently touched her shoul-der. "We're all afraid, Marla, but we owe it to those who have perished to go on. I was heartened by

Ambassador's Worf visit, because now we know from a firsthand account that a person *can* survive in a transporter for a long time. Plus we have experienced fighters on our side, if fighting is what we have to do."

"I suppose," answered the regent, feeling unconvinced. "Captain Uzel, what is our status?"

"Impulse engines are maintaining power to the satellites," answered the captain as he leaned over his science officer's shoulder. "All of the ships bearing satellites report stability, which should last as long as we don't tax our engines too much. By the way, several of the smaller ships wish to talk to you."

"About what?" she asked.

"Mostly looking for instructions," answered the silver-haired captain. "One small runabout, the *Klamath*, says it's urgent that they speak to you. This ship has Federation registry."

"Federation?" asked Marla, rubbing her tired eyes. "Did they say what they wanted?"

"No, but they dropped a name they said you would know," the captain answered. "Does the name Vilo Garlet mean anything?"

"Vilo Garlet," she echoed, jumping to her feet and moving toward the viewscreen. "Put the captain onscreen."

A few moments later, Karuw and everyone else on the *Darzor* bridge was astounded when the pointy-eared countenance of a Vulcan appeared on their overhead screen. Then she remembered that this was a Federation ship, inexplicably caught in Aluwna's catastrophe.

"I am Regimol, captain of the *Klamath*," he began. "Am I addressing Regent Karuw?"

"Yes," she answered. "Is Vilo Garlet on your vessel?"

"He is, and so is another Aluwnan who may be of use to you. I must go elsewhere, and I request permission to transfer my two passengers to your ship."

"We're packed beyond capacity," Captain Uzel reminded her.

"We can take these two," she answered. "Yes, Captain Regimol, transfer them directly to our bridge. Do you have our coordinates?"

"I do," answered the Vulcan somberly. "Please accept my regrets over the tragic destruction of your planet. Preparing to transport passengers. Live long and prosper. *Klamath* out."

The first Aluwnan to materialize on the bridge of the *Darzor* was her old colleague Vilo Garlet, and she was thrilled to see him, although she maintained her reserve. Marla was surprised when the other passenger turned out to be a very young woman wearing a Federation-issue jumpsuit.

"Vilo, I'm glad to see you made it to safety," said the regent, warmly clasping the scientist's hand. "You'll be able to help us after all."

"I suppose so," he answered noncommittally.

"And who's your friend?"

"This is Candra," he answered, presenting the

young lady. "We just met, but she's a very good friend of the new seeress consort."

"Is that so?" asked Overseer Tejharet with interest. "I haven't even met my new family member yet."

The girl stared at him, awed by the presence of the monarch. "Pleased to meet you," she answered with a gulp. Then she turned to Marla and asked, "Are you the new regent?"

"Yes, my dear," she answered with a smile. "And you're a very lucky young lady."

"I know," said Candra humbly. "Did it . . . did it happen?"

"Yes, it's all over," replied the regent, casting down her eyes. She took a breath, lifted her chin, and declared, "With the help of the Klingons, we're going to return home very soon. And with the help of my friend Vilo, we're going to remake Aluwna into the paradise it once was."

The girl twisted her hands together and looked at the overseer. "Can I see my friend Farlo? He married the seeress . . . at the Institute of Devotion."

"My wife's shuttlecraft is out there somewhere," answered Tejharet, pointing toward the ragtag fleet floating in the vastness of space. "We know he's on board, but we haven't spoken to them yet. Let's allow the captain and his crew to attend to urgent matters, and we'll have our reunions later. In the meantime, you two must be tired. If we could find you a place to sleep—"

"We have no empty quarters," said Captain Uzel.

"Candra can stay with me," replied Marla Karuw, taking a liking to the young woman, who seemed very unpretentious for a person who associated with Vulcans, scientists, and high-bred royalty. "And, Vilo, you can stay in the laboratory."

"My lot in life," said the grizzled physicist with a shrug. "You know, Marla, what you want to do won't be easy. We haven't perfected the chromasynthesis process, and we've never done anything large-scale before."

"This is the time to do it," answered the regent. "We won't know what we have to deal with until we see it, but we have a huge canvas, and a whole world to re-create. So let's get started."

Worf swung his *bat'leth* and connected hard with the practice weapon of his opponent, feeling a shudder run up the length of his brawny forearms. Before the big Klingon could recover, his helmeted foe whirled around, ducked, and jabbed him in the ribs. Despite his protective armor, Worf grunted and had to gasp for air, while his opponent laughed and circled the training room. Anger rising, Worf tried to smash his foe in the head, but his adversary was too fast and lithe, easily dodging the overhead shot. Snarling like a *targ*, the ambassador swept the *bat'leth* along the deck, trying to catch his foe's foot and trip him. Once again the youth was too quick, and he easily made a vertical leap while he slashed at Worf's weapon arm, dealing a blow that numbed the Klingon from wrist to elbow.

Clearly outmatched and losing momentum, Worf went into parry mode. He relied on footwork to keep out of reach of the weapon, while he did his best to neutralize his opponent's frantic flurry of blows. His foe had always been quick, but the ambassador was surprised at how strong he had become since their last training exercise.

Using every trick to avoid another painful strike, Worf tried to figure out how to counterattack. Sensing victory, his opponent pressed forward, lunging, slashing, and trying to overpower the older fighter. Worf was careful to feint and jab, trying to keep him honest while retreating. Grunting with the effort, he was tired, and he pretended to be even more tired. When his foe tried an overhead kill shot, Worf lifted his *bat'leth* as if to parry again, but instead he pulled it back and stepped aside, allowing his off-balance opponent to stagger forward. That was when Worf stuck out a big foot and tripped him. The enemy somehow maintained his balance until Worf swept his weapon like a scythe and connected with the back of the lad's neck. That blow sent him sprawling onto his stomach.

Panting and grinning, Worf yanked off his helmet and said, "If this was a sharp *bat'leth*, your head would be bouncing across the deck."

His opponent rolled over and pulled off his own helmet, revealing a shock of blond hair and a handsome human face. Jeremy Aster rubbed his neck painfully, but still laughed as he looked up to his foster father. "I thought I had you that time!"

"You did," said the Klingon sternly, "but you are too impatient. Toward the end, you were so anxious to finish me that you were off-balance and out of control. Had you been content to wear me down, you would have done so, and soon. I may be old and slow, but I am patient."

He reached down and helped the young man to his feet. Although technically the *R'uustai* ceremony had made them brothers, their difference in age—and the boy's need for a father figure—had allowed Worf to treat him like a son.

"It's a pain being the only human on this ship," complained Jeremy. "None of the other crew members will fight me. They think it's beneath them."

"You would probably best some of the younger ones," answered his father, "if you kept your patience. I will teach you how to challenge them in such a manner that they cannot refuse. By the time you finish the Officer Exchange Program, you should know a great deal about Klingons."

"Can we go again?" asked the energetic youth, lifting his wooden *bat'leth* and begging for more.

Worf sighed wearily. "No, not right now. We must clean up and dress for dinner. Your brother is coming over from the *Ya'Vang*."

"And he won't fight me either!" complained Jeremy.

"Alexander has much to do lately," countered Worf. "They just made him third-shift duty officer in engineering, and he is studying our culture and language."

"Yeah, well." Jeremy sighed. "I'll never get a promotion. I don't think Captain Kralenk likes me."

"What did I just tell you about patience?" snapped Worf. "I was the only Klingon on a Starfleet ship, and do you know how many years it took *me* to get a promotion? But once the promotions started coming, they came rapidly. Now I have such influence that I can demand that both my sons serve with me, and here you are. But I wish this were a happier assignment."

"At least Starfleet ended the threat," said Jeremy.

"Yes." Teeth clenched, Worf shook his fist and added, "I wish I had been there to kill the ones who unleashed it."

Jeremy smiled slyly. "Dad, you don't really like being an ambassador, do you?"

Worf looked around and lowered his voice to answer, "No. I would gladly trade places with you and be a junior weapons officer. So you see, promotions are not all they are cracked up to be."

"But we have a hundred weapons officers on this ship," muttered Jeremy, hefting his *bat'leth*. "It's hard to get noticed."

"Believe me, they notice you," answered the Klingon. "You're hard to miss."

The com panel on the bulkhead made a sharp squeal, and a voice said, "Bridge to Ambassador Worf."

He walked across the training room and tapped the com panel. "Worf here."

"This is Science Officer Jagrow," came the reply,

"and we have received data from the probes we sent to Aluwna."

"Go on," said Worf with interest.

"First, all probes are functioning as normal, so the captain assumes it's safe to proceed into the solar system. Secondly, Aluwna is still a habitable planet, although the atmosphere is hotter and more humid than our records show. Plant life has increased oxygen levels in the atmosphere by twenty percent. Carbon dioxide, hydrogen, and helium levels have slightly decreased but are holding steady."

"Plant life?" asked Worf curiously. "I thought the planet had been razed."

"This is *new* plant life," replied the science officer, "growing at an accelerated pace. Most unusual of all is a reading of a hundred thousand humanoid-sized life-forms."

"What kind of life-forms?" asked the ambassador.

"They match nothing in our database," answered Jagrow. "The sun in the solar system is also undergoing increased thermonuclear fusion, which may be adding to the accelerated growth. Without firsthand observation, we can't tell if these trends will stabilize or continue to mutate into an unreliable ecosystem. Considering the number of life-forms, Captain Kralenk wishes to proceed in battle readiness."

"Agreed," answered Worf. "Inform Regent Karuw on the *Darzor* of these findings, and prepare to get under way. As before, we will have to tow the Aluwnan ships and their satellites."

"Yes, sir. Bridge out."

The big Klingon frowned and looked at his foster son. "It appears that dinner with your brother will have to be put off. However, it also appears that you may have a chance to fight someone else besides me."

"Good!" said Jeremy Aster with a broad grin. "I'm looking forward to it."

twelve

"I can't stand being cooped up in here anymore!" yelled Seeress Jenoset, slamming the back of the seat where Farlo Fuzwik was sleeping fitfully. The lad blinked himself awake and gazed up at the regal blond woman, who had spent many units pacing back and forth in the short aisle of the shuttlecraft. The pilot, the copilot, and the pilot's family cowered from her anger, while Seeress Consort Padrin yawned wearily.

"Darling," said Padrin, "we could have gone on one of the larger ships, but you insisted on having autonomy."

"But they could keep us informed!" railed the monarch. "What is the point of sitting here, surrounded by Klingons? When are we going to go home?"

"I've been hailing the *Darzor*," said the pilot, Hajhor Kanow. "They say there is no news and no orders. But several units ago, the Klingons fired probes toward Aluwna. I presume we're waiting to hear the results."

"You presume a lot," muttered Jenoset. "Perhaps the Klingons are making demands, or that bungling regent is being too cautious. In truth, we don't know *what* is going on."

"We know our world has been destroyed," said Farlo simply. "And millions and millions of people are dead."

That brought Jenoset's tirade to a halt, and everyone on the small craft lowered their heads in quiet introspection. Farlo had lost as much as anyone, but he didn't think it was fair to complain when everyone in this barren region of space was lucky just to be alive. He also felt sorry for those millions more suspended in the transporter satellites, because that was almost death.

"I owe you my life," he told Seeress Jenoset, "but you're wrong to be angry at anyone. All of us here . . . we should feel nothing but grateful."

Jenoset patted her newest husband on the shoulder and said, "You're wise for one so young. Very well, I'll sit down and wait, but not for long."

"Maybe it won't be long," said Farlo. Through the bow viewport he could see one of the big Klingon warships edging slowly forward. "The Klingons are starting to move out there."

The seeress stepped toward the cockpit. "Kanow, get confirmation on whether we're getting ready to move."

"I am," answered the pilot, working his board. After a moment, he reported, "There's lots of traffic on the com frequencies. It would appear that the Klingon vessels are activating their tractor beams. We must be getting ready to move out."

"Good," said Seeress Jenoset, returning to her seat. "We'll be home by tomorrow."

"But what will home be like?" asked Padrin. His fellow passengers diverted their eyes, because nobody had an answer for him.

Flanked by Overseer Tejharet and Captain Uzel, Marla Karuw gazed at the lush green planet on the overhead viewport. It looked perfectly habitable, with its plethora of plant life, gleaming polar ice-caps, and azure veins of rivers and deltas. Nevertheless, they were all stunned after their day-long journey home, because this was a planet none of them recognized.

"There's got to be a mistake," rasped Marla. "That can't be Aluwna. I didn't expect to see cities, but where are the oceans? Where are the deserts?"

"There's no mistake," said Vilo Garlet, peering at the sensor readings scrolling across his science console. "This is exactly where Aluwna should be. The mass, diameter, and axial rotation are the same. That *is* our homeworld."

"We were told to expect this," said Tejharet softly.

Marla Karuw snarled with anger. "This isn't *terraforming*! This is a completely different planet." She stopped her rant and rubbed her eyes, trying to control her emotions. "All right, the first order of business is to get the satellites back into their geosynchronous orbits, then we'll have to erect new transporter stations . . . lots of them. We can save power by making them unidirectional—down to Aluwna only."

"Shouldn't we go there and explore first?" asked Tejharet. "We may find that Ambassador Worf is right . . . that we should relocate."

Marla scoffed at the suggestion. "Why should we relocate to another new, untamed planet that isn't our own? We've got one of those right here, and it already belongs to us. Besides . . . Vilo, tell them what you told me earlier."

The other renegade scientist in the group looked up from his readouts. "According to Federation data, the closest planet that would be suitable is almost fifteen light-years away. It would be dangerous to haul the satellites that far, and we can't be guaranteed that the Klingons will be here to help us tomorrow or the next day. For all we know, this could be the beginning of some huge war. Overseer, Regent—you did all you could do under the circumstances, but we had better make do with this world. It's the only one we've got."

"We need to commandeer all the shuttlecraft and orbiters," ordered Marla Karuw. "Get technicians on them and begin to put the satellites back into orbit. Hail the *Doghjey* and ask them for help—they must have shuttlecraft, too."

"Yes, Regent," said Captain Uzel with a slight bow. "This will take some time."

"Then let's get started," replied Karuw. "Time is not our ally. Assemble the work crews and the shuttles. I want to see what it's like down there firsthand. When the Klingons send an away team down to the planet, I want to be with them. Until then, Vilo and I will be in the laboratory."

She nodded to her fellow scientist, and the two of them strode quickly off the bridge.

"What do you mean, they want to commandeer my shuttlecraft?" snapped Seeress Jenoset. "Do they know who I am?"

"They don't seem to care," replied the pilot, Kanow. "These orders come directly from the regent. We're supposed to enter the shuttlebay of the *Darzor* immediately, and all passengers are supposed to vacate."

"The impertinence!" cried Jenoset.

Farlo Fuzwik watched his much older wife, thinking that he would like to see her when she wasn't angry and indignant. At their wedding ceremony, she had been polite and courtly, and then she had wept like a child when they left Aluwna. Those were the only two times when Jenoset had not been outraged over imagined and real injustices. If he was going to be married to her, he at least wanted to like her a little.

While the seeress continued to sputter in anger, Padrin gently took her hand. "Come on, my dear, you've been dying to get off this craft for two days now. It's finally time to see something else and I, for one, am ready. What about you, Farlo?"

"I'm ready," said the lad, jumping to his feet. "Do you think we'll go down to the surface soon?"

Padrin shivered at the idea. "I hope they build some facilities first. I've never been good at camping out in the woods."

"Will everyone please take a seat," ordered the pilot. "We'll be entering the shuttlebay soon."

Farlo took his seat along with the other passengers, all of whom were trying to avoid the seeress, who was still pouting. It had been night when their shuttlecraft left Aluwna in a big hurry, and he hadn't gotten a chance to see the planet from space. The lad had no frame of reference to know what was missing, or what had been added, but it looked like a wild, primitive place from way up in orbit. He was still gloomy over losing Candra and so many other friends in the capital city, but it was strangely exciting to return and face a new beginning. Farlo kept hoping that everyone had been wrong about the Genesis Wave, and maybe it hadn't wreaked as much havoc as they thought it would. Maybe some people had been spared.

It was also thrilling to ride the small ship into the shuttlebay of the royal yacht, and he was amazed by how gracefully the pilot eased the craft into the dock. As soon as the vessel came to rest, a mass of people emerged from double doors, and most of them were carrying equipment. Farlo wanted to do something to help, but everyone thought of him as just another high breed, worthless except for making more high breeds. Maybe in the new Aluwna there wouldn't be a leisure class of people, he told himself, and everyone would have to work. There certainly wouldn't be much need for thieves anymore, as there was probably nothing to steal.

"I hope they have proper quarters for me," grumbled Seeress Jenoset as they filed out of the shuttlecraft.

"You might have to sleep with your husbands," joked Padrin. Although Farlo smiled, the seeress narrowed her eyes with annoyance at Uncle Padrin.

The boy wasn't expecting any kind of welcome, so he was amazed when someone charged out of the waiting crowd and ran toward him. "Farlo!" cried a voice.

His breath caught in his throat, and he blinked in amazement—because it was a ghost. "Candra?" he rasped in disbelief.

There was nothing ghostly about the hug she gave him, and both of them dissolved into tears as they clung to each other.

"Move along!" said an impatient technician, shoving them out of the way so he could load his equipment. Seeress Jenoset also fixed him with a baleful glare, but she said nothing to spoil the happy reunion. She was met by an older, regally dressed man, who must have been the overseer, although he looked

older and more gaunt than he remembered. Farlo
didn't care about any of the high breeds, the workers,
the crew, or anyone else on the ship—not as long as
his best friend, Candra, had returned to him.

"How . . . did you . . . Are you okay?" he stammered.

"I'm okay," she answered with a grin. "I'll tell you
how I got out when we're alone."

"New passengers to the mess hall for assignment,"
announced a crew member. "Please move along,
because we've got more shuttlecraft to bring in."

The two young people dashed off ahead of the others, with Candra anxious to tell Farlo her story. As
soon as they were out of earshot, she said, "I was really
mad after I left you, and I almost threw away the
brooch and the black tube. It was a good thing I
didn't, because they saved my lives. There was a lot of
screaming and fighting after the lottery survivors were
announced, and I broke into a store."

"I bet you were looking for something to eat," said
Farlo with a grin, "like you always are."

Candra laughed. "I was! Hey, why shouldn't I be
comfortable if I'm going to die? But there was already a
mob of people in there, and they didn't want anyone
else. They chased me down and cornered me, and I
tapped the brooch to save myself. I didn't expect it to
work, but it did! A few instants later, I was in a
Federation runabout with two men, and they really
wanted this."

She held up the small ebony tube the two of them

had stolen days ago. "But this is *yours*," she whispered. "You're the one who really needs it."

"A perfume mister?" asked Farlo puzzledly. "I don't think I need—"

"Believe me, you do." Candra stopped to look around the crowded corridor; then she pulled her friend into a doorway and cupped her hand to whisper into his ear, "You aren't really a high breed. Sniffing this before Padrin tested you is what made them think you had all that royal blood. You sniffed it, right?"

Farlo nodded in astonishment. "Yeah, I did. But I don't get it—"

"Listen to me." She stared pointedly into his eyes. "One of the men is a genetic scientist named Vilo Garlet—he's on this ship—and he made this device in order to fool their DNA sensors. And it works! You're proof of that. You have to sniff it again whenever they want to test your breeding. Otherwise, you'll be a nobody again."

She pressed the small cylinder into his hand, and Farlo gaped at his friend. "But if they know it's fake, won't they tell someone?" he asked.

"No," answered Candra. "The other man was a Romulan—people here think he's a Vulcan—and he's gone home. Vilo Garlet promised me that he would keep your secret from everyone, because the Genesis Wave made his plans pointless. We both owe our lives to this little black tube."

Holding his breath, Farlo lifted the object and

stared at it. "I wondered about that," he breathed. "I never felt like a high breed. But I'm still married to the seeress."

"Yeah, I know," muttered Candra. "We can't do anything about that now, but maybe soon we can run away . . . or something."

Farlo carefully hid the tube in the inner breast pocket of his fine silky tunic. "Thanks, Candra. You're the best friend anybody ever had."

"I know," she answered with a chuckle. "You tried to help me, too, but I was too stubborn. I didn't want to share you with that older lady. Have the two of you, er . . . have you done anything?"

"No, and we can't," muttered Farlo with sudden realization. "If I did get her pregnant, she'd have a low-breed baby, and everyone would know I was a fake."

"Well, keep away from her as much as you can," cautioned Candra. "Come on, I'll show you where the mess hall is. We're all pretty crammed together on this ship, but they'll probably give *you* a nice room."

"I deserve it," joked Farlo, his spirits soaring. With Candra back at his side, he could enjoy this crazy adventure, no matter what happened.

"I warn you, Father, I wouldn't use the transporters to go down there," said the young Klingon on the viewscreen. Alexander Rozhenko was slightly built for a Klingon, but he had a presence and outspokenness that belied his youth. "There's too much residual radiation from protomatter fission and thermonuclear reaction, and our biofilters may not be familiar with any of the microbes. I say we take a shuttlecraft down."

"We?" asked Worf with amusement. "Are you coming on the away team with us?"

"I thought I would," answered the young Klingon, who was raised on Earth, like his father. He had been slower to embrace Klingon customs and heritage, but he was making up for lost time by serving in the Klingon Defense Force. "You'll need somebody on tricorder."

"There is a growing list of people who want to go," said Worf, "including Jeremy, the overseer, and Regent Karuw." The ambassador frowned in thought, then added, "The regent is not going to be happy to hear that we can't use transporters, because she wants to get her people out of those pattern buffers."

"I know," replied Alexander, "but it's not safe yet. Perhaps by the time we return all the satellites to orbit, it will be. So when do we go down to Aluwna?"

"All of our shuttlecraft are being used to maneuver the satellites back into orbit," answered Worf. "Realistically, I would say another two hours, after we run more scans. I'll inform you and your captain when it's time to go."

"Very well, Father. Rozhenko out." The image faded from the viewscreen in Worf's spartan quarters on the *Doghjey*, and the big Klingon sat back in his seat and smiled. There had been a time, not long ago,

Genesis Force   **165**

when his biological son could hardly stand to be in the same room with him. He hadn't even wanted to serve on the same ship with Worf during the Dominion War, but that time together had started healing the wounds. Marrying Jadzia Dax and giving Alexander a prominent role in the wedding had further cemented their growing bond. Now it was like they had never been apart, and Worf relished these days together, no matter how fraught with danger they were. He knew that circumstances would probably separate them again, sooner or later, but he was going to enjoy the time until then. That is, if one could enjoy anything to do with the Genesis Wave.

Grunting because his ribs were still sore from his *bat'leth* match with Jeremy, Worf rose to his feet and stretched. Serving with both his boys had taken him back to his early days aboard the *Enterprise*, when he had been young, headstrong, and somewhat romantic. *Well, I'm still headstrong*, thought Worf. He was cautious enough to make sure that the majority of crew on the landing party to Aluwna would be warriors, armed to the teeth, and he was taking no chances with his two sons and various Aluwnan dignitaries along for the ride. Worf hoped the Aluwnans' return to their world would go smoothly, but he felt an ominous dread that it wouldn't.

For some time, Farlo and Candra just sat in the mess hall with other refugees, most of them family of the *Darzor* crew. Of course, they sat apart and were waited on by servers from the kitchen, owing to Farlo's elevated status, which made both of them chuckle. Farlo was relieved to hear that he wasn't a real high breed but that he was playing some kind of complex scam on the royal family, because that fit in with his concept of himself as a young rogue. With Candra at his side, it was like old times, living by their wits and coming out on top, when so many others had perished. Let them think he was stuffy and high-bred; now that he knew he was playing a role, he could enjoy it.

The lad kept his best ally hidden yet close to him, feeling often in his interior pocket for the black perfume mister. This was all that he needed to succeed, and he planned to keep playing the game until he and Candra could escape undetected. Figuring that his status would allow them to tour the ship, he was about to suggest they leave when the door whooshed open, and all conversation in the mess hall ended. Everyone turned to see the new regent, Marla Karuw, enter the crowded hall with two constables at her side.

Candra quickly whispered in his ear, "I'm staying in her room, and she seems to like me. Everyone else is scared of her."

"I'm used to dealing with those kind," said Farlo with a sly smile. They stopped their conversation, too, because it was clear that Regent Karuw was headed in their direction.

She stopped at the table and looked directly at the

young lady. "Hello, Candra, I see you found your friend."

"Yes, I did," said the youth gratefully. She looked at her old chum and asked, "What is your title?"

"Seeress Consort Farlo Fuzwik," he answered gravely, trying not to smile. He nodded at the regent and asked, "Would you like to join us?"

"I would," she answered, glancing at a constable, who immediately procured a chair for her. She nodded at the guards, and they moved a few steps away but kept watchful.

"I had never met you," said the regent. "In all the activity, it was kind of odd for the seeress to marry again, when she had been with two husbands for so long."

Farlo shrugged. "Well, these are uncertain times. Maybe she wanted to get her quota . . . in case she lost one or two of them."

Candra laughed, nearly snorting up her drink. "Oh, you are always so funny, Farlo. You know that the seeress had her eye on you for a long time. Besides, the others are so old—it was time she had a young husband."

"I'm that, if nothing else," said Farlo smugly.

The regent sighed and lowered her eyes. "Well, I was under arrest for a few cycles, so I didn't keep up with social doings. But they say you are very high-born . . . ninety-six percent suzerainty."

"Let's just say I've never had to work," answered Farlo, trying to sound like his uncle Padrin. "Now I've got the post I was intended to have."

"And what are you going to do with that post?" asked Marla Karuw bluntly. "Do you aim to stay in the shadow of Seeress Jenoset? Or do you wish to be overseer?"

"Whoa," said Farlo honestly, thinking that this conversation had taken a strange twist. "We've got an overseer, right? And we've got someone who is doing his job and has his powers—you. So why would you need *me* for that?"

"We wouldn't . . . not now," answered Karuw. "But as you say, you have youth on your side. The overseer, myself, and others in charge are old. According to some very musty traditions, there are circumstances in which you could become the rightful heir. By the way, who are your parents?"

Now I'm on slippery ground, thought Farlo, and he answered softly, "My parents aren't important. They're dead now." No doubt that was the truth, he decided glumly.

"I'm sorry," answered Marla Karuw. "It's . . . it's beyond belief what has happened to us. I just want you and Candra to know that you have a friend and ally in me. I'm high-bred myself, although it hasn't always done me a lot of good. Seeress Jenoset is an important part of our government, and we want to maintain our traditions in this time of turmoil. I have to be very careful of this, since I'm regent with—"

The communication device attached to her epaulet beeped, and she said, "Excuse me." Karuw flipped a switch on the device and said testily, "Komplum, I left word not to be disturbed."

"Sorry, Your Regency," he answered, "but Ambassador Worf is insisting that we must load the shuttlecraft now. One has been recalled to pick us up in the shuttlebay, and anyone who is going to the surface should report there now. I've already informed the overseer."

The regent scowled. "Why can't we use transporters?"

"Radiation . . . protomatter . . . microbes . . . general caution," answered Komplum. "I've got a detailed report from them, but the short answer is that the Klingons want to land in a shuttlecraft. They'll have more firepower, if they need it."

"Very well," concluded the regent. "I'm on my way."

"Can we go?" asked Candra excitedly.

"Sounds like fun!" seconded Farlo.

"No. It's likely to be very dangerous. Nice to meet you, Seeress Consort. We'll talk more later." Regent Karuw rose from her seat and walked briskly toward the door.

After they were gone, Candra gazed at Farlo and whispered in amazement, "That's why she wanted to talk to you. If they all get themselves killed, and there's just you—what will happen?"

Farlo scoffed. "You don't think I'll end up overseer of Aluwna?"

"I don't, but she brought it up." The girl frowned

and shook her head. "These are insane times—anything could happen."

"We'll go down to the planet on the next trip," vowed Farlo Fuzwik. "And let's hope they make it back from this one."

thirteen

Marla Karuw had lived long enough to see many storms and bouts of bad weather on her native Aluwna, but she never expected to see anything like the tempest currently lashing this part of the planet. Even three of the largest Klingon shuttlecraft were buffeted mercilessly as they tried to land. It didn't help that there was no flat part of the planet that wasn't covered with teeming, churning plant life, much of it towering into the air. The sky was a swirling morass of dust, sleet, and purple-orange clouds, and the wind was ferocious, whipping at the new flora like a hurricane. Volcanoes belched ash and fire in the distance, and huge geysers spewed brackish water eighty meters into the air, forcing all three shuttles to circle slowly, looking for a place to set down.

"Ambassador Worf?" called Marla over the roar of

the wind crashing against their vessel. "Isn't there someplace more hospitable to land?"

"We've looked, but our sensors haven't found such a place!" answered the Klingon. He went back to huddling with two young aides, a fellow Klingon and a handsome blond humanoid. Finally Worf said, "Pilot! You may have to blast out a landing pad."

"Yes, sir," agreed the veteran Klingon pilot. "Let me inform the other shuttles, so we can concentrate our firepower."

The shuttlecraft continued to bob in the furious storm until all three vessels aligned themselves and selected a target. Then they cut loose with disruptors, blasting an overgrown stand of gnarled trees and sending a fireball of sparks and debris swirling into the turbulent sky. With relentless disruptor fire, they finally scorched a huge red welt on the planet's surface, and the first shuttlecraft set down in a ring of fire. Its landing struts sunk into the smoldering soil, making it appear that the ground was still somewhat liquefied. After the vessels exchanged frantic messages, it was determined that this was as safe as it was going to get. Marla Karuw held her breath and gripped the arms of her chair as their shuttlecraft dropped into the riotous jungle.

With a thud they landed, and the craft tilted to starboard. They fired some thrusters and managed to right themselves before Worf gave the pilot permission to cut the engines. Three heavily armed Klingon security officers took positions at the hatch, planning to be the first ones out. The rest of the party on this shuttle consisted of Worf, his two young aides, plus Marla Karuw and Overseer Tejharet.

The overseer looked ashen with fright from the horrendous sights and rugged landing, and the regent leaned across the aisle to tell him, "You don't have to get out. I think we can see from here what we face."

Tejharet stared out the viewport at an incredible jungle of freakish new life. Ferns and evergreenlike plants grew in abundance, unfurling long pistils and colorful red blooms. Misshapen trees towered above them, casting swaying shadows, while fast-growing vines tried to reclaim the earth they had just scorched. Buffeted like a kite in a hurricane, the third shuttle-craft managed to land in the burned-out clearing, and the frantic chat on the com channel died down to a hum.

"I will walk on Aluwna," vowed the overseer, his voice sounding old and worn.

"Open the hatch!" ordered Worf.

Grunting as he struggled against the fierce wind, a security officer managed to push open the hatch and keep it open long enough for his two fellow guards to stagger out. Wretched odors of ammonia, sulfur, charred vegetation, and rotting decay rolled into the tiny craft, and Marla Karuw nearly gagged. Still she kept her resolve as she lurched to her feet. Tejharet did the same, and they gripped each other's hands for both physical and moral support. By the time the two Aluwnans reached the hatch, the Klingons had formed a circle of protection around the landing party, while Worf offered a hand to help them.

Upon leaping out, Marla felt her feet sink into the charred mire, and she was nearly knocked to the ground by the furious wind. She and Tejharet gripped each other tightly, just trying to keep their balance. Putrid fog and slimy sleet rolled over them in waves, and there were alternating gusts of warm and cold air, as if the weather couldn't make up its mind. Marla gasped in alarm, because the ground was crawling with wormy, fishy slugs which had somehow survived the disruptor blasts. She tried to avoid stepping on the repulsive creatures, but that was impossible, because the ground was alive with them.

"Tricorder readings inconclusive!" reported the young Klingon to Ambassador Worf. "Maybe this accelerated growth will slow down, but it hasn't yet. The residual protomatter is creating havoc with the sensors!"

"Sheesh, this is nasty!" shouted the blond humanoid, hefting his disruptor rifle and scanning the swaying treetops, which seemed to be covered with blankets of hanging moss. Beyond the trees was a range of jagged black mountains, most of which were spewing smoke and flame. "What are we looking for?"

"A place to erect our transporter booths," answered Marla Karuw, trying to keep them focused on the task. The Klingons glanced at one another as if a person would be crazy to want to set foot in this tortured limbo. "You see," she continued, "the transporters in the satellites can't direct-beam just anywhere—they have to be targeted and activated by booths on the ground. We can make these enclosures one-way to save power, but they've got to be here first."

"First we set up a base," countered Worf. He looked with disgust at a vine that tried to curl around his ankle, and he finally smashed it with the butt of his disruptor rifle. Then he shook some slimy creatures off his boot and scowled. "It's hard to imagine someone set out to create this. Alexander, what about the big life-forms the probes detected?"

The young Klingon studied his handheld device and reported, "They're all around us—mostly in the trees. But they could be parasitic plants. With this interference, I'm not sure anymore what I'm reading."

Overseer Tejharet staggered on his feet and gripped Marla's arm for support. "I need to go back to the shuttlecraft," he rasped.

"Go ahead," she said with encouragement. "I'll let you know if we find anything of interest. Ambassador Worf—what about those shelters?"

"Right," answered the brawny Klingon. He had twenty security officers under his command, and he ordered half of them to start the process of taking back the planet for humanoid habitation.

They ducked into the largest shuttlecraft and pulled out several prefabricated metal sections, which they started to assemble in the feeble windbreak between the vessels. It was almost humorous to watch the strapping Klingons struggle to make a shelter in this gale, but Marla Karuw couldn't allow herself even a smile. This was worse than she had ever imagined, and rebuilding would take a lifetime. An immediate concern was food, and she wondered how much of this rampant, swarming plant growth was edible. Or would it eat them before they could eat it?

In due time, the Klingon warriors managed to construct a small geodesic dome, which kept trying to blow away. Only by sinking numerous stakes and poles in the sludge could they even get the structure to stand still, and it wasn't until several of them carried heavy equipment into the dome that it appeared to be stable. Despite the futility of their efforts, Marla Karuw was heartened by the sight of the first new building on their ravaged homeworld.

None of the big, brave Klingons looked as if they wanted to leave the scorched clearing and the shelter of their shuttlecraft. Marla had a small receptacle for taking samples, and she knelt down and scooped up a handful of earth, complete with squirming slugs. She put the whole wriggling mass in her sample jar and secured it just inside the hatch of the shuttlecraft. As she did, she caught a glimpse of Tejharet staring numbly out the viewport at the swirling sleet- and mist-shrouded trees. He looked beaten, discouraged, and she knew she would have to be strong for both of them . . . for every Aluwnan.

After glancing out the hatchway to make sure the Klingons were occupied, Marla went to the overseer and gently rubbed his shoulder. "Don't worry, we have a plan to return our beloved planet to normal."

He looked at her as if she were crazy. "Normal? The air is breathable, if you can stand the smell, but our people aren't Klingons or pioneers. They can't carve a civilization out of this madness. Look at those trees— they're growing right before my eyes! This is not Aluwna . . . this is some cursed abomination!"

Marla took a deep breath and fought the temptation to slap the overseer. "This is our home," she replied evenly. "If it were just you and me and a few hundred people on the royal yachts, we could go anywhere and resettle. But it's not just us. The satellites are already going back into orbit, and we owe it to those eight million people to free them. We owe it to all those who died to reclaim our world. Beside, the Klingons are helping us, and maybe we can get more Federation help, now that the immediate threat has ended."

"Federation help?" rasped Tejharet, laughing disdainfully. "It's *their* technology that ravaged our planet and turned it into a wasteland. And you expect *them* to save us?"

"No," answered Marla Karuw gravely, "I expect to use them until we can stand on our own. We dare not tell them how we plan to terraform the planet."

Before the regent could say more, the hatch opened again, and a foul-smelling wind swirled inside the cabin. Ambassador Worf entered, shaking the snow off his hair and shoulders, and he was followed by the young blond man he called Jeremy, who sat at the pilot's console.

"Overseer . . . Regent," he began, "we need to contact our ships and blast out a bigger clearing for our base. We're getting overrun out there by the plant growth. Do you have any objections to this course of action?"

"No," answered Karuw. "Clear as much area as you can."

Diffidently, Tejharet waved his approval.

At the console, Jeremy reported, "I've sent coordinates to the *Doghjey* and the *Ya'Vang* to clear an area the size of three hectares. We can coordinate the bombardment from here."

"Is it all right if we return to our ship?" asked the regent. "We've still got all those satellites to oversee."

Worf nodded. "Yes. Remain here, and I'll send a pilot to take you." He nodded to the young man, and the two of them staggered back outside, braving the ferocious elements.

"Blast the whole planet," muttered Overseer Tejharet.

"Maybe they will," answered Marla Karuw, her jaw clenched tightly. She picked up the sample jar that contained the charred, mutated soil of their homeworld, plus some very unwelcome new inhabitants. "They'll do what they can, but it's up to *us* to save our world."

Alexander Rozhenko covered his ears as explosions ripped through the riotous jungle one kilometer away, sending great plumes of smoke and plant debris swirling into the atmosphere. From space, the Klingon task force continued to pound the selected spot with disruptor beams, obliterating the profuse vegetation and no doubt making massive craters. Their destructive fire almost rivaled that of the great volcanoes in the distance. *It's not going to be pretty ground, but at least it will be bare ground*, thought the young Klingon, *with all the roots, seeds, and spores totally obliterated*. That's what they needed—a campsite free of the encroaching underbrush and towering trees.

Alexander wasn't sure if it was his imagination or just the contrast with the massive explosions, but the weather seemed to have calmed somewhat since their arrival two hours ago. The domed shelters they had hurriedly erected were now staying put, and the snow flurries and freezing sleet had abated, although the fog was worsened by the bombardment. Fortunately, Klingons were handy with *bat'leths* and other bladed weapons, and the warriors were hacking away at the rampant brush on the outskirts of Base One, trying to keep it clear until the new campsite was ready.

Although Aluwna was a dangerous, wildly primitive place, it held a certain attraction for the young warrior. When the pressures of living as a Klingon among humans had grown too intense for him, he had often escaped to the wilderness areas of Earth. There he could be alone to think, surrounded by nature, which never cared about his race or circumstances. This world reminded Alexander of those simple times when life boiled down to finding food and shelter. Still, he had never seen plants grow like this, curling upward right before his eyes.

The Genesis Wave was a cowardly, spiteful weapon that killed without discrimination or compunction, but one had to respect any force that could unleash this kind of power. He could now understand why the Klingons of an earlier generation had coveted the Genesis weapon and had almost gone to war with the Federation to obtain it. Alexander could also understand why the Federation had gone to such great lengths to protect its secret, even if all their precautions had ultimately failed.

He had fought in the Dominion War, but that had been a fight against a recognizable foe with clearly defined objectives. *What is the point of this invasion?* Alexander wondered to himself as the disruptors emblazoned the twilit sky. To terraform a planet that was already livable—that made no sense. Where were the invaders who could make use of such a wretched, overgrown wilderness? Wouldn't it have made some sense to at least leave some buildings and infrastructure standing? Worriedly, he scanned the sky, almost expecting the unknown conquerors to arrive at any moment.

Then he heard a shout, which wrenched him out of his uneasy thoughts. One of the guards at the edge of the clearing drew a hand disruptor and began firing into the brush, while shouting something incomprehensible. Alexander's Klingonese wasn't perfect, so maybe he misunderstood the panicked guard. He jumped to his feet and jogged toward the spot, as did his father and foster brother, Jeremy, who had been setting up scanners in one of the shelters. All three of them reached the area at the same time, and Alexander saw nothing that warranted such a reaction—just the twisting vines that constantly tried to reclaim this patch of mutant dirt.

"Cease fire!" barked Worf. "Put your weapon away."

"But . . . there! I saw it . . . right there!" stammered the officer, who looked like a grizzled veteran.

"What did you see?" demanded Worf.

Other Klingons were poking around the spot, and one of them jumped back in alarm. "Creatures!" he shouted.

They used their *bat'leths* and knives to slash at the underbrush, revealing a nest of grotesque man-sized slugs. The horrendous creatures were the color of mottled gruel, and they were flopping and squirming like fish suddenly plucked from the water. For mouths, they seemed to have circles ringed with tiny teeth, like lamprey Alexander had seen on Earth. Slimy feelers lined their misshapen bodies, and it was hard to count the number of eyes they had. But they definitely knew they were under attack, as they writhed and twisted through the teeming vines and underbrush.

"Capture one!" ordered Worf, shouting over the distant disruptor blasts.

Klingon warriors, who weren't usually so squeamish, gawked at their commander with distaste. "Couldn't we just kill them?" asked one.

"Capture one, and kill the rest," ordered Worf pragmatically. "These may be the life-forms that have registered on our sensors."

That made sense, thought Alexander, and if so, it meant that these ugly organisms might be the invaders they expected to discover.

Alexander took a pair of heavy gloves from his pack and put them on. "Come on, Jeremy, let's show them how to do it. Are we not sons of Worf from the House of Martok?"

His blond brother grinned at him and pulled out his own pair of studded gloves. "Yes, we are," he answered proudly.

The two of them reached into the squirming, twisting mass of slime and grabbed the fattest specimen. The thing felt like one entire slab of muscle as it writhed out of their grasp, and they had to wade farther into the morass. Their comrades hacked at the vines, thorn plants, and giant slugs to keep them at bay, while the two boys finally wrestled the big specimen out of the nest and onto bare ground. It snapped and twisted and lunged at them, but they were laughing as they tied cords around its head and tail, gradually reducing it into a lumpen slab of ooze.

"Well done," said Worf with a laugh. "I wonder if these things are good eating?"

"I bet it would be good with a little drawn garlic butter," suggested Jeremy with a smile.

"That's *not* what I saw," muttered the old warrior who had started this ruckus.

"What did you see?" asked Jeremy.

"Rrrgh!" He snarled defensively at the human, turned on his heel, and strode away.

In the next moment, the bombardment ended, and the landing party stopped to listen to the relative silence. The wind was still howling, and massive tree branches draped with moss rustled ominously; plus geysers continued to spew their foul contents into the darkening sky, adding to the reek of the sulfurous fog.

"Take that thing to shuttlecraft five," ordered Worf. "We are sending men back to the ship for supplies, and they might as well take the beast with them."

"Yes, Father," replied Alexander, and he grabbed one arm of the cord and Jeremy grabbed the other. They dragged the slimy thing over the charred dirt and tossed it unceremoniously into the small vessel. Alexander was glad they wouldn't have to be riding in the shuttle with the beast, because it was beginning to stink.

Glancing at the ambassador's sons with a slightly elevated measure of respect, two Klingon pilots boarded the shuttlecraft and prepared for takeoff. The boys walked back to join their father, who was conversing over the com channel with a distant party.

"Thank you, Captain Kralenk," said Worf. "I am sure you have cleared enough land for our base."

"And we made sure that *nothing* is going to grow there for a while," boasted the voice of the captain. "Will you be spending the night on the planet?"

"I believe we must," answered Worf. "There is a certain amount of exploration to be done here before we can allow the Aluwnans to return. Shuttlecraft five is on its way back to the *Doghjey* for supplies, and they are also bringing back a rather large specimen of animal life we have captured. When our science officer has had a chance to inspect it, I would appreciate hearing a report."

"We can do that," answered Captain Kralenk. "I will also send a landing party to Base Two to start erecting shelters."

"Wait until morning," suggested Worf, "it's starting to get dark here. With the added supplies, we'll be fine for the night."

"Very well. Kralenk out."

A roar sounded, and Alexander looked up to see the departing shuttlecraft streaking over the treetops. He glanced around the motley camp, which consisted of two geodesic domes that had been pounded into the charred soil, plus two muddy shuttlecraft. His father, Jeremy, and the remaining warriors were making a slow walk around the perimeter, occasionally hacking at the vines that continued to encroach upon their hard-won spit of land. Even though the wind continued to howl and the temperature grew colder, the sunset gave the swaying trees and rugged mountains a golden glow that made them beautiful, in a primitive fashion. He couldn't imagine the kind of creature who would find this place to be a custom-built paradise, but he could see promise in its raw forest and fiery terrain. Gazing at the sheer force of life in this place made a person feel alive.

Twilight was a strange time anyway—a delicate stage between two different worlds of light and dark, visible and invisible. Alexander had often felt like that, suspended between two worlds, sometimes rejecting both of them. He was thinking about all he had missed, and why, when he heard a soft voice calling to him from the unruly jungle.

"Alexander," said the feminine voice, "I am here."

He whirled around to see if anyone else had heard the mysterious voice, but Worf, Jeremy, and the others were on the far side of the clearing, partly obscured by a shuttlecraft. They weren't paying any attention to him. He peered into the swaying boughs of the primeval forest and thought he saw a figure, somewhat obscured by the lengthening shadows of dusk.

As she strode toward him, the vines and thornbushes seemed to part for her, and Alexander recognized her long hair, beautiful face, and prominent head ridges. She stopped just at the edge of the forest and smiled at him, and he heard her soothing voice in his mind.

"Alexander," she said, "it's so good to see you again."

"Mother!" he croaked, hardly believing his eyes. He hadn't seen K'Ehleyr since he was a lad, but he remembered that calm, implacable face and quiet authority. He wanted to run and grab his father's hand and show him that his beloved mother had returned. But then something in his mind clicked, and he remembered an important fact.

K'Ehleyr was dead.

"Come with me," she urged, holding out her hand. More than anything in the universe, he wanted to grab that hand and be with his mother, even in this tumultuous world, because he missed her so much. Her murder had been the one huge turning point in his life, and not for the good. Her appearance seemed to represent a way to turn back time and make up for all the wrong that had happened in his life. Alexander held out his hand, longing to be with her, even as the logic centers of his brain screamed out that this couldn't be real.

A disruptor blast startled him, and he turned to see two officers shooting something in the brush just off to his right. That broke the spell, and he staggered backward. In desperation, Alexander turned to look for his mother, but she was gone, consumed by the shadows that were gradually swallowing the great forest. He almost screamed in anguish over losing her again, and a hand caught his arm as he staggered.

"Brother," said Jeremy Aster with alarm. "I hardly ever see Klingons look pale, but *you* look pale."

"Did you see her?" he asked, gripping the human's shoulders. "She was just out there . . . in the forest."

"Who?" asked Jeremy with confusion. The blond man peered into the gloomy jungle along with his brother, but there was nothing to be seen, except rampant plant growth and wispy fog.

"I was just thinking about her," muttered Alexander, "and there she was." He shook his head, feeling as if he had just awakened from a dream and was in between reality and imagination, unsure of either one.

"What were they shooting at over there?" he asked, pointing to the officers to his right.

Jeremy shrugged. "I don't know . . . phantoms. It's getting dark, and people are seeing things in the shadows."

"Where's Father?" asked Alexander. It was suddenly urgent that he see Worf, to make sure he was alive, still flesh and blood.

Jeremy pointed to one of the shelters, and the young Klingon jogged in that direction. He entered the geodesic dome and found Worf entering data onto a padd. "What is it, son?" asked the Ambassador.

"I don't know," answered Alexander, shaking his head. "Come with me, please. It's urgent."

Worf nodded and set down his padd on a small table. Seeing the wild look in his son's eyes, he picked up his *bat'leth* on the way out.

They strode to the edge of the forest, where Jeremy was still standing. Now it was Alexander's turn to be shocked at the human's appearance.

"I saw her!" exclaimed Jeremy, pointing wildly into the underbrush. "She *was* out there!"

"Who?" asked Worf.

"My mother." As soon as Jeremy said the words, he shook his head in confusion, realizing that couldn't be true.

"We share a bond," said Alexander, "because both of our mothers died when we were young. Yet we saw both of them here tonight."

"What are you talking about?" asked Worf worriedly.

Alexander gripped his father's forearm and said, "Think about my mother, K'Ehleyr, and call to her."

"This is stupid," said Worf bluntly.

"No, it's not," answered Alexander. "Clear your mind, except for K'Ehleyr, and call to her."

Frowning deeply at such nonsense, Worf did as he'd been told. "K'Ehleyr," he whispered. "K'Ehleyr."

Man-sized shapes began to emerge from the forest, moving toward them in a ghostly procession. One of them was K'Ehleyr, another was Jeremy's mother, whom Alexander recognized from old photographs, and a third was K'mtar, a strange visitor from the future Alexander had once encountered. None of them should exist.

"By the beard of Kahless!" said Worf with a gasp. "It *is* her! Your mother—"

"Gowron!" shouted a voice to the right of them, and Alexander turned to see a Klingon security officer drop to his knees before one of the wispy figures emerging from the fog. Although the officer saw a dead Klingon leader, Alexander again saw his mother in the same apparition. Everywhere he looked, he saw his mother—dozens of them, all smiling beatifically.

"Come with me, Worf," said the beautiful K'Ehleyr, holding out her arms. "We are waiting for you."

fourteen

"We've got to get out of here!" shouted Alexander, grabbing his father's arm and trying to drag him away from the shadowy, ghost-filled jungle of Aluwna. "Something is affecting our minds!"

When Worf refused to move, Alexander clenched his fist and slugged him in the jaw. That staggered the big Klingon and nearly dropped him to the ground; it also shattered the hold that the apparition had on the ambassador, and he stared in alarm at his son.

"Jeremy!" yelled Alexander, trying to pull the human away from the edge of the forest.

"I can't leave her now," insisted Jeremy Aster. "My mother—"

"It's not your mother!" shouted Alexander. "Your mother's dead."

"Everyone to the shuttlecraft!" ordered Worf. "Immediate evacuation! Everyone to the shuttles!"

That took some doing, since so many of the officers were entranced by the ghostlike beings emerging from the forest. In desperation, Worf ran up to one of the creatures and cut it in half with his *bat'leth*. What fell to the ground was a weird clump of moss and gray-green vegetation. The enraged Klingon, whose dear one had just been dispatched with such cold-blooded ruthlessness, turned on Worf and drew his knife. Alexander feared that his father would be killed, but Jeremy leveled a Starfleet phaser and hit the officer with a stun beam. He slumped to the ground, unconscious.

"We are under attack!" bellowed Worf. He pointed to his fallen comrade. "You two, pick up that officer. Everyone to the shuttlecraft! *Now!*"

Those who were too enchanted to obey orders were stunned into unconsciousness by Jeremy's phaser. Dragging, cajoling, yelling, and slugging it out with each other, the small force of Klingons and one human somehow retreated into the two shuttlecraft. Worf wouldn't allow them to take off, however, until he made sure that the pilots were possessed of their full mental faculties. After the pilots had reported to Worf, confirming their fitness, he ordered the two shuttlecraft aloft. Through the viewport, Alexander could see an army of shadowy beings emerging from the trees to reclaim the burned-out clearing.

As they rose over the dense forest of Aluwna, Worf tapped his com medallion and said, "Worf to *Doghjey*—urgent."

"Kralenk here," answered the captain. "What is it, Ambassador? You are deserting your post."

"We were under attack," reported Worf, "by creatures which could assume the appearance of people we know—loved ones who are dead or certainly not on Aluwna. We are returning to the ship, but I request quarantine measures."

"Very well," answered the captain, sounding unhappy. "This will set back our timetable. We'll turn on the forcefields in the shuttlebay, and I'll have a medical team meet you. Worf, are you saying that the planet is inhabited?"

The big Klingon frowned in thought for a moment, then replied, "Let us just say that something lives here besides trees, bushes, and slugs. I suggest you contact Starfleet and see if they've had similar experiences on the other Genesis planets."

"Acknowledged. Kralenk out."

Heaving a sigh of relief, Worf sunk back in his seat; then he glanced at his son across the aisle. Alexander shook his head wistfully and said, "I had forgotten how beautiful my mother was."

"K'Ehleyr's death is seared in my memory," answered Worf. "But that wasn't your mother. I hope to find out exactly what it was."

From the seat in front of Worf, Jeremy turned around. "When you killed that one . . . it looked like vegetation."

"That won't be the last one we kill," vowed Worf. "Next time we go down in force."

* * *

On the bridge of the royal yacht *Darzor*, Marla Karuw paced angrily, slamming her fist into her palm. "This is an absurd directive from the Klingons," she muttered. "We still cannot transport down to Aluwna—why not? Unless we can transport to the planet, eight million survivors are in jeopardy. Now they say that we can't even go down there in shuttle-craft! Who are *they* to tell us we can't walk on our own world?"

"They are looking out for our safety," said her aide, Komplum, twisting his hands nervously. "Maybe we should err on the side of caution."

"Caution?" she scoffed. "Caution will get eight million people killed! You are aware that the temperature of the bioneural networks on some of the satellites has dropped another two degrees, and there are other signs of degradation. Those satellites have been through a lot, and we are not going to be able to keep our people stored in them for seventy-five Terran years. I want our people to be freed in a few days, at the latest."

She turned to Captain Uzel, who had been watching the regent with interest. "Captain," she asked, "now that most of the satellites have been disconnected from our engines, do we have enough power to use our transporters?"

"Very sparingly," he answered. "What do you have in mind, Regent?"

"I want to prove our Klingon friends wrong," Marla

declared. "I'm going to go to the transporter room and beam down to the planet." She started for the corridor at the rear of the bridge.

Both Komplum and the captain shouted after her to stop. "What if the Klingons are right?" asked Uzel. "At least ask for a volunteer!"

"I *am* a volunteer," she replied, pausing in the doorway. "I wouldn't ask anyone else to do what I wouldn't do myself. It's essential that we be able to transport down to the planet. If we can't do that . . . then all of our rescue efforts have been in vain. Tell them I'm coming."

Marla Karuw turned on her heel and walked down the corridor to the transporter room, which was only a few doors away. When she arrived, the transporter operator was ending a conversation over the com channel. "Yes, Captain, we'll be careful," he promised. "Transporter room out."

He stepped behind his console and asked the regent, "Do you have a specific destination in mind?"

"Do you have the coordinates where the Klingon shuttlecraft landed?" she asked.

The officer checked his board and nodded. "Yes, I do. The shelters are still standing, but the Klingons pulled out only a short time ago. It's also night there."

"It doesn't matter," Karuw answered, climbing aboard the transporter platform. "This is simply an experiment, and I won't be down there long."

The operator left his post for a moment to hand her a small device to be worn on her wrist. "Press this

alert when you are ready to return. That will get you
back the quickest."

"Thank you," she said, granting the young officer a
smile as she strapped the device to her wrist. "Proceed
when ready."

"Yes, Regent." He worked his board, and she felt
the slight tingle that indicated that her molecules
were being dispersed. As she nervously caught her
breath, Marla realized that this might be the last
breath she would ever take. But someone had to
prove that it was safe to transport. Either she would
do that in the next few instants, or she would join the
seventy million souls who had perished on Aluwna.

When Marla smelled the awful ammonia-and-
sulfur-tainted air, then shivered from the cold, she realized that her transporter experiment had been a success.
What did those stupid Klingons know? They were
supposed to be so brave, yet they had deserted their
camp only half a day after settling it. She looked at the
two domed shelters, which were the only things which
stood out in the Aluwnan night, and she wondered
what their rush to evacuate had been. The distant
mountains were tipped with fire from volcanic eruptions, but the wind had died down along with some of
the more malevolent plant growth. She still was afraid
to look at the squishy things on the ground, but it was
too dark to see them, anyway.

No, there was almost a peace here now that gave
her hope that they could resettle Aluwna and make it
their home once again. More than anything, Marla

Karuw just wanted to know that the desperate acts she had committed were necessary and would pay off in the long run. There were likely to be more desperate acts, such as this transporter experiment, but she was heartened to know that her luck was still holding.

Marla heard an odd shuffling noise behind her, and she turned around to see a slight, bent figure walking toward her. "Hello, Regent," said a familiar voice.

No, it couldn't be! Marla gasped and stumbled backward a few paces. "Curate Molafzon!" she croaked.

"Yes, I am here," said the elderly clergyman, "even though you tried to kill me."

"But how?" she rasped, shaking her head with disbelief. "It's really *you?*"

"I have friends," he answered calmly, "friends who spared my life and made sure I could be here to greet you upon your return."

"And you're living . . . *here?*"

The curate shrugged. "Where else would I be living but our beloved home? I want you to know that I bear you no ill feelings. You did what you had to do, and I am proud of you for fulfilling your vision and saving so many. I have revealed myself to you, because I want you to know that it is safe for our people to return to Aluwna. The sooner the better, as you always say."

"Don't worry, I will make sure all the survivors return," promised the regent. "But now I must go back to the ship. And you should come with me."

"No," he answered quickly. "You are not the only one who thinks I am dead, and it's best for you to keep our secret for now. I am perfectly safe here, as will all of our people be. Once again, I forgive you for what you tried to do to me."

He held out his wizened hand, and Karuw dropped to her knees and gratefully kissed it. "You are truly the instrument of the Divine Hand," she said with immense respect and admiration.

There was rustling in the brush, and she thought she saw other figures moving in the dark forest. "You are not alone?" asked Marla.

"Never am I alone," he answered. "But all of this must be our secret. You continue with your plans to return our people to their home, and all will be revealed in time."

"Thank you, Curate," answered Marla, rising to her feet. "I was feeling so guilty—"

"Don't," he answered. "All of this is part of the Divine Plan. But the strangers—"

"The Klingons?"

"I don't trust them," said the elder. "Beware of them. Now you may return to the ship."

"Yes, Curate." Bowing gratefully, Marla Karuw pressed the alert button on her wristband, and her molecules swirled upward in a shimmering column of refracted light.

Worf paced sullenly in the confines of the brig on the *Doghjey*, where he, Alexander, Jeremy, and the other members of the landing party had been direct-beamed from the shuttlebay. He was proud to be a Klingon—and to have the responsibility of directing this task force—but there were times when he missed the luxurious sickbay on the *Enterprise*. A Klingon sickbay was hardly better than this brig, and it didn't possess any quarantine facilities. Klingons were expected to fight and perform duties as normal when wounded, and if they were too wounded to be useful, they might as well be dead. The medical staff consisted of one doctor and two part-time medics, and it often took forever for them to deal with a complicated medical problem.

"Dad," said Jeremy, "all that pacing isn't going to get us out of here any sooner. And you're the one who insisted on quarantine. Klingons don't normally believe they can get sick."

Alexander cast a jaundiced eye at his brother. "And humans think they're sick when they have a stuffy nose and a slight headache."

"We're not sick," answered Worf. "At least I don't feel sick. But seeing dead people is not the mark of a healthy person."

"And it's something which affected all of us," added Alexander.

"Like mass hysteria," suggested Jeremy.

Worf stopped pacing and scowled at his adopted son. "Klingons do not get hysterical. I was just taking normal precautions."

"Of course," answered Jeremy with a smile. "But

something was coming out of that jungle, and it couldn't be who we thought we saw."

Alexander scratched his chin thoughtfully. "The odd thing is, I was just thinking about my mother, and what her death meant to me, when she appeared. That can't be a coincidence."

"I saw Chancellor Gowron," muttered one of the veteran officers in another cell. He shook his head in disbelief. "I had recalled that it was Ambassador Worf who killed him, and then he was there!"

One by one, the hardened Klingons admitted to seeing loved ones or important figures from their past, some of whom were dead and all of whom could not possibly be on Aluwna. In fact, nothing could exist on Aluwna, except whatever devilish spawn the Genesis Wave had brought. Illness or madness, there was something terribly wrong with the lifelike apparitions on the planet, and not a single crew member complained about being locked away in the brig.

"Could they be Founders from the Dominion?" asked Alexander.

"I don't believe even Founders could live through the Genesis Wave," answered Worf. "And our sensors are now calibrated to detect Founders, ever since they infiltrated the High Council."

"Besides," said Jeremy, "they didn't really succeed in doing anything but scaring us off. It was like a dream—or a nightmare—one of those encounters that doesn't make any sense."

The outer door opened, and the squat, gray-haired

Captain Kralenk entered, followed by an elderly, white-haired doctor named M'Lorik. The doctor's face was deeply scarred, and he walked with a limp, as if he had once been a warrior until an injury had forced him into the less strenuous field of medicine. The captain and doctor stopped just outside the force-field that contained the members of the landing party, and any germs that accompanied them.

"Ambassador Worf," said the captain, "you showed good judgment in suggesting this quarantine. The doctor will tell you what he has discovered from your tissue samples, and I can tell you that Starfleet is making similar discoveries."

The old doctor cleared his throat and consulted a medical padd. "All of you are suffering from a fungal infection in your brains and lungs. This fungus does not appear to be fatal, although it is fast-moving and airborne, making it very contagious. Fungi of this sort can cause fevers and hallucination, but it is treatable."

"These were not hallucinations," said Worf, bristling. "Perhaps that was a part of it, but I thought I killed one of these ghosts."

M'Lorik nodded sagely and said, "An airborne fungus could transmit information . . . perhaps even allow another creature to read your mind, if it were close enough. You were probably affected in the first hours on the planet's surface. The captain has more information."

"Starfleet should have warned us what we were dealing with," grumbled Captain Kralenk. "But we are only now receiving reports from other Genesis planets. This was not an isolated incident—both Starfleet and Romulan forces have experienced similar encounters, hallucinations, or whatever you want to call them. Some of them have resulted in much worse consequences, such as a Starfleet vessel that was taken over by officers under the influence of this fungus."

"Have you continued to send them reports about our situation here?" asked Worf.

"Yes, I have," replied the captain. "They promised to send some help as soon as they resolve their own problems. As yet, there's no set procedure for dealing with these ghosts, so we can proceed as we see fit."

"I see fit to eradicate them," answered Worf determinedly. "Until we do, we should wear protective suits to minimize exposure to the fungus. And make sure we keep the Aluwnans from going down there."

Captain Kralenk scowled. "That may be easier said than done. I've sent them directives, but they keep demanding that they be allowed to erect transporter booths—so they can start freeing their people in the pattern buffers."

"I will talk to them," said Worf, starting for the door of his cell.

"Halt!" ordered Dr. M'Lorik. "None of you will go anywhere until we rid you of this fungus. My staff will be here soon with an antibiotic which should work; then there will be more tests and examinations. You are the first cases of this type, and we want to make sure you are the last. So rest and resign yourselves to an indefinite stay in the brig. Those are my orders, and you are now under *my* command."

"Hmmm," muttered Worf disgruntledly, "now you sound like a Starfleet doctor."

"I will take that as a compliment," said the old healer with a smile.

"Captain," asked Alexander Rozhenko, "what about that creature we sent you?"

"It was relatively harmless," answered the captain, "although it was also infected by the fungus and a related parasite. Our science officer considers it to be a food source."

"A food source for *what?*" said Worf ominously. They all looked at one another, but nobody ventured a reply.

Feeling energized and optimistic after her visit to the planet, Marla Karuw walked into the dimly lit laboratory on the *Darzor*, where her master scientist, Vilo Garlet, was at work on a prototype transporter booth. It looked much like one of the blue enclosures that had been ubiquitous on Aluwna before the cataclysm, although it was smaller and could accommodate only one person at a time. The reduction in size was intended to make it possible to beam the booth itself from the ship's transporter room to the planet. That would make it possible to install hundreds of the transporters in a relatively short time. Despite feeling better about their prospects since seeing Curate

Molafzon again, Marla had no doubt that their time to act was running out.

"Good work, Vilo," she said as she admired the apparatus. "Does it meet all of my specs?"

"Yes," answered the scientist with a weary nod. He pointed out various features. "Here are the solar power cells and the wireless receiver. As you requested, it has a chromasynthesis emitter hidden in the base, which we can program and activate remotely. Without a considerable amount of testing, however, I'm not quite sure what chromasynthesis will do to the current flora and fauna on the planet."

"We may not need it," answered Karuw, "because this new world may yet prove to be hospitable. Still I would like to have the option to terraform, if necessary."

"Without informing the Klingons?" asked Vilo Garlet.

The regent scowled. "It's our planet, and we can do what we want with it. I trust they'll understand that, or leave. I won't brook any interference from the Klingons, the Federation, or anybody else."

fifteen

As Admiral Alynna Nechayev sat at the dining table in her stateroom aboard the starship *Sovereign*, she tried not to look in the mirror on the far bulkhead. Instead she concentrated on the padds, printouts, and transparencies spread across her table, trying to catch up with dispatches and reports from all over the region devastated by the Genesis Wave. Whenever her gaze traveled in the direction of that mirror— or any mirror—the result was too shocking to contemplate. One half of her face was weathered by decades of command, hard decisions, and strife, and the other half was as smooth and pristine as a teenager's complexion. On one side, the bags, wrinkles, jowls, and discoloration of her years were prominent; on the other side, they didn't exist. One half was spotted with age, and the other half was freckled with youth.

In a desperate attempt to save her life on Myrmidon, Commander Geordi La Forge had applied a glob of still-mutating Genesis material to her wounds; now she had to live with it, until she reached Starfleet Medical Center on Earth. Nechayev was a walking billboard for the wonders and horrors of the Genesis technology, and so were all these frantic pleas for help spread before her. What could she tell them? They had vanquished the moss creatures who had tried to remake the Alpha Quadrant in their own image, but that had been too late for dozens of inhabited worlds and billions of innocent beings. Her security arrangements to protect Dr. Carol Marcus had failed, making her personally culpable for all that had happened.

They could put her face back to normal, but they couldn't excise her guilt.

It had been several hours since the *Sovereign* had left the *Enterprise* crew on Starbase 302, and it seemed as if the worst should be over. But the mountain of requests on this table made it clear that the repercussions of the Genesis Wave would continue for some time. Already she had dispatched a special operative, Regimol, to investigate the existence of a portable Genesis device. That was frightening enough, but now reports were coming in from all over that the moss creatures were flourishing on several of the planets they had transformed.

It seemed inevitable that there would be a second round of wholesale destruction and murder, except on

one previously uninhabited planet where the moss
creatures would be allowed to exist, never coming into
contact with humanoid species. Everywhere else, they
would have to be hunted down and destroyed. And
that would have to be done with extreme caution,
considering the telepathic and pseudo-shapechanging
properties of these beings. As intelligent parasites, they
were not really able to control their predatory behavior, but sympathy couldn't enter into the equation. As
more survivors tried to return home to their ravished
planets, more victims would fall prey to these unwit-
ting monsters, and this new threat had to be stopped
before more damage was done.

To that end, she had asked another passenger on
the *Sovereign*, Dr. Leah Brahms, to issue a report to
all the survivors of all the worlds affected by the
Genesis Wave. Nobody knew more about the wave
and its horrible aftermath than Leah Brahms, who
had rushed halfway across the Alpha Quadrant trying
to warn people. Also her phase-shifting radiation suit
had saved countless lives at the height of the disaster.
Nechayev had the feeling that they would be dealing
with the fallout from Genesis for some time to come,
and she was thinking about forming a special force to
deal with such problems. Leah Brahms was the logical one to lead such a team. Judging from the mountain of paperwork on her dining-room table, there
was a lot of work to do.

What she didn't want to do was scare off Dr.
Brahms, when she needed her so badly. Leah had

been left somewhat traumatized by her husband's death and all she had witnessed, but she was a strong woman. And Nechayev had never been averse to using people under difficult circumstances—even pushing them beyond their endurance—for the greater good.

Her door chime sounded, and the admiral lifted her chin and said, "Enter."

The door whooshed open, and the attractive but somewhat gaunt figure of Leah Brahms entered her quarters. Her shoulder-length, chestnut-colored hair was not unkempt but looked a little matted. "You sent for me, Admiral?" asked the engineer.

"Yes, Leah, please have a seat," said Nechayev pleasantly. She motioned to the food replicator. "Do you want something to eat or drink?"

"No thank you." Brahms took a seat at the table, averting her eyes so as not to stare too much at Nechayev's remarkably altered face.

"I read your report," said the admiral. "Short and to the point, yet stressing what dangers we still face. I ordered that it be distributed immediately, although it still has to go through channels."

"I understand," replied Brahms. "Thank you."

Nechayev sighed heavily and sat back in her seat. Then she motioned to the piles of documents before her. "As you can see, we've still got a ton of work to do. Most of these are dispatches from Genesis planets where there are concerned survivors. Your report will answer many of their questions, but some of them face arduous tasks in resettling their planets."

Brahms winced. "I don't know that I would want to live on one of those planets. Aren't there any alternatives?"

"For some of them, no," answered Nechayev. She rifled through the documents and picked up a padd, glancing at it to make sure it was the right one. "Take this compilation of reports, for example. It's about a planet named Aluwna, which was hit late in the wave's cycle. We've heard from their government and from the Klingons who went to help them, but arrived too late. We weren't able to reach them with your phase-shifting technology, so they were forced into extreme measures. Why don't you read it, while I catch up on some of these others."

She handed the padd to Leah Brahms, who read it with interest. Nechayev perused another document, while she glanced occasionally at the engineer. From her furrowed brow, it was clear that Brahms found the report fascinating.

"Wow," she said somberly, setting the padd on the table, "this is amazing. All those people trapped in transporter buffers. I can think of a million things that could go wrong, especially if they're trying to return these people to a new Genesis planet."

"You're right," agreed Nechayev. "The Klingons are helping them, and they can handle the moss creatures. But I believe the Aluwnans could use some technical help."

Leah narrowed her eyes. "Like me?"

"You're all I have," said the admiral with a smile. "This ship is returning to Earth, where I have an appointment with Starfleet Medical. But we'll pass fairly close to Aluwna, and I can put you on a runabout and get you there fairly quickly. As more personnel are freed up, I'll send them along to help you."

"I didn't know that I worked for you," said Leah.

Nechayev absentmindedly touched the youthful side of her face. "I have more than a few special operatives working for me, and none of them ever complain that the work is boring. I know you're at loose ends, and sometimes hard work is the best antidote to grief. I'd be honored if you would join my team. What do you say, Dr. Brahms."

"Can I quit anytime?"

"But of course," answered Nechayev. "This is strictly voluntary."

"Then I'll go to Aluwna," replied Leah Brahms. "And we'll take it from there."

"Thank you," said the admiral with a broad smile. She rose to her feet and offered the younger woman her hand. "Welcome aboard."

Farlo Fuzwik squirmed uncomfortably in his seat as he sat in the presence of Overseer Tejharet, Seeress Jenoset, and his fellow seeress consort, Padrin. He had wanted to bring Candra with him to this private dinner in the royal stateroom, but Jenoset had insisted—with steely resolve—that this was a dinner for members of the royal family only. Even the regent had not been invited, although it was clear that Marla Karuw was very busy, running to and from the planet, meeting with scientists, and overseeing the satellites. It was the first opportunity for him to spend any time with the overseer, who at first was shocked by his youth. Then it became clear that very little the seeress did could shock him for very long, and he had grown sullen and distracted.

They made small talk as they ate, with Jenoset and Padrin complaining about the food and their accommodations on the ship, although it all seemed grand to Farlo. They also bemoaned the loss of so many cultural institutions and people they knew, especially a curate named Molafzon. For a moment, the overseer became animated as he wondered how Curate Molafzon had disappeared or gotten lost in the chaos of the evacuation, and what a loss it was. After that, he lapsed back into sullen retrospection. Although this wasn't a cheerful dinner party, it was clear that these three people were comfortable in each other's presence, and Farlo wondered if he would ever fit in so easily.

After dessert, Seeress Jenoset sat stiffly in her chair and said, "I suggested we have dinner together for a reason. I want to discuss when and how we should go about returning the traditional power of government to the royal family, where it has rested for eons of peace and prosperity."

The glaze left the overseer's eyes, and he sat up to listen as the seeress went on to say, "I realize we turned over the reins of government to a regent for very good reason, although no regent has ever held power in any of our lifetimes. In the past, a regent has served only when the overseer was too young or incapacitated, and that is not the case. I salute Marla Karuw for her daring and successful evacuation of Aluwna, but the threat is over. There is no immediate emergency, just a great deal of work to do. We must face the prospect of rebuilding our homes and society, and the people will be helped in this great task by a sense of tradition and continuity with our past."

"Absolutely," agreed Padrin. "It will encourage them to step off our transporters and see the power structure they have come to trust. Plus any ill feelings over the lottery and those passed over can be attributed to the regent. Don't get me wrong, she did a great job—but the overseer has an opportunity to rise above those difficult decisions."

Overseer Tejharet sniffed disdainfully. "What do you want to do with Marla Karuw? Simply toss her off with a handshake?"

"Husband," said Jenoset sweetly, "may I remind you that not long ago, Marla Karuw was convicted of heresy. Considering the seriousness of her crimes, she should be grateful for the pardon you granted her. In other words, she was paid in advance for her work during this crisis. Our universities and laboratories are gone, so we can't give her a prominent post—but I'm sure we will find a way to dutifully honor Marla Karuw."

Jenoset's eyes narrowed as she added, "However, leaving her permanently in charge of Aluwna is pointless. It would also endanger any future transfer of power. If we have a reign of regents, who would choose them after we're gone? Thanks to the Hand of the Divine, our family has remained untouched by this horrendous disaster." The elegant seeress glanced pointedly at Farlo and granted him a smile. "In fact, we have gained in number, and the future of our line is assured. This is not the time to toss out our most noble traditions. Tejharet, you made her the regent, and you could return power to its rightful place, whenever you wish. I urge you to do so immediately."

Farlo and everyone else in the room turned to look at the overseer, who shifted uneasily under their gaze. He looked older, almost confused, and for a moment Farlo wondered if Tejharet was up to the task of ruling during these bizarre times.

"We still need Marla Karuw," he finally said. "As long as our people are trapped in those satellites, we still need her leadership. As soon as they are freed, I will review this decision."

The overseer rose unsteadily to his feet and rubbed his eyes. "Now I'm tired—if you would leave me, I'd like to go to bed."

"Let me rub your back," offered Jenoset. "That will ease your tension." She looked pointedly at Padrin and Farlo.

Padrin jumped to his feet at the signal and grabbed Farlo by the collar of his silky tunic. "Come on, lad, let's go watch the shuttlecraft put the satellites back into orbit."

As Uncle Padrin hustled him out of the royal stateroom, Farlo breathed a sigh of relief. This would apparently be another night when he would not be required to perform any consort duties. He felt for the ebony tube in his pocket, to make sure he still had it. Until he and Candra were back on Aluwna, and life was less uncertain, he had to remain a high breed.

"Ambassador Worf, you and all the members of the landing party are free to go," announced a security officer as he turned off the forcefield in the brig of the *Doghjey*. "The doctor says the treatment worked, and you are cleared."

"It's about time," muttered Worf as he strode from the cell, followed by his sons, Alexander and Jeremy, plus a dozen warriors.

The officer added, "The captain is assembling a squadron of warriors to return to the planet and secure Base Two. If any of you wish to participate, report to the shuttlebay at ten hundred hours."

"Good, that gives us time to eat," said Jeremy with a grin.

Worf turned to Alexander, who was not the most avid fighter. "Perhaps you'd prefer to return to your ship."

"No thanks, Father," answered the young Klingon. "Last time I fought at your side, I didn't appreciate it. This time, I will."

Worf nodded, allowing himself a smile. *"maDo'-choH,"* he said warmly.

From the moment their shuttlecraft landed roughly in an overgrown crater, which had been cleared of vegetation only yesterday, Alexander Rozhenko knew they were in for a difficult fight. Huge vines and vine-like creatures wrapped around the small craft and obscured the viewports, and the warriors had difficulty moving in their gray environmental suits. Klingons weren't used to wearing much protection, and every one of them bristled at the restrictions forced upon them by the suits, especially the helmets. But the necessity had been drummed into them. At least the environmental headgear had special biofilters that allowed them to breathe ambient air and talk to one another.

Through the blurry, leaf-streaked window, Alexander could see four of the other ten shuttlecraft plunk down in the three hectares supposedly cleared by yesterday's bombardment. Some of them were immediately encased in a cocoon of thorny vines and thick boughs, and monstrous beings shuffled from the jungle and marched toward them en masse, shifting into recognizable shapes as they came. Unable to read their minds, the bizarre creatures took on the forms of the few humanoids they had learned about the night before, so there was suddenly an army of Gowrons and K'Ehleyrs striding toward them. Alexander recoiled in horror as his dead mother suddenly peered at him through the window.

"Remember, take no prisoners!" shouted Worf. "Kill everything that moves, unless they are wearing one of our suits! *Dalegh wa' yIHoH!*"

Rising with difficulty and bumping into each other, the suited Klingons moved clumsily toward the hatch, disruptors leveled for action. Worf pushed the hatch open and was instantly encircled by thorny green tendrils and the naked arms of fake K'Ehleyrs. He was pulled from the craft and engulfed, but Jeremy was right behind him. The young human blasted the leafy heads of the enemy, and a blazing fire erupted in the hatchway. Ignoring his own safety, Jeremy jumped out and began clubbing the clinging, flaming arms of the enemy, as Worf rolled to the ground to allow others to jump out. High-pitched, unholy screams rent the air as the creatures burned and died, but countless more were right behind them, engulfing the warriors in nets of ungodly moss laced with humanoid arms and legs.

Every centimeter of ground was fought over with blazing intensity, and it took Alexander almost fifteen minutes just to get out of the shuttlecraft. The battleground was chaos, and the entire crater was ablaze and filled with embers and smoke, whipped by the wind. The Klingons looked as ghostly in the choking haze as did the horrendous plant creatures. Dozens of brave warriors were pulled to the ground, and some had their helmets and suits ripped from their bodies. Alexander was one of those who carried a Starfleet phaser set to stun, and it was his job to incapacitate those who might be infected and used by the enemy. Before their minds could be raped, he blasted his own comrades, felling them where they lay.

"Switch to *bat'leths*!" shouted Worf, which made perfect sense, because the fire and smoke was aiding the enemy and hindering the Klingon advance. The call echoed across the charred craters to switch to blades, and the warriors fought like crazed farmers, trying to cut down a field of tall cane which was on fire and moving swiftly at the same time. On Earth, Alexander had often heard of the underworld land called Hell, and he couldn't imagine that it could be any worse than this, especially with having to watch his mother be brutally hacked to pieces a hundred times over.

It seemed as if they fought for days, advancing only a few steps every hour. The enemy realized that this was the first but most important battle—if the suited invaders could be stopped here, the world of Aluwna was theirs forever. The vile, shapeshifting beasts must have mustered their forces from every corner of the planet, because they came in waves. Even some of the man-sized slugs got into the fight, snaking their way through the morass to latch on to legs and fallen comrades. Klingons were strangled by thick vines, burned by flaming tendrils, and bled by the giant lampreys; many fell to the phasers on purpose and the disruptors by accident. Despite the horrific carnage, not a single Klingon ever retreated.

They pushed onward, hacking, blasting, and rending; and their cries and grunts echoed over the bloody ground. There was no doubt this was going to be a fight to the death.

Alexander used his phaser to stun more than one comrade who was dying, and he often switched the weapon to full to blow apart a wall of swarming creatures. He cringed as he destroyed the visage of his mother, holding her arms out to hug him.

Someone started lobbing explosive shells behind the enemy lines, to reduce their incredible number of reinforcements. Whipped by the wind, these explosions set the whole forest on fire, and they were soon fighting inside a ring of flames. Somehow the Klingons' circle continued to widen even while their numbers lessened, and the enemy was on the retreat by the time dusk drew a curtain over the dreadful slaughter. The shadows were a welcome sight to Alexander, because the sights on this killing field were too awful for the harsh light of day.

With their blood at high boil, the Klingons pursued the creatures into the flames, risking their lives in order to hack them to pieces. Even after the battle had been won and the base secured, the berserk warriors continued to slice the enemy to bits, no matter what form they took. Smoke wafted across the battlefield, and so did the howls of many Klingons as they performed the death ritual over their fallen comrades.

Manning a tricorder to check for vital signs, Alexander ran from one wounded fighter to another;

he tagged those still alive with a com medallion. "Father!" he called as he ran. "Father! Where are you?"

"Over here!" shouted a weary, hoarse voice.

Alexander's heart sank to his bowels when he saw Worf bent over a fallen figure—one considerably skinnier than the brawny Klingons. Jeremy was not moving, and his suit was badly burned.

Alexander gulped as he knelt down beside Worf. "Is he . . . is he alive?"

"Barely," answered the ambassador, bowing his helmeted head.

"Despite the directive against transporting," said Alexander, "we've got many wounded who need to get back to the ship immediately. Can you give the order?" He placed his last com medallion on the chest of his human brother.

Worf nodded and tapped the com device on his wrist. "Worf to Captain Kralenk on the *Doghjey*."

"Kralenk here," answered the familiar voice. "You have been down there a long time. What is the outcome?"

Worf lifted his chin and said, "We have won a great victory, killing countless hundreds of these monsters. But we have many dead and wounded. Since we cannot spare a single warrior or shuttlecraft, in case the enemy returns, I request permission to have the badly wounded beamed to the ship. My son has tagged them with com devices."

"Certainly," answered the captain. "Tonight we

will sing your praises over a goblet of bloodwine. Kralenk out."

Alexander stood wearily, thinking he wasn't a full-blooded Klingon yet, because he didn't feel like singing or praising. He felt more like weeping.

"I hope the Aluwnans appreciate what we are doing for them," grumbled Worf as he staggered to his feet. He put his arm around his son and said, "Join me in the death howl, the same as we did for your mother."

Alexander nodded solemnly, and he and his father threw their heads back and bellowed their grief and pride to the dusky, smoke-filled sky.

sixteen

Her jaw clenched in rage, Marla Karuw leaned over the shoulder of her assistant, Komplum, who was manning the science station on the bridge of the *Darzor*. Both of them watched the curious sensor readings from Aluwna scroll across the screen.

"What in the Divine are those crazy Klingons doing down there?" she asked with a scowl.

"It appears to be a battle," answered Komplum. "In the large area they bombarded yesterday."

Captin Uzel stepped to her side and added, "They must be fighting something on the planet . . . perhaps the creatures they've been telling us about."

"Creatures?" asked Marla in confusion. "The only ones down there are—" She stopped, because she was about to say that Curate Molafzon and his followers were already living on Aluwna, but that was a secret she had vowed to keep.

"Haven't you been reading the dispatches from Starfleet?" asked Captain Uzel.

"No," the regent answered brusquely. "Who has time to read all that drivel?"

"It isn't drivel," answered the captain, eyeing his leader with mild disapproval. "These Genesis planets are dangerous places, according to Starfleet."

"That's our home you're talking about," said Marla Karuw. "Whatever is down there, we can learn to live with it . . . or change it. Komplum, bring up the latest status of the satellites. Are they all in place yet?"

"No," answered the young scientist worriedly. "We've had outright failure in a handful of satellites when they went off solar power during the night."

"What!" she shouted. "And you didn't tell me?"

Her assistant cringed. "You were so busy in the laboratory with Professor Garlet, and we thought we had it isolated to a few bad plasma cells. I still don't think it's a systemwide failure, but we've slowed down putting them back into orbit until we could run diagnostics on all of them."

Captain Uzel cleared his throat and said, "The delay was partly my doing, Regent. We've had shuttlecraft pilots and technical teams working around the clock since we returned, and I approved a few hours of rest for them."

"There's no time for rest!" snapped Karuw. Hearing her own shrill voice, she stopped to massage her aching head. "I'm sorry, but we've got so much left to do. Not only do we have to stabilize those satellites and get them back into orbit, but we've got to get the replicators on every ship making parts for the transporter booths. Then everyone will work to assemble them. We've got a new compact design—have you seen the prototype?"

Uzel shook his head. "That's one thing I haven't had time for. But it seems to me that before we can put up hundreds of transporter booths, we need the Klingons to make Aluwna safe. Regent, I urge you to read the dispatches from Starfleet. For one thing, they're sending us an expert on Genesis planets."

Marla Karuw furrowed all six of her eyebrows at him. "Oh, *now* they send us experts. First the wave, and then someone to explain it? After our eight million survivors are safe, I'll listen to their experts and their excuses." The regent paced anxiously across the small bridge.

"Captain," she ordered, "get your crews and your shuttlecraft back to work. Komplum, we haven't got time to run diagnostics on every satellite, and we don't need to—I know they're degrading, and so do you. Way back in the Summer Palace, you told me that the biological components would degrade, and I knew you were right then. We didn't have any choice then, and we still don't have any choice—we must keep moving ahead or sacrifice those eight million souls, half of whom are children."

"Three of them are *my* children," said Captain Uzel, gazing pointedly at her.

"Well, if you ever want to see them again, get those

satellites in place." Marla Karuw turned and headed for the doorway at the rear of the bridge.

"Where are you going, Regent?" asked Komplum.

She scowled. "Down to the planet to see what the Klingons are doing."

"You're going to beam down again?" asked the captain with concern.

"I've proven that we can use our transporters," she answered. "What have the Klingons proven, except that they can blow things up and set the forest on fire?" She strode into the corridor.

"Regent Karuw!" called the captain. "The Klingons said that everyone going to the planet must wear an environmental suit."

Marla sniffed with disdain. "They don't sound as brave as they're made out to be."

Halfway to the transporter room, a sultry blond woman dressed in a dinner gown stepped from a doorway and moved in front of Marla. "Regent Karuw, may I have a word with you?" asked Seeress Jenoset.

"I'm very busy," answered Karuw, trying to slip past the elegant but useless monarch.

"I've asked you politely," said the seeress, mustering her considerable charm. "The overseer is not well, and I'm worried about him. You know, if he dies, one of my other husbands will become overseer, and they could rescind the decree making you regent."

That stopped Marla Karuw dead in her tracks, and she whirled on the elegant autocrat. "Are you threatening *me*? Or the overseer?"

"I'm threatening no one," answered Jenoset pleasantly. "I only asked to have a word with you. In private, not here in the hallway. Surely you can spare a few moments for your benefactor's wife. For your *lover's* wife."

Marla tried to keep a composed expression on her face; but she must have failed, because the seeress smiled in triumph.

"Oh, you didn't think I knew about that," said Jenoset. "Well, I did. I chose not to bring it up at your heresy trial, because we had so much other evidence against you. But I can tell you that we could still use that information to have you removed from office. I don't wish to do that—I only wish to talk to you. Woman to woman. Is that too much to ask?"

Karuw glanced around to see if anyone had overheard; then she pointed down the corridor. "I'm headed to the transporter room. We'll ask the operator to leave. Then we can talk there."

"Lead on," said the seeress with a smile.

A few moments later, they entered the transporter room, where the prototype of the new booth was already awaiting its trip down to the planet. One technician was working on the enclosure, and another was at the console. They stopped work immediately upon the arrival of the two most powerful women in their society.

"Officers, could I ask you to leave for a few minutes?" asked Karuw. "Take a short break, please."

They glanced at one another, nodded, and shuffled

out of the room. When the door whooshed shut, Seeress Jenoset turned to the regent and crossed her arms. "First of all, I've been impressed with what you've done," she began. "And I'm not saying that to curry favor or—"

"We're far from done," warned the regent, "and I'm short of time."

"I know that. But someday we will be done, and we will still need you—but not for you to have all the power in the world. What has happened to us is bad enough, without completely overturning the order of our society as well. We Aluwnans have never been technocrats who need to be governed by a scientist, no matter how brilliant that scientist is. My husband is the rightful ruler."

"I thought you told me he was sick," said Karuw.

"Sick at heart," answered Jenoset, her beautiful face frowning with concern. "It's like he has no reason to live. I've never seen him like this. If you don't believe me—"

"I believe you," said the regent. "And, as you say, I love him, too. But do you think a man who's severely depressed is the one to rule us right now?"

Jenoset held her palms out, begging. "What we need is to get back to normal as soon as we can."

"Normal?" scoffed the regent. "You haven't been down to Aluwna to see what it's like, have you?"

"No," admitted Jenoset hesitantly.

Marla Karuw moved toward the transporter console and pointed to that platform. "Go stand over there.

We're going down to the planet to see what our Klingon friends have been doing."

"Now?" asked Jenoset in horror, tugging at her elegant scarlet gown. "I'm not dressed for it."

Marla smiled. "You'll be an inspiration to the Klingon warriors. Go ahead, get on the platform."

Hesitantly, Seeress Jenoset stepped onto the transporter pad, and Marla Karuw fought the temptation to scatter her molecules into the stratosphere. She had already done that once with Curate Molafzon, and the guilt still haunted her, even if he had somehow survived. More and more, seeing the curate on the planet's surface seemed like a dream, and she was beginning to wonder if it had actually happened. But of course it had.

"All right, I've laid in the coordinates, and we're on a short delay." Regent Karuw strode over to the platform and took her place beside the seeress, who was trembling.

"I thought we were told we shouldn't use transporters," said Jenoset.

"Don't believe everything you're told," answered Marla. "I don't. I want you to see with your own two eyes exactly what we face." The transporter sequence began, and the two women steeled themselves as their corporeal forms became disembodied for a moment.

Freezing, foul-smelling wind assaulted them as they materialized on the planet's surface in the middle of a snowy blizzard, with immense trees shaking all around them. Within seconds, they were surrounded by towering figures, armored from head to toe and carrying disruptor rifles. Seeress Jenoset had been trembling when they left the *Darzor*, and now she was shaking more than the windblown trees. It was dark, except for lanterns and the lights from several shuttlecraft, but they could still see blasted craters and pockets of fire burning on the ground and in the misty forest.

"Who goes there?" grumbled a deep voice, pointing the business end of a disruptor at Karuw's midsection.

"The rulers of this planet," answered the regent imperiously. "Is Ambassador Worf here?"

"You must wear headgear and environmental suits," answered another Klingon, as if he hadn't heard her. He motioned to a comrade, who hurried off to a waiting shuttlecraft. Karuw noticed what looked like bodies stacked outside the vessel, and she shivered.

"What if we don't want to wear your suits?" asked Jenoset indignantly.

"Then we will transport you to the *Doghjey* and put you in quarantine in our brig," answered the masked officer. "No exceptions, because there's a dangerous fungus on this planet which can affect your mind."

"I want to see Ambassador Worf," demanded Regent Karuw.

"I *am* Worf!" barked the armed Klingon. His underling returned with suits and headgear and handed them to the women. Because she was cold, Marla Karuw didn't argue anymore as she pulled on the overly large protective gear. Her teeth chattering, Jenoset was even quicker to obey their orders.

"Haven't you read our dispatches?" asked Worf angrily. "The Genesis Wave also brought invaders to this planet. They killed seven of our officers and wounded fifteen others."

"How many of them did you kill?" asked Karuw, her voice sounding muffled in the helmet she had just donned.

Worf picked up a handful of moss from the ground and held it out to the women. "That is difficult to say when this is their true appearance. However, they can take on the form of persons known to you, which is why they are so dangerous."

"Really?" asked Karuw, trying not to let the fear show in her voice. "Have you . . . have you seen anybody else down here?"

"Any other creatures?" asked Worf, misinterpreting her question. "There are some rather large food animals—I can show you their carcasses, because they were involved in the battle."

"That's all right," said Karuw, waving off the question. "Our main concern are the people stored in our transporter satellites. We have to start setting up transporter stations and beaming them down immediately."

"That is impossible now," answered Worf. "We have no idea how many of these creatures there are—there may be millions of them."

"And there are millions of *my* people trapped in those satellites!" said Karuw heatedly. She took a deep breath, trying to control her anger. "This area is big enough to put up some shelters and start bringing down our people. Please, Ambassador, our time is extremely limited—the bioneural network in those satellites is already degrading. They've been through a lot."

"I can't guarantee their safety," said Worf.

"Neither can I," countered Regent Karuw, "and that's the problem. Down here, they've got a fighting chance. Up there, they've got no chance at all if the computers fail."

The big Klingon considered her request for a moment, then nodded. "Very well, we will speed up our timetable. We'll start erecting shelters, and you can erect the transporter platforms you need. By daylight, we should be ready."

"Thank you," answered Karuw with a grateful sigh. More than ever, it seemed, they would have to terraform the planet to make it safe.

"Don't leave this clearing," warned Worf.

"Don't worry, we won't. Thank you, Ambassador."

Worf motioned to his comrades, and the Klingons dispersed, going back to their grim business. Marla turned to look at Seeress Jenoset, whose stunned face was barely visible behind the visor in her helmet. It took a great deal to keep Jenoset quiet, but she had barely said a word since setting foot on Aluwna, or what had become of it. Karuw wasn't sure, but she thought she saw tears in the pale eyes of the seeress.

"Are you ready to go?" she asked.

"Yes," Jenoset answered hoarsely. "I didn't think . . . it would be so changed."

"Rest assured, we'll change it back to the paradise it was," vowed Marla Karuw. "Are you going to leave it to me, or burden Tejharet with these tasks?"

Jenoset bowed her head and replied, "You are in charge, Regent. No one is going to fight you for this job."

"I didn't think so." Warmly Marla Karuw wrapped an arm around the slender shoulders of her nemesis and said, "Let's go back to the ship."

Overseer Tejharet tossed fitfully in his sleep in the royal stateroom aboard the *Darzor*, hearing a babble of voices inside his head. At first, he thought they were the crew members and passengers on the crowded ship, but then he remembered that his stateroom was solidly soundproofed, as befitted a monarch. The more he drifted in and out of sleep, the more he realized that the voices were part of a nightmare—the voices of all those millions of subjects he had abandoned to their fate. They were the voices of the people in the square outside the Summer Palace, begging him to be saved. He had sat in his darkened quarters listening to them right up until the moment when his aides had come to pack him off to the yacht. They were the voices of his loyal servants, who had been locked out of the palace by his guards, because they had hounded him with pleas for mercy. They were the voices of the children who were too poor and disenfranchised to make it onto the sacrosanct list.

By leaving all the decisions up to Marla Karuw, he had abdicated his power to save anyone, including himself. The distraught overseer had turned his back on countless millions, because he was too cowardly to make the tough choices himself. There might have been other options, if he hadn't given up so quickly. Perhaps he could have cajoled the Federation into giving Aluwna more help; perhaps he could have been more proactive, knowing that even a perfect world could be threatened with destruction. He should have built more starships during his reign—he should have reached out to more interstellar neighbors. He should have done *something* for all those whose voices now rang in his ears.

Shivering with the sweat of guilt and remorse, Tejharet reached across his bed for Jenoset, but his wife was no longer there. Her kisses and caresses had brought him some respite from his agony, no matter how briefly, and now she was gone, too. He knew he could get out of bed and roam the corridors of the ship like a ghost, but what good would that do? Who wanted to see him—the ghost of a former ruler? They didn't need him anymore.

Perhaps they never did.

"Open your door," said another voice, soft and feminine. "And turn out the lights."

In his addled state, it took Tejharet several moments to realize that this was a *real* voice, one coming from the com panel outside his door. Of course, he was alone, so anyone wishing admittance to the secure stateroom had to ask for it. The lights were already out, although the darkness did nothing to help him sleep or assuage his grief. He touched the panel on the table at his bedside, and the door whispered open.

A curvaceous figure shrouded in flowing silk padded into the room, and the door slid shut behind her. He recognized the perfume, and he breathed a sigh of relief. Jenoset had returned to him!

"My darling," he rasped, reaching for her in the darkness. "I need you so badly."

"I know," she said huskily as her barely clad figure slithered into his arms. "Kiss me, my overseer."

Eagerly seeking warmth and redemption—and a measure of forgetfulness—Tejharet probed her supple lips with his own. She tasted oddly bitter, not like before, but perhaps she had drunk something bitter. It suited his mood, this bitterness, and he momentarily lost himself in their mutual passion.

Then his chest began to constrict, as if he had been running too fast, too far. Before he could fill his lungs, the constriction in his chest turned to stabbing pain, and he couldn't draw a breath at all. As he began to cough and gag, his lover pulled away from him and left him grasping for both her body and the air. He wanted to move, to speak, to scream—and he tried to reach for the com panel by his bed—but the muscles in his arms were frozen, just like his lungs and heart.

Tejharet knew he was dying, and that no power on or off Aluwna could save him.

Then the babble of voices sounded again, and they welcomed him to the grip of the Divine Hand, where he deserved to be. *Poetic justice*, he thought with the final synapses of his brain neurons before everything in his body shut down permanently.

As the door of his stateroom whooshed open and a shadow slipped out, the vaunted Overseer of Aluwna, who had ruled for three generations of peace and prosperity, collapsed in his bed and died.

seventeen

Alexander cringed when he saw his brother, Jeremy, lying in a sickbay bed aboard the *Doghjey*. The burns on his face and body were very serious, although no longer life-threatening, and Dr. M'Lorik and his overburdened staff had done as much as they could for him without resorting to reconstructive surgery. Even now, the doctors were working on other patients with more urgent injuries. Warriors were lined up in the corridor, waiting to be treated for fungal infections they might have suffered during the battle, due to torn environmental suits. All in all, the medical staff on the *Doghjey* had not been geared up for a combat situation, but they were doing the best they could under the circumstances.

Jeremy looked up at his brother and tried to smile. His voice was a throaty crackle as he said, "They burned off all my nice blond hair. The girls back home are going to be disappointed."

"I heard you're going to see home very soon," said Alexander.

The young human grunted. "I don't want to, but a Starfleet runabout is dumping someone off here. Put in a word with Dad, will you, and tell him I'm okay—I can stay here."

"Come on," said Alexander gently, "you know you'll get better treatment at Starfleet Medical." He lowered his voice to add, "These guys are sawbones. Nobody ever accused Klingons of being great healers."

Jeremy grunted in pain as he shifted slightly. "I know," he rasped. "They keep asking me why I don't have two or three of every organ, like you do."

Alexander laughed and changed the subject. "We got reinforcements on the planet, so Dad sent a big force to march from Base Two to Base One. Now that we're using just bladed weapons, we had a lot fewer casualties. Those things don't stand up well to *bat'leths*, and they're not very smart or organized. We need to establish a bigger perimeter and enlarge the two bases, because the Aluwnans want to start bringing their people down."

"They're braver and crazier than Klingons," observed Jeremy, shaking his bandaged head. "I would just leave this place to the giant slugs and move on."

"I guess that's not an option," answered Alexander. "Hey, at least you got to fight alongside Dad."

"Yeah, that's a blast," agreed Jeremy, mustering a pained smile. "Is he . . . is he coming to visit me?"

"He's meeting the specialist Starfleet is sending us, so he'll be there to see you off."

"Good," croaked the injured human, slumping back in his bed. "But I don't really want to go."

"Orders are orders." Alexander tapped Jeremy gently on the shoulder. "Now you've got to rest, brother. When I get back to Earth, I want you to be well, so I can beat you in one-on-one."

"Basketball?" rasped Jeremy, closing his eyes. "In your dreams."

"Yeah, in my dreams," agreed Alexander with a smile. He stepped away from the bed and wound his way through the crowded sickbay and into the corridor, where he was met by a shuttlecraft pilot.

"Alexander Rozhenko?" asked the pilot.

"Yes, that's me," answered the young Klingon. "Are you here to take me back to the planet?"

"Not the planet," answered the pilot. "Your orders have changed, and you are to report to the Aluwnan vessel *Darzor*."

"Why?" asked Alexander puzzledly.

"There is some sort of emergency there," answered the pilot. "They have requested a Klingon representative, and you are the closest and most able, according to Ambassador Worf."

Alexander suppressed a smile, amused that his father considered him so capable. Then he wondered what sort of emergency could be so urgent to the Aluwnans when they had been mired in the worst crisis imaginable for almost a week. "Will you take me there?" he asked.

"Yes, I am due to report to the *Darzor*, anyway, to pick up a work crew."

"Lead on," said Alexander Rozhenko.

Fifteen minutes later, a Klingon shuttlecraft slid into the shuttlebay of the *Darzor*, and Alexander stepped off as six Aluwnan technicians carrying equipment waited to board. He was met by the two strong-willed women he had seen the night before: the older, scholarly regent, Marla Karuw, and the regal beauty, Seeress Jenoset. Alexander had lived on Earth, fought in the Dominion War, and served with a variety of forces from different worlds—so he supposed he was qualified for this duty.

Plus Alexander had received a strange visitor from the future once, who had assured him that his destiny would be in diplomatic service. For the present, anyway, he was content to serve in engineering.

Marla Karuw scowled at him as she asked, "And you are?"

"Duty Chief Alexander Rozhenko of the *Ya'Vang*," he answered. "Son of Worf, House of Martok."

"And your father couldn't come?" asked the regent.

"My father is busy securing the planet for your people," he answered. "What is the emergency?"

Seeress Jenoset sniffed back a sob, and he noticed that her eyes were red. "My husband, Overseer Tejharet, is dead."

"We fear he's been murdered," added Regent Karuw in a hoarse whisper.

The young Klingon frowned at this revelation,

wondering what he could do to prove or disprove this serious allegation. "I'm an engineer," he said, "not a policeman."

The two women immediately pointed at one another and said in unison, "She did it!"

Alexander shook his head and held up his hands. "Ladies, what do you want me to do?"

"I can explain," said a male voice behind Alexander.

He turned to see a handsome Aluwnan of middle age and fine clothing come striding toward him, followed by an entourage consisting of an even younger male and several uniformed officers. "Excuse me for being late," said this new arrival. "I had some urgent documents to sign. I am Overseer Padrin."

"Alexander Rozhenko, Son of Worf, House of Martok," replied the young Klingon again. "You have succeeded the dead overseer?"

"I have," answered Padrin, gazing pointedly at Marla Karuw. "And I have relieved Professor Karuw of the title of regent and assumed her duties and powers."

"You can't do this now!" shrieked Karuw, her hands balled into fists. "You've got to let me finish my work. You're condemning eight million people to death!"

"I'm doing no such thing!" snapped Padrin angrily, glaring at the former regent. "Marla, you're lucky that you're not in custody. Under the circumstances, you can proceed with all the tasks you have to do—

nobody wants to stop you. But you are a suspect in the overseer's death."

Padrin looked fondly at Seeress Jenoset. "You are also a suspect, my dear. I'm sorry, but you must be confined to quarters until the inquiry is complete, and I don't know how long that will take . . . with everything else going on."

He turned again to the young Klingon. "I'm sorry to burden you with this, Alexander Rozhenko, but we aren't equipped at the moment to do any kind of proper inquiry. This death puts what's left of our government into chaos, and our people need to know there's still some authority and order. You Klingons represent that to us now. If your father can't help— and I understand why he can't—I welcome any help *you* can give us."

"I see," said the young Klingon, his mind working furiously. *If I'm ever going to be a diplomat*, he decided, *this is a good time to start.* "Can I see the body and the evidence—to understand *why* you think one of these esteemed ladies murdered Overseer Tejharet?"

"Absolutely," answered Padrin with relief. He turned to the cadre of uniformed officers behind him and said, "You two constables, accompany the seeress to her quarters and make sure she stays there. You two, accompany Professor Karuw to the laboratory and make sure she stays there . . . to do her work."

"This is preposterous," replied Karuw, shaking her head in disbelief. "Why would I kill him, when he made me regent?" She turned on Seeress Jenoset and said, "You told me you wouldn't do this to me, not in the middle of this nightmare."

"I didn't do anything!" answered Jenoset through clenched teeth.

"Marla, you don't need to be regent to succeed," interjected Overseer Padrin. "We'll continue to help you, but you can't be regent with this cloud hanging over you. Everyone, go where you're supposed to be, and concentrate on the job at hand. We've lost one life, but we have eight million more to save."

These final words ended the conversation, and the two strong-willed women and their escorts left the shuttlebay. Remaining behind were Alexander, Overseer Padrin, and the young lad who had accompanied the group.

"Who is this?" asked the Klingon, pointing to the boy.

"This is Farlo, the seeress's third husband," answered Padrin. "It is typical for our well-bred females to have three husbands, and he and Jenoset wed on the day we left Aluwna."

The towheaded lad smiled at Alexander and said, "I'm pleased to meet you, Alexander Rozhenko. I'm just as confused as you are, but I'll help you any way I can."

The Klingon smiled back, liking the lad immediately. "Are you the next in line to be overseer?"

Farlo shrugged. "I guess so. But it doesn't look like it's a healthy job to have."

Overseer Padrin blanched at those blunt words.

"Let me show you the body and the place he died."

The *Darzor* was a relatively small ship, and it only took them a few minutes to walk down the main corridor to a door that was guarded by more constables. They saluted the new overseer and opened the door for him. As they entered the darkened stateroom, Alexander was struck by the luxury of the furnishings and also the odor of a very opulent perfume. If he wasn't mistaken, it was the same scent that Seeress Jenoset had been wearing in the shuttlebay.

In bed lay the gaunt body of an older and quite dead Aluwnan, who must have been the late overseer. He was attended by another elder, who wore a white gown, such as those favored by technicians.

"Dr. Gherdin," said Padrin, "has no one touched the body?"

"No one but myself," answered the doctor.

"You know the seeress consort," said Padrin, pointing to young Farlo. "This is Alexander Rozhenko, a representative of the Klingon Empire. To make sure our inquiry into the overseer's death is unbiased, he is in charge."

Once again, Alexander wanted to tell them that he was an engineer, not a policeman, but he kept his mouth shut. "Doctor," said Padrin, "please tell him what you told me."

The medical man took a deep breath and consulted a handheld device before answering. "Tejharet was poisoned," he said bluntly. "There are traces on his lips of ilzeden, a very fast-acting nerve agent which is often used in large-sized pest eradication. There are known antidotes, which are taken by those who work with ilzeden on a regular basis. What I couldn't tell from my examination is whether he was poisoned or whether he committed suicide."

"What was his frame of mind recently?" asked Alexander.

"Poor," answered Padrin. "Of course, none of us have had any reason to be happy lately."

"He was really miserable at dinner last night," added Farlo. "I don't think he liked giving up his powers to the regent."

The Klingon nodded sagely and said, "Then wouldn't it be logical to assume that he *did* commit suicide?"

"It would be," answered Dr. Gherdin, "but there's no trace of ilzeden in this room. If he administered it himself, what did he do with it? Plus he had a visitor late last night."

"A visitor?" asked Alexander. "Who?"

"We don't know, but she was female," said Overseer Padrin. "Our ship is packed with passengers, and one of them saw her in the corridor. The lights were dimmed, because it was the late shift, and the witness couldn't give us a description— except to say it was a female wearing nightclothes. We know that the overseer and the seeress came back here alone for one unit of time after dinner and then the seeress and the regent went down to Aluwna."

"Where my father and I saw them," added Alexander.

Padrin nodded. "Indeed. Then the seeress returned to the ship, apparently was alone for some time, then spent the rest of the night with me."

"And who discovered the body?" asked the Klingon.

"I did," answered Dr. Gherdin. "The overseer was taking some medicine for his depression, and I administer it myself. When I chimed at his door this morning, he didn't answer, although the ship's computer verified that he was in here. I had the captain override the door security, and he was like this when I found him. You'll notice that his clothing is disheveled, as if he were . . . with someone. The time of death coincides with the sighting of the woman who was seen coming out of here. She could not have entered unless he opened the door for her, so it must have been somebody he knew."

Alexander took a deep breath while he collected his thoughts, then he glanced at young Farlo, who also sighed heavily. With everything else that was happening on Aluwna, he wanted to tell them to forget this lone death and concentrate on their urgent business. But this was their leader who had been poisoned, and their world was already in a fragile state.

"I know very little about your society," began Alexander, "but in Klingon society, there is an old tradition of claiming power by murder and violent duels to the death."

"We have nothing like that!" answered Padrin, sounding aghast at the very idea. "We have a very orderly transition of power based on bloodlines and DNA. Nobody has to commit murder to claim power. Besides," he muttered, "who would want to be in charge during these troubled times?"

"You benefited," said the Klingon, "and Regent Karuw suffered. Why was your first act to relieve her of duty? And why would you suspect her of murder, when she was the first to suffer from his death?"

Padrin pursed his lips, as if he were hesitant to answer. He finally said, "Regent Karuw and Overseer Tejharet were lovers, and she and Seeress Jenoset were enemies—due to that and many philosophical matters. Before she was made regent, Marla Karuw was imprisoned for several years. Despite all she has done for us recently, I'm not sure of the regent's loyalty or her sanity. She and Jenoset were seen arguing last night, and the question of returning power to our family was bound to be a problem, no matter what else happened. I thought it was best to remove that friction from the equation. If she really wants to do her work, she can help Aluwnans without being regent."

"So you and Jenoset got your way," concluded Alexander.

Padrin shook his head. "Not *my* way. I was happy being the seeress consort—I never wanted this job. And now Jenoset will forever be under suspicion, even though I know she loved Tejharet a great deal."

Alexander rubbed his eyes, feeling way over his head. He would rather be down on the planet's surface, battling those fiendish moss creatures, than steering his way through this morass. That thought brought him to a disturbing conclusion.

"Doctor," he said, turning to the white-suited figure, "you need to make sure that no one on this vessel—or any of your ships—has been infected by the fungus we encountered down on the planet. If you haven't read our dispatches, I urge you to do so. You have to test everyone on this ship."

"Do you really think that's necessary?" asked the doctor in alarm.

"I do. It might explain what happened to the overseer." He glanced at the ashen figure lying stiffly in the bed. "Let's do something about this body."

"Yes, let me handle it," said the doctor. "I was only waiting until you could see it. We can put the overseer in stasis in our sickbay until we beam enough people down to the planet to have a proper ceremony."

"Are you going to stay here with us?" asked Farlo, looking eagerly at the young Klingon.

Alexander furrowed his bony brow. "I hadn't thought about it, but I've been awake for three days straight."

"Can he stay with us?" Farlo asked. "We've got room. You'll be moving into this big room, won't you, Uncle?"

"I suppose," answered Padrin, looking distraught at

the idea of taking both the dead man's position and his quarters. "May the Divine Hand be with us."

In the laboratory on the *Darzor*, Marla Karuw tried to forget her anger and grief long enough to concentrate on her work, but it was almost impossible. All she had the capacity to do was monitor the progress of the work crews rushing to put the satellites back into orbit at the same time that they attempted to stabilize the bioneural networks. That was going as well as could be expected, despite several troublesome readings. Karuw also had to oversee the manufacture of several thousand compact solar-powered transporter booths, to be transported to the planet as soon as the Klingons secured a big enough area.

Fortunately, slaving at her side was Vilo Garlet, who must have been sent by the Divine, because he was able to fulfill all the development work on the transporters, especially their secret purpose to re-terraform Aluwna. If anyone had any questions about the unusual circuitry in the base of the enclosures, they kept it to themselves. The chances were good that nobody asked because nobody had time to consider anything. It was full speed ahead, and damn the consequences.

At first, Marla was a bit annoyed to see Candra, the young friend of the new seeress consort, working alongside Vilo Garlet. But her colleague trusted the young lady, having saved her life, and Marla was in no position to make him mad or turn down capable help.

In fact, young Candra went about her duties tirelessly and in good spirits, and she was willing to do the fetching and grunt work they both required. As the units of time passed, Candra became more and more of a fixture in the laboratory, and the former regent thought very little about her. Still she made certain never to discuss her secret plans with anyone but Vilo Garlet, and she was careful to keep their discussions out of earshot of anyone else.

"How is the programming going on the chromasynthesis box?" she whispered during one break when they were alone.

Garlet nodded wearily and said, "As far as I can tell, fine. But with no testing—" He shrugged, letting her finish the sentence.

"But you're certain that it won't harm humanoid life on the planet?"

"It's not Genesis," he said, bristling at her suggestion. "It doesn't take existing life as its source of raw material, but it does supplant anything alien that's not in our matrix. In that way, you could call it the 'anti–Genesis device.' However, our flora and fauna will be layered on top of the existing Genesis growth, with results that I can't entirely predict. This won't be the Aluwna we knew, but it will be much closer than what's there now. At this point, my main concern is the coverage. We've got to make sure to get one of these boxes at every hundred measures for it to be successful."

"Right," said Marla with a frown. "I'll have to come up with a good excuse for spreading the enclosures across the planet, instead of concentrating them. Something the Klingons will buy."

Garlet rubbed his chin thoughtfully and replied, "Since the transporter component is solar-powered and unidirectional, tell them that we must have complete coverage in order to keep them working around the clock. And they have to match up with the satellites."

"Good idea," Marla answered with a smile. She glanced at her timepiece and frowned again. "Starfleet's expert is due to arrive soon. Do you think they'll let me out to meet her, or will I have to remain a prisoner in my own lab?"

"What they're doing to you is insane," he muttered angrily. "We've got to overthrow this stupid hereditary system."

"It seems to be self-destructing," said Marla grimly. "I wonder who killed him?"

Candra and the other assistants were starting to file in from their break, so Karuw stepped away from her co-conspirator in order to check her progress reports. The next two days would be crucial, she decided, because they would either prepare the planet to receive the eight million survivors—or they would lose them all.

Worf stood in the cavernous shuttlebay of the *Doghjey* with both of his sons at his side, waiting for the arrival of a Starfleet runabout. Neither one of his boys was in particularly good humor. Jeremy lay on an antigrav gurney that floated at waist level; the young human tried to be brave and upbeat, but he was miserable at the prospect of returning home on his back, wounded. In that respect, he had become a Klingon during his service aboard the *Doghjey*, and Worf was proud of his adopted son, although he would miss him.

Standing at the ambassador's other side, Alexander was preoccupied with his new assignment among the Aluwnans, for which Worf felt a pang of guilt. Still he was certain that he had sent the right diplomat to handle the situation, even if Alexander wasn't so sure. While they waited for the arrival of the runabout, Worf and Jeremy listened to Alexander's account of the overseer's suspected murder. Worf could offer little advice or succor. For a Klingon, the murder of a weak, ineffectual leader sounded like the normal course of events. Grief and mourning were to be expected, but undue worry and incriminations . . . that was pointless. The old man had not been governing, anyway, and the Aluwnans were nobly carrying on without him.

"Just do your best," said Worf. "His family will find out in time who killed him, because such secrets can never be kept forever. Then they can wreak their revenge."

"Father," said Alexander, "these aren't Klingons we're talking about. Violence is not part of their culture, and I think they're mostly upset that a female carried out the crime. The Aluwnans place their upper-caste women on a very high pedestal."

"Like that regent," rasped Jeremy. "She's the real power."

"Not anymore," replied Alexander. "She's been relieved of her office, although she's still in charge of the rescue effort. She's also a suspect in this crime. Father, can't you give me more help and guidance?"

Worf turned to look at his son by blood, and he slowly shook his head. "You are asking the right questions, which is all I or anyone else could do. If you ask the right questions, the right answers will come. You are just the mirror—*they* are the ones who must look into it."

His thick brow furrowed in thought, Alexander nodded slowly.

"Stand clear for docking!" announced a voice, and the heavy doors of the shuttlebay slid open. Because all the Klingon shuttlecraft were gone, helping the Aluwnans with their transporter satellites, there was plenty of room for the larger runabout to enter and find a place to set down. Protected by forcefields, Worf and his sons waited at the rear of the bay and watched the graceful, lozenge-shaped vessel come sweeping into the hangar. Captured by more forcefields, its thrusters shut off quickly, and it dropped to the deck.

After the outer doors shut and the thrusters stilled, the forcefield was deactivated. Worf gently pushed Jeremy's gurney forward, while Alexander gripped the side bar and helped to steer. The hatch of the runabout opened, and an attractive woman stepped forward to meet them. It had been many years since Worf had seen Dr. Leah Brahms, and she looked somewhat older and thinner, even gaunt, as if she had been suffering. Her chestnut-colored hair was shorter than he remembered and now had strands of gray in it.

"Hello, Mr. Worf," she said with a smile. "Glad to see you again."

"You, too, Doctor," he said with a nod of his head. "These are my sons, Alexander and Jeremy."

She held out her hand to engage in the human custom of the handshake, and she was very gentle with Jeremy's bandaged appendage. "Pleased to meet you. I've been reading about what you've been going through here. I wish I could say it was unusual, but it's not. What is unusual is the plight of the Aluwnans."

"I understand your husband died on Seran," said Worf, bowing his head. "My sympathies."

"It seems like ages ago," said the engineer sadly. "Another lifetime." Brahms looked around, as if expecting to see someone else in the welcome party. "Regent Karuw could not be here?" she asked.

"I'm afraid not," answered Alexander. "She's in confinement on an Aluwnan ship, because she's suspected of committing a crime. But she's still leading their rescue efforts."

Another crew member hopped out of the runabout and stepped toward the gurney. "Is this our patient?" he asked. "I hate to rush you, but we're on a tight schedule."

Jeremy twisted his head around and asked, "Dad, do I really have to go? I'm feeling much better."

"You don't look any better," said his father bluntly. "We'll get back to Earth as soon as possible, I promise. All those wounded or killed in the battle on Aluwna will be decorated for bravery. You'll be the only one on your next ship wearing the Klingon *Degh van'a'quv*."

"I'll wear it with honor," said the young man with tears welling up under his bandages.

"Good-bye, brother," said Alexander. "Pump up your basketball."

"And sharpen your *bat'leth*," answered Jeremy hoarsely.

Worf nodded to the crewman, who grabbed the antigrav gurney and steered it through the hatch into the runabout. Leah Brahms and the two Klingons moved off to allow the runabout to prepare for take-off.

"Since there are no Aluwnans to meet you," said Worf, "we should beam down to the planet and show you what we're doing."

"I would still like to see Regent Karuw," said Leah. "I was very impressed with her solution to this crisis— I feel like she's a kindred spirit."

Alexander interjected, "I'm going back to the royal yacht, the *Darzor*, and I'll arrange a meeting. She's a very forceful woman."

"I would guess so," answered Leah Brahms, "if she could convince eight million people to stake their lives on transporter buffers."

"What is the *Enterprise* doing?" asked Worf.

"Admiral Nechayev has sent them on a separate mission," answered Brahms. The engineer looked around to make sure no one was in the immediate vicinity, then she added, "Apparently, there's a portable Genesis device in the hands of some deluded Bajorans, and they're trying to stop them from using it. That's supposed to be classified information. I've asked that the *Enterprise* be sent here as soon as they're done, but we'll see."

Worf shook his head with disbelief. "A portable Genesis device—is there no end to this madness?"

"Make ready for launch!" announced a voice, and the three of them stepped into the observation area behind the protective forcefield. They watched silently as the runabout lifted off the deck and cruised into space.

"Let's end it here," said Leah Brahms with determination. "Far too many have died."

eighteen

Leah Brahms never thought she would see Klingon gardeners, but there they were—an army of them hacking their way with scythes, *bat'leths*, and machetes through the thick, gloomy jungle of Aluwna. It wasn't just brush removal, because the morass of vines, roots, trees, bushes, and succulents was alive and fought back, making their chore more enjoyable for them than it looked. It was difficult to tell how many of the moss creatures they shredded along with innocent shrubs, but nothing stood in the way of their sharp blades. Where mounds of dirt or giant slugs interfered with their progress, the gardeners stepped back to allow warriors armed with disruptor rifles to blast the impediments into dust and flaming embers. If the resulting fires grew too smoky and dangerous, firefighters armed with extinguishers put out the flames, and the scythes and machetes were quickly put back to work.

Wave after wave of well-organized Klingons assaulted the forest, carving a path thirty meters wide and two kilometers long in less than an hour. Cleanup crews followed behind, spraying an herbicide on the residue of the defeated plant life, making sure it didn't grow back any time soon. It helped that the Klingons were wearing environmental suits, or else they might have suffered ill effects from this deadly poison. Leah Brahms followed the column at a safe distance, marveling at their efficiency. Still it would take them a lifetime to tame the entire planet in this fashion.

As Worf had explained to her, they were only trying to clear a belt of land to allow the Aluwnans to erect their transporter booths. Behind them, the locals were beaming down blue enclosures almost as fast as the Klingons carved up the forest. Technicians pounced on each box as soon as it arrived, making it ready for immediate use. As soon as the technical crews moved on, the boxes began to disgorge confused survivors. Medical teams were standing by to inoculate these poor souls with anti-fungals the moment they were freed from their silicon prisons in orbit around the planet. Even though almost ten days had passed, for the evacuees it was just an instant since they had left their beautiful world, only to emerge upon this overgrown, foul-smelling hellhole. If they were looking for shelter, there was none—just an environmental suit.

Frantic activity was everywhere, and Leah knew that other Klingon bands were hacking their way through other regions of the planet. Even if this strange scene was being repeated everywhere at once, the progress still felt too slow to Leah. At this rate, it would take weeks to free all the people in the transporter satellites. Brahms didn't need a computer model to know that they were racing against time, and moving at a snail's pace. If anything were to go wrong—

"Dr. Brahms," said a familiar voice, and she turned to see Alexander Rozhenko, accompanied by an Aluwnan female dressed in an environmental suit identical to her own. "Dr. Brahms, this is Marla Karuw."

"Are you responsible for the Genesis technology?" asked Karuw in an accusatory tone.

"No," answered Leah calmly, "I'm responsible for fighting it. The ones responsible are these moss creatures the Klingons are killing at an impressive rate."

"But it is Federation technology," insisted Karuw, obviously using this opportunity to vent her rage. "They told me you were an expert on Genesis."

Leah took a deep, calming breath before replying, "We abandoned the Genesis technology ninety years ago, long before either one of us were born. Unfortunately, we didn't protect the secrets of Genesis well enough. These invaders can impersonate close friends and family members, if you're not protected from their fungus, and they were able to kidnap the one actual expert we had."

Marla Karuw backed off a step and seemed somewhat mollified by this news. "I was infected by the fungus," she admitted.

"You were?" asked Worf's son, sounding shocked at this revelation. "Have you received treatment?"

Karuw nodded. "Yes, I have, and I feel much better. Thanks to you, Alexander, our doctors have been testing and treating everyone on our ships. We'll continue that practice with all the survivors. I guess I'm looking to fix blame for this somewhere, and I don't know where."

"Welcome to the club," said Leah Brahms. "I really came here to see if I could help you with your transporter satellites, but I guess you have—"

A bloodcurdling scream cut short her words, and the three of them whirled around to see two Aluwnan technicians scurrying away from a newly arrived transporter booth. One of them ripped off his protective headgear and vomited on the charred ground, and the other collapsed to his knees. Most of the Klingons were some distance away, still slashing through the jungle, so Leah, Alexander, and Marla Karuw rushed to see what had caused this consternation.

The door of the compact transporter booth was open, as if another shocked survivor were about to step out at any moment. Instead a wisp of steam curled from the enclosure, and Leah slowed her step to approach cautiously. Alexander and Marla Karuw did likewise, and the young Klingon drew a disruptor pistol from his belt. When they peered into the angular blue box, Leah's stomach heaved so drastically that she feared she would also be ripping off her helmet. Alexander held out an arm to brace himself against the box, and Marla Karuw whimpered and held her hand over her mouth.

There on the floor of the small transporter platform was a steaming, oozing pile of skin, hair, blood, bones, viscera, and unrecognizable biological matter, mixed with fabric and writhing maggot-like things. The horrible mass quivered, as if it still possessed some spark of life.

"What is it?" muttered Alexander.

"One of my countrymen," rasped Marla Karuw. She tore herself away from the awful sight and slumped against the enclosure, even while she tapped the com device on her wrist. "Karuw to Vilo Garlet," she said. "Vilo, answer me, please!"

"Yes, Professor, I'm here," replied her colleague.

"Stop transporting from the satellites immediately!" she ordered. "Something has gone terribly, terribly wrong."

Karuw dropped to her knees and checked the base of the enclosure for a serial number. Mustering her poise, she said, "I'm at booth one-six-zero-eight-five, and there's been an accident. The subject beamed down . . . dead. In fact, mutilated. Whatever satellite it came from, it must be diagnosed immediately. I'm returning to the lab as soon as I can, although I won't be transporting. Do you understand all this?"

"I do," answered her assistant somberly. "Do you want to stop putting up the transporter booths?"

"No, we have to proceed, or we'll fall way behind schedule. Just stop until I get there. Karuw out." She turned to Alexander and asked snidely, "I'm in your custody—is it all right if I go back to my ship?"

"Of course," answered the young Klingon. "I'll commandeer a shuttlecraft to take us." He rushed off toward the large group of Klingons, who were still clearing the rabid jungle.

"What can I do to help?" asked Leah Brahms, feeling totally helpless.

Karuw scowled and lowered her head. "I hate to turn this . . . tragedy . . . over to you, but the Klingons have scientific facilities. Perhaps you could analyze it for me."

"I will," promised Brahms, dreading the task. "Do you have any idea what caused this?"

She shook her head. "It could be a dozen things. Alexander has been warning us not to use transporters at all, for anybody, due to residual radiation from the Genesis Wave. Some of the bioneural networks have been slowly degrading ever since we left the planet, even before we returned. Perhaps there's a malfunction with this transporter unit alone. I don't know, but we have to find out."

"I'll do what I can from here," promised Leah, "but don't you think it would be wise to suspend—"

"No!" snapped the Aluwnan. "It's crucial that everybody keep working. This is a momentary setback." She turned to the two technicians who had made the gruesome discovery and said, "The two of you assist Dr. Brahms. Alexander!"

"I'm coming!" called the young Klingon. He hurried to her side and said, "We can use shuttlecraft number five."

"Let's hurry!" insisted Marla Karuw, marching off into a swirling snowstorm.

Back in the laboratory on the *Darzor*, Marla Karuw felt hemmed in—trapped—by so many people around. Not only were Vilo Garlet, Candra, and numerous assistants present, but Alexander Rozhenko, two constables, and two shuttlecraft pilots also watched her every move, as if expecting her to crack up or confess to being a murderer. It was true, Marla felt as if she were on the verge of a nervous breakdown, but she couldn't allow herself any kind of respite from her duties, not even the sanctuary of insanity. In truth, she was a murderer, but she hadn't killed Tejharet.

They had used the Klingon shuttlecraft to drag the aberrant satellite back into the laboratory, where they studied it as best they could without cutting the power. Losing power could cause the death of the four thousand people stored in the satellite's pattern buffers, and she tried not to consider the possibility that they were already dead . . . or maimed beyond recognition like that poor individual in the transporter booth. Millions were depending upon her, and what they found out here could affect the success of the entire rescue operation.

After she bumped into a constable on the way to a computer terminal, Marla stopped, balled her hands into fists, and almost screamed. "Will some of you people get out of here? Alexander—I can't work like this. Help me!"

"Who do you want to leave?" asked the young Klingon.

"I want everybody to go but Vilo," she answered. "If we can't find out what's wrong, nobody can."

"Alexander," said Vilo Garlet, "we do need one person to help us. Will you please fetch Dr. Gherdin?"

Karuw looked puzzledly at her colleague, wondering why they needed a medical doctor, but she didn't question him. She simply stared at Alexander, expecting him to obey the order.

"All right, everybody out!" bellowed the Klingon, sounding much like his father. "We need to make room here—everybody out!"

"But the overseer's orders," protested one of the constables. "We're supposed to stay and—"

"I'll take responsibility," Alexander assured him. "I don't think the professor is going anywhere."

When they were mercifully all gone, and Marla could draw a breath without bumping into someone, she turned to look at Vilo. "Why do you need Dr. Gherdin?"

He scowled at the satellite spread across two workbenches, its colored lights and beeping sounds making it seem alive. "With all the biological components in this thing, it's as much a sick patient as it is a sick machine. I want the doctor to verify a hunch, or tell me I'm crazy."

Venerable Dr. Gherdin arrived a short time later, and he had already heard about the unfortunate accident in the transporter booth. Marla wearily took a seat while the two men discussed Vilo's hunch, whatever it was, and the healer took out his diagnostic instruments and began to inspect the satellite. Deprived of sleep for days, Marla drifted off to slumber while she sat in the chair, and a fitful dream overtook her mind. In this nightmare, a group of children were behind bars—in the same cell where she had spent so many recent cycles—and they were begging her to let them out. But she couldn't find the key to open the lock. She looked everywhere, including the old haunts of her own childhood, but the secret to freeing the children was gone. Marla was almost in tears by the time Vilo shook her awake.

"Marla," he said gently. "Marla?"

"Huh!" she exclaimed, jerking awake. "Oh, thank the Divine it was just a dream. I was asleep."

"I noticed," he answered with a sympathetic smile. "Dr. Gherdin just left, but he confirmed my suspicions. It's bad news, but at least we have a cause for what happened."

She bolted to her feet. "What is it?"

Vilo pointed back to the satellite and said, "The biological components . . . they're infected by the same fungus that's found on the planet."

Marla gasped and sunk back into the chair and buried her face in her hands. "Oh, no . . . the fungus! Was that one of the satellites—"

"Yes," he answered grimly, "it's one of the satellites you handled personally when we were experimenting. But you mustn't blame yourself, Marla—you didn't know. How could you know?"

Her voice was almost a sob as she replied, "That trip I took alone down to the surface. I was so stubborn and cocksure . . . and I jeopardized everything!"

"No," he said sympathetically, shaking his head. "You were only in contact with two or three satellites, and we know exactly which ones they are."

"But others came into contact with them . . . and could have infected them. The Klingons, our own work crews—we didn't start to take precautions until a few days ago." Karuw jumped to her feet and began to pace frantically. "We'll never know how many are infected by this fungus, until we try to bring the people back."

Vilo gulped hard and said, "The doctor has plenty of medicine, and he can treat this. He's already given this unit a preliminary treatment, and we'll keep monitoring it."

"That damnable Genesis Wave!" cursed Karuw, shaking her fist in the air. "Even after they say it's gone, it keeps haunting us! I hate everything about the planet that Aluwna has become. We must kill the alien plants and microbes, and put it back the way it was."

"We're working toward that," said Vilo meekly.

She fixed him with a baleful glare. "Working toward it is not enough. As soon as the last transporter booth is on the surface of Aluwna, I want to start the chromasynthesis process."

Vilo gaped at her. "Before our people are even down? Before we even run a single test?"

"I won't bring my people to that monstrous inferno!" she declared, stomping across the laboratory. "We have it within our power to undo the horrors of the Genesis Wave, and we must. You know, we've replanted some of our native flora, and those damned vines and roots strangle them every time! If we want to save Aluwna, we can't go halfway with any of our measures."

Marla Karuw stopped pacing and clenched her fist. "Tell no one our plans—but be ready to act as soon as the last box is in place."

"Yes, Professor," replied Vilo Garlet with a bow. "The new Aluwna has no room for the hereditary monarchy either."

"You're right," she answered, "we'll destroy it, too."

"It's fascinating!" said Candra as she sat down across from Farlo in the mess hall of the *Darzor*. "We had Klingons in the lab, and scientists and shuttle-craft pilots, because one of the new transporter booths went really crazy. I didn't see it, but I guess it turned one of the people from the satellites into a steaming lump of flesh. Regent Karuw—well, I guess she's not the regent anymore, but she went totally crazy and kicked everybody out but my friend, Vilo. It sounds like Aluwna is a nasty mess, and nobody can live there . . . except Klingons. Maybe I'll get to go down there soon!"

Farlo scowled and picked at his food. "It sounds like you're having more fun than I am. I don't do anything but sit around and tell Padrin and Jenoset that everything will be okay. Ever since the overseer died, they keep thinking they'll be next. It's very depressing. You don't think they'll try to kill *me*, do you?"

"You?" asked Candra in amazement. She wrinkled her triple row of eyebrows. "No, because you haven't done anything."

"What did Overseer Tejharet do?" asked Farlo.

"It's what he represents," she said. "When all of this is over, we need a fresh start, with new leadership."

Farlo sat up and stared at his best friend. "Who have you been talking to? You never cared about politics before."

Before she answered, Candra looked around to make sure no one was listening, then she leaned forward to whisper, "My friend Vilo. You know you wouldn't be a high breed if he hadn't invented that black tube, and he did that to throw the whole hereditary DNA testing into confusion. Of course, the Genesis Wave came and threw everyone into even more confusion."

"But everyone thinks Seeress Jenoset killed the overseer," whispered Farlo, "and I know that's not true. But nobody trusts her now, and constables are keeping her in her quarters. I mean, is that fair?"

"Is it fair that she married you, a young boy?" Candra's lips pouted, and her eyes narrowed at him.

"I'm *not* a young boy," he answered angrily. "I'm not any younger than you, and look at the clothes you wear now. And look at the things you do."

"And what do I do?" she asked testily.

"You hang out in the laboratory with that Vilo person, and you plot against the government. Once you're in it, like I am, you realize that it's a hard job, an impossible job. Especially now." He shook his head sadly. "I don't know . . . it seems like we're on two different sides."

Candra frowned deeply at this thought and glanced away from her best friend. "I'm sorry about that, Farlo. I'd better go back and see if they need me."

Grabbing the leftovers of her meal, she hopped to her feet and walked away. To his shame, Farlo watched Candra's backside as she moved, thinking that she had indeed grown up and was a woman now. Almost no man would think of her as a child anymore, just as Padrin had immediately sent her to the pleasure palaces of the esplanade.

She could fool a man, he thought somberly, *almost any man . . . even an overseer.*

During her odyssey across the Alpha Quadrant, fleeing from or chasing the Genesis Wave, Leah Brahms had spent many nights in strange places, from a Klingon bird-of-prey to the moss creatures' homeworld of Lomar. But she could not recall a more eerie place than Aluwna by night. Thick clouds, which looked like curdled milk, floated eerily over the lush treetops, and the vines and shrubbery rustled in the chilly breeze, as things slithered through the roots and shadows of the rutted soil. More than once, Leah ground wormy slugs under the heel of her boot. Bonfires burned in front of geodesic domes in the Klingon camp, and displaced Aluwnans sat in front of them, looking like ghosts in their ill-fitting environmental suits. The Klingons themselves were only now returning from a day spent hacking through the jungle. The hulking, weary figures looked like abominable snowmen tromping their way back to the base.

Leah herself had dug a small grave and buried the indecipherable remains found in the bottom of the Aluwnan transporter booth. The sample she had taken had revealed its secrets quickly to a medical tricorder—it was crawling with the dangerous fungus. Perhaps someday this planet would be habitable, even pleasant, but that day seemed a long way off, when one couldn't even breathe unfiltered air without an inoculation she had not had time to get, and that worked poorly on her Klingon colleagues, if at all. The ones she felt sorriest for were the refugees sitting by the lonely campfires. They were alive, but their planet and civilization were dead. All of them must have lost family members and friends, and the fate of millions of Aluwnans was still uncertain. It was a blessing, thought Leah, that she couldn't see their distraught faces, even if their defeated body language spoke volumes.

The good guys had won, and the enemy were dying by the thousands in their customized world—but this did not seem like victory.

"Is that you, Leah?" asked a deep voice.

She looked up to see a hulking Klingon in an environmental suit, wearily holding a *bat'leth* at his side. The double-bladed weapon was streaked and caked with greenery, reminding her of the lawnmower blades she had seen as a child. "Hello, Worf, how goes the war?"

"Tiring," he grunted. "I don't want to use too much herbicide, but the plants here grow like a *targ*'s mane." He looked around and noted the gloomy Aluwnans. "I see some natives have returned."

"They were beaming them down quickly, until one of them got mangled in the transporter," said Brahms, wincing behind her face mask. "There was fungus all over the remains—it wasn't pretty, you can ask Alexander. I would guess that the bioneural network in the satellite was infected by the fungus. I wonder how many others are?"

The big Klingon dragged over a camp chair and slumped down beside her in front of the fire, warming his hands. "The flames keep the moss beings away," he explained. "And there is a lot of rubbish to burn."

"I was wondering about all the campfires,"

answered Brahms with a wan smile. "But it does make the camp a little more cheery."

They sat in silence for a moment, and she added, "Listen, Worf, there's something I meant to tell you before now. You may hear that it was the Romulans or the *Enterprise* who stopped the wave and those responsible, and they helped. But the one who really stopped them was an old Klingon warrior named Maltz. He had a personal blood oath against Genesis, and he pursued it all the way to the end. Maltz saved the Alpha Quadrant, and died doing it."

Worf nodded slowly and intoned, "Maltz celebrates his victory with Kahless the Unforgettable in *Sto-Vo-Kor*."

"Yes, he does," agreed Leah, gulping down a lump in her throat. "Someday I want to write his story, and that of my husband."

"I will help you," promised Worf. "It will be a good change of pace . . . from this."

After a few moments of listening to the crackling fire and the subdued conversation all around them, Leah Brahms asked, "Worf, did we arrive too late?"

He shrugged his beefy shoulders and didn't give her an answer.

PART THREE

REVENGE

nineteen

Captain Jean-Luc Picard stood stoically on the bridge of the *Enterprise*, a smile plastered to his face as he listened to a harangue from Vedek Orojop, whose stout physiognomy took up most of the viewscreen.

"This report you have sent us is woefully inadequate," complained the clergyman from Bajor. "What exactly happened to Vedek Yorka on Solosos III? Why in the name of the Prophets were you and the Federation meddling in our affairs, anyway? On one of our most hallowed historical sites! As far as I can tell from this muddled mess, you killed a member of the Vedek Assembly while destroying a precious gift from the Prophets—the Orb of Life!"

Captain Picard took a deep breath and tried to maintain his temper as he replied, "Our actions were in response to a grave threat, and I myself was somewhat incapacitated during this incident. But I can assure you of one thing, Vedek, the so-called Orb of Life was *not* an Orb of the Prophets. It was called that—for better or worse—as a sort of publicity stunt."

Vedek Orojop scowled. "A publicity stunt? I can assure you, Captain Picard, that the Vedek Assembly does not perform publicity stunts. If the orb wasn't an orb, what was it?"

"A small, portable Genesis device," answered Picard, shifting uneasily on his feet. "With all due respect, Vedek, I am uncomfortable discussing this matter on an open subspace channel, because many aspects of this incident are classified. When we arrive on Bajor and I can address the Vedek Assembly directly, I will answer all questions and supply all pertinent data. These events were an unfortunate offshoot of the terrible disaster that struck the Alpha Quadrant. Many inhabited worlds and billions of innocent people have been completely wiped out, which makes the death of a handful of profiteers unfortunate but minor, in comparison."

"Minor?" roared the vedek. "This is twice now that the Federation has devastated Solosos III. Do you know what that planet means to us? The martyrs of the Maquis made their last stand there."

Picard tried to resurrect his smile, realizing he had lost both it and his temper. "Yes, I know all about that. When we meet, I look forward to giving the Vedek Assembly a full explanation," he lied. "But there is really nothing else I can say at present."

The stout vedek scowled and sputtered for a moment; then he said, "Very well. But if I were you, Captain, I wouldn't be surprised if the Chamber of Ministers didn't put out a warrant for your arrest."

"I will face that prospect when it occurs," said the captain cheerfully. "Respectfully, Captain Jean-Luc Picard of the *Enterprise* out."

When the image finally faded from the overhead viewscreen, Picard let his shoulders slump with relief. He turned to the rest of his bridge crew and found his first officer, Will Riker, suppressing a smile. Riker turned quickly to Deanna Troi, seated beside him in the second command seat; and La Forge, Data, and the rest of the crew went about their business as if they hadn't heard the laborious conversation. *It wouldn't be so bad*, thought Picard, *if I hadn't been under the spell of that Elaysian and could remember everything that had happened.*

With resignation, he ordered, "Conn, set a course for Bajor."

"One moment, sir," said Data at the ops console. "I am receiving a hail from Admiral Nechayev on the *Javlek*, and she requests an audience before we get under way."

"I'll take it in my ready room," answered Picard, moving toward his private office off the bridge.

Data looked up and cocked his head quizzically. "That is unnecessary, sir. She wishes to address the entire bridge crew."

"Very well," said the captain, returning to the spot

where he had been standing during the vedek's lecture. After having made a romantic fool of himself the last few days, he was willing to make amends. "On screen," he ordered.

Admiral Nechayev's visage appeared on the viewscreen, and Picard was relieved to see that she was back to her pinched-faced, stiff-backed self. "Hello, Captain Picard, Commander Riker, and the rest of you," Nechayev began. "I was able to listen in to your conversation with Vedek Orojop, and I admit to feeling a pang of guilt. You've been through so much lately that I hate to subject you to the wrath of the Vedek Assembly. When it comes to being obtuse and argumentative, very few species can challenge our friends the Bajorans. I also happen to have another diplomatic mission, with scientific overtones, which I was going to attend to myself. I thought I would give you a choice of the two missions."

Picard glanced at Riker, and the big first officer raised an eyebrow as if to say, "This is unusual."

"One of the planets devastated by the Genesis Wave was Aluwna," the admiral continued. "That's a nonaligned world that has always been cordial to the Federation, but I don't think they hold much love for us now. They're in a desperate situation, because they've got eight million people stored in a network of transporter satellites. And they're battling to reclaim a world overrun with moss creatures and everything else endemic to a Genesis planet."

She went on to give a few more details, concluding

with a promise to send them reports and dispatches. "Ambassador Worf is already there with a Klingon task force," she added, "and Leah Brahms arrived there three days ago."

Geordi La Forge looked up with interest from his engineering station, and he watched the viewscreen intently with his ocular implants.

"Let me understand," said Picard. "We have the choice of dealing with the Bajorans and the Vedek Assembly, or joining Worf and Leah Brahms in helping this unfortunate planet?"

"That's correct," answered the admiral. "Do you need to take a poll?"

"I don't think so," answered Picard with a slight smile. He turned to his shipmates and said, "Does anyone object to going to Aluwna?"

He never saw so many heads shake "no" so quickly. "Admiral, we volunteer to go to Aluwna," replied Captain Picard.

"Very well, maintain your position," answered Nechayev. "I want to beam Raynr Sleven and Regimol back to your ship, because I feel they might be useful. In fact, Regimol was on Aluwna just before the wave struck. Both of them are now mission specialists assigned directly to me. We should rendezvous with you in less than half an hour. I'll give your regrets to the Vedek Assembly, but they'll be happier to get an admiral. Don't worry, I'll set them straight on the Yorka incident."

Picard suddenly felt some pity for the Bajorans,

because he knew that Nechayev could be brutal in setting people straight. "Thank you, Admiral."

"Nechayev out," she replied, and the screen went dark.

The captain crossed to the ops station. "Mr. Data, see what you can find out about Aluwna and this transporter network of theirs."

"Yes, sir," answered the android, his fingers skimming across his board with blazing speed.

Picard again strode toward his ready room. "Conn, set course for Aluwna and get under way at maximum warp just as soon as Regimol and Raynr Sleven are on board. I'd like to see both of them in my ready room when they arrive."

"Yes, sir," answered the Deltan at the helm.

Data reported, "We are receiving data transmissions from Admiral Nechayev."

"I'll read them in private," said Picard. "Make sure everyone on the staff gets a copy."

Picard entered his ready room, sat at his desk, and brought up the newly arrived reports on his terminal. Frowning with concern, the captain read about Aluwna's Genesis experience, as told in their own voices and by Worf, Nechayev, Brahms, and others. It was a tragic story that had been related a dozen times over, from Seran to Hakon to Myrmidon, and on countless planets that had been uninhabited until becoming incubators for the moss beings and their version of paradise. But each new iteration of this story had its own sorrows and triumphs, heroes and villains.

This Marla Karuw is a fascinating character, decided Picard, *having come out of obscurity in an Aluwnan jail to lead her people in a desperate evacuation*. Despite her daring actions and difficult decisions, the success of the evacuation was still in doubt, and she was under investigation for the murder of the overseer, the person who had yanked her from obscurity. Had power corrupted her, or had the natural politics of a beleaguered world turned against her?

One thing was clear: At the moment, Aluwna was no more than a handful of ships, thousands of transporter satellites, and a world under siege by frightening new life-forms. Only the Klingons, Leah Brahms, and Marla Karuw stood between partial success and total disaster.

Riker notified him that they were en route to Aluwna, so Picard prepared himself for the arrival of Regimol and Raynr Sleven. Both of them had undergone extreme changes from where they had started in life, but they had ended up in the same position— hired guns for Admiral Nechayev. He wanted to make sure that they understood their role in his crew, because each possessed unusual attributes that could present a problem.

His door chimed, and he rose to his feet and said, "Come."

The door slid open, and a distinguished-looking Romulan entered his ready room, followed by a hulking but humble Antosian, his raven hair tied in an elaborate topknot. Both of them wore nondescript jumpsuits without any insignia or ranks. Regimol gave the captain an insouciant smile, and Raynr Sleven lowered his head submissively.

"Captain," said Regimol, "it seems that our departure from the *Enterprise* was premature."

"Hello, Captain Picard," said the Antosian sheepishly.

"Hello, gentlemen, welcome back," began the captain, choosing his words carefully. "Regimol, I know that Admiral Nechayev has considerable faith in you, and that you are accustomed to operating independently. But I want you to know that as long as you are on this ship, you are under my command. We had a very disturbing incident with another Romulan who was wearing an interphase generator, and I want you to curtail walking through walls and becoming invisible while on this ship, unless I give you an order to do so. Is that understood?"

"Perfectly, Captain," answered the Romulan, his smile fading. "That other Romulan stole my invention—it was never intended to be used for espionage against Starfleet. That's the main reason I broke with the Romulan Star Empire."

"I understand that," said Picard, mustering a smile. "And I'm very glad you're on our side. It's just that past events cannot be ignored, and there may be some on this ship who harbor ill feelings about that device you wear on your chest."

Regimol furrowed his brow, forcing his angular eyebrows downward. "You know, the Romulans have put a high price on my head, and they are always looking for a way to kill me. I reserve the right to use my invention to save my own skin."

"I don't think that will be a problem while you're on the *Enterprise*," answered Picard succinctly.

Now he turned his attention to the large, almost childlike Antosian, who looked away with embarrassment. "Mr. Sleven," he began, "I was hoping that you would never have to see Alyssa Ogawa and her family again, because she definitely harbors ill feelings toward you."

"And I don't blame her," insisted the Antosian. "You rescued me and saved my life, and I repaid Nurse Ogawa by impersonating her husband. I won't do it again. I hate what that treatment did to me—sometimes I wish I had died on the *Barcelona*."

Picard pursed his lips together, troubled by this outburst of emotion. "Mr. Sleven, there's an old Terran saying: 'What doesn't kill us makes us stronger.' In your case, the cellular metamorphosis has granted you the power to shapeshift, without destroying your mind, and that has made you a valuable operative to Admiral Nechayev and Starfleet. However, this gift carries great responsibility, which you are learning. As I just told Regimol, your powers are not to be used on this ship, unless I order you to do so."

The Antosian nodded humbly. "I promise, Captain, I won't. I also promise to stay far away from the Ogawas."

"I'll assist you in that," answered Picard, "by assigning you to guest quarters ten decks away from them. I also want you to continue the counseling treatments you began with Counselor Troi, because I think you have some distance to go before you fully accept what's happened to you."

"I'll look after him," promised Regimol, patting his colleague on his broad back. "I feel like we're kind of a team now."

One of the most dangerous teams in the galaxy, thought Picard, but he didn't say that. Instead he went to his computer terminal and selected adjoining staterooms for the two of them on deck nineteen. After he gave them their assignments, he said, "I don't want to restrict you to quarters, but I would suggest you keep your interaction with the crew to a minimum. How much do you know about our mission to Aluwna? I understand you were there, Regimol."

"Yes, and a quite delightful planet it was," he answered with an emphasis on the past tense. "They weren't without their political intrigue, of course, and their class structure wasn't fair by Federation standards. Still it reminded me a lot of Romulus, if you could turn the Romulans into a peaceful, insular people."

"Their overseer was recently murdered," added the captain.

Regimol shrugged. "See, reminds me of Romulus."

"They hate us, you know," said Raynr Sleven.

Both the human and the Romulan looked quizzically at him. "How do you know that?" asked Picard.

"Technology we invented killed nine-tenths of

their population," answered Sleven. "How could they not hate us?"

For that question, the captain had no answer.

"It's taken me *three days* to get in to see her," complained Leah Brahms, crossing her arms and looking expectantly at Alexander Rozhenko. "Is she under house arrest or what?"

The young Klingon shrugged his shoulders and said, "Marla Karuw is under confinement in her laboratory, but she's allowed to see people. The fact is, she doesn't want to see anybody. She's desperately trying to get the last of the transporter booths down to the planet, and she says she'll entertain visitors after that. It's been difficult for me, because I've got a murder investigation to conduct."

Leah could clearly see that getting transporter booths to the surface of Aluwna was more important than anything else at the moment, because the transporter room of the *Darzor* was filled with the ubiquitous blue enclosures. Every minute or so, brawny Aluwnans loaded a new one onto the transporter platform, entered coordinates, and sent the box to some forsaken spot on the planet, where Klingons were hurriedly hacking, burning, or poisoning the rampaging plants into submission. It was almost a miracle that they had even stopped long enough to allow her and Alexander to board the royal yacht. They certainly didn't go out of their way to make them feel welcome.

"I came here to help," said Leah evenly. "The planet is ringed with these boxes, but I haven't seen anyone get out of one for days."

Alexander nodded. "Ever since . . . the accident."

"But aren't the Aluwnans getting ahead of themselves?" she asked. "They're filling the planet with transporter booths when they don't even know if the survivors are still alive."

"I've been told that they're working on that, too." The young Klingon lifted his hands helplessly. "What do you want me to do, barge in there and insist that she see you, when she's kicked out everybody else?"

"That would do for a start," answered Brahms. "I could offer her something."

"What?" asked Alexander doubtfully.

"Asylum," answered Leah Brahms. "Even if you find her guilty of the murder of Overseer Tejharet, I could offer her asylum in the Federation. Or perhaps this rescue effort will fail, and she wouldn't mind a change of scene."

Alexander furrowed his bony brow at the diminutive scientist. "You could do that? You *would* do that?"

"Yes, to both questions. My boss, Admiral Nechayev, could authorize it. I believe we owe these people something, especially Marla Karuw. If they won't take our help, perhaps they'll take our charity."

"Come," said Alexander, heading for the door of the transporter room. "I'll let you relay that message."

The laboratory was only a few doors down the corridor of the royal yacht, and the lab was locked until

Worf's son identified himself. Reluctantly, a weary female voice said, "Yes, come in, Alexander."

They entered the laboratory, which looked more like a factory with a variety of parts, blue metal enclosures, and circuitry spread all over the place. The only people present were three Aluwnans, one older female and one female who was quite young, plus a wild-haired male who looked like a typical mad scientist. All three stared at her as if she were a bug-eyed monster stepping off a flying saucer.

"Not you again," muttered Marla Karuw. "Alexander, I told you that I didn't want any onlookers or guards."

"I'm not a guard," answered Leah, bristling but maintaining her calm. "I came here to help you, but I understand you don't want our help. So I'm willing to offer you something else you might want."

"I only want to get on with my work," snapped Karuw, turning her back on the visitor.

"I'm here to offer you asylum in the Federation," answered Brahms, ignoring the snub. "No matter what happens here, no matter what happens in the murder investigation, you will be welcome to spend the rest of your days on a Federation world, conducting whatever research you care to conduct."

The former regent turned slowly to face the newcomer. "Do you think I need asylum? Do you think I even need the Federation?"

"Well," said Leah, "you asked us for help many days ago, and we arrived too late to give it to you. Because you shouldered the burden by yourself, I'm trying to make it up to you."

"And what's your connection again?" asked Karuw angrily. "Aren't you one of those scientists who helped develop Genesis?"

Leah met her gaze and answered, "No, I'm one of those scientists who lost her husband, all her friends, her homeworld, and everything I hold dear when the wave wiped out the planet of Seran. We didn't save nearly the number of people you saved—we had *two* survivors from our entire population, and I was one of them. If you want to be noble and pretend that this didn't happen anywhere but Aluwna, that's fine . . . but it's also wrong."

Karuw's tough exterior cracked a bit, and she lowered her head. "I'm sorry. You had no warning?"

"None," answered Brahms. "And for the first three days, I was the only one warning anybody. I was at the beginning, and you were at the end—and there were a lot more in between."

Marla Karuw waved to the Klingon, who had remained silent and respectful during this conversation. "Thank you, Alexander. This woman is welcome to stay with us . . . for a while."

Looking relieved, the Klingon nodded and slipped quietly out the door.

After he was gone, Leah Brahms said, "I noticed that you haven't rescued anyone from the satellites in a few days . . . ever since the transporter incident. If you'll recall, I was there."

Wincing, Karuw rubbed the rows of eyebrows lining her troubled brow. "Yes, we've been afraid to try it again, until we're ready to bring everyone down. Time is running out, and we're not sure how badly the fungus has spread along the bioneural network. It's my theory that if we can minimize transfers and bring everyone down quickly, we can avoid the worst side effects."

"Well, I've got a theory, too," said Brahms. "I presume you've still got the satellite that malfunctioned?"

Karuw nodded. "Yes. After we checked it out and found out about the fungus, we returned it to orbit."

"Good," said the human. "We've got a million of those giant slug creatures down on the planet, and we could certainly spare one or two for testing purposes. They're about the size and weight of a humanoid. I say we beam one of them into the pattern buffers on the affected satellite—or any satellite you want to test—then beam it back to the planet and see what happens. If it re-integrates properly, you'll know it's working."

Karuw considered the proposal for a moment, and the only male in the room finally spoke up: "That's a good idea, Marla. It wouldn't be hard to do either."

"You're Vilo Garlet?" asked Brahms.

He nodded and gave her a grudging smile. "Yes, I am."

The human turned to the young girl. "And you are?"

"Candra," she answered shyly. There was an eva-siveness around the girl's eyes that bothered Leah, but she didn't say anything. If this girl was welcome into Marla Karuw's inner circle, then so be it. These Alwunans were suspicious people; maybe they hadn't always been that way, but they were now.

Leah started to the door. "I'll go back to Aluwna and ask Worf to capture one of those creatures. Beam down to Base Two when you're ready to conduct the experiment. Some of the Klingon shuttlecraft have transporters, and we can use one to beam it up. Then we can use any of your blue boxes to return the crea-ture."

"Thank you, Dr. Brahms," said Karuw. "We appre-ciate your help."

That brought the first smile to Leah's face in many days, and she headed for the door and stopped. "Oh, one more thing—there's more help on the way. The *Enterprise* is supposed to arrive tomorrow."

"*Enterprise?*" asked Karuw. "Is that supposed to mean something?"

"If you were in the Federation, it would," answered Brahms. "That's our most celebrated starship, and we can't give you any better help than that. When you're ready, I'll see you below."

After Leah Brahms had left the laboratory, the smile melted from Marla Karuw's face. "That's just what we need," she muttered, "more meddlers from the Federation."

"Still this experiment is a good idea," said Vilo Garlet. "It will tell us if we have a chance to save our people."

"Oh, we'll have more than a chance," vowed Karuw with determination. "We're going to save our world, and get even for what was done to us."

Still feeling overwhelmed, Alexander Rozhenko walked down the corridor, headed to the quarters he'd been assigned on the *Darzor*. He alternated his time between Aluwna, the *Doghjey*, and his own ship, the *Ya'Vang*, but more and more he found himself spending his days and nights on the royal yacht. If diplomatic service meant sleeping in strange beds almost every night, he might have to give more thought to pursuing that calling, because the young Klingon had already moved around too much in his life. Right now, he just wanted to sit quietly for a few minutes and collect his thoughts.

As he approached his door, he noticed that it was open a few centimeters, and bristles on the back of his neck stood at attention. This wasn't really a cause for alarm, he tried to tell himself, because the *Darzor* had poor security, with doors that opened easily and didn't always shut automatically. Because the *Darzor* was so crowded with refugees, he was sharing quarters with two Aluwnan constables, both of whom were assigned to watching Seeress Jenoset. One of them was probably in the room, he decided, and had merely forgotten to shut the door.

Still Alexander slowed his pace and put his hand on the butt of the disruptor in his holster. A murder had taken place on this vessel, and he was leading the investigation. Of course, if anyone knew how little he had found out, they wouldn't be concerned enough to bother him. He approached the door and touched the panel on the bulkhead; the door slid open to its normal width, and he peered inside. Although he was sharing a room, his quarters were more spacious and luxurious here than they were on the *Ya'Vang*. The captain on a Klingon vessel didn't live as well as a servant on an Aluwnan yacht, he thought ruefully. Clearly there was nobody in the room at the moment, which hardly explained why it was open. Perhaps there was a malfunction in the door.

The Klingon entered cautiously, looking for signs of unauthorized entry. He found such a sign rather quickly, when he noted that a padd he had left on his desk was now missing. Then his ears picked up a telltale sign that most humanoids would have missed—the sound of someone breathing, and that someone wasn't him. There were two closets and space under the bunk beds where a person could hide, but Alexander fought the temptation to tear the room apart. He remained calm and pretended that he hadn't noticed anything amiss. After all, if someone was going to attack him, they would have done so by now. No, the entry had been to gather information—to snoop, as humans called it.

So Alexander calmly washed his hands in the basin, spent a few seconds grooming himself, then walked out, making as much noise as possible. He made sure to shut the door behind him all the way, then he pressed himself against the bulkhead in the corridor and waited.

It wasn't long before his patience was rewarded, and the door slid open again. When a slight figure slipped out, he pounced like a Capellan power cat, grabbed the intruder by the neck in the crook of his arm, and almost snapped his neck. The padd dropped to the deck, and Alexander increased the pressure of his grip. Gasping and flailing, his foe never had a chance to resist, and he was whimpering within seconds.

"Don't kill me!" he rasped. "Please . . . I didn't mean any harm!"

Realizing it was the young seeress consort, the one named Farlo, Alexander released his death hold and hurled the youth against the opposite bulkhead. The young Aluwnan bounced off the cold metal and dropped to his knees, gasping for air, tears in his eyes.

"Explain yourself!" ordered Alexander, his voice nearly as deep and forceful as his father's.

The boy heaved great breaths and tried to collect himself. "I . . . I wanted to see . . . if you had found out who did it."

"You mean, who murdered the overseer?" asked the Klingon. "Don't you think I would tell you if I found out?"

"Well," said Farlo, looking up with plaintive eyes,

"maybe you wouldn't ... until you found out for sure."

"You have a mouth," roared Alexander, "so you could *ask* me. You don't need to snoop around in my quarters. Your explanation is insufficient, and I've got a good mind to put you under guard with the rest of your family."

"Overseer Padrin would let me out," claimed the boy, glaring defiantly at Alexander.

The Klingon scowled. "Not if I grab you by the scruff of your neck and drag you to a Klingon vessel, where I would put you in irons! Give me a good explanation right now, or I'll do it."

Farlo gulped and said, "I ... I want to help you."

Alexander narrowed his eyes at his young captive, realization sweeping over him. "You know who did it, don't you?"

"I have a suspicion."

"Who?"

Moving as quickly as a targ surprised in the bush, Farlo jumped to his feet and dashed down the corridor. Alexander took a step after him, but he realized that he could never catch the lad before he reached the safety of the cabin he shared with Overseer Padrin. When it came time to explain, it would be his word against the boy's, and Padrin liked the boy. Scowling, Alexander bent down and picked up his padd.

Actually, it was a relief to know that *somebody* on this crazy vessel had an idea who had committed the crime. Farlo was confined to the *Darzor*, so he couldn't run far. There would be another opportunity to corner the lad and extract the information— Alexander would just have to plan it well. As his father had said when assigning him this murder investigation, such secrets could not be kept forever.

twenty

The Klingons had killed so many of the giant slug creatures that Worf feared they might have trouble finding one for Leah Brahms' experiment. Ever since they had discovered that they were indeed good eating, the Klingons assigned to the planet had been eating them in everything from stew to barbecued shish kebab, and they had even given them a name, *nujgharg*. The flavor was almost addictive, despite the distasteful necessity of cooking the slugs to kill the fungus. Of course, they had to cook them outside but eat them in the shuttlecraft, because they were still wearing protective gear.

The ground troops had gone so far as to transport select cuts of the delicacy back to the ships, so that their mates in orbit could share in the bounty of the land. But it was one thing to wade into the bog with a lance or *bat'leth*, kill one, and drag it back to camp, and it was quite another thing to capture one alive. Their large, suckerlike mouths were ringed with sharp teeth, and when one latched on to a leg or arm, its head had to be cut off and the teeth pried open with a knife. More than once, a nasty *nujgharg* had been responsible for sending a warrior to sickbay, howling in pain.

Worf had let his men decimate the local food animal, because it helped to eradicate the moss creatures, who had also acquired a Klingon name, *poch'loD*. Following a trail of dead *nujgharg* dragged along the ground, the starving *poch'loD* would shamble out of the forest into ambushes set by the Klingons, who would proceed to hack them into confetti before they knew what had hit them. There were great stretches of the planet where no one had set foot, and Worf imagined that both species still existed there in abundance. But for one Aluwnan day, he had seen nothing of the moss creatures or the big slugs. His men were starting to grumble, because this Genesis planet was getting too tame. It was no fun to fight plants that didn't fight back.

So it was that Worf now led a small band of six warriors fairly deep into the jungle from Base One. As usual, it was slow going in the thick brush and the awkward environmental suits, and they took turns slicing the path. Worf was beginning to think that they could do without the suits, but he couldn't take the chance on anyone getting infected and losing their minds. Although nothing seemed more dangerous than a renascent vine at the moment, Aluwna was still a very dangerous place.

The brawny warrior ahead of him suddenly got his *bat'leth* stuck in a vine as thick as a tree trunk, and he was so tired he could barely pull it out. That was Worf's cue to relieve him, and he was the next in line and fairly fresh. After helping his comrade extricate his blade, Worf said, "I will take the point."

"Where have all the *nujgharg* gone?" muttered his comrade, stepping back into line.

"They're hiding," answered another member of the group. "They've gotten smart."

"Remember," said Worf, "if we find one, we need it alive. Do you still have the pole?"

"Yes, sir!" panted the warrior at the rear, who was carrying a coil of rope and a large metal pole and having some difficulty maneuvering it through the thick branches and boughs.

"What good is a live *nujgharg?*" wondered a warrior aloud.

"To test their transporter boxes," answered another. "We don't want any more steaming goo coming out of them."

Worf was too busy hacking and slicing his way through the grotesque undergrowth to talk. Swinging his blade in time to his grunts, he was working too hard to pay full attention to the terrain, and he suddenly stumbled into a hole and was waist-deep in foul, slimy water. "I need aid," he muttered, reaching back for his fellows.

No sooner had the words left his mouth than a monstrous tentacle whipped out of the brown sludge and wrapped around his neck. It tightened like a noose and yanked him face-first into the mire, and instinctively he swung his *bat'leth* at the greasy appendage. It was so thick that he cut only partway through the massive knot of muscles, and he might have drowned immediately if his comrades hadn't waded into the bog, blades flying. In high spirits, the Klingons slashed and stabbed at the massive creature hidden under the roiling waves, and the battle seemed to go on for a long time before Worf could surface, sputtering for breath.

More tentacles whipped from the water, spraying globs of mud everywhere, but the thing was clearly in retreat from the flurry of slashing blades. Spitting up sludge, Worf finally crawled out of the brackish pool, still wearing the severed tentacle around his neck like an outrageous necklace. Panting heavily, he lay on a bed of roots and leaves until he coughed up enough water to breathe. He glanced over his shoulder and saw his comrades pursuing the unseen monster through the bog, and he yelled at them, "Let it go!"

"But this one would feed us for a month!" shouted his lieutenant.

"Let it go!" he repeated. "If it's not dead yet, it's too dangerous to hunt."

Worf staggered to his feet and inspected his suit; it was torn in three places, and the faceplate was cracked, which meant that he had to get back to the shuttlecraft as soon as possible. He had received treatment for the fungus, but who knew what other dangerous, insanity-provoking microbes lived in this prickly swamp? Luckily, the path hacked through the jungle remained clearly visible, and it wouldn't be grown over for at least an hour.

"I've got to go back to camp," he said, "because my suit has been compromised. The rest of you proceed for a hundred more meters along the bank of this bog, and be careful not to fall in. If you can't capture a *nujgharg* by then, head back to camp. Don't take any chances."

Trudging wearily, Worf retraced his steps, wondering how his adopted son, Jeremy, was faring back on Earth. It would have been pleasant to keep Jeremy with him a little while longer, but this bizarre duty wasn't destined to last forever, he hoped.

"Dad!" called a voice. "How are you?"

Worf stopped and whirled around, only to see his blond-haired son smiling at him. He was cured from his injuries, but he wasn't wearing a protective suit, per orders. Worf was about to scold him when he realized that Jeremy couldn't be here on Aluwna—no matter how realistic this facsimile was, it wasn't the young man he had taken into his family.

But for the moment, he needed something, and Worf was willing to play along. "Jeremy, I'm hungry. I need a *nujgharg*. Can you point one out to me?"

The young human frowned at him. "Come on, Dad, haven't you and your friends taken enough meat creatures? Haven't you killed enough harmless beings on this planet? It's time for all of you to go home, and I've come back to tell you that."

Worf had been in enough negotiations to know that one had just begun. "What do you offer us if we go home?" he asked.

"Peace," said the young man, stepping forward. "Nostalgia and comfort. Wouldn't you like to be with K'Ehleyr again? Or Jadzia Dax? What about Tasha Yar and all the old comrades you have served with and miss so much. You don't have to fear us—we could be a source of great comfort in your world."

"Stop!" growled Worf. "We don't want fakes and false comfort, or benign enslavement. Klingons, humans, Aluwnans—we are not your meat creatures which crawl upon the ground and are content to play hosts to parasites. Life is not easy for us, and we don't want it to be. When our loved ones are gone, they are gone . . . except for living in our hearts and memories."

The false Jeremy looked troubled by this. "We didn't know it would be so difficult to connect with you. Jadzia had a parasite within her, so what is the difference?"

"The difference," said Worf, "is that she *chose* to be joined with a Trill. That's a huge difference, and one which you haven't offered us."

"Worf!" cried an alarmed voice from the forest. He looked over Jeremy's shoulder to see his cadre of warriors stopped on the path twenty meters away. They carried a squirming *nujgharg* tied to a pole slung across their shoulders, and several of them were drawing disruptor pistols.

"Hold your fire!" he ordered. "I know it's one of them. It is leaving and taking a message." Worf turned back to the shimmering creature, which momentarily looked like Jadzia Dax. "Gather your race and take them to the farthest reaches of Aluwna. If we never see you again, perhaps you'll be spared. But you must leave us completely alone, or you'll be hunted down and killed, every last one of you."

"Very well, Worf," said Jadzia, her long dark hair flowing behind her strong, lovely face. "But you don't know what you are giving up."

"I know," he replied, "but I would rather have real pain than false pleasure. Go quickly."

"Good-bye," she said, fading into the thick vines and brush of the Aluwnan forest.

Worf staggered, feeling faint, and his lieutenant rushed forward to steady him. "We must get you back to the doctor," he said. "What were you doing, talking to that monster?"

"My job," answered Worf somberly. "I'm an ambassador, remember."

"But that *thing* . . . it's dishonorable."

"The enemy is beaten," he said with an odd sense of certainty. "And they know it."

The big, sawtoothed slug writhed in the charred dirt of the base camp, trying to escape back to the jungle, and a Klingon prodded it brutally with a pole.

The creature contracted like a giant amoeba, and Leah Brahms almost felt sorry for it.

"How are we going to get that thing into a shuttle-craft and onto a transporter platform?" she asked.

"I can stun it," answered Alexander Rozhenko, drawing his Starfleet phaser. He turned to Marla Karuw and asked, "Is that acceptable?"

"I suppose," answered the former regent, crossing her arms. "Stunned or alert, it shouldn't affect the experiment. By the way, where is your father?"

"Ambassador Worf had to return to the *Doghjey* for medical attention," answered Alexander. "They had an encounter with some kind of swamp creature, and his suit got torn. Then he had a discussion with a *poch'loD*."

"A what?" asked Karuw.

"That's what the Klingons call the moss creatures," said Leah Brahms with a smile. "I think it means 'plant man.'"

"I'll be glad when all the plant men are turned into mulch," said Karuw with a scowl. She held up an iso-linear chip and showed it to Alexander. "I have an emulation program which should turn your shuttle-craft transporter into one of our blue booths, com-plete with preset coordinates for the satellite we're testing. Can I run it to make sure?"

"Go ahead," answered Alexander, waving her toward a waiting shuttle. "This craft is at your dis-posal."

The two of them entered the small vessel, leaving

Leah Brahms outside, shivering in the cold. It was midday, and the snow flurries were particularly heavy. Or maybe they were ash flurries from a nearby volcano that had stepped up its activity, turning the sky an unpleasant shade of burnt umber with black streaks. The odors of sulfur and ammonia were also prominent today, even through the filters of the headgear she wore. The more time Leah spent on Aluwna, the less she was convinced that anything could be done to save the place. It pained her to think that her longtime home, Seran, was just like this, only there was no one left to try to reclaim it.

While she waited, Leah tried to concentrate on hopeful signs. The rate of plant growth had slowed somewhat, suggesting that the Genesis effect was approaching maturity. The areas that the Klingons had cleared were staying clear, except for what might be called normal encroachment, and blue transporter booths ringed the planet. Still she watched the Aluwnans who had already returned, and they moved like sullen ghosts through the unfriendly, unfinished landscape. More than once, the Klingons had caught depressed Aluwnans wandering about without their headgear, communing with moss creatures who pretended to be dead friends and family. The sickbays of every ship in orbit were filled with Aluwnans unable to cope with the devastation and hopelessness. Given the grimness of their reality, it was hard to blame them for seeking refuge in these prefabricated fantasies.

"We're ready," said a voice, breaking her out of her troubled thoughts. "The emulation works."

Leah turned to see Alexander changing the setting on his phaser, and the Klingons who were guarding the big slug backed away. A Klingon doctor had treated the *nujgharg* with the same antibiotics given to everybody else, and it was supposedly free of the fungus, or at least in remission. As the monstrous beast tried to squirm away from its captors, Alexander aimed his phaser and zapped it with a brilliant blue beam. At once, the creature became still, lying in the dirt like a limp, slimy fish.

It took two Klingons to drag the dead weight into the confines of the shuttlecraft, and Leah Brahms remained outside. Even though this experiment had been her idea, she was now having second thoughts, because there was a finality to what they might discover here. The harsh reality wasn't only in the howling winds and impenetrable jungle of Aluwna, it was also in the unseen pattern buffers on those satellites, floating silently in orbit. This might be the moment of reckoning for all who had toiled so long and hard to resurrect the eight million souls trapped in the ominous sky.

Marla Karuw jumped out of the shuttlecraft and dashed to the nearest blue enclosure on the edge of the clearing, and Leah followed close behind. As she ran, Karuw barked into the com device on her wrist, "All right, Vilo, the test subject has been beamed into test satellite one. Do you show it on your monitor?"

"Yes," answered a tinny voice. "Biosigns look normal. I'm ready to beam back on your command."

The energetic Aluwnan stopped at the blue booth and checked the status panel inside. "All right, it's on and ready. Proceed!"

Leah Brahms lifted her tricorder, ready to check the slug's health, although failure would be readily apparent. Both women held their breaths as the booth lit up and hummed with power, and a slight chime sounded. When the activity stopped, Karuw hesitantly opened the door to reveal . . .

The *nujgharg* lying on the transporter pad, unconscious but breathing. Brahms let out her pent-up breath and looked at Karuw. "Success?" she asked.

"Yes, but that was a satellite we expected to be successful," she replied. "One which hadn't shown any degradation. Now we're going to send it to the one which malfunctioned."

While she reported the results to Vilo Garlet on the *Darzor*, two brawny Klingons picked up the stunned beast and carried it back into the shuttlecraft. The blue boxes were one-way only, because transporting a life-form required considerably more power than receiving one. Leah Brahms paced in the snow flurries while Marla Karuw, Alexander, and the ever-helpful Klingons repeated the first part of the experiment.

After a few tense minutes, Karuw returned to the transporter booth, issuing commands to her subordinate. "Okay, Vilo, it's in test satellite two. Are you reading it?"

There came an uncomfortable pause, and Garlet finally reported, "Readings are erratic. Remember, the plasma packs have fallen below the threshold in that satellite, and we haven't gotten strong readings for a week. The pattern buffers show normal capacity, though, and the solar-power readings are within normal parameters."

"There's no way to know unless we try it." Marla Karuw heaved her shoulders and glanced at Leah; then she ducked into the blue enclosure to check its status. While she was doing this, Alexander Rozhenko walked to Leah's side and gave her a concerned look. Anxiety was thicker in the air than snow and ash.

Karuw stepped out and barked, "Proceed!"

Again the blue enclosure hummed and crackled, and static electricity raised the hair on the back of Leah's neck. When it was over, they pushed the door open, and there lay the slug creature, looking none the worse for wear.

"Success!" shouted Marla Karuw, raising her fists into the air. At once, she was back on her com device, saying, "Vilo, let's get ready for stage two. How many more boxes do we have to put down?"

"Fifty-five," came the answer. "We can be done before nightfall."

Something about the slug didn't look right to Leah, however, and she turned on the medical tricorder in her hands. She had taken readings before the beast was stunned, after, and then before it was beamed into orbit the second time. The readings this time were quite different.

While everyone was congratulating each other, Brahms felt like the messenger who was about to be shot. "Marla," she said, "there's a problem."

The Aluwnan was too busy issuing orders to respond, and Leah had to shout, "It's dead, Marla! The creature is dead."

That brought all immediate conversation to a halt, and the former regent whirled and stared at her. "Are you sure?"

"Look for yourself," said the human, shoving the tricorder under her nose. "No life-sign readings. Now it's just a hunk of cold meat."

Karuw didn't fully believe this conclusion until she pulled her own instrument from her belt and took her own readings. Then she slumped into the dirt and sat for a moment, legs crossed, staring down.

"We aren't really familiar with these beasts," said Alexander, sounding overly optimistic. "Perhaps the stress of transporting—"

"It survived the first time," rasped Karuw. "It should have survived the second time. This means that every satellite which has dipped below the threshold is in doubt. We have to act no later than tomorrow."

"What are you going to do?" asked Brahms.

"First," she answered somberly, "we don't need the Klingons anymore. It's best to let them go home."

"The *Enterprise* will arrive soon," said Leah helpfully.

Marla Karuw gave her a strange smile. "Then they'll be here to see stage two."

Sitting on an examination table in sickbay, Worf looked quizzically at the cryptic message he had just received from Marla Karuw. It also bore the seal of the new overseer, Padrin, which made it official. The message read succinctly, "Ambassador Worf, please accept our profound gratitude for all that you and the Klingons have done for Aluwna. You can do no more, and we respectfully request that you withdraw your ships and forces."

He turned to the com officer who had delivered the electronic missive. "When did you receive this?"

"Exactly three minutes ago," answered the young female Klingon, snapping to attention. "Do you wish to send a reply?"

"Yes," answered Worf. "Acknowledge receipt of message, and inform the overseer that all Klingon vessels will withdraw except for the *Doghjey*, which will remain in orbit to meet the *Enterprise*. Inform the other ships in the task force to recall their shuttlecraft and crew members from the planet. Tell them to withdraw to the outer planet in the solar system, where they will await my orders. Do you have that?"

"Yes, sir!" she answered sharply. "All ships to withdraw to the outer planet of the solar system, except the *Doghjey*. I believe that outer planet is called Aluwna Minor."

"One more thing," said Worf. "Tell my son,

Alexander, to remain on the planet. Inform the captain of the *Ya'Vang* that he's still assigned to me."

"Yes, sir! Anything else?"

"No," grumbled Worf, "I think that's more than enough."

The young ensign hurried off, leaving the old veteran to ponder this sudden change in their relationship with the Aluwnans. Yes, they had cleared enough of the jungle to erect all the transporter booths they wanted, but Klingons weren't so easily dismissed. He didn't know why exactly, but the hackles on the back of his neck were starting to rise. Worf felt danger in the troubled atmosphere of Aluwna.

twenty-one

The *Enterprise* cruised majestically into orbit around the lush green planet, which was ringed by vivid volcanoes and thick gray clouds, and framed by foreboding polar icecaps. The ring of satellites was clearly visible on the overhead viewscreen, and Captain Picard gave orders not to establish orbit too close to the fragile satellites. His ship didn't need geosynchronous orbit, because they could make adjustments automatically to keep in a fixed position. He had expected to see several Klingon vessels, along with the dozen or so Aluwnan vessels, but the stratosphere was oddly empty.

"Data," he said with a puzzled frown, "where are the Klingons?"

"Only one Klingon ship is in orbit," answered the android, "and that is the *Doghjey*. They are making their way toward our position at one-quarter impulse."

"Ambassador Worf is hailing us," reported the officer on the tactical station.

With a smile, Picard strode to the center of the bridge. "Put him on screen."

A moment later, the familiar if somewhat dour face of Starfleet's first Klingon officer appeared on the overhead viewscreen. "Hello, Ambassador," said Picard cheerfully. "I was expecting a bigger welcoming party."

"Good to see you, Captain," answered Worf. "We are all that remain of the Klingon task force. By request of the Aluwnan authorities, the rest of my ships have withdrawn."

Picard nodded thoughtfully. "Does that mean the mission has been a success?"

"Hardly," answered the Klingon glumly. "Only a few hundred Aluwnans have been reconstituted from the satellites, and only one percent of the habitable land area has been reclaimed."

"What is going on?" asked Picard.

"Permission to come aboard with my son, Alexander," replied Worf. "We could brief you and the rest of your staff in the observation lounge."

"Certainly," answered the captain, his smile returning. "It will be like old times."

"We can be in transporter range in approximately twenty minutes," said Worf.

"Make it so. Picard out." After the screen had gone blank, he turned to La Forge at the engineering station. "Geordi, run a scan on the Aluwnans' satellites

and see what you can find out about their status.
Data, give him a hand. By the look on Worf's face, I
think something peculiar is going on."

Farlo Fuzwik peered through the double doors into
the shuttlebay of the *Darzor* and saw the seeress's
royal shuttlecraft, which had just returned from being
pressed into service herding satellites around. The
pilot and copilot stood outside the hatch, chatting
with two of the shuttlebay personnel.

"Yes!" the lad whispered in triumph, pumping his
fist into the air. Their means to get off this ship and
back into hiding had just returned, and he was going
to make the most of it. Ever since that annoying
Klingon had caught him snooping in his quarters—
and he'd let it slip that he knew who had killed
Overseer Tejharet—Farlo had been keeping a low
profile and waiting for an opportunity to escape. But
not alone—that would be no good. He couldn't use
the transporter room, because that was crowded and
under use constantly.

The boy wished he knew how to pilot a shuttlecraft
himself, but he didn't. He had watched the pilot's
actions and had tried to pick up the procedures, but
they were unusually complicated. Flying in space was
something that very few Aluwnans had ever accomplished, or even tried, and he told himself he would
learn it someday. But for now, he just had to use his
regal position and imperious manner, which he had
learned to wield effectively.

Smoothing the wrinkles out of his satin tunic, Farlo lifted his chin and strode into the shuttlebay. He marched right up to the pilot and said, "Kanow, I'm sorry, but you can't go off-duty yet."

The man looked quizzically at him but didn't show his displeasure. "Why not? I've been on duty for twenty units straight." He glanced at his copilot and added, "We're both exhausted." She nodded in agreement.

"You're not done yet," replied Farlo indignantly, "because the seeress wishes to go down to the planet."

"Now?" muttered Kanow. "There's nothing down there but a bunch of huts where Klingons have been sleeping." From the distasteful wrinkle of his nose, he made it clear that Seeress Jenoset wouldn't find a Klingon sleeping hut to be very pleasant.

"I'm just relaying the message," answered Farlo, feigning boredom. "You wouldn't like to make the seeress mad, would you? I am your superior."

"Yes, you are," admitted Kanow grudgingly.

"Then wait here while I fetch Seeress Jenoset," ordered Farlo. "We'll be quick."

Trying to look dignified, Farlo exited the shuttlebay and hurried down the corridor to the laboratory, where he figured he would find Candra. Two constables were waiting outside, and he turned his overbearing manner upon them, too.

"Excuse me," he said, brushing past them. "I have to go in there."

The constables glanced uncertainly at one another, but this youth was now the second most important male in their society. If anything happened to Padrin, he would be their next overseer. So they stepped aside and opened the door for him.

Farlo strode inside and looked around to see who was present. He was relieved to find that Marla Karuw was nowhere to be seen, and the only ones in the lab were Candra and her dangerous friend, Vilo Garlet. He didn't need a scorecard to know that Vilo Garlet was responsible for turning Candra into a murderer.

"Farlo!" said the young lady in surprise. "What are you doing here?"

"I've got to talk to you," he replied simply. Then he cast his imperious gaze upon Vilo Garlet. "Alone."

The crazed scientist scowled and looked as if he would say something unkind, but Candra nodded to him and said, "It's okay."

"I need a bathroom break," muttered Garlet, brushing close to Farlo on his way out. "Don't be long," he warned.

"Take your time," Farlo shot back. After the door whooshed shut and they were finally alone, he gripped Candra's shoulders. "Listen," he said urgently, "you've got to come with me, and we've got to get off this ship."

"Why?" she asked bluntly.

"Can't you just trust me?" he begged. "We're best friends—I wouldn't suggest this unless it was necessary. You're in danger here."

"I am?" Candra asked suspiciously. "But we were just about to—" She stopped suddenly and shook her head. "I don't want to leave. Besides, where would we go?"

"Anywhere we want!" answered Farlo. "I've got a shuttlecraft and a pilot. We could go down to Aluwna and hide there."

Candra looked away. "Why do we have to hide?"

"You know why," he answered sharply. "You could pretend to be Seeress Jenoset—you've done it before."

At those words, she whirled on him. "What do you mean?" she asked defensively. "I . . . I didn't do anything like that."

Farlo held out his hands, pleading, "Come on, Candra, they'll catch you! Worf's son, Alexander, he's going to figure it out sooner or later."

"The Klingons have all left," she snapped, moving away from him.

"No, they haven't. Worf and Alexander are still here, and so is that big Klingon warship." He chased her halfway across the cluttered laboratory, pleading with her. "No one will be able to save you—not Vilo Garlet or Marla Karuw—not when they find out what you did. You *killed* the overseer!"

Now Candra stopped, hid her face in her hands, and began to cry. "They didn't tell me . . . not that he would die. It was an accident . . . he was just supposed to get sick!"

"Then they lied to you," whispered Farlo. "They're

using you. Listen, I'm the only one who's looking out for you now, Candra, and we've got to get out of here."

The door slid open, and Vilo Garlet entered with Marla Karuw at his side. The two of them looked suspiciously at the young seeress consort.

"What are you doing here?" asked Karuw, staring at Candra as she wiped her eyes.

"This is part of my domain," answered Farlo grandly. "I came here to ask my friend to have dinner with me tonight. In fact, right now, if she's available."

"We've got lots of work to do," said Vilo Garlet.

"Surely you can spare Candra for a short time," said Farlo, trying to muster some regal charm. "A big starship from the Federation has just entered orbit—maybe they can help you."

Garlet narrowed his eyes at the lad, but Marla Karuw brushed him off with a smile. "I think we can oblige the seeress consort. Go ahead, Candra, enjoy yourself."

"Thank you," said the girl, her voice a hoarse whisper.

Farlo instantly grabbed his friend's hand and pulled her toward the door. "Come along, my dear, we're having your favorite dishes."

Vilo Garlet stepped in front of them, blocking the door, and he gave Farlo a rapacious grin. "Remember, boy, I know your secret."

"I'm not the only one who has secrets," answered

Farlo, "but I am the only one who Overseer Padrin trusts." As Garlet's eyes flashed angrily, the boy slipped past him, dragging Candra behind him.

When they reached the corridor, Farlo laughed out loud, because nothing was better than being with his best friend, running a crazy scam, like the old days. But Candra looked frightened.

"I can't do it," she said. "I can't really look like the seeress, except in the dark. They'll spot me!"

"No, they won't," answered Farlo with a wave of his hand. "I've got it all figured out. Nobody goes down to Aluwna unless they're wearing a suit that covers them from head to toe. And I stole two of those suits—they even have the royal crest on them. All you have to do is wear this suit and yell at the pilot. Tell him to hurry or something. I guarantee, he'll think you're Jenoset. I'll do all the talking—you just look important."

"All right," she said, a smile creeping across her pretty face. "Where will we live down there? What will we do?"

"I have no idea," answered Farlo. "But I know I'm sick of living on this stupid ship."

"Me, too!" exclaimed Candra with a giggle. They took off running down the corridor, holding each other's hands.

"That girl knows too much," muttered Marla Karuw as she leaned over the spare transporter console she had requisitioned from supply. She was in the process of modifying the console to remotely control the chromasynthesis emitters hidden in every transporter box on Aluwna. In another hour, they would be able to set off a chain reaction from the laboratory on the *Darzor*.

"She won't talk," said Vilo Garlet. "Not unless she wants to stand trial for murdering the overseer."

Karuw nearly dropped the spanner in her hand, and she bolted upright. "Are you telling me that girl was the one?"

"With my help," answered Garlet proudly.

Marla fought the temptation to use the tool in her hand to bash in his head. "I know you hate our hereditary system, and so do I—but did it ever occur to you that I had control over Tejharet? And I don't have any influence with Padrin or Jenoset. Or that boy."

Garlet shrugged. "Accidents can befall all of them. Besides, now that the Klingons are gone, who's to stand in our way? We'll turn Aluwna back into a paradise, free our people, and claim our rightful place as rulers of this planet."

"In the name of science?" asked Marla, shuddering.

He nodded his bushy head of hair. "In the name of science."

Feeling much older, Marla stared somberly into space and said, "We started out as saviors, and now we're murderers. Or maybe we've always been murderers."

"What are you talking about?" asked Garlet. "It's

the Federation who are the murderers. *They* invented Genesis."

"Yes, and they also thought they were scientists," she answered gravely, wishing she could laugh at the irony. Instead she felt like crying. "Maybe if you invent something of such great power, you can't control it. It controls you."

"You think too much, Marla," said Garlet, taking the spanner from her hand. "Come on, we want to be done with this by the time dawn comes to the camps."

"We didn't have time to test it," she said, panic suddenly gripping her. "We don't really know the full results—"

"We'll know tomorrow," he assured her.

Every seat at the conference table in the observation lounge of the *Enterprise* was filled. There were several usual faces, noted Captain Picard—Will Riker, Beverly Crusher, Deanna Troi, Data, Geordi La Forge, plus one glowering face which had been missing for a few years, Worf. There were three observers present who had never been there before—Regimol, Raynr Sleven, and Worf's son, Alexander Rozhenko. All listened intently as Worf related the Klingons' experiences on Aluwna, and Picard was particularly fascinated by the cast of characters in the Aluwnan hierarchy: Overseer Tejharet, now deceased; the new overseer, Padrin; Seeress Jenoset; the young seeress consort, Farlo; and of course, Marla Karuw, who was like a lightning rod for everything good and bad that had happened in the last two weeks.

When he was finished, Worf turned the floor over to Alexander to discuss the murder of Overseer Tejharet, which had resulted in half of the central figures being under suspicion. The young Klingon revealed that he had a potential witness in the youthful seeress consort, who seemed to know more than anyone else about the crime. But the murder and internal politics were overshadowed by the tremendous drive and determination of Marla Karuw, plus the unknown fate of eight million Aluwnans trapped in a fragile string of satellites circling the planet.

"Any idea why they asked your task force to leave?" queried Picard.

"None," answered Worf. "The Aluwnans have never been forthcoming with information, just demands. We have done all we can to help them—perhaps it is time to leave."

"Where is Leah Brahms?" asked Geordi, not hiding his concern very well.

"I presume she's still on the planet," answered Worf. He turned to his son for confirmation.

Alexander nodded. "Yes, Dr. Brahms and I were down there this morning when they conducted the last experiment with the transporter booths." The young Klingon shook his head. "It didn't go well, and Marla Karuw was very upset. She took off, and the next thing we knew, we were asked to leave. Leah

Brahms wanted to stay down there and do what she could to help, but they haven't exactly welcomed her."

"They spurned her help," said Worf bluntly. "I have no doubt they would spurn yours as well."

"We still have a handful of warriors down there," Alexander added, "and there are maybe three hundred carefully inoculated Aluwnans living in the shelters we erected. As you can imagine, life is hard on Aluwna."

"The moss creatures?" asked Beverly Crusher. "Have they been much of a problem?"

"Not anymore," answered Worf. "We've been killing them since we got here, and they are mostly vanquished. A few of us were infected by the fungus, but we've taken precautions."

Will Riker sat forward and asked, "These transporter booths; are they ready to be used?"

"As far as we can tell they are," answered Worf. "They've got thousands of them, ringing the planet. I don't know why they're waiting."

"They're afraid," said Alexander. "But I heard Marla Karuw say they would beam everyone down tomorrow. I think it would be a surprise if everyone in those pattern buffers survived."

"I see." Captain Picard stroked his chin thoughtfully, then turned to La Forge. "What did our sensors tell you about the satellites?"

The engineer shook his head doubtfully. "They've got a bioneural network and lots of biological components, and the readings were all over the place. I don't think the satellites are in very good shape. If it were me, I wouldn't wait another minute."

"Is there anything we could actually do to help them?" asked Picard.

"It is unlikely," answered Data. "This was an existing transportation system, and the satellites' emitters and beam conduits are all keyed to individual transporter booths. Without considerable modification to our transporters, we could not extract any of the survivors from the pattern buffers."

"Then we can't do anything but wait," said Riker, "and see what they do tomorrow."

"Captain Picard," said the dignified Romulan, Regimol. "Raynr and I could slip aboard their ship and find out more information."

The captain waved the suggestion aside. "I'm not ready to interfere yet, unless we're asked. We tried hailing the *Darzor* but didn't get an answer, but we can keep trying. In the meantime, I think we should send an away team down to the planet to check out the conditions for ourselves. Number One—"

Riker jumped to his feet and smiled at an old comrade. "I haven't been able to say 'Worf, you're with me' for a long time. But now I have to ask politely, because you could say no."

"I'm with you," answered Worf, granting the first officer a slight smile. "My old job is looking more appealing all the time. And you, Alexander?"

"I'd like to get back to the *Darzor*," answered the young Klingon, "and find that boy, Farlo, to ask him a few questions. This may be the last chance I get to solve this murder."

"Watch yourself," warned his father.

"Commander, can I go with you?" asked La Forge, rising to his feet.

"Sure, Geordi," said Riker with an understanding smile. "Data, you, too."

"Yes, sir," answered the android. "I suggest we take a shuttlecraft for mobility and protection."

"All of you wear environmental suits," ordered Dr. Crusher. "Except for you, Data. And if you see any dead people, or people you know can't be on Aluwna, get right back to sickbay."

While the lounge began to empty, Regimol sidled up to Alexander and said, "Does Marla Karuw have an assistant named Vilo Garlet?"

"Yes, I believe she does."

The Romulan nodded slyly. "Look to him for information. He's been plotting against the Aluwnan royal family for a long time."

"Thank you," said the young Klingon. "Is there anything else I should know?"

"As your father says, be wary."

Leah Brahms sat in front of the campfire, studying the night sky over Aluwna. For the first time in the several days she had been there, the cloud cover was wispy, and she could see a panoply of stars scattered across the heavens. *All those solar systems,* she mused, *where the Genesis Wave is just a rumor or com-*

pletely unknown. They don't know how lucky they are.

Still, on a night such as this when the blizzards and howling winds were strangely absent, the new Aluwna could be almost beautiful in its primitive, unspoiled state. Since all but a few Klingons had pulled out, the camps were also oddly quiet, missing the loud camaraderie and bantering that had signified their presence. Armed Aluwnans patrolled the perimeter of Base Two, but they were hardly as reassuring as the Klingons had been. Even so, it didn't feel as if the moss creatures were massing to attack them. For the first time, it felt as if the planet were settling down into an almost normal existence.

Every hour or so, a shuttlecraft would land or take off from the clearings. One bearing the Aluwnan royal seal had landed a few minutes ago to let off two passengers. She had to respect those Aluwnans who could have stayed in the comfort of their ships in orbit but instead chose to brave this dark, primeval world. Of course, they might consider that they had very little choice—between this and death.

"This seat taken?" asked a polite voice, breaking Leah out of her reverie. She turned to see a handsome young Aluwnan—at least he looked handsome and young through the faceplate of his environmental suit. He pointed to the empty camp chair beside her.

"Please, sit down," she answered.

He settled his slender frame into the chair and peered curiously at her. "What race are you?"

"Human," she answered sheepishly, because that

meant she was from the dreaded Federation, which many Aluwnans held to blame for this disaster. "My name is Leah Brahms. I came here to help, but I'm mostly sitting around."

"Me, too," he answered. "My name is Komplum."

"I've seen you before, haven't I?" she asked. "Weren't you assisting Marla Karuw?"

"I was," he answered with a shrug, "but she replaced me a few days ago. I mean, not officially. Nothing is really official around here. But she turned to other assistants—I think because I asked too many questions."

"About what?" asked Leah.

He shook his head apologetically. "I shouldn't complain, because she's got a lot on her mind. Professor Karuw spent a long time on trial and in jail, and that's made her a bit secretive. Once we get our people out of the satellites, I'm sure things will be less tense around here."

"When is that due to happen?" asked Leah.

"I heard them talking about tomorrow morning," he answered. "She's got to start bringing them back, whether things are perfect or not."

"Yes," agreed Leah Brahms. "Holding out for perfection around here is pointless."

The sound of thrusters overhead alerted her that another shuttlecraft was arriving, and Leah peered into the night sky. She expected to see one of the foreboding gray Klingon shuttles, or one of the boxy blue Aluwnan shuttles—instead this one was a familiar lozenge shape of silver and gold. As it settled down into one of the burnt craters that passed for civilization on Aluwna, Leah Brahms jumped to her feet.

"That's a Starfleet shuttlecraft!" she said with excitement.

"Really?" asked Komplum, rising more slowly.

The two of them approached the glistening craft just as the hatch popped open and the first Starfleet officer she had seen in days stepped out. From his broad shoulders and peculiar gait, Leah identified him as Commander Riker, and she waved. Then came Worf, wielding his *bat'leth* and looking around warily. The third officer to emerge was even more familiar, and she instantly recognized his dusky skin and bionic eyes.

"Geordi!" she cried, rushing forward to meet him. There was no reserve or pretense as the two of them embraced awkwardly in their environmental suits. "It's great to see you!" she exclaimed.

"Hi, Leah!" he said, beaming. "I thought it would be ten months before I saw you again." He looked around at the charred ground, twisted roots, and monstrous trees and added, "This isn't exactly Paris, is it?"

"No," she admitted, "I'd almost rather be in a boring lecture than this."

The lights dimmed on the shuttlecraft, and Data stepped out, dressed as usual in nothing more than his normal uniform. He paused in the chill air to study a tricorder, while Riker lifted a nightscope to his eyes and studied the perimeter. Worf strode to a tiny encampment of Klingons, but Geordi did nothing but stare at Leah.

"Oh," she said with some embarrassment, "this is one of the local scientists, Komplum. We were just talking before you got here."

Geordi tried to shake the Aluwnan's hand, but there were cultural differences as well as thick gloves getting in the way. "Pleased to meet you," said the human engineer, finally giving up on the handshake.

"Pleased as well," answered Komplum. "You arrived after all the excitement—you should have seen the battle at this spot between the Klingons and those plant creatures. After that, they began to clear the land."

"No sign of the moss creatures lately?" asked Geordi.

"Not for a few days," answered Leah.

"I am picking up only minute, airborne traces of the fungus," said Data, joining their group. "In my opinion, humanoids could reside in this area without the environmental suits, but please do not tell Dr. Crusher I suggested that."

"I won't," promised Geordi with a smile. "So what is there to do for fun around here?"

"Sitting by the campfire," suggested Leah. "It's not bad if you've got someone to snuggle with."

"Can we sing cowboy songs?" asked Data.

Leah wasn't sure if the android was serious or not, but Geordi laughed. "All we've been hearing about are the blue transporter booths," he said. "Could I see one of them?"

"You can see a thousand of them, if you walk far enough," answered Leah. She waved and led them toward the perimeter, with Geordi and Data following.

"I think I'll sit by the fire," said Komplum, staying behind. "It was a pleasure to meet you."

"Likewise," answered Geordi. As soon as they were out of earshot, the engineer asked, "He's a scientist, but he's just standing around down here, doing nothing?"

"Aluwna is kind of a one-woman band," answered Leah, "and Marla Karuw is the conductor, too. You're not here long before you find that out. I don't think there's any reason for us to stay . . . beyond tonight."

She reached the nearest blue transporter enclosure, stopped, and pointed to it. "There it is. Every ship in orbit has been running replicators and making these for over a week, and they just put the last one in place a couple hours ago."

"This appears to be a very compact and efficient design," remarked Data, opening his tricorder and taking some readings. "Solar power, plasma gel packs, autosequencing, receive function only—no matter-stream transmission. There is some unusual circuitry in the base which I cannot identify."

"Does it have quantum resolution or molecular resolution?" asked Geordi. "What about biofilters? Does it use the Doppler compensation sync?"

"I'm no expert on transporters," admitted Leah, reaching for the door handle. "But I've heard them say that it comes complete with everything, including a—" She opened the door of the booth and promptly screamed with shock and surprise, because slumped on the floor, mouth agape in a horrible manner and looking badly decomposed, was a dead naked body.

"Complete with corpse," said Data, finishing her sentence.

twenty-two

Alexander Rozhenko paced in the corridor outside the royal stateroom on the *Darzor*, eyeing the two Aluwnan constables angrily. He stopped and said through clenched teeth, "Please tell the seeress that it's urgent I see her."

"We are sorry," answered the Aluwnan, "but she left orders not to be disturbed."

The Klingon tried to control his rising anger as he answered, "Overseer Padrin put me in charge of the murder investigation of Overseer Tejharet. You both know that. Seeress Jenoset is a suspect, but I really don't want to see her. I want to know where the seeress consort is—the youth called Farlo. He's not in his cabin. Is he in there with her?"

The two constables looked uncertainly at one another, and it was difficult to tell if they knew but refused to answer, or didn't know. "I didn't see him go in," answered one. The other guard shook his head.

"Ask her, will you?" demanded Alexander.

"She left word not to be disturbed," insisted the constable.

"Arrgh!" groaned Alexander, rushing up and banging on the door himself. When the constables moved to stop him, he bashed one in the head with his elbow and dropped him to the deck, then he ducked the stun stick wielded by the other. Having been attacked with a weapon, Alexander went into full battle mode, smashing his two attackers with fists and elbows until he bought himself enough time to draw his disruptor. Then he blasted them both where they stood, and the Aluwnans were soon lying on the deck, unconscious.

Growling, he banged on the door again. "Open up, Seeress!"

The door slid open, and a sleepy-eyed but still fetching blonde dressed in filmy nightclothes answered the door. "What is all the commotion?" she demanded. When she saw the tall, young Klingon, still panting from his battle with her guards, her demeanor changed completely. "Hello, Alexander," she said in a sultry voice. "Would you like to come in . . . for a while?"

He gave her a leering smile. "Are you alone?"

"Yes, I am," she replied in a come-hither tone of voice, raising three eyebrows expectantly.

"That's all I needed to know," answered Alexander, returning to a businesslike manner. "I'm looking for Farlo—he's disappeared."

"Disappeared?" she said in shock. "But I saw him, just a few units ago."

Alexander ticked off on his fingers as he answered, "He's not with you, not with Padrin, not in his cabin, not in the mess hall or any of the places I've seen him."

"The ship's computer can locate him," she replied with concern. "Please come in."

This time, Alexander obeyed, and the two of them strode across her sumptuous stateroom to her terminal. "Computer," said Jenoset, "where on the ship is Seeress Consort Farlo Fuzwik?"

After a moment, the computer's polite voice responded, "Farlo Fuzwik is not on the ship. His last known location was the shuttlebay."

"The shuttlebay?" asked Alexander curiously. "Has your shuttlecraft taken off recently?"

"Not that I'm aware," the seeress answered indignantly. "Listen, before you assume he's left the ship—and I don't know why he would—check the laboratory. He has a friend who's been working there with Marla Karuw."

"I know who you mean," said Alexander, "I will check there. Thank you, Seeress."

"Anytime," she replied in a sultry voice, "and I mean it. By the way, I didn't kill Tejharet."

"I never thought you did," answered Alexander as he rushed out the door.

A minute later, he reached the laboratory and found three armed constables waiting for him. Apparently, they had found out about the way he dealt with their comrades. "You are not welcome here," warned the biggest of the Aluwnans. "You had better leave."

"I don't want a confrontation," said Alexander. "I'm looking for Farlo, the seeress consort."

"He's not here," answered the big Aluwnan, taking a threatening step toward the Klingon.

"What about his friend, the girl named Candra?"

The Aluwnans looked at one another with surprise, as if they hadn't expected that question. "She left with the seeress consort," answered one of the constables, "about one unit ago."

"Thank you," said Alexander with relief. "You can stand down now."

He turned to leave, although he wasn't sure where he was going from here, when the laboratory door suddenly opened. Out strode Marla Karuw, looking enraged, her white lab coat rustling stiffly. Vilo Garlet poked his head out of the laboratory and shouted, "Professor, you can't go now!"

"I have to confront them," she replied. "You know what to do if you get my signal."

"Professor," said a constable, stepping in front of her and brandishing his stun stick, "you aren't allowed to leave without permission."

"Damn!" muttered Karuw. Realizing Alexander was there, she turned and pointed to him. "*He* can give me permission to leave."

"Yes, I can," answered the Klingon. "Where do you want to go?"

"To Aluwna," she answered, crossing her arms.

Alexander nodded and said, "One quick question—where are Candra and Farlo Fuzwik?"

"I have no idea," she answered. "They left and never came back."

"That's enough for me," said the Klingon, motioning her down the corridor. "I'll go with you."

"I don't need an escort!"

"Perhaps not, but we're both going to the same place." A few moments later, they strode into the transporter room, which was now quiet after the frenetic activity of the last few days. There were only a few partially built transporter booths lying around and one weary operator, who lunged to his feet upon their approach.

"Regent!" he said in shock. "I mean, Professor."

"It doesn't matter what you call me," snapped Karuw as she bounded onto the transporter platform. Alexander moved quickly to stay at her side. "Send us to Base Two on the surface."

"Yes, Professor," responded the operator, entering the coordinates on his console. "You know, it's the middle of the night down there."

"I'm aware what time it is." Karuw scowled and crossed her arms, making it clear that she wanted to go now, without any further ado.

"Wait a minute!" said Alexander with alarm. "Don't we need environmental suits?"

Karuw scoffed at him. "And they told me Klingons were brave."

"Brave, not stupid."

"They have plenty of suits down there," she answered, "if you're afraid."

Alexander crossed his arms stubbornly and said, "Energize."

The two of them vanished from the warm confines of the *Darzor* and materialized a moment later in the chilly wasteland of Aluwna, surrounded by campfires, temporary shelters, and a few scattered shuttlecraft. Alexander wanted to ask Marla Karuw what was so urgent, but he figured if he followed her, he would soon find out. She stalked across the burnt grass and gnarled roots of the crater, ignoring the few despondent Aluwnans who greeted her. Alexander had to run to keep up. Their destination was soon apparent, because several crouched figures were gathered around one of the blue transporter booths, looking at a body lying prone on the ground.

Marla Karuw strode up to the figures, who were unrecognizable in their environmental suits, except for the android, Data. Alexander realized that this was the away team from the *Enterprise*, and he soon identified his father, Riker, and the others. They had apparently discovered a badly decomposed body, but it looked too old to have arrived on the planet since the Genesis Wave struck. Where had it come from? he wondered.

Karuw took one look at the body and gasped, stepping back, her hand over her mouth. This was the strongest reaction Alexander had ever seen from the unflappable professor.

"Curate Molafzon," she said, looking as pale as if she had seen a ghost. "But how . . . here?"

"Obviously, you can identify the body," said Commander Riker. "You are Marla Karuw, aren't you?"

"Yes," she answered, lifting her chin and mustering her composure. "The curate . . . he went missing before the wave struck. Where did you find him?"

"In the transporter booth," answered Leah Brahms. "Are you ready to let us help you?"

Karuw's back stiffened, and she glowered at the newly arrived visitors. "I think the Federation has done quite enough already. I know you mean well, but everything is under control."

"That's not the impression we get," said Geordi La Forge. "We've run scans on your satellites, and many of those pattern buffers are destabilizing at an alarming rate. If I were you—"

"You aren't me!" she snapped, again looking flustered, especially whenever she glanced at the wizened body on the ground. "Yes, I begged you for help, but that was weeks ago . . . when help would have done us some good. Now we're ready to reclaim our planet . . . for Aluwnans, not the Federation."

She turned to Worf and said, "Ambassador, you sent me that story . . . about the ancient Terran named Noah. You didn't think I would read it, but I did. You were right—it did give me inspiration, because it was about a lone person who listened to his inner voice, the Divine. That voice told him to build the ark, and he ignored everyone else on the planet, all those who thought he was a fool. Single-handedly, he brought his world through turmoil and saved all the species on the planet. One person! Yes, I could identify with Noah. Now we are finally at the end of the storm; the clouds are parting, and the flood waters are receding. I can't believe that anything will stop me from my victory."

"Something might," said Data, stepping forward. "The unusual circuitry you have in the base of your transporter booth is sapping the solar power cells. If you could explain to us the purpose of these emitters, perhaps we could find a way to increase energy efficiency. If not, I fear the power cells will fail under heavy usage."

A dark cloud passed over Marla Karuw's weathered face, and she lifted her left wrist and squeezed her communications bracelet. It beeped, sending out a signal. "I'll show you what those emitters do," she said calmly, "because I can't let you meddle in our lives anymore."

The transporter booth suddenly came alive, beeping, whirring, and glowing with an eerie amber light. When Marla Karuw ran at full speed away from the enclosure, the away team looked uneasily at one another, except for Data, who studied his tricorder intently.

"There is a large buildup of kedion particles,"

said the android, "I suggest vacating the area. Do not use transporters."

That was enough for Riker, Worf, La Forge, Brahms, and Alexander, who ran at full speed through the camp, waving at everyone. "Run!" they shouted. "Take cover! Get away from the transporter!"

The warning came too late for most of the stunned refugees, because the transporter booth suddenly erupted with amber light, like a sun going nova, and a shock wave resonated outward in every direction. The ground shuddered, the trees rippled and wilted, and the oxygen was sucked out of the air. The shock wave knocked Alexander to the ground, and Worf landed with such force that his protective helmet flew off. They could do little more than grasp roots and rocks, while their lungs screamed for air. Alexander looked up and marveled at the way Data stood in the center of the maelstrom, light and strange energy ripples flowing all around him while he continued to take readings. The Klingon's lungs were starting to burn when they abruptly filled with air that he could breathe.

"Where is Marla Karuw?" shouted his father, glaring over his shoulder into the misty darkness, which seemed to be shimmering from the passing of the energy beam. But neither one of them could see much of anything, because the campfires and lights on the shuttlecraft had all gone out. The transporter booth was dark again, too.

A mighty tree from the edge of the jungle suddenly toppled over and fell to the ground with a resounding crash. Alexander hoped there was nobody under it. More trees began to fall, as if a thousand lumberjacks were working overtime. Without warning, the ground beneath him turned to mushy mud and then slimy quicksand, and he was sinking.

"Help!" cried Alexander, reaching for his father.

"Don't struggle," ordered Worf, gripping his hand. "Try to float on top!"

That was easier said than done, because first he had to extricate his limbs from the muck. Alexander could hear frightened cries and screams in the darkness, and he wanted to help them—but he could barely help himself.

"The ground is liquefying!" shouted Commander Riker somewhere in the blackness. "Try to float! Don't struggle!"

Others took up the chant, and the word quickly spread across the clearing. "Float on top! Float!"

Floating was possible, Alexander discovered just as soon as he stopped panicking. Unfortunately, that was all he or anyone else was able to do, while the ground continued to shudder, and trees tumbled in the forest like grain under a scythe. His irrational mind almost thought it was the Genesis Wave again, but he was still alive—so that wasn't it.

"Marla Karuw!" his father yelled angrily. Even his great bellow was barely audible over the screams, shouts, and collapsing forest.

He blames the right one, thought Alexander, because he remembered Karuw telling Vilo Garlet to wait for her signal. *What have those crazy Aluwnans done?*

Geordi La Forge and Leah Brahms held each other tightly as the liquefied ground quaked beneath them. They didn't sink, because they had jumped upon a sheet of metal from a fallen shelter. They wanted to assure each other that this wasn't the end, but neither one of them had any idea what it was. All they could hear were the faceless cries to "Float! Don't struggle!" And the only struggling they did was to drop to their knees and grip each other as the undulating earth tried to drown them.

At the edge of the forest, two youths held each other in the same fashion as they crouched under a hollow log. The forest, which had seemed so lush and vibrant only a few instants ago, was melting away like snow caught in a warm downpour. They could hear the leaves crackling and withering as they died.

"What is going on?" breathed Candra.

"I don't know," answered Farlo honestly. "Did you see that light?"

"How could I miss it?" Even though it was dark, the whole planet seemed to have a strange golden halo. The ground quivered after a tremendous tree collapsed just behind them, and they gripped each other even more tightly, waiting for the end of everything.

* * *

On the bridge of the *Enterprise*, the normal running lights went out, plunging them into darkness, and Captain Picard banged his knee on his own command chair. A moment later, the emergency reds went on, bathing them in eerie but functional light. Picard turned to look at Beverly Crusher, who was on bridge duty as acting first officer, and her eyes widened in amazement. It wasn't often that the power went off unexpectedly on the immense starship.

Picard hit his combadge and said, "Bridge to engineering. What is going on?"

"Unknown, sir," came the reply. "Computers are down. All systems are down . . . except for communications and emergency—"

Without warning, the transmission went dead, and Picard continued to slap his combadge with no result. "Bridge to engineering." No answer came, and the captain started to feel light-headed and light of foot. In fact, his feet lifted off the deck.

"Conn," he ordered, "get us out of here."

The helmsman held himself in his seat with one hand and tried to work his board with the other, to no avail. "Helm is not responding," he answered. "We're losing all ship's systems, including artificial gravity."

Picard felt hands gripping his biceps, and he turned to see Beverly Crusher giving him a brave smile. "We could lose warp containment," she said. "Want me to get down there and see what's happening?"

The captain looked instinctively at the main

viewscreen, but it was dark. He wasn't sure, but he thought he had seen a flash of light from the planet just before everything went haywire.

"No, Beverly, stay with me," he said, floating closer to her. "By the time you crawled there and back in the Jefferies tube, we might lose the warp core and our orbit. We'll have to assume that someone will make their way here from engineering."

Before he floated too far away, Picard hooked the arm of his chair with his foot and pulled himself down to his command panel. There weren't too many orders he could issue from this small console, but there was one which seemed appropriate. Under the fading red light, he entered his private access code and a shipwide alert.

An emergency klaxon sounded, and a computer voice intoned, "All hands, abandon ship! Proceed to escape pods. All hands, abandon ship!"

The *Darzor* pitched back and forth, losing altitude and helm control, and Vilo Garlet was slammed against the transporter console he had just used to unleash the chromasynthesis process. "Slipstream particles!" he muttered to himself. "Feedback overload . . . how do I stop it?"

He began pounding commands into his board, but the process had already terminated. There was no way to turn it off, because it was over. Whatever strange side effects had rippled back along the control waves to the ships in orbit, the anti-Genesis device had already done its job on the planet. He wanted to take sensor readings of the planet, but his controls were frozen as the royal yacht continued to heave and yaw like a rowboat caught in a hurricane.

The laboratory door slid open, and Overseer Padrin and Seeress Jenoset charged into his domain, fear and anger in their eyes. "What's happening?" shouted Padrin with alarm. "What have you done?"

"Where's Marla?" demanded Jenoset, her hands balled into fists.

"She's on the planet," answered Vilo Garlet, staggering from behind his console. He suddenly felt as if the temperature had gone up twenty degrees, and he tugged at his collar. "And I don't know what's happening!"

As the ship pitched again, Jenoset nearly fell into him, and both of them suddenly floated off the deck. "What have you done!" she screamed. "What have you done?"

"What had to be done," he answered, pleading for understanding. "We had to get Aluwna back to normal."

Jenoset reached for the rebellious scientist just as an awful squawking noise sounded over the shipwide intercom system. That was followed by a voice battling against static: "This is Captain Uzel . . . we're losing altitude. We're trying to compensate, but . . . we've lost control! We're reentering the atmosphere. All hands, brace for impact!"

"You have destroyed us!" wailed Overseer Padrin.

As he floated to the ceiling of the laboratory, the short-lived ruler of Aluwna began to weep.

Streaking out of control toward Aluwna, the sleek yacht *Darzor* careened into the atmosphere, with fire blazing along its entire length. The craft gradually turned into a giant fireball with a long tail of smoke, and it burned for several seconds before shattering into a billion burning embers. The pieces of the unfortunate craft floated through the dark sky over Aluwna, looking like the finale of a stunning fireworks display.

twenty-three

Deanna Troi peered out the small viewport on her escape pod at a remarkable sight. The planet Aluwna was no longer a big ball of greenery with impressive polar icecaps; now it was striped like a zebra with alternating bands of chaotic Genesis growth and barren brown wasteland. It was green and tan, like a round watermelon, and there were brackish bodies of water where before there had been only jungle. The polar icecaps were smaller and were also ringed with barren patches. Of the hundreds of planets she had seen across the universe, she had never seen one that looked like this. In fact, Aluwna had not looked like this yesterday. It was like a dog with striped mange eating up its fur.

She had wanted to stay aboard the *Enterprise* with Captain Picard and Beverly Crusher, but he had made it clear that an all-hands evacuation meant all hands.

Besides, he wanted there to be leadership down on the planet, where there was bound to be mostly chaos. The escape pods would be coming down in a centralized locale but still separated from each other, perhaps by several kilometers. Half of the senior staff was already down there, but their situation was unknown. All that was known was that some unfamiliar particle stream from the planet's surface had blasted every system on the ship, and the warp core was oozing deadly radiation. Even the warp-core ejection system was disabled, or else they could save the *Enterprise* by dispatching the core. But that wasn't an option.

All of them seemed to be caught in Aluwna's ongoing nightmare.

"We'll be safe on the planet, won't we?" said a small voice. Troi turned to look at one of three children strapped into the pod with her, along with their teacher, Valerie, who gave Deanna a game smile.

"I'm sure we'll be safe," answered Troi, "although it may be quite an adventure. We'll have to work together and do as we're told."

"What will we eat?" asked a boy about eight years old.

"Emergency rations," said Troi. "Packaged food."

"What about my mommy?" asked a little Delta girl.

Troi gave her a reassuring smile. "I'm sure she's on one of the other escape pods. When we have to leave the ship quickly, everyone goes to the closest pod."

The little Deltan nodded as if this made sense to

her; then her lips pouted in the beginning of a sob. Before she could break into tears, the escape pod hit turbulence in the upper atmosphere, and they were buffeted about. Troi's stomach flew somewhere above her head, and all of them gasped.

"Hold my hands," said the counselor to the two closest children. "I'm afraid."

Their teacher said the same thing, and they were all holding hands during the frightening tumble through the atmosphere. Deanna glanced out the viewport and could see no more than a blur of clouds and sparks. With a loud whoosh, the parachutes deployed, which brought another stomach-churning shift, frightened gasps, and renewed clutching of hands. Troi explained what was happening, and the children were very brave as the pod's plummet to Aluwna finally began to slow.

When Troi saw trees and rocks outside the window, she said, "Brace yourselves—we're coming down."

The landing was surprisingly soft after the frenetic free fall through the atmosphere. There was a bump and a few moments of settling, and then the hatches popped open—one above their heads and another beneath their feet, which only opened partway because it was stuck in thick vines and branches, which were choked with velvety leaves. The shaken passengers were relatively calm until a mass of tentacles and squirming, fist-sized maggots began to ooze through the crack in the lower hatchway. Now the children cried in earnest, and the teacher began to scream.

"Stay calm!" ordered Troi. "We'll get out on top." She unfastened her restraints and leaned forward far enough to reach the manual controls on the bulkhead panel. First she closed both hatches, crushing a dozen squirming tentacles and countless wiggly grubs, which continued to writhe just beneath their feet. Getting the hang of the controls and flashing back on her emergency training, the counselor managed to open only the upper hatch, leaving the lower one shut tight against the disturbing elements. She braced herself on the rungs of a small ladder and unfastened her restraints, then climbed to the nose cone of the escape pod and peered out at the new Aluwna.

Troi tried not to gasp too loudly, but it was a stunning sight, even in the early dawn. They were mired in the thickest, sweatiest morass of brush she had ever seen, but ten meters away lay a desolate plain of caked soil. It looked like a drought-stricken desert right next to a luxuriant park. The desert wasn't totally devoid of life, because there were blackened roots and stumps, and small buds appeared to be growing from them. Buzzing like an alarm clock, a huge flying insect dove from nowhere at her head, and Deanna had to duck back into the escape pod and pull the hatch shut.

The children and their teacher stared at her, and she tried to smile. "I think we'll stay in here awhile," she said, "until they find us. Who wants some rations?"

Floating weightlessly, Captain Picard climbed out of the gloomy Jefferies tube into the corridor outside engineering, which was lit like a tart's boudoir in hot red light. Clanging behind him on a tether was a large white suit, so bulky it was like a statue of some forgotten golem or perhaps an example of ancient deep-sea diving gear. Following the Genesis Wave threat, they were supposed to have returned all the Brahms radiation suits to the Romulans, because Leah Brahms had infringed upon Romulan phase-shifting technology to make her protective garment. But Geordi La Forge had saved one suit as a souvenir, and Picard had just liberated it from Geordi's quarters. Similar suits had saved millions of lives during the height of the Genesis Wave, Brahms' own life included, but this was the purpose for which it had been designed—to enter a room contaminated with lethal radiation.

A small device on his belt squawked loudly, followed by Beverly Crusher's tinny voice. "Jean-Luc," she said, "the last escape pod is away, and I think all hands have been evacuated. There's one pod left for you and me, and I'll meet you on deck six. Over."

Since the com system was down, they were using old-fashioned walkie-talkies, such as those issued in emergency kits for away teams. The captain pulled the device off his belt and stopped to collect his thoughts before he pushed the Talk buttom. "Beverly," he said forcefully, "don't wait for me. Get in the escape pod and launch. Over."

"What?" she said angrily. "I'm not going to leave you here."

"It's the captain's prerogative to go down with the

ship," he reminded her. "Besides, I'm not done yet. I have the Brahms radiation suit, and I'm going into the warp chamber to try manual ejection of the core."

"You'll be killed," Beverly warned solemnly. "Besides, that's a two-person job at the very least. Get on the escape pod with me—it's your only chance."

"With the Brahms suit, I won't be killed unless I fail," he replied, his lips thinning. "Beverly, get into the escape pod and launch—that's an order. Picard out." He turned off the walkie-talkie before she could argue with him further.

Pushing off the bulkhead, he glided weightlessly toward the sealed door of engineering, where he stopped to strip out of his uniform. Carefully but with a sense of urgency, he climbed into the bulky white suit. All of them had undergone brief training with the Brahms gear, and Troi, Riker, and others had worn duplicate suits during the crisis. The gel interior molded to the contours of his body, shrinking or expanding as needed. Picard was glad he had paid attention, because operating the complicated apparatus with its interphase generators, self-contained life-support, computer, and robotic attachments was no trivial task. The controls were in the fingers of the gloves, and the upper right-hand corner of the face-plate gave him a reflective viewscreen of instructions and readings.

The captain activated the suit, which gave him one immediate advantage—magnetized soles on the boots, which allowed him to walk again, albeit slowly and deliberately. He was relieved to see that the power levels were sufficient for ten minutes of operation, and he hoped that would be all he needed. The interphase generators kept him oscillating in and out of the temporal plane, allowing him to interact with physical objects yet avoid the most immediate physical dangers. He walked up to the sealed door of engineering and entered his security access code at the panel, which allowed him to override the emergency precautions.

With a whoosh, the hatch unsealed, and the door creaked open a few centimeters. He pushed it open some more and then gasped as the unequal air pressure caused a bloated corpse to crash into him. The dead engineer's skin was peeled off, and his eyes bulged grotesquely. Picard gulped and pushed the weightless cadaver out of his way. Sensor readings were scrolling frantically in the reflective viewscreen in the corner of his faceplate, but he didn't need to read them to see that it was lethal to be in here. Half a dozen other bodies floated ominously in the carvernous hold of engineering.

Red emergency lights glimmered all around him, but his eyes were drawn to the towering warp coil in the center of the circular silo. It looked like a neon Christmas tree, ablaze with white branches of pure energy and crackling beams that looked like lightning. Picard had to get a grip on his fear, because he had never seen a warp core in such bad shape before. It looked as if it could blow apart any second, turning the *Enterprise* into a gaseous cloud and spreading antimatter and radiation throughout the atmosphere. That alone might kill all life on the planet. Even if they didn't eject the warp core, the ship would soon lose orbit and burn up in the atmosphere. Once launched, the core had a self-contained guidance system that would steer it harmlessly into space.

"We'd better hurry," said a voice behind him, reflecting his thoughts. Picard turned around as quickly as he could in the radiation suit, but there was no one there.

With a touch of a button in his left-hand glove, Picard activated a speaker system inside the suit. "Who's there?" he asked.

"It's me—Regimol." For a fleeting instant, the Romulan appeared, then disappeared, and the captain realized that Regimol had activated his own interphase device. Whether it fully protected the Romulan from the radiation, the captain didn't know, but here was the help he badly needed.

"The manual controls are over here," said the ghostly voice, moving toward the glowing, pulsating warp core. "Hurry."

Picard knew where the emergency ejectors were, and he also knew how they could be operated, minus computer control. There were three innocuous-looking, hand-turned wheels: one to jettison the exterior hull plate, another to disengage the pylons holding the towering warp core in place, and a third to feed rocket fuel to the thrusters, which ignited when reaching threshold. All of it had to be accomplished in a matter of seconds, which was why he couldn't have done it alone, which he now realized.

Under bursts of radioactive steam and the unearthly blue-white crackle of the warp core, Picard could see the flickering image of a humanoid, turning the first wheel. "Hurry!" he croaked. "Get the second!"

A distant clanging sound told Picard that the exterior hull plate had been jettisoned, and he grabbed the second disk and turned it with all his might. The wheel groaned like a creaking old hatch on a rusty submarine, and Picard's arms and back ached from the effort to turn it. Gradually, the wheel turned more smoothly, and towering metal struts and sparking cables fell away from the shimmering warp coil. The glowing structure began to tremble like a rocket about to take off, and the captain ducked from a flying cable. The ghostly figure of Regimol moved to his other side and began to turn the third wheel, but it barely budged.

"Losing strength!" he groaned. "Help me!"

The captain pressed his shoulder against the Romulan's and took a firm grip on the disk. As the warp core shuddered and Klaxons and steam blasted in their ears, they turned the grating wheel one centimeter after another, until they could hear the roar of thrusters firing all around them. From the deafening noise, it sounded as if the entire warp chamber would launch from the ship. Suddenly the core erupted in flames and dropped straight down through a monstrous hole in the deck. Now Picard had to grip the wheel with all his strength just to avoid being sucked out, along with the towering cylinder of flame and several of the bodies. It was like a rocket from the twentieth century being blasted the wrong way into the center of the earth.

He gripped his comrade, Regimol, by an invisible arm and breathed, "You saved the ship . . . come on!"

"One more thing," the Romulan croaked. "To restore emergency power to the helm, override the driver coil assembly and patch EPS power to the auxiliary computer core. I can't move—you'll have to do it." He briefly turned visible and pointed to the emergency engineering console.

Picard didn't question these orders, but he had to wonder how a Romulan knew so much about the engineering systems of a Federation starship. Moving as fast as the Brahms suit would allow—and realizing that he had less than two minutes of time left before the suit stopped working—Picard lumbered to the console. He tried to clear his mind of extraneous thoughts and concentrate on the job at hand. Without the warp core about to suffer an imminent breach, which took all the ship's resources to contain, the auxiliary computer systems gradually came back online. Picard entered the instructions, breathed another huge sigh of relief, and turned to look for Regimol.

He found the Romulan floating at the wheel they had just rotated, tethered there by the cable of his interphase generator. Hoping he wasn't too late to save the hero's life, the captain shuffled across the deck, freed the Romulan's body, and carried him to the doorway. Once outside in the corridor, he let Regimol's body float for a moment while he entered commands to close the door and seal it.

At the same moment, a beep sounded inside the Brahms radiation suit, and a tinny computer voice said, "Power failing. Please replace power cell immediately. This suit is inoperative." The screen, the faceplate . . . everything went dark, and Picard felt as if he were wearing a hundred kilos of weight. He realized the artificial gravity was back on, and he lowered Regimol's unconscious body to the deck.

"Jean-Luc!" cried a feminine voice, and he turned to see Beverly Crusher emerge from the Jefferies tube and come running toward him, a medkit in her hand. Another person crawled out right behind her.

The captain collapsed to the deck, his back against the bulkhead. With considerable effort from his aching arms and back, he managed to extricate himself from the suit and stare gratefully at the doctor. "You've got to help Regimol," he wheezed, pointing to the fallen Romulan.

"Regimol?" asked a voice curiously. Picard looked up to see the Romulan standing behind Beverly, with the other Regimol lying prone at their feet. The hero of the day suddenly materialized in full, and all three of them gasped. Even with his horrendous burns and horribly disfigured face, they could recognize the soft-spoken Antosian, Raynr Sleven. His once immaculately coiffed hair was now singed black all the way to his scalp.

With a tearful mixture of anger and grief, the real Regimol barked at his friend, "You idiot! You stole my interphase box."

"Had to do it," rasped the former Starfleet technician. "You wouldn't have known what to do."

Looking distraught at the seriousness of his injuries, Dr. Crusher opened her medkit and prepared a hypospray.

"There's no point, Doctor," said the Antosian, a look of peace coming over his scarred face. "I should have died days ago on the *Barcelona*. I couldn't save that ship . . . but I saved this one. Please tell Alyssa Ogawa . . . I am sorry."

"Try to hold on," insisted Picard, gripping the ship's savior by the sleeve of his tattered uniform. "We'll get you to sickbay, where we can—"

Raynr Sleven slowly expelled his last breath of air, and peace came to his charred body and tortured soul.

Beverly hung her head and dropped the hypospray into her medkit. "He was dead the moment he went in there. The phase-shifting protected him just long enough to do the job."

Regimol sniffed back a tear and muttered, "I have known very few honestly good and simple people in my life . . . here lies one." The usually glib and cocksure Romulan covered his eyes and wept.

Picard staggered wearily to his feet and looked around at his intact but deserted ship. "Thanks to

Raynr Sleven, I won't be going down with her after all. At least not today. There were dead bodies in engineering."

"I estimate six dead shipwide," said Crusher, brushing back an errant strand of hair. "That includes Raynr. It could have been much worse."

"Now we've got to find out what caused this," replied the captain, his jaw clenched in anger. He tapped his combadge and said, "Picard to away team. Are you there, Number One?"

"Captain!" answered a surprised voice. "We've been trying to contact you. I'd all but given up. Yes, we're here, but something fried the circuits in the shuttlecraft, and it's halfway submerged in mud, anyway. We saw the escape pods coming down and have been trying to collect the crew . . . but things are pretty strange down here."

"Things are strange up here, too," muttered the captain. "We just manually ejected the warp core. Do you have any idea what caused this?"

"It's something that the Aluwnans did," answered Riker testily. "They tried to reverse the Genesis effect . . . or something. We won't know exactly what they did until we find Marla Karuw."

Former regent, professor, and lover to an overseer, Marla Karuw sat dumbfounded on a worm-ridden log and surveyed the sun coming up over . . . not the paradise she had envisioned . . . not the overgrown chaos of Genesis . . . but something much worse. This was neither beast nor fowl—it was the unholy conglomeration of two biological experiments that had both failed, and together they had produced the equivalent of a two-headed, mutant baby. Oil and water didn't mix; neither did the overlay of Genesis technology and their own chromasynthetic, DNA-laced terraforming. Vilo Garlet had been right in one respect, though wrong in many others: unleashing widespread chromasynthesis without testing was tantamount to killing an already ill patient.

She had destroyed what she set out to save.

Marla couldn't even bear to look in the other direction, where there was nothing but a cracked, baked salt flat. Even the rocks were gone, and the wind bore reeking scents of ammonia and methane. She couldn't even decide which half of the split world was supposed to be the real Aluwna—neither one looked like anything she had seen before, and that included the Genesis jungle. She squeezed the com bracelet on her left arm, and it beeped to say it was trying to contact the *Darzor*, but there hadn't been any response from them since the fateful signal she had sent to Vilo.

How can I call myself a scientist when I released a planetwide scourge, without testing? The Genesis effect was still evolving . . . and I should've brought my people down first.

Something rustled in the brackish, leaf-covered swamp in front of her, and Marla looked up but didn't move—she was too tired and despondent to move. She watched transfixed as a mammoth serpent with long tentacles and three beady, blistered eyes rose from the depths. Its arced neck and bulbous head towered over the trees, which had been blasted into gnarled twigs and bare branches. A lot of trees had fallen, such as the one upon which she sat. In their place rose the primeval vision of a behemoth that had existed before any creature walked on two legs. Or maybe it would never exist, except in this unique time and place.

"Go ahead and kill me," she told the beast as it hovered ever closer, showing her rows and rows of interlaced picklike teeth. It studied her as if she were an unfamiliar but possibly delectable morsel. "I deserve to die—for my arrogance," Marla informed the monster. "I have failed my people . . . and myself."

Staring at death in its most hideous and primal form, her life memories assaulted her. It had been a life of great promise, great opportunities, and an almost psychotic urge to battle authority whenever possible. Every time she had been given an opportunity, she threw it away because of hubris, and this disaster was the worst example of all. She had squandered her people's faith in her, and she had introduced murder where there was none.

In fact, it had been the sight of the wizened corpse of Curate Molafzon that had tipped her over the edge. And even now she wondered if it had been but a vision, conjured by a failing, guilty mind. Marla gazed up to see the basilisk, cocking its fearsome head at her and watching her wallow in pity. She looked for a rock to hit it with, but many of the rocks had been pulverized and crumbled in her hands.

"Come on, finish me off!" she challenged the beast.

Almost smiling, the creature nodded and lunged its massive head toward her, jaws agape. A flash came out of the jungle and hit the beast a glancing blow near the base of its neck. It roared in terror and primal rage, shaking what few leaves were left off their branches, then it ducked quickly out of sight while another shot went wild and set a bush at water's edge on fire.

"Bless me," said a startled voice behind her, and she turned to see her former assistant, Komplum, wielding a Klingon disruptor rifle. His helmet was gone, and what was left of his environmental suit was soiled and ripped. "That should have killed it—what a monster!"

"And you deprived him of his dinner," said Marla glumly, throwing her legs over the log and staring at her young apprentice. "If you've come here to capture me, you might as well *shoot* me. Go ahead. Unlike that animal, I'll make sure to die."

Komplum took the weapon off his shoulder and set it uneasily on the ground. "I've been watching you since you came back to camp with Alexander, and I saw where you ran when . . . whatever you did . . . happened. I stayed in camp, wandered around, listening . . . and I picked up this disruptor from a dead Klingon. There's been lots of death lately."

"So why don't you leave me alone?" she asked, turning away from him in embarrassment. "Spare me the speeches—just kill me or leave me alone."

"I'm not completely blameless," muttered Komplum, hanging his head. "I was the one who put the curate's body in the transporter booth."

"What?" she shrieked, jumping to her feet and roaring as in days of old. She glared at him, tried to talk, and sputtered, "I didn't know how . . . it scared me. What . . . where . . . explain yourself!"

"You killed him," said Komplum frankly. "That did more harm than everything else you did. Or at least it made you the False Divine, making life-and-death decisions without consulting anyone or any power. You ran roughshod over everyone else, including me. You never even officially fired me, just banished me down here, while you depended on Vilo."

"Stop!" she grumbled. "I know my crimes. Of course, you're right. So shoot me with that Klingon stick."

"No, you don't get off that easily," snapped Komplum. "You told those people you would save them—you put them into the care of machines, and now you have to free them. The satellites are dying, and the people will die, too. Don't you care?"

That stung her, and she turned toward him, her eyes glistening red. She couldn't refute him, so she just listened.

Komplum pointed into the distance. "The Federation personnel didn't deserve this. They're out there now, trying to finish *your* work . . . while you desert us. Before this, you've made every decision for a good end, but now you're so selfish you can't even do that much."

"I'm sorry," muttered Karuw. "When I saw the curate's body . . . how did you get it?"

"I announced him into your study, remember?" asked Komplum. "He came out, went with the constables, and was never seen again. You weren't paying much attention to me even them, so I retrieved him with the transporter. He was quite dead and desiccated, of course, and I thought I would hold him . . . as a kind of insurance, in case you tried to leave me behind. You weren't that cruel to me, until Vilo Garlet came aboard. I knew the two of you were planning something, but you never took me into your confidence. Then, I guess, you got nervous about me and sent me here. I stashed his body in one of the booths to be sent down—it beamed down yesterday to replace the one with the accident. Strange, eh?"

"That crime was waiting to be discovered," grumbled the professor, "or for me to acknowledge it." She stared into the bleak, foreboding forest, smelling what seemed like sulfur and creosote. "I knew his murder would come back to haunt me, but I had nothing to do with Tejharet's death."

The young scholar shook his head sadly. "By that time, the Cursed Hand was loose upon us, and it was mixed with fatigue and the thirst for revenge."

Vigorously Marla Karuw stood up and lifted her

chin. "You're right, we have to get them out of those satellites. I'll go back to camp with you and confess to the murder I committed. I hope they'll let me advise them."

"Let me speak for you," said Komplum, picking up his disruptor rifle. "The key person now is Worf—he's in charge of this brutalized planet, which I have a hard time calling Aluwna. He'll be very glad to see you."

twenty-four

Worf scowled as he paced through the ooze of Base One, or what was left of it. The survivors of the second catastrophe on Aluwna had staked out a new camp on the high ground, although most of their shuttlecraft, shelters, and equipment were mired in a meter or two of mud. Some were underwater completely in the bog that was once a crater and before that was part of an extinct civilization. It was time these inhabitants learned to live with what had happened, although it was hard to blame irrational behavior on those who had suffered so much. Now the Aluwnans had dug their hole that much deeper, and more than anything Worf just wanted to get off this chameleon planet.

The snow and ash had been replaced by grit and sand from the new strips of desert wasteland, but the wind blew as fiercely as ever. The moss creatures were a distant memory, and Worf felt no fear or psychic pull from them. Everyone had discarded their headgear, but most were still wearing their enviro suits for protection from the cold. The sun was shining red through the salmon clouds, as if it could see its former paradise and was as mad as Worf.

The transporter booth had been moved beside their half-submerged shuttlecraft, and broken metal walls from the geodesic domes had been laid down to walk upon. Leah Brahms, Geordi, Data, and most of the away team toiled down there, trying to figure out what to do for the people trapped in the satellites. With the ships in orbit out of commission or gone, there was very little they could do to help anyone on the ground. Alexander and two of the Klingons were trying to calm the panicked Aluwnans, while gangs of Aluwnans and Klingons were salvaging what they could from the new wave of wreckage.

Will Riker stood on a nearby sand dune, staring upward at the angry amber sky. He spoke into the wind, then tapped his combadge. Seeing Worf looking at him, Riker waved, then skidded down his heels toward the Klingon's position. "The *Enterprise* has resumed orbit and is almost back online," he reported. "But transporters are still iffy."

"That is the truth," muttered Worf. "I feel like Reg Barclay—I never want to see another transporter."

"Now that it's daylight," said Riker, "we've got to send out more parties to find the escape pods. They're probably having a harder time than we are. At least now we can coordinate with the *Enterprise*'s sensors."

"Yes, let's organize—" Something caught Worf's eye coming out of the bedraggled forest at the edge of the green zone, and he peered more closely. It was an Aluwnan female, about the right age and station to be Marla Karuw; an Aluwnan with a disruptor rifle was guiding her toward camp. "Come with me," said Worf.

The two of them strode toward the approaching pair. A hush went up around the scattered refugees, and everyone knew something important was happening. By the time Worf and Riker reached Marla Karuw and her escort, others had stopped what they were doing to gather around. Members of the away team, Alexander and several Klingons, and a number of Aluwnans walked solemnly up the barren ridge, their scarves and tattered garments whipping in the wind.

"Marla Karuw," intoned Worf in his best wrath-of-God voice. "You have sabotaged our efforts and your own. I'm placing you under arrest."

"Ambassador Worf," said the young Aluwnan with the disruptor rifle. "I am Komplum, her assistant, and I captured her. By captor's right in the Klingon canon, I can determine what's done with this prisoner, as long as confinement is guaranteed. That might include her serving as a vassal to me. If she attempts to escape, the next captor would have the right to claim her. Even if she goes to trial for her crimes, she remains in my custody until the fate for her crime is determined."

"That is a very old law," grumbled Worf, clenching his teeth.

Data cocked his head and said, "I believe that law is the fundamental statute in the Klingon bounty-hunting industry."

"True," muttered Worf.

"The most important thing," Karuw said, "is to get our people out of the satellite buffers. If we can just contact the *Darzor*—"

Worf scowled. "The *Darzor* was lost with all hands on board. You killed about half of your own survivors with that senseless act of yours."

"Oh, my, the Hand of—" Karuw touched her forehead and wobbled on her feet. Komplum and Alexander rushed to steady her, and they seated her gently in the cracked sand.

"You nearly destroyed the *Enterprise*," Worf continued. "Only heroic acts saved her. Fortunately, the *Doghjey* had shields up, although we still took damage. We have impulse drive and were able to move off to a safe distance. There are no ships in orbit which can save us . . . from whatever you did to this poor world."

"We were just trying to reverse the Genesis effect," she muttered in shock. "To bring back our native species—like Noah did. It was wrong . . . stupid . . . I'm sorry."

"You will stand trial for your acts," vowed Worf, staring pointedly at Komplum.

Drawing on reserves of strength, the professor rose to her feet and looked the Klingon squarely in the eye. "I'll gladly take whatever punishment you deem fit. I've committed crimes you don't even know about, but first *please* help me free the survivors from our transporters."

"We've been trying," said Geordi. "The solar power cells in the booths have to recharge. Even if they do, we've got no way to patch into your system."

Marla retrieved an isolinear chip from an inner pocket of her enviro suit. "Here, this is the emulation program I used to send a test animal to our satellite yesterday. It should enable us to tap into the system from any of your shuttlecraft transporters."

"Our shuttlecraft is without power," replied Data. "As are the Klingon shuttles. What were those energy particles you released?"

Karuw sighed and answered, "A process that is unique to our science, I believe, called chromasynthesis. We hadn't tested it on such a widespread application, and it must have reacted badly to some of the protomatter left over from Genesis."

"That is putting it mildly," said Data. "The kedion particles transmitted the energy into space, where all of our ships were badly affected. We must assume that your satellites were also adversely affected."

Marla Karuw's face was an inscrutable mask of determination. "I'm not proud of anything I've done recently, but I put those people into those satellites, and I'll get them out . . . with your help. How badly damaged is the *Enterprise?*"

"She's coming back online slowly," answered Riker.

"Can she launch a shuttlecraft?" asked Karuw.

The first officer looked doubtful. "There are plenty of shuttlecraft on board, but hardly any crew. Our captain, our doctor, and the Romulan—that's all there are."

"Regimol can fly a shuttlecraft," said Karuw. "He was piloting a runabout when I met him. I want to analyze a few of the satellites in orbit, and try to get the return sequence started. It has to come from a transporter booth or the main controller . . . and that was on the *Darzor.*" She cast her eyes downward and kicked at the calcified soil.

"May I?" asked Data, holding out his hand to take the isolinear chip, which Karuw surrendered reluctantly. "I would like to understand your transporter algorithms and matrices. I can analyze this aboard the shuttlecraft."

"I'll contact Captain Picard," said Worf. He turned to Riker and added, "This is a diplomatic mission, and I'm the lead diplomat. And we're clearly on the ground with the locals."

"We're at your service," answered Riker with a quick smile as he patted Worf on the back. "Just don't ever come back to work for me."

"If there are any more missions like this—" muttered Worf, not finishing his sentence. He looked around at the tattered, dirty band of several hundred, who had been marooned on a schizophrenic planet with no food or shelter. He wondered aloud, "Who is now the head of the government?"

Marla Karuw looked as if she wanted to raise her hand but couldn't.

"The seeress consort," answered Alexander, stepping toward his father. "Now that Padrin and Jenoset are dead, he's the only member of the royal family left. He also has the highest breeding of anyone, according to their DNA ranking. I know he escaped from the *Darzor*, because I followed him down here."

"Take some men and find him," ordered Worf. As his son gathered Klingons and a few able-bodied Aluwnans, the ambassador slapped the com medallion on his chest and bellowed, "Worf to *Enterprise*."

When the stuffy air, pathetic whimpering, and aching joints grew a bit too much for Deanna Troi, she knew they had to get out of the cramped escape pod. They couldn't hang forever in the netting, like sides of beef, and they couldn't step on the muddy hatch below them for fear it would pop open and let in more tentacles and slimy critters. They had to stretch their legs and search for other evacuees from the *Enterprise*, because it wasn't clear that help was on the way.

Troi turned to the three children and their teacher, the young human named Valerie, and she said, "We're going out the top. We can't stay in here anymore."

"I agree," said Valerie, and the tearful children nodded as well.

Deanna had learned all their names by now: Skyler, the precocious seven-year-old human; Taylen, the

Deltan girl who was quiet but large for her age; and
Cody, the curious eight-year-old boy. They were all old
enough to know that living in space was uncommon,
even in this day and age. Most of the crew members'
children shuttled back and forth between the
Enterprise and a more mundane planetary existence, so
they knew how special—and dangerous—it was to live
on the *Enterprise*. To their credit, they didn't speak
much about the parents and caregivers they were separated from, and both the teacher and the counselor did
their best to talk about other subjects.

While they hung in the escape pod, Troi had told
them many of the exciting stories that led to ending
the Genesis Wave threat, although she left out the
more gruesome details. It was hard to deal with the
magnitude of death and destruction it had caused,
and was still causing.

"Okay, I'm going out." Deanna Troi opened a
small locker and took out a personal hand phaser,
making no pretense or mention of it to the children.
They had seen such weapons before, and it was a survival tool stored with the other rations, fuel cells,
flares, implements, and water pouches. A phaser could
start a fire, warm rocks for heating, and do all sorts of
things that Deanna hoped she wouldn't have to show
them. She stuck it in her utility belt, along with some
flares and a flashlight, even though it looked like
morning outside. It was hard to tell by looking out
the viewport, because of all the muck smeared across
the window.

No sooner did Troi unstrap herself from the harness than something struck the side of the pod and dropped her to the bottom. She landed on both rotting and living tentacles stuck in the half-open hatch, and the pod promptly fell to its side and slammed her against the bulkhead. She just missed landing on top of Skyler, who began screaming at the top of her lungs. Troi twisted around to see a grotesque stingray-like creature with huge flaps of slimy, scaled skin trying to squirm its way into the pod. The counselor drew her phaser, took careful aim, and zapped the encroaching animal with a blue beam that rendered it unconscious.

She didn't know what had tipped them onto their side, but now that the bottom hatch was open, they might as well escape that way. Deanna figured they would have to brave slimy things in whatever direction they headed, but she knew there was clear land only a few meters away. At least the flapping ray had plugged up the entrance for the moment, although more mud was slopping in. The teacher, Valerie, was hanging upside down, so Deanna concentrated on freeing her from her harness first. As soon as Valerie dropped to the bulkhead, both of them began to free the children. Soon they all were crouching in the curve of what felt like a short pipe sinking into the mud.

"What else should we take?" asked Valerie.

"Keep your hands free in case you have to climb or move branches," answered Troi. "But stuff some rations into your pockets. We can always come back to get more stuff, but we have to close the hatch behind us . . . so these crawlers don't get in."

Troi waited until the children had armed themselves with packets of food, and the teacher grabbed a medkit that could be carried over the shoulder. "Valerie," ordered Troi, "you help me close the hatch. The rest of you wait until we find the open ground. That's where we're headed—open ground. Let's go!"

She kicked open the hatch, pushing the stunned ray-creature out of the way. Then Troi turned around and crawled out, braving the sulfurous, foul-smelling, oily goop that seemed to crawl up her arms and legs. Some of the children screamed in terror as the slop ran into the pod, and Deanna wrinkled her nose and crawled through the miasma. As she hauled herself into the chilly air, Deanna peeled off the black leeches that tried to cling to her arms.

"Don't look at them, just hurry!" she shouted to the others. Beyond the hatchway, Troi staggered to her feet and shielded her eyes from the blazing sun. It probably wasn't that bright, but it looked that way to someone who'd just spent hours stuck in a can. She held open the hatch and helped the kids out; they were troupers, even though Valerie was nudging them from behind.

Once they all got out, both women did a head count and reached for the hatch. They kicked out the clumps of mud and maggots and did their best to squeeze out the slop until they finally managed to shut the hatch. Troi was about to search for the clearing when Skyler screamed. All three children dashed into the woods, distracting Deanna and making her catch her breath before she could turn around.

A scream lodged in her throat as she stumbled backward from an ungodly giant amoeba, as tall and as wide as an elephant but curiously flat. Clumsily it reared up, swaying like a great puckered flag, and tried to collapse on top of them. Because Deanna and Valerie were running as fast as the children, all it caught was the helpless escape pod, which it covered, tried to absorb, and then slid off, recoiling.

"This way!" yelled little Cody, and both Deanna and Valerie stumbled in a new direction, following the child's voice. Being small and agile, the kids made their way through the fallen timber and burnt stumps better than the adults. A moment later, all five of them emerged into the clearing, as ordered.

That swiftly turned into a mixed blessing, because it wasn't solid ground but a meter of fine dust that rippled like a slow motion wave with their slightest movement. With too much movement, the fine talc rose upward and caught in their noses and mouths, especially the children, who were closer to the ground. They were soon choking and coughing and had to flail away in thick clouds which rose up to engulf them.

Calling to them between coughs, Deanna gathered up small hands and was joined by the teacher, who was carrying the Deltan girl. She waded through the ocean of talc and led them to the muddy bank where the green zone began. They hauled themselves onto roots and mutant pads of fungus, trying to ignore the worms and maggots. Crying, coughing, and spitting up, they were a sorry lot, lying on the gelatinous beach. Still no one complained until a strangled roar issued from the jungle; it was so anguished that it had to be the cry of a dying animal, or a beast bearing children.

"I want my mommy!" complained Skyler.

They huddled together on the dividing line between two worlds, while Deanna Troi kept watch on the ominous forest. The reeking smells, the chilblain cold, and the general sickly milieu of the planet made her realize that they wouldn't be exploring on their own anytime soon.

"We're going to stay here for a little while," she said, shivering from a blast of arctic air. "And I'll show you how to make a fire. How does that sound?"

A crashing sound from the forest didn't soothe their nerves, and they all huddled together. Two of the children whimpered, and Valerie couldn't stop coughing. "Shhh!" the Deltan girl told them, and their noise level faded to panicked breathing.

That was when the swarm of insects attacked, and they were about as big as Deanna's hand—primeval dragonflies buzzing so loudly it was like an attack of flying alarm clocks. They were suddenly everywhere, biting ferociously, and everyone in the group just cowered and screamed. Deanna set her phaser to a dispersal pattern and shot straight into the air above them. Dozens of bat-sized bugs suddenly blazed with red sparks and blue flames, and they dropped upon the cowering survivors, to be set upon by dozens of their ravenous fellows. Valerie led the terrified children farther along the bank, while Deanna did her best to extricate herself from the feeding frenzy. Shooting another wide beam, she singed another score of the flying things before she managed to crawl away. Even so, her face and exposed arms had tiny bite marks from the rapacious creatures.

Panting heavily, staring over her shoulder, Troi rejoined her party as they clung to gnarled roots and dripping gray fungus. All of them were now more in shock than panic, because the adventure had turned into a waking nightmare.

"The pod puts out a signal," she told the children. "They'll find us."

"Yeah, they'll find us," muttered little Cody, "but what *else* will find us?"

As unseen things rustled and slithered all around them, Deanna Troi had no answer; so she kept her phaser pistol ready and her eyes on the branches, which trembled as much as she did in the sulfurous mist.

In a sickly part of the jungle, surrounded by majestic but fallen trees, Farlo and Candra sat in a circle of about ten Aluwnans who had managed to start a fire out of brittle wood and branches. Now they had a good-sized conflagration going, even though the sparks threatened to catch some of the neighboring brush on fire. It was still warm and communal, and they scooted back when the flames got too hot, as others joined their circle. It was easier to stare into the mesmerizing fire, even at midday, than to gaze at the ghostly remains of their homeworld. Farlo looked around, wishing he could do something to lift their spirits, but his spirits were down too. They had been safe on the ship, and now he was beginning to second-guess his decision to bring Candra down here.

Nobody in the despondent group felt like talking, except for one older constable, who felt like ranting. *"They* did this to us!" he harangued the others. "The blasted Federation, because they wanted to take over our planet. And you know who invited them in? The stupid royal family, that's who! First they turn us over to that dunderhead regent—what's her name? And she puts us into satellites, so we won't make trouble. But where's our families? Where's the rest of us?"

He started mimicking someone he had never seen. " 'I'm afraid we can't get you out now . . . so sorry,' says the regent and the friendly Federation. Truth is, they don't want too many of us here, because they can't control us then. I heard that the Klingons wanted to rescue us, and the Federation turned them away . . . told them to come back later. And that's why they killed Overseer Tejharet and made that fop into the overseer. Just to have a puppet."

"Old man, you're daft!" blurted Farlo. "That's not the way it happened. You think Padrin wanted to be overseer? Ha!"

The grizzled constable fixed him with a rheumy gaze and lifted his stun stick. Fortunately, thought Farlo, he was on the other side of the fire. "And why, young one, is the Federation here? And how do you know so much?"

"We were passengers on the *Darzor* with the high breeds," said Candra, kicking Farlo in the shin to get him to shut up. "They were stunned by the overseer's death, and the Federation wasn't even here yet. I'm sure whoever did that feels truly bad." Candra blinked a couple times and stared into the fire.

"You didn't answer about the regent!" the constable declared, as if making a point. "She's the one who's in league with the Federation. I heard that she unleashed that second Genesis Wave on us, too! Didn't you hear that, boys?"

He turned to the miserable refugees, looking for verification, and a few of them nodded somberly. "We heard that," one muttered.

"I heard that all the royal family is dead," said a newcomer to the fire circle, and two more nodded to that.

Farlo sat upright, despair on his face. "What do you mean, dead?"

"We heard that the *Darzor* was destroyed when that second pulse went off," said the newcomer. "Well, they might as well be dead for all they care about us. They sent away the Klingons, who were the only ones keeping us going."

Candra squeezed his hand, and he knew she sympathized. If that was true, they had both lost friends on the *Darzor*, and friends were hard to come by out here among this bitter lot.

The old constable looked teary eyed as he rasped, "Seeress Jenoset dead? Now there was the brains and beauty of the outfit. The Federation probably killed her, too!"

Farlo could tell that Candra wanted to keep arguing, and so did he—but it was his turn to kick her in the leg. It was best to lie low, because there wasn't any advantage to be had in being the seeress consort down here. That wouldn't make the air smell any better or make the wormy grubs stay off his leg. This talk of more death and worse destruction—it sunk Farlo's spirits even deeper, and he just wanted to curl up somewhere. He had honestly liked Padrin and was beginning to like Jenoset, despite her selfishness. She had wanted to make him into a man, but there had been no time for marital bliss in these desperate days.

"Now I know who you are!" shouted the old constable with the stun stick, and he pointed his weapon straight at Farlo. "You not just lived on the *Darzor* . . . you're one of *them!* You're the young seeress consort, the one she plucked off the streets before we cleared out!"

Now all eyes were riveted upon him, and Farlo appraised his surroundings from the corner of his eye, trying to pick the best escape route. If he broke free from all the adults sitting around the fire, they probably wouldn't be able to catch him. He felt Candra tense beside him.

"Yeah, right!" responded Farlo with a big laugh. "Sure, I'm the seeress consort! Who are you— Overseer Padrin?"

Others in the circle laughed uncertainly at his joke, but he saw their eyes glaze over as if the absurdity of the old man's claim discredited everything he had said. Sure, they were sitting around with the seeress consort, who was probably stone-cold dead with the rest of them . . . and almost everybody else who had ever lived on this forsaken planet.

"Sit down, Barbo!" cried one of the men. "You're seeing ghosts. Those children are refugees, like all of us. Survivors, although I wouldn't call us living. Whatever they were before, that's what they are now."

The veteran constable sputtered some old curses but finally sat down and shut up. The brief debate, which had lapsed into absurdity, had made them all weary and sad. It was best not to talk. Someone threw more charred wood onto the fire, and it flared up, forcing everyone to scoot back a seat-length, which made room for others to sit down. They went back to staring mournfully into the flames, thinking of all those who had gone to be with the Divine. They almost seemed like the lucky ones.

The Starfleet shuttlecraft cruised within twenty meters of the impressive wingspan of the satellite, which looked much the worse for wear, with a broken solar panel and many scratches and scorch marks on its casing. In the cockpit, Regimol piloted the craft, while Leah Brahms glanced over the shoulders of Geordi, Data, Marla Karuw, and Komplum, who were huddled around a bank of sensor readouts. Data had interfaced Karuw's isolinear chip with the shuttle's sensors and transporter and was running the emulation program. Leah told her that this was one of the Federation's more advanced shuttlecraft, *Navigator*-class, and if it couldn't tell them the condition of these satellites, nothing in their fleet could.

"With this program, can we trick the satellite into letting us initiate standard diagnostic routines?" asked Data. "Otherwise, we have no healthy data to compare with our current sensor readings."

"I know the general levels," said Marla Karuw, "and the lowest thresholds. But you might as well run the diagnostics, because that's the first step in making a satellite recognize the shuttlecraft as one of our enclosures. If we can do that, maybe we can patch into the main system. We've got to pop the satellites in series and keep them regulated—and all those subroutines were on the *Darzor*."

"I'm running the emulation now," said Data, punching commands onto his board at blazing speed. He read the binary data just as quickly. "Satellite acknowledges us—is still operational, in standby mode."

Marla Karuw frowned. "That's actually bad,

because they're supposed to be in 'ready' mode. Standby is a low-energy setting, which is typical when a satellite is in darkness and not recharging, but this one is in the sun."

"Then why would it be in standby?" asked Geordi.

"Emergency conservation of power," she answered. "Only the volatile memory is kept alive—that's where our people are trapped. Everything else must be shut down."

"Be careful before you bring it out of standby," warned Komplum. "If there's not enough power, you could have a fatal emergency shutdown."

"A level-two diagnostic should give us more data," said Karuw. "Can I enter that command?"

"Be my guest," said Data, stepping aside and letting her have the console. After a moment, the android looked pleased with the increased stream of information. "Yes, that is useful to know."

"Freeze it!" said Karuw, and Data instantly tapped the controls and froze a graph on the screen. As she read, the Aluwnan's face registered disbelief. "No, those temperature and pH factors can't be correct. The electromagnetic pulse is below threshold, too. The plasma gel packs must be damaged, or the readings couldn't sink that low."

The professor grabbed Data's shoulder and said urgently, "We've got to get them out! When everything fails, they'll die."

"There is reason to believe the volatile memory is still intact," the android reminded her. "It will take some time to interpret this data. We could activate the satellite and beam off the first life-form in the pattern buffer, but that would put the satellite in active mode. According to your assistant, that could be fatal."

"Of course," said Marla, rubbing her head wearily. "I don't know what got into me . . . just worry. To bring everyone off as quickly as possible, we've got to get the satellites up to full power, and I don't think we can wait for the sun to do it."

"Thanks to you," said Leah Brahms, "the transporter booths are depleted, too. Everything's recharging . . . or slowly losing power. What's the step below standby? Good-bye?"

"I know it's my fault," grumbled Karuw. "You don't need to remind me. And standby is the lowest power setting . . . before shutdown. It can't last more than ten units before a recharging source is needed, or the satellite will lose power. That's about twelve of your hours. If we found out when they entered this mode, that would tell us how much time they have left."

While everyone kept their thoughts to themselves, Data continued to scroll through screens of sensor readouts. "This satellite entered standby five units ago, which would coincide with your chromasynthesis discharge. We will check more satellites, and I assume we will find this effect repeated. Using your theory, we have five units left, or about six hours."

"How can we recharge everything in time?" muttered Karuw, brushing back her graying hair. "We're beaten. Anything we do will be a disaster."

Leah Brahms looked at Geordi, and he shook his head glumly, fresh out of ideas. "The *Enterprise* has no reserve power," he said. "They can't help us, and they're the only ship in orbit."

"Our people are doomed," breathed Karuw.

twenty-five

Alexander Rozhenko waded through the rubble, burnt twigs, and scorched bushes of the once-luxuriant forest, a handful of Klingons and Aluwnans behind him. They were following a trail after having heard of an encampment of Aluwnans inside the forest. Clambering over fallen trees was the hardest part of the search, but they could smell the smoke from a fire as it wafted through the misty gorge. Then again, there were fires everywhere, and everything smelled of smoke and strange industrial solvents, as if the planet had been scoured clean of some particularly bad stain.

His tricorder picked up an electrical pulse several meters off to the right of the trail, and Alexander waved to his comrades to follow him. There were a few uncertain birdcalls in the forest, and he wasn't sure he had heard those before Karuw's scouring of the planet. Also there were numerous insects as big as his fist, and they bedeviled the party as they slogged along through the thorny underbrush. The signals on his tricorder were getting stronger, and he soon understood why when he spotted two unlikely beacons of technology in this devastated wood.

In a clearing lay a blue transporter booth tipped on its side, and resting next to it was an escape pod from the *Enterprise*. A canopy of trees still stretched over this part of Aluwna, and this grove looked like strong hardwood trees, such as the maples and oaks of Earth, not the droopy, spooky, moss-ridden plants left by the Genesis Wave. Alexander holstered his phaser beside the disruptor on his belt and made for the escape pod with increased speed. The whole band could see what he had found, and they were following close behind, the Klingons keeping a wary eye on the forest.

Alexander carefully approached the escape pod, which appeared to be closed at both ends, and he tapped on it. From within came frantic pounding—a tool on metal—followed by muffled voices, which he couldn't understand. "Can I open the hatch?" he bellowed.

"Look out!" he heard a cry from inside the pod. "Look out! Above—"

The young Klingon leaned down to hear more at the same moment that someone in his band cried out in alarm. A huge shadow swept over their position, and Alexander stared upward to see what looked like a massive blanket falling on top of them. It flapped as if it had wings, dropping directly on top of the booth, the pod, and seven members of the rescue party, including Alexander. The air instantly turned foul, unbreathable, and Alexander was lucky that he had the pod for protection. Where the massive flat creature was able to encompass the Klingons completely, they began to smother, dropping to the ground unconscious.

Alexander drew his disruptor and shot straight upward into the slimy membrane of the beast, blasting a big hole wide enough to put his arm through. That caused the monster to contract involuntarily, drawing the booth, the pod, and unconscious men with it. In pure survival mode, Alexander just wanted to get out, and he used the disruptor like a laser cutter to slice a gruesome escape flap in the filmy flesh. Burning bits of viscera rained down on him as he blasted away in the dark, and Alexander could hear muffled shouts and another sizzling whine—a second beamed weapon. Someone else was also trying to cut his way out, but it didn't help as the creature writhed powerfully, dragging everything and everyone trapped underneath it to the center.

Climbing on top of the escape pod, Alexander took the fight straight to the beast, relentlessly trying to blast his way through the unctuous guts and thick membrane, finally succeeding enough to free part of a fin on the escape pod. As if blasting his way upward through a tent, the Klingon finally managed to make a gooey hole and stick his neck and shoulders through it. The monster was now trying to escape, with Alexander stuck partway inside of it, and he could understand why.

Outside, a large group of Aluwnans had gathered around the smother beast and were bombarding it with tent poles, sticks, rocks, and whatever bladed weapons they could find. Leading them was a fresh-faced youth and his young friend, and Alexander sighed gratefully, because his search was over.

"Come on!" yelled Farlo, hacking at the slithering blanket with a scythe. "Keep attacking—it's trying to run off!"

Alexander ducked back into the wretched darkness under its belly, because the reinforcements had put the enemy on the run. He had come to rescue Farlo, and instead the boy had rescued his party. The Klingon tried to find his men in the darkness, and he dragged a few of them to the relative shelter of the escape pod. From his pack he took a flare and lit it, and that turned the underbelly of the creature a bright bloodred. It allowed him to find another Klingon and an Aluwnan and get them to safety.

This strange melee seemed to go on for hours, but it was probably only minutes before the creature dragged its bloody, burnt carcass off of them. It slithered maybe thirty meters into the forest, where it succumbed to continued attacks by the Aluwnans. In their ferocity, they seemed to work off some of their grief and lethargy, and they were laughing and congratulating each other when they returned to help

Alexander's party. With all of them working together, it wasn't long before his men and the *Enterprise* crew members in the escape pod were freed. There were introductions and hearty slaps on the back all around.

Seeing that the Aluwnans all seemed to know Farlo, Alexander decided to impress them a bit. When the lad approached him with a grin on his face, Alexander dropped down to one knee and bowed his head. "Overseer Farlo," he intoned as his father would, "we thank you for rescuing us. We came to tell you that your world needs you to rule."

Farlo looked around with some embarrassment, and Candra grinned at him, while the other Aluwnans looked astonished. Alexander had thought they knew who he was, but maybe not. "All of you come back to camp!" said Alexander, rising to his feet. "Welcome your new leader and all those being freed from the transporters!" The young Klingon had no idea if that was a factual statement, but it got the band of refugees all moving in the same direction.

"He really is the overseer!" cried an old constable, pointing triumphantly at Farlo. "See, I told you! I told you!"

"Barbo, I'll never doubt you again," muttered a second constable.

As they walked back to the path, Farlo sidled up to Alexander and whispered, "I can't be the overseer! I'm not even really a high breed. I have this tube—"

"I don't care," snapped Alexander, quickening his step and making the lad keep up. "People need authority in time of crisis, and they need to feel a continuity in their society. For whatever reason, you're the last one left, and Marla Karuw has taken herself out of consideration. Don't worry, we'll be here to help you. For now, there won't be a lot of governing—more like survival, rescues, and searching for hope. So just smile and look confident, as you did back there when you came to our aid. We Klingons have a saying: 'Wear the sash.' It means act the part, and people will think you were born to be the overseer."

He winked at the boy. "Come on, you're a con artist. You can do it."

"I guess so," answered Farlo with a game smile. He pouted thoughtfully, then added, "Can I make your father regent?"

"Regent Worf," Alexander repeated with amusement. Then he shook his head. "I'm afraid Worf is trying to get out of the diplomacy business. I believe him when he says he wants his old job back."

"Then I'll make *you* regent!" said Farlo cheerfully.

"You keep the power for now," advised the Klingon. "Don't confuse your people. But I will tell you what you should do as your first official act—join the Federation. I'm sure they're guilty enough to take you without question, and you'll get lots of aid and technology. Trust me, they'll be more useful for rebuilding Aluwna than we Klingons."

"That's after we save our people in the transporters," said Farlo with determination. "We're going to do that, right?"

"We're trying."

"Um, Alexander," said the lad meekly, "are you still investigating Overseer Tejharet's murder?"

The Klingon gave him a sidelong glance. "Yes, I am."

Farlo jumped in front of him and looked at him with pleading green eyes. "Can you believe me when I tell you that the *real* murderer died on the *Darzor?*"

"I know that all our evidence is gone," said the Klingon with a scowl. He eyed the young ruler appraisingly. "Perhaps I will conclude my report by saying that our primary suspects perished on the *Darzor*. I will consider it."

"Thank you," answered Farlo with a sigh of relief. "Then I'll take the overseer job and do the best I can."

Deanna Troi crawled over the fallen logs, making sure the children and Valerie were right behind her. They had to brave a return to the escape pod, even though the giant amoeba creature was nearby and seemingly attracted to it, along with every crawly worm and slug for a hundred kilometers. There wasn't really time to analyze the wildlife, as interesting as it was. They needed to make sure the com array on the pod was sending out its homing signal and distress calls, because they were definitely in distress.

When Troi stepped into the area plowed clear by the crash of the escape pod, she looked up to see what she thought was the parachute, mired in the trees. Instead she gasped and froze like a statue, because that was no parachute but the monstrous membrane creature, hanging from the boughs and looking like an ominous spider's web. She heard one of the children whimper behind her, and she turned to see the Deltan staring toward the pod itself. There stood a vision from some prehistoric nightmare.

It was a large sea serpent—that was all to which she could liken it. It had a long rangy neck, toothy head, and a sleek black body with paddles for legs. Long tentacles writhed like a wreath of snakes around the creature's massive haunches, making its appearance more frightening yet. The beast nudged the escape pod curiously, then turned to look directly at Deanna and her frightened brood.

"Back up," she whispered to Valerie and the students. "Don't get under that thing in the trees."

"It's . . . it's coming closer!" warned Cody, and the ground suddenly trembled as the behemoth moved a few footsteps toward her. Deanna had recently communicated with tortured beings in another dimension, and her psi skills were at their apex, better than they had ever been before. Perhaps she wasn't a full-blooded Betazoid, but she was highly experienced with species not her own. So she stood her ground and let the basilisk come as close as it wanted. Besides, if it intended to kill them, it wouldn't take much effort to chase them down first. They were at this creature's mercy, and she doubted that her phaser would be able to stop it should it charge in earnest.

Deanna tried to send out soothing thoughts,

because she sensed a strong intelligence that belied its fearsome appearance. The beast felt more than attraction for her and the escape pod; it seemed to recognize both of them at a primal level—the technology and the humanoids. Then she realized that the giant amoeba was probably up in the trees because of the sea serpent—it was their protector.

Her eyes were half-shut from the waves of emotion, and when she opened them, the creature was a meter away, staring at her with three curious orbs. Instinctively Troi reached out to touch its scaly skin; the telepathic impulses came much stronger as soon as her fingertips brushed its hide.

I know you, said the creature.

We are friends from long ago, she answered, unsure of the details but certain of the sentiment.

On the shuttlecraft, Leah Brahms plugged diligently away at a rear auxiliary console, assuming they would make a desperate attempt to free the survivors before the satellites went dead. In her opinion, nothing would work unless they could jump-start the whole satellite-booth connection in one fell swoop, and keep it running as long as the power would allow. All they knew for sure they could do was to beam someone into the system from the shuttle's single transporter pad, and she kept looking at that potential. Geordi had returned to the *Enterprise*, where he was needed on more than one front; Komplum had gone to the surface to brief Worf, leaving Regimol, Data, Marla Karuw, and Leah in orbit. She felt at home on the little craft, after having spent the first part of this odyssey on one not much different.

Suddenly cheers went up from the cockpit, and Leah looked up from her figures. She didn't know it, but folks applauded on the ground and the *Enterprise*, too, where different teams were working on different solutions. "What happened?" she called out.

"The beautiful Klingons have returned," answered Regimol, putting the impressive fleet up on his viewscreen. "The *Doghjey* and all the ships in the task force are back in orbit over Aluwna. Eight warships strong!"

Brahms looked at her chronometer—three hours and forty-five minutes left. "We'll do plasma discharges from all the ships in orbit," she said, "along the satellite belt. The longer the better, and we can send instructions to the machines to fast-charge. That should give a substantial boost to all the birds, as long as their solar collectors are still intact. It might even help the booths on the ground, although that's not as crucial."

Data cocked his head thoughtfully. "It can do no harm, and it could potentially do a great deal of good."

"Easy to do, too," said Karuw. "Isn't the venting of plasma standard procedure—routine maintenance for the ships?"

"Yes," answered the android as his digits took over

the main console. "I am sending your recommendation to all ships, asking the *Doghjey* to coordinate."

"Thank you, Dr. Brahms," said Marla Karuw gratefully. "What else have you been working on in silence back here?"

The human shifted in her chair and pointed to a schematic. "I know one foolproof way to jump-start the system—to fool it into thinking this is a regular day, time to transport eight million people like we usually do. Anything fancy could only delay start-up, and we don't have enough energy to risk that. So we give the system exactly what it expects to get."

"I'm listening," said Karuw. "I had been thinking the same thing."

Brahms pointed to the small transporter platform a meter away. "We know we can send an animal through from here, like you did with that test. So we ask for a volunteer to beam into the system, and at the same time we use your emulator to issue the repeat command—like several people are going at once. Unless I have this wrong, the full satellite should try to lay off the workload on down the line, and that trips the system into full autosequencing, which is what we want. It should wake up the rest of them . . . to start beaming down."

Karuw nodded excitedly. "Yes, absolutely! An Aluwnan must transport in, because that's what the system expects—and those bioneural networks can be very picky. You know, it's doubtful we'll have a way to get your volunteer back."

"Uh, yes, there's that complication," agreed Brahms.

The Aluwnan whispered, "Don't mention that to anyone, will you? They might not allow us to do it, and we do have a volunteer." The older woman looked pointedly at the younger.

Leah gulped and shook her head. "I don't think we can allow you—"

"I spent years in a cell already," she said through gritted teeth, "and I'm not going back. I don't mind paying for my crimes if we can get the people out. We'll pick a satellite that was emptied of a few passengers, so there might be room to store my pattern."

"You'll get out last," added Leah, "at the end of the queue."

"That sounds good to me," answered Marla Karuw, leaning over Brahms' console. "Now let's see what else we can do to get more power to those satellites."

"Move them into the clearing!" called Riker, motioning to the work crew of Aluwnans and *Enterprise* crew members to carry the transporter booth out of the trees. They bore the enclosure on two poles slung over their shoulders, and Riker motioned them to lug it to a sunny area that had been filled with dry dirt and graded level. As soon as they got the box erected in place, Komplum's crew took over, checking diagnostics and making it ready for action.

Scores of similar crews were working all along the

wide strip of land where the transporter booths had been erected over the last few days. Most barren areas had survived the anti-Genesis weapon better than the forest, although some blue boxes had sunk into the quicksand. Ships in orbit were using tractor beams to free the sunken enclosures, while other crews rushed to set them upright. The Klingons were beaming helpers down, and their numbers were growing every hour. In fits and starts, the workers rushed against the looming deadline.

Riker and his crew were jogging through chalky mud to the next location when a shuttlecraft zoomed over their heads and turned around to land in their path. When Riker saw it was a Starfleet shuttle, he waved his hand and led the way through the muck. At least running kept the blood flowing, he decided, and a person didn't get as cold.

When he saw Worf jump out of the craft and head toward him, Riker quickened his pace. Panting and bent over from exertion, he reached his old comrade, who held up his hands and said, "At ease. You've got a few minutes to wait here, then we'll take you to your next site."

"Thanks," said Riker, grabbing his canteen. "Why are we waiting?"

"The first of the plasma bursts is due any moment," answered Worf. "They told me I had better land the shuttle for it, and I was looking for you. My son found the new ruler, so they'll have someone to welcome them back to Aluwna."

"I hope they'll have counselors with them," said Riker, looking around the daunting wilderness. "I wonder . . . will they ever forgive us for what Genesis did?"

"Someday, if we prove worthy." Worf squinted into the grayish, overcast sky. "Did you see a glimmer?"

Riker looked upward just as the heavens were infused with light, like a lightning bolt that's frozen at its peak discharge. The whole sky seemed to pulsate with light, and more than a few Aluwnans ducked for cover. Riker heard muttering, and he told his work crew, "It's okay! We're doing this to recharge the satellites!"

Even though he knew it was harmless, the artificially bright sky seemed ominous after all that had befallen this poor planet. He couldn't blame people for ducking, especially when the ships vented their plasma for almost a minute. Shortly before it ended, a light rain began to fall, and a glorious rainbow arced across the sky for several seconds. That cheered everyone, and the work crew was enthusiastic as they climbed aboard Worf's shuttlecraft.

No sooner had they taken off than the pilot spotted something on the ground. "Ambassador Worf!" he called. "Take a look out the port window."

The pilot banked around in order to give everyone in the rear a chance to look out and see what he saw. Riker was seated right behind Worf, and they jockeyed to fit both their big heads into the small window frame. The battle was worth it, because below them, slogging through the sand at the edge of the forest, was an amazing prehistoric beast—like a cross between a dinosaur and a sea serpent. If that weren't astounding enough, people were riding the beast, and they waved as the shuttlecraft cruised overhead.

"Did that look like Deanna to you?" asked Worf.

"There's one way to find out." Riker tapped his combadge and said, "Riker to Troi. Are you in the vicinity?"

"Troi here," she answered happily. "I'm right below you. We picked up some native transportation."

"I can see!" exclaimed Riker. "You're headed toward our camp, and we'll meet you there when we finish."

"Take your time, we're having fun. Troi out."

"You should marry her," said Worf, intruding into Riker's thoughts. "You never know how long you will be together, and you should spend your time with passion."

"Yeah, I guess you're right," replied the human thoughtfully. "I really can't see letting her go again. But I won't be able to get away without having a big wedding . . . maybe a couple of them."

"Well then, never mind," said Worf.

The human knew his friend was kidding, although Worf kept his most dour poker face. "Pilot!" called the Klingon. "Status?"

"We've passed two booths that are reported to be in good shape, and we're about to land near one that needs repair," answered the pilot.

"Take us down," said the Klingon. "Gently. And look for bedrock, not quicksand."

"Aye, sir."

The shuttlecraft dropped in altitude and swept over majestic trees on the edge of a muddy stream that was trickling through the bottom of the wash. It was silt-ridden now, but the more it rained, the clearer it would flow. Maybe the zebra effect wouldn't last forever, thought Riker, but for now there was cleared land and plenty of fallen lumber, side by side.

In space, the rarefied atmosphere blazed with a light that was almost crystal in its fragility and purity, but it grew brighter as the particles danced through the cloud cover of Aluwna. The great Klingon warships soared swiftly over the string of satellites, expelling bursts of plasma that had built up through countless warp excursions. They had even performed a quick warp maneuver at inefficient loads to have some more plasma to vent on this second round. There had proven to be little else the Klingon task force could do on such short notice, with the minutes ticking off at high speed.

The *Enterprise* also followed a row of satellites, venting as much plasma as she had, considering her warp core was gone. Captain Picard still had a skeletal crew, because he was also in a recharging and refitting mode. Almost all the shuttlecraft had launched to aid in the rescue effort, but he didn't want to risk using transporters. The majority of the crew were safer on the ground, although there were disturbing reports of evacuees encountering large, predatory beasts on the new Aluwna.

"We're out of plasma," complained La Forge from the engineering station on the bridge. "That's the second burst, and we won't be any good if they want a third one."

"Report to central command on the *Doghjey*," replied Picard, his lips thinning worriedly. "How much time is left?"

"Forty-five minutes," answered Geordi. "They're cutting it close, because they'll need some running time."

"Only half a unit left," muttered Marla Karuw from the copilot's seat of the shuttlecraft. "That's barely enough time to let everyone out of the buffers. We can't wait any longer."

Leah Brahms turned to look at Data, who was ostensibly in charge of this craft and this mission. He hadn't seemed adverse to command, and he made instantaneous decisions. At the controls, Regimol cut the thrusters and let the shuttle drift toward a metal flower suspended in space—an Aluwnan transporter satellite in very good condition. Twenty-one people had been released from this bionic machine during the first round, days ago.

"Distance?" asked the Romulan.

"Twenty meters," replied Data. The android looked up at the two women, and Leah Brahms tried to figure out his inscrutable expression. "You have been discussing what to do," he said, "so I presume you can do it without our help."

"Yes, we can!" vowed Marla Karuw, jumping to her feet. "Um, I'm going to transport into the satellite, while Dr. Brahms sends the repeat command. Some of the satellites won't kick on until the sun reaches them."

"No need to explain," said Data with a placid smile of understanding. "I have very good hearing. Give me a moment to alert the ships and the ground teams."

"It's been a pleasure serving with you, Professor Karuw," called Regimol. "We'll stay here to see if you beam back."

"Thank you," answered the scholar with a heartfelt tremble in her voice. She bounded onto the small transporter pad in the rear of the cabin, across from the lavatory.

"You are cleared to transport," said Data. "However, Komplum may be mad, because you are technically still his property."

"Give him my regrets," answered Karuw, her voice cracking.

Leah took a big gulp of air and cleared her throat. "Are you sure—"

"Have you got the repeat command ready?" asked Karuw, lifting her chin. "If so, energize."

Leah Brahms nodded, because Marla Karuw and the repeat instruction were going together to the shiny bird with half a dozen open wings. When she punched the activation code, Marla Karuw's body swirled into a tubular rainbow, such as those they had been seeing all morning in the plasma-induced rain. At the same instant, the satellite blinked on, and several of their sensors kicked into high gear, spewing readouts onto all their screens.

"It's working!" cried Leah Brahms, thrusting her fist upward. "Have we gotten the whole chain working?"

"On either side of us, we've got machines coming on," answered Regimol. "We're sending *something* to the planet—we'll just have to hope the cargo is in good condition."

Worf held his breath as the transporter booth closest to camp—the one in which Curate Molafzon's body had been discovered—blinked on and began to hum. Riker, Alexander, and Overseer Farlo also stepped to his side and stared at the whirring blue box, and dozens of Aluwnans and Klingons stopped what they were doing to approach the blinking enclosure. The ambassador straightened his spine, expecting trouble and ready to deal with it, because he knew what horrors could come out of these boxes. He wished the Aluwnans well, but they were on a fragile footing emotionally, so he had to be ready to quell a riot.

The door of the enclosure shook, then opened, and a dazed child about ten years old stepped out, followed by an Aluwnan woman who gripped the child protectively. A huge cheer went up, and everyone in camp broke into hoarse cries and hooting applause. This did very little to calm the survivors, and Farlo and Alexander rushed forward to lead the small family away from the booth, so more survivors could exit. Farlo took them to see the huge beast which Deanna Troi had ridden into camp, and that was acceptable to Worf. That behemoth was making more friends than any other creature on Aluwna.

All over the planet, dazed survivors were stepping out of transporter booths and meeting welcoming parties, who tried to explain the strange sights and smells. It seemed as if there was a plethora of constables and children among them, but all were given water and rations. Dr. Crusher and other medical teams were standing by, but the vast majority of evacuees suffered more from shock, grief, and denial, for which there was no medical cure. Although they were alive after having survived a power loss, a fungus, and other dangers, for them it was but an instant since they boarded the transporters in their cities and towns. All those places were gone; in return they had inherited a bizarre wilderness, which only accentuated their loss.

Still there was great joy among all those Aluwnans who had come days earlier, either by ship or by the first transporter release. They had thought they would never see so many of their fellow Aluwnans again, and their good spirits lifted the newcomers. There were also wonders to be seen in this strange world:

amazing growth and destruction, incredible animal life, and lush forests bordered by great plains which were already growing grass. Apparently, this grass was a wild grain, which the Aluwnans knew how to cultivate and harvest. Worf and the Klingons maintained a watch for the moss creatures, but they were never seen again on Aluwna.

"No more moss creatures at all?" asked Jeremy Aster, sitting up in his hospital bed at Starfleet Medical Center in San Francisco. His wounds were almost entirely healed, Worf was glad to see, and even his facial scars were going away. "What did you call them?"

"*poch'loD*," answered Alexander with a grin as he sat on the side of Jeremy's bed. "But you were right, because those big slugs—we called them *nujgharg*— were very good eating. The Klingons ate so many that they were going extinct even before the anti-Genesis thing went off."

"Our crew was getting quite addicted to them," said Worf with disapproval. He lowered his voice to add, "Don't tell Starfleet, but some Klingons are planning a hunt for *nujgharg* on one of the other Genesis planets. Rare, dangerous to catch, and quite tasty— they might become a Klingon delicacy."

"The Aluwnans seem to like their new overseer, too," said Alexander with some pride. "Although he's just a lad, he's got a good head on his shoulders, and he wants to do well. There's lots of raw materials to

rebuild, food is growing, and the Federation will continue to assist."

Worf nodded his head solemnly. "We freed ninety
percent of the people trapped in their satellites,
which is an extraordinary achievement. I wish the
person who made it possible could have seen it."

"And the *Enterprise?*" asked Jeremy. "What happened to them?"

"They're still in orbit around Aluwna," answered
Worf with amusement, "waiting for Starfleet to bring
a new warp core."

Alexander laughed, and shook his head. "But I
don't think they mind—it's almost like shore leave at
this point, with lots of romantic, isolated places to
visit. Geordi La Forge and Leah Brahms looked very
happy, and so did Commander Riker and the counselor."

"That is true," said Worf with satisfaction. "I keep
looking for something good to happen from all this.
Maybe now."

With a sigh, the big Klingon took a step closer to
the bed and patted Jeremy gently on his shoulder.
"Now, son, you must rest so the doctors will release
you on schedule. You can rejoin the officer-exchange
program next week, and I'll do what I can to get you
back on the *Doghjey.*"

"*Qapla'!*" said Jeremy, holding out his fist to the
two Klingons. With gusto, the family joined fists and
echoed the sentiment: "*Qapla'!*"

KNOW NO BOUNDARIES

Explore the Star Trek™
Universe with Star Trek™
Communicator, The Magazine of
the Official Star Trek Fan Club.

Subscription to Communicator is
only $29.95 per year (plus shipping and handling)
and entitles you to:

- 6 issues of STAR TREK Communicator

- Membership in the official STAR TREK™ Fan Club

- An exclusive full-color lithograph

- 10% discount on all merchandise purchased at
  www.startrekfanclub.com

- Advance purchase preference on select items
  exclusive to the fan club

- ...and more benefits to come!

So don't get left behind! Subscribe to STAR TREK™
Communicator now at www.startrekfanclub.com